MW01152729

LOVED BY A DUKE

LOVED BY A DUKE

Christi Caldwell

Copyright © 2015 by Christi Caldwell

All rights reserved. No part of this book may be reproduced in any form by any electronic or mechanical means—except in the case of brief quotations embodied in critical articles or reviews—without written permission.

The characters and events portrayed in this book are fictitious. Any similarity to real persons, living or dead, is purely coincidental and not intended by the author.

License Notes
This eBook is licensed for your personal enjoyment only. This eBook may not be re-sold or given away to other people. If you would like to share this book with another person, please purchase an additional copy for each recipient. If you're reading this book and did not purchase it or borrow it, or it was not purchased for your use only, then please return it and purchase your own copy. Thank you for respecting the hard work of the author.

For more information about the author:
christicaldwellauthor@gmail.com
www.christicaldwellauthor.com

ISBN: 1514387913
ISBN 13: 9781514387917

DEDICATION

To Sarah.
On this writing journey I embarked upon, finding you and
your friendship has been one of the greatest gifts. You are
my meme master, the eyes upon my drafts, and more…
a friend and mother with whom I can celebrate the great,
and also lean upon when times are hard. Thank you.
For *Everything*.

PROLOGUE

Leeds, England
1805

At just eleven years of age, Lady Daisy Laurel Meadows, in all her infinite wisdom, realized the inherent silliness of her name. Everyone knew it. She frowned at the adults scattered about the table, breaking their fast, and then settled her glare on the two people responsible for that silliest of names. Her parents, otherwise engrossed in conversation with the Duke and Duchess of Crawford, failed to note her displeasure.

That is, everyone knew it…*except* for her mother and father, the Marquess and Marchioness of Roxbury. *They* seemed to think there was nothing wrong in naming one's daughter, Daisy. While her surname was Meadows.

She propped her elbows on the table. Silly name. From across the table, the cluster of three girls looked over at Daisy, giggling behind their hands. She picked up the buttered roll from her plate and tore it with her teeth.

Of course, her mother chose that precise moment to glance up. She gave Daisy a pointed look. Daisy chewed the warm, flaky bread then swallowed. She dropped the remainder of the roll onto her plate.

Someone set hands upon her shoulders and she jumped. A smile split her lips as she stared up at her older brother. "Lionel!"

He whispered close to her ear. "They're just jealous, Daisy."

"You came." She wrinkled her nose. "And no, they're not." They had golden curls and perfect porcelain white skin while she had plain, brown hair and too many freckles.

"Do you imagine Mother and Father would have allowed me not to come to their annual summer party?"

She snorted. "Certainly not."

He tweaked her nose. "And yes, Daisy. Those young ladies are indeed green with envy. Someday you're going to realize just how lovely you are." He glanced over at his two friends, Marcus, Lord Wessex, and Auric, Lord Ashburn, future Duke of Crawford. "Isn't that right, gentlemen? She's perfectly lovely, isn't she?"

Lord Marcus yawned and wandered over to the sideboard. His answer was quite clear.

Lord Auric winked at her. "Perfectly lovely." He leaned down. "In fact, when you have your Come Out, I'll gladly make you my future duchess."

Her heart tripped a little beat.

"See that, Daisy?" She whipped her head around to look back at her brother. "You'll become a duchess someday when all those other, unkind, girls find themselves with mere future marquesses such as myself."

She swatted his arm. "Don't be silly. I'll not let you wed a single one of those nasty creatures."

Lionel cuffed her on the chin. "Well, you will be a duchess, so you'll be able to command even me with a single look." He knocked his friend on the arm. "Granted, when you make your Come Out, Auric will be one of those old dukes with a quizzing glass to his eye."

Lord Auric opened his mouth to say something when a flurry of whispers and another round of tittering carried from across the room. Lady Leticia, one year younger and a million times prettier than Daisy, stuck her finger in Daisy's direction and giggled. Lord Auric glowered in her direction and the little girl's blue eyes formed moons in her face. He slid into the empty seat beside Daisy while Lionel claimed the chair on her opposite side. The trio fell instantly silent.

"Serves them right," Daisy muttered and grabbed her roll once again. She ripped into it with her teeth.

"Daisy," her mother chided from across the table.

She dropped the roll. She knew all the nonsense ingrained into her by Mrs. Wimpleton, her ancient governess, but really those tiny shredded pieces and nibbling bites were better suited to a small mouse than a human child.

Lord Auric picked up the partially eaten roll from her plate. He yanked an enormous piece off with his teeth and winked at her once more.

She grinned. He really was quite charming. And dashing. And all things wonderful. With a soft sigh, she propped one elbow onto the table and dropped her chin into her hand. With her free hand she reached for her glass of water. Her fingers brushed cold silver.

Shrieks erupted about the table, as the silver candelabra tipped sideways. The marquess yanked her hand back, even as several footmen rushed forward to blot out the small flames that now licked at the white, Italian lace tablecloth.

Lord Auric turned her hand over in his much larger one studying for marks. "No burn," he murmured.

"Daisy Meadows!"

Her mother took her by the forearm and steered Daisy to her feet. She allowed herself to be dragged from the slightly charred tablecloth. Another round of tittering from the trio of mean girls trailed after her. While her mother quietly scolded her, Daisy cast one last glance over her shoulder at the young marquess now fully engrossed in conversation with Lionel.

She sighed. She really didn't need the future Duke of Crawford. Just Auric would do.

ONE

London, England
21 April 1816

Lady Daisy Meadows was invisible.

Oh, she hadn't always been a shiftless, shapeless figure overlooked by all. In fact, she'd been quite the bane of her poor mother and father's existence, and prone to all manner of mischief, since a young girl had about as little hope of being made Queen of England as accomplishing the whole invisibility feat. And yet, she'd managed it with a remarkable finesse, through no help of her own. She could point to the precise moment in time when she ceased to be.

She plucked the copy of *The Times* from the rose-inlaid, mahogany table and scanned the words on the front page; so familiar she'd already committed them to memory.

> *Duke of C in the market for his duchess, thrown over by the Lady AA, etc., etc.,*

Offended by the blasted page, Daisy stuck her tongue out at the mocking words and threw the paper onto the table. *Thwack!* "Market for a duchess," she muttered under her breath. "As though he's hunting for a prime piece of horseflesh."

The Duke of C. None other than the illustrious, sought after, Duke of Crawford. Sought after by all…She glanced down at the page once more. Well, not all. After all, the then Lady Anne Adamson had rejected his suit in favor of the roguish Earl of Stanhope. The fool.

A fool Daisy was indebted to. But a fool nonetheless.

With a growl of annoyance she grabbed for the embroidery frame. She picked up the needle and jammed it through the screen with such zeal she jabbed the sharp tip into the soft flesh of her index finger. "Blast." She popped the wounded digit into her mouth and sucked the drop of blood. When she'd become invisible, she'd also taken to embroidering. She had been doing so for nearly seven years. She was as rubbish at it as she was at winning the heart of a certain duke.

With needle in hand, and greater care on her part, she pulled it through the outline of the heart...she wrinkled her brow...or, it was intended to be a heart. Now it bore the hint of a sad circle with a slight dip in the middle. She tugged the needle through once more with entirely too much zeal and stuck her finger again. "Double blast."

Giving up on the hope of distraction, she tossed the frame aside where it landed upon the damning page with a quiet *thwack*. She hopped to her feet then made her way over to the hearth. A small fire cast soothing warmth into the chilled room. She rubbed her palms together and contemplated the flickering flames.

It shouldn't matter what the scandal sheets reported about a certain duke in the market for a wife. She'd known it was an inevitability he would wed and had long ago accustomed herself to that sad, sorry truth that it would not be her but instead a flawless English beauty such as the Lady Anne. There had been whispers of a fabled heart pendant given by a gypsy and worn by the lady to win the heart of a duke. Nothing more than whispers from romantic ladies who believed in such silly talismans. It wouldn't have mattered if Lady Anne had been in possession of an armoire full of magic pendants. With her golden blonde curls and a remarkably curved figure, she could have had any duke, marquess, or in the lady's case—earl, she wanted. Unlike plump, unfortunately curved Daisy. To Auric, the 8th Duke of Crawford she was just as invisible to him as she was to everyone.

She picked her gaze up and stared at her reflection in the enormous, gold mirror. A wry grin formed on her too large lips. Odd, how a lady cursed with dark brown hair and a shocking amount of freckles, and of such a *plump* form should ever achieve the whole invisibility feat, and yet she had. "Now, I," she said to the creature with enormous, brown eyes. "I require some enchanted object." Nothing short of a gypsy's charm would help her win Auric's stubborn, blind heart.

Shuffling footsteps sounded in the hall, calling her attention. Her mother stood framed in the doorway gazing with an empty stare at the parlor, as though she'd entered a foreign world and didn't know how to escape it. It was the same blank look and wan expression she'd worn since they'd learned of Lionel.

Her brother. Her protector. Defender. And champion. Smiling and tweaking her nose one day. The next, lost in the most brutal manner imaginable. With his senseless death, he'd taken her parents' only happiness with them, and with his aching absence, left her invisible.

"Mother." There was a pain that would never go away in knowing, as the living child, Daisy could never restore happiness to her mother's world.

The marchioness blinked several times. "Daisy?"

"Yes." As in the woman's daughter and only surviving child.

"I…" Mother touched her fingertips to her temple as though she had a vicious megrim. "I have a bit of a headache." She glanced about the room. "Is Aur—?"

"He is not here," she interrupted. Following her husband's death two years earlier, the Duke of Crawford had become the only person her mother left the privacy of her darkened chambers for. In his presence, she somehow found traces of the mother, hostess, and person she'd been before her, nay *their*, world had been torn asunder.

"He is not," her mother repeated, furrowing her brow. With his visits, it was as though the cloak of misery she'd donned these years would lift, and the woman would show traces of the proper hostess she'd been once upon a lifetime ago. But with his departure, she'd settle into the fog of despair once again.

"No, Mama," she said gentling her tone as though speaking to a fractious mare. Auric hadn't been 'round in nearly a month. Three weeks and six days to be precise. But who was counting? "Surely you do not expect he'll visit forever?" There was no reason for him to do so. "He'll take a duchess soon." She hated the way her heart tugged painfully at that truth.

A flash of lucidity lit the marchioness' gray-blue eyes. "Do not be rude, Daisy."

"I'm not being rude." She was being truthful. Even as she longed to be the reason for his coming 'round, she'd long ago accepted that his visits were out of a ducal obligation to the dear friends of his late parents. And through it all, Daisy remained invisible. "His visits are merely an obligatory social call, Mother."

"I can't think when you speak like that." Her mother clenched her eyes tight and rubbed her temples, pressing her fingers into the skin. "I…"

Remorse flooded her and she swept across the room. "Shh." She took her mother by the shoulders and gave her a gentle squeeze. "You should rest."

The older woman nodded. "Yes. Yes. That is a very good idea. I should rest." She turned away woodenly and left in a sea of black, bombazine skirts. The only time she replaced her mourning attire was when she was forced out into Society with her still unwed daughter.

With a sigh, Daisy wandered back to the hearth and stared down into the orange-red flames. The fire snapped and hissed noisily in the quiet of the room. When she'd been a small girl, she'd loved to hop. She would jump on two feet, until she'd discovered the thrill of that unsteady one-footed hop. Then her mother had discovered her hopping and put a subsequent end to any such behavior.

At least when there was a hint of a possibility of Mother being near. Now, with her father gone, dead in his sleep not even two years ago, and a mother who'd ceased to note her existence, Daisy would quite gladly trade her current state for that overbearing, oft-scolding mother.

She gently tugged up the hem of her gown and jumped on her two slippered feet. A smile pulled at her lips as the familiar thrill of the forbidden filled her. Even if it was only the forbidden that existed in her mind, from a time long ago. Did she even remember how to hop? She'd not done so in…she searched her mind. Seven years? Surely not. Entirely too long for any person to not do something as enjoyable as jump or hop.

4

Daisy held her arms out at her side and experimented with a tentative hop. She chewed her lips. Boots had been ever so much more conducive to this manner of enjoyable business. "How utterly silly," she mumbled to herself. It was silly. Quite juvenile, really. And yet, despite knowing that and all the lessons of propriety ingrained into her, giddiness filled her chest. With a widening smile she hopped higher, catching her reflection in the mirror, a kind of testament to the fact that she was, in truth, visible. Still real. Still alive when the loved, cherished brother no longer was. "I am here," she said softly into the quiet of the ivory parlor. Daisy lifted her skirts higher and hopped up and down on one foot. Her loose chignon released several brown curls. They tumbled over her eye and she blew them back.

Ladies did not hop. Invisible ones, however, were permitted certain freedoms.

Her smile widened at the triviality of her actions. For many years, she'd been besieged with guilt for daring to smile or laugh when Lionel should never again do either. Eventually, she had. And along with guilt there was also some joy for the reminder that she was in fact—

"Ahem, the Duke of Crawford."

Daisy came down hard on her ankle and, with a curse, crumpled before the hearth. Her heartbeat sped up as she caught a glimpse of Auric's towering form, over the ivory satin sofa, at the entranceway. He wore his familiar ducal frown. However, the usually stoic, unflappable peer hovered blinking at her in her pile of sea foam green skirts.

She mustered a smile. "Hullo." She made to shove herself to her feet.

He was across the room in three long strides. "What are you doing?" Not: *how are you?* Not: *Are you all right?* And certainly not: *My love, please don't be injured.*

She winged an eyebrow upward. "Oh, you know, I'm merely sitting here admiring the lovely fire." His frown deepened.

Then in one effortless movement, he scooped her up and set her on her feet. A thrill of warmth charged through her at his strong hands upon her person. "Are you hurt?"

Well, there, a bit belated, but she supposed, better late than never. "I'm fine," she assured him. Her maid appeared in the doorway. "Agnes, will you see to refreshments?"

The young woman, who'd been with her for almost six years, turned on her heel and hurried to see to her mistress' bidding. Agnes had come to know, just like every other servant, peer, and person, that there was no danger to Daisy's reputation where the Duke of Crawford was concerned.

She took a tentative step, testing for injury.

"You'd indicated you were unhurt," he spoke in a disapproving tone, as though perturbed at the idea of her being hurt.

Goodness, she'd not want to go and bother him by being injured. "I am all right," she replied automatically. Then, "What are you doing here?" Mortified heat burned her cheeks at the boldness of her own question.

He gave her an indecipherable look.

"Not that you're not welcome to visit." *Shut up this instant, Daisy Laurel.* "You are of course, welcome." He continued to study her in that inscrutable way of his. Sometime between charming young boy of sixteen and now, he'd perfected ducal haughtiness. Annoyed by his complete mastery of his emotions, she slipped by him and claimed a seat on the ivory sofa. "What I intended to say is," *I,* "my mother missed your visits."

There was a slight tightening at the corners of his lips. Beyond that, however, he gave no indication that he either cared, remembered, or worried about the Marchioness of Roxbury.

She sat back in her seat. "Would you care to sit?" *Or would you rather stand there glowering in that menacing manner of yours?*

He sat. And still glowered in that menacing manner of his. "What were you doing?"

Daisy blinked at this crack in his previously cool mask. "What was I doing?"

"Prior to your fall." Auric jerked his chin toward the hearth. "It appeared as though you were," he peered down the length of his aquiline nose. "Hopping." The grinning Auric of his youth would have challenged her to a jumping competition. This hard person he'd become spoke to the man who found inane amusements, well...*inane*.

She trilled a forced laugh. "Oh, hopping." Daisy gave a wave of her hand that she hoped conveyed "what-a-silly-idea-whyever-would-I-do-anything-as-childlike-as-hop?" To give her fingers something to do, she grabbed for her embroidery frame and cautiously eyed the offending needle.

Auric shifted in the King Louis XIV chair taking in the frame in her hands. "You don't embroider."

No, by the weak rendering upon the frame, he'd be correct in that regard. For as deplorable as she was, she really quite enjoyed it. Her stitchery was something she did for herself. It was a secret enjoyment that belonged to her and no other. A secret Auric now shared. "I like embroidering." In the immediacy of Lionel's death, when the night-mares had kept her awake, she would fix her energy on the attention it took her to complete a living scene upon the screen. Some of her more horrid pieces had kept her from the gasping, crying mess she so often was in those earlier days.

An inelegant, and wholly un-dukelike, snort escaped Auric, and just like that, he was the man she remembered and not the stern figure he presented to the *ton*.

"What?" she asked defensively, even as she warmed with the restored ease between them. "I do." To prove as much she pulled the needle through the fabric, releasing a relieved sigh as it sailed through the fabric and, this time, sparing her poor, wounded flesh.

"Since when do you embroider?" Auric looped his ankle over his knee.

Out the corner of her eyes, she stole a peek at him. "For some years now." Seven, to be precise. Not giving in to dark thoughts, she paused to arch an eyebrow. "I expect a lofty duke such as you would approve of a lady embroidering." And doing all manner of things dull.

Except, he refused to take the gentle bait she'd set out for him and so, with a little sigh, she returned her attention to the frame. Auric had always been such great fun to tease. He would tease back. They would smile. Now, he was always serious and somber and so very *dukish*.

The awkward silence stretched out between them, endless, until her skin burned from the impenetrable gaze he trained on her. She paused to steal another sideways glance and found him trying to make out the image on her frame, wholly uninterested in Daisy herself.

Invisible.

"What was that?" his low baritone cut into her thoughts.

A little shriek escaped her as she jammed the needle into her fingertip. "What was what?" She winced and popped the wounded digit into her mouth.

"You said something."

Daisy gave her head a firm shake and drew her finger out to assess the angry, red mark. "No, I didn't." Not intentionally, anyway. She'd developed the bothersome habit of talking to herself and creating horrible embroideries. "I daresay with you having not been to visit in some time," three weeks and six days, but really who was counting? "you've come 'round for a reason?" Her question, borderline rude, brought his eyebrows together. Then, powerful dukes such as he were likely unaccustomed to tart replies and annoyed young ladies.

"I always visit on Wednesdays."

"No," she corrected. Before he'd inherited the title of duke, a year after the death of Lionel, with a carriage accident that had claimed both his father and mother, he'd been a *very* different man. "No, you don't." He always *had* visited. This Season he'd devoted his attentions to duchess hunting—which is where his attention should be. Her lips pulled in a grimace. Well, not necessarily on finding a wife, but rather on himself and his own happiness. She'd never wanted to be a burden to him, never wanted to be an obligation.

It wasn't always that way...

Auric drummed his fingertips on the edge of his thigh and she followed the subtle movement. Her mouth went dry as she took in the thick, corded muscles encased in buff skin breeches. He really possessed quite splendid thighs. Not the legs one might expect of a duke. But rather—"You're displeased, Daisy."

His words jerked her from her improper musings. "What would I have to be displeased with?" Displeased would never be the right word. Regretful. Disappointed. For the years she'd spent waiting for him to see more where she was concerned, he continued to see nothing at all. To give her fingers something to do, Daisy drew the needle through the frame, working on her piece, all the while her skin pricked with the feel of being studied.

"What is it?"

She jerked her head up so swiftly, she wrenched the muscles of her neck. Daisy winced, resisting the urge to knead the tight flesh. "What is what?" She glanced about.

Auric nodded to her frame.

"This?" Oh, drat. Why must he be so blasted astute? She alternated her attention between his pointed stare and her embroidery frame then pulled it protectively to her chest.

His firm lips tugged with a nearly imperceptible hint of amusement. "Yes, what are you embroidering?"

Then knowing it would be futile to casually ignore his bold question, she turned the frame around. Even as she revealed her work, her cheeks warmed with embarrassment over her meager efforts.

"What is *that*?" His sharp bark of laughter caught her momentarily unawares. The sound emerged rusty, as if from ill use, but rich and full, nonetheless. She missed his laughter. She'd still rather it not be directed *her* way.

"Oh, hush." She jerked the frame back onto her lap. Then she glanced down eyeing the scrap. It really wasn't *that* bad. Or perhaps it was. After all, she'd spent several years trying to perfect this blasted image and could, herself, barely decipher the poor attempt. "What do you think it is?" She really was quite curious.

"I daresay I'd require another glance."

Daisy turned it back around and held it up for his inspection. Silence stretched on. Surely, he had some manner of guess? "Well?" she prodded.

"I'm still trying to make it out," he murmured as if to himself. Lines of consternation creased his brow. "A circle with a dip in the center?"

"Precisely." Precisely what she'd taken it as, anyway. Daisy tossed the frame atop the table, inadvertently rustling the gossip sheet and drawing Auric's attention from one embarrassment—to the next.

As bold as though he sat in his own parlor, he reached for the paper. With alacrity, Daisy swiped it off the table just as his fingers brushed the corner of the sheets. "You don't read gossip." She dropped it over her shoulder where it sailed to the floor in a noisy rustle. "Dukes don't read scandal sheets."

"And you have a good deal of experience with dukes, do you?" Amusement underscored his question.

She didn't have a good deal of experience with any gentlemen. "You're my only duke," she confided. Couldn't very well go mentioning her remarkable lack of insight with gentlemen.

His lips twitched again.

A servant rushed into the room bearing a silver tray of biscuits and tea, cutting into whatever he intended to say. The young woman set her burden on the table before them and dipped a curtsy, then backed out of the room. Daisy's maid, Agnes reentered and took a seat in the corner, with her own embroidery. The servant was far more impressive with a needle than Daisy could ever hope to be.

"How is your mother?"

Ah, of course. The reason for his visit. Auric, the Duke of Crawford, was the ever respectful, unfailingly polite gentleman.

"She is indisposed," she said with a deliberate vagueness. Only Auric truly understood the depth of her mother's misery and, even so, not the full extent of the woman's sorrow. Daisy would not draw him into her sad, sorry, little world. She reached for the porcelain teapot and steeped a delicate cup full, adding milk and three sugars. She ventured he had enough of his own sad, sorry, little world.

Auric accepted the fragile, porcelain cup. "Thank you," he murmured, taking a sip.

"Well, out with it." Daisy poured another, also with milk and three sugars. "After your absence, there must be a reason for your visit."

"Am I not permitted to call?"

She snorted. "You're a duke. I venture, you're permitted to do anything you want." Just so the new stodgier version of his younger self knew she jested, Daisy followed her words with a wink.

Daisy stared expectantly back at him.

Auric considered her question. *Why do I visit?* Repeatedly. Again and again. Week after week. Year after year.

The truth was guilt brought him back. It was a powerful sentiment that had held him in an unrelenting grip for seven years and he suspected always would. Selfishly, there were times he wished Daisy was invisible. But she wasn't. Nor would she ever be. No matter how much he willed it. "Come, Daisy," Auric took a sip and then provided the safe, polite answer. "I enjoy your company. Surely you know that."

She choked on her tea. "Why, that was a bit belated."

He frowned, not particularly caring to have the veracity of his words called into question—even if it was by a slip of a lady he'd known since she'd been a blubbering, babbling babe.

"I referred to your response," she clarified, unnecessarily. Then, like a governess praising her charge, Daisy leaned over and patted him on the knee. "It was still, however, very proper and polite."

"Are you questioning my sincerity?" Having known her since she'd been in the nursery, and he a boy of eight, there was nothing the least subservient or simpering about Daisy Meadows.

"Just a bit," she whispered and winked once more. Then a seriousness replaced the twinkle of mirth in her eyes. "I gather you've not come by because you're still nursing a broken heart over your Lady Anne." Lady Anne Adamson—or rather the former Lady Anne Adamson. Recently married to the roguish Earl of Stanhope, she'd now be referred to as the Countess of Stanhope in polite Society. The young lady also happened to be the woman he'd set his sights upon as his future duchess.

"A broken heart?" he scoffed. "I don't have a broken heart." He'd held the young lady in high regard. He found her to be a forthright woman who'd have him for more than his title, but there had been no love there. Daisy gave him a pointed look. "Regardless, what do you know of Lady Anne?"

"Come, Auric," she scoffed. "Just because I made my Come Out years ago and disappeared from your life doesn't mean I've not always worried after your happiness." At her directness, a twinge of guilt struck him. She'd always been a far better friend to him than he'd deserved. Daisy's initial entry into Society had been cut short by the untimely death of her father. She and her mother had retreated into mourning and had only reemerged this year.

He shifted in his seat, not at all comfortable discussing topics of his interest in another woman with Daisy. She was…was…well, *Daisy*. "I thought you didn't read the gossip columns?" he asked in attempt to steer the conversation away from matters of the heart.

"Ah, I said *you* didn't read the scandal sheets." She held up a finger and waved it about. "You're a duke, after all. I'm merely an unwed wallflower for which such pursuits are perfectly acceptable."

"You're n—"

"Yes, I am," she said simply, as though no more concerned with her marital state than she was with her rapidly cooling tea. "I'm very much a wallflower and quite content." She took a sip.

"Must you do that?" he groused, even as it was not at all dukelike to do something as common as grouse. She'd always had an uncanny ability to finish his thoughts, as he had hers. Still, it was quite unnerving when that skill was turned upon a person.

"Yes, there simply is no helping it. I'm afraid I'll have Season after Season until—"

"I referred to finishing my sentences."

Daisy set her teacup on the table in front of them and leaned forward, her palms pressed to her knees. "I know, Auric," she whispered as though imparting a great secret. "I was merely teasing. Though, I expect you're unaccustomed to people going about teasing you."

He took another sip and thought once more about the only lady who'd managed to capture his attention. The Lady Anne Adamson, now Countess of Stanhope. There had been nothing fawning about the lady, which had been some of the appeal to the now wedded woman.

Daisy patted his hand. "You are better served in her belonging to the earl. You'd not wed a woman who is in love with another."

A dull flush heated his neck at the intimate direction she'd steered their discourse once more. Words of love and affection and hearts had no place between him and Daisy. Theirs was a comfortable friendship borne of their families' connection and strengthened by a loss they shared. A friendship that would likely not be if she learned the role he'd played in her brother's death. She'd certainly not be smiling and teasing him as she now did. Pain knifed at his chest. With a forcible effort, he thrust back his dark, regretful thoughts. "I've quite accepted Lady Anne's decision." There, that was a vague enough response. He felt inclined to add, "Nor was my heart fully engaged."

Daisy let out a beleaguered sigh. "If that was the romance you reserved for the lady, it is no wonder she chose another."

Instead of rising to her baiting, he asked, "Are you a romantic now, Daisy Meadows? Dreaming of love matches?"

"What should I dream of?" She sent a dark eyebrow sweeping upward. "A cold, emotionless union to a gentleman who'd wed me for my dowry?"

Auric stilled and looked at the girl, Daisy, and conceded, in this moment with talks of hearts and love matches and unions, that she was no longer a girl, rather a woman. "You've always been something of a romantic." A woman who, if one sorted through her entrance, and disappearance, and then reemergence into Society, was on her third Season, no less. She professed herself to be a wallflower. He eyed her a moment. He took in the dark, curled hair piled atop her head, the shock of freckles on her cheeks and nose, her too full mouth. Uniquely different than the Incomparables, she'd never be considered a great beauty by Society's rigid standards, and yet certainly interesting enough to make a match with a proper gentleman. "You desire love then, do you?" he asked, hating that it was not Lionel here having this discussion with her—for so very many reasons.

Auric expected her to debate the charge. Instead, she again sighed and picked up her embroidery frame. "You always were entirely too practical." She paused. "And clever. You are indeed, correct. I'm a romantic." Daisy looked down a long moment at her embroidery frame and then turned the ambiguous needlepoint toward him. "You really cannot tell what it is?"

"No idea," he said succinctly. On the heel of that was a sudden, unexpected, and *unwelcome* possibility. "Has some gentleman captured your affections?" Whoever the blighter was, he was unworthy of her.

She paused, for the span of a heartbeat. "Don't be silly."

His shoulders sagged with relief. He didn't care to think of Daisy setting her affections on some gentleman because it would require Auric to take a role in determining that man's suitability as her match and he did not welcome that responsibility. Not yet. Oh, as she'd pointed out, with her out a second time, it was likely she'd need to make a match soon. However, it was not a prospect he relished. There was too much responsibility that went with seeing to her future. Auric finished his tea and set aside his cup. He tugged out his watch fob and consulted the timepiece attached.

"You have business?" she asked with a dryness to her tone that hinted at her having identified his eagerness to take his leave.

"Indeed," he murmured as he stood. "Will you give my regards to your mother and send her my apologies for not visiting in—?"

"Three weeks?" Daisy rose in a flurry of sea foam skirts, that silly embroidery in her hands. "I shall." With her chocolate brown gaze, she searched his face. For a moment she opened her mouth, as though she wished to say more but then closed it.

He sketched a bow and started for the door.

"Auric?"

Her quietly spoken question brought him to a stop and he froze at the threshold. He cast a questioning glance back over his shoulder.

Daisy folded her hands, one gloved, the other devoid of that proper garment. He eyed her fingers a moment; long, exposed, graceful. How had he failed to note what magnificent hands she possessed? With a hard shake of his head, he concentrated on the lady's words. "You needn't feel an obligation to us. You've responsibilities. My mother and I, we know that." A pressure tightened his chest. She held his gaze. "Lionel would have known that, too," she assured him, unknowingly squeezing the vise all the more, making breathing difficult.

The polite and, at the very least, gentlemanly thing to do was assure Daisy that his visit was more than an obligatory call. But that would be a lie. His debt to this family was great. He managed a jerky nod and swept from the room, feeling the familiar relief at each departure from the Marchioness of Roxbury's home awash in memories.

Auric strode down the long, carpeted corridors, past the oil canvas paintings of landscapes and bucolic, country scenes.

Except with the relief at having paid his requisite visit, there was guilt. A new niggling of guilt that didn't have to do with his failures the night Lionel had been killed, and everything do with the sudden, staggering truth that Daisy Meadows was on her third Season, unwed, and…he shuddered, romantic.

Bloody hell. The girl had grown up and he wanted as little do with Daisy dreaming of a love match as he did with a scheming matchmaking mama with designs upon his title. The pressure was too great to not err where she was concerned.

He reached the foyer. The late Marquess of Roxbury's devoted, white-haired butler stood in wait, Auric's black cloak in his hands. "Your carriage awaits, Your Grace." There was much to be said for a man who'd leave the employ of the man who inherited the title and remain on the more modest staff of the marchioness and her daughter.

"Thank you, Frederick," he murmured to the servant he'd known since his boyhood.

The man inclined his head as Auric shrugged into his cloak and then Auric hesitated. As a duke he enlisted the help of very few. He didn't go about making inquiries to servants, particularly other peoples' servants, and yet, this was the butler who'd demonstrated discretion with his and Lionel's every scheme through the years. A man who'd rejected the post of butler to the new Marquess of Roxbury following the other man's death and remained loyal to Daisy and her mother. "Tell me, Frederick, is there…" He flicked an imaginary piece of lint from his sleeve. "Has a certain gentleman captured Lady Daisy's attentions?"

"Beg pardon, Your Grace?"

"A gentleman." He made a show of adjusting his cloak. "More particularly an unworthy gentleman you," *I*, "would worry of where the lady is concerned?" A gentleman with dishonorable intentions, perhaps, or one of those bounders after her dowry, who'd take advantage of her whimsical hopes of love. He fisted his hands wanting to end the faceless, nameless, and still, as of now, *fictional* fiend.

Frederick lowered his voice. "Not an unworthy gentleman, Your Grace. No."

Auric released a breath as the old servant rushed to pull open the door. Except as he strode down the handful of steps toward his waiting carriage, he glanced back at the closed door, a frown on his lips as the butler's words registered through his earlier relief.

*Not an unworthy gentleman…*Not. *No.* Not. *There is no gentleman who's captured the lady's affection.*

That suggested there was, in fact, a gentleman. And Daisy, with her silly romantic sentiments required more of a careful eye. "Bloody hell," he muttered as he climbed inside his carriage. He had an obligation to Lionel, and to Daisy, his friend's sister.

Whether he wished it or not.

TWO

Seated at the edge of Lady Harrison's ballroom floor, Daisy fiddled with her skirts. Couples whirled past in an explosion of colorful satin gowns. She eyed the dancers longingly and tapped her slippers noiselessly to the one-two-three rhythm of the waltz.

...it doesn't matter that you're a horrid dancer. When you love something enough as you do, it will come. Now focus. One-two-three. One-two-three...

The gentle chiding words spoken long ago whispered around her memory so strongly she glanced about, almost expecting her brother to be there, staunch, supportive, and at her side as he'd always been. Alas, the delicate chairs alongside hers remained fittingly empty. The aching hole that would forever remain in her heart throbbed and as she rubbed at her chest. She searched for one particular gentleman whose reassuring presence always drove back the agony of missing Lionel. Alas, every other unwedded young lady waited in breathless anticipation for the Duke of Crawford's rumored arrival as well. Except, with the rapidity in which he'd taken flight that afternoon, as though her townhouse was ablaze and he was bent on survival, Daisy was sure she was in fact, the *last* person he cared to see.

She sat back in her seat and sighed. For all the bothersome business of being invisible, there were certain benefits. She touched her gloved fingers to her bare neck as the silly thought that had taken root earlier that afternoon had since grown. The pendant. She required a necklace. Nay, not any necklace, but that whispered about heart worn by the Countess of Stanhope and the woman before her—the countess' twin sister.

Both strangers to Daisy. She slowly stood, shifting her gaze to her mama locked in conversation. Eyes blank, lips moving, the marchioness was her usual empty shell and certainly wouldn't note if her invisible daughter did something as scandalous as slip away from the ballroom. Alone. Unchaperoned. Nor would she likely care if she *did* note such a shocking aberration from Daisy's predictable self.

From across the room, a flash of burnt orange skirts stood vibrant amidst the sea of whites and ivory. Daisy's heart kicked up a swifter beat as the lovely, golden-blonde woman stole an almost searching glance about and then took her leave of the ballroom.

Before her courage left her, Daisy skirted the edge of the dance floor and slipped from the crush of Lady Harrison's annual event. Her slippered footsteps silent on the carpeted floors, she stole down her host's corridor. She fixed her gaze on the burnt orange satin skirts as they disappeared around the corridor and quickened her step, detesting her rather short legs that tended to complicate the whole hurrying about business. Daisy reached the end of the hall and turned in time to see her quarry slip inside her host's conservatory.

No good could really come to a lady sneaking off to her host's conservatory. She lengthened her stride and made her way down the passageway. Then, a good deal more freedom was permitted married women. Daisy, on the other hand, flirted with ruin sneaking about her host's opulent townhouse.

She paused outside the room and peeked her head inside. The young woman with pale golden ringlets sat on a bench examining a torn hem. Slim, blonde, with blue eyes and flawless skin, the beauty represented everything plump, freckled, Daisy with her plain, brown hair would never be. She'd accepted her lack of uniqueness amongst diamonds of the first water. Yet, in this instant, in this very moment, she would trade her two smallest fingers for a smidgeon of the perfect, English beauty possessed by the young woman.

"Blast and double blast," the woman muttered.

Daisy paused. For with that single curse, it removed the air of perfection Daisy had ascribed to the lady and made her human, and more…approachable. She cleared her throat. "My lady?"

18

Lady Stanhope shrieked. The bench beneath her tipped precariously backward and, for one horrifying, infinitesimal moment that stretched to eternity, Daisy suspected the woman would tumble backwards.

Then miraculously the bench teetered forward and righted itself.

Filled with horror, Daisy rushed over. "Oh, my lady, forgive me." Mortified heat blazed in her cheeks. She'd nearly upended the lovely countess. Accustomed to the cool rigidity of other ladies of the *ton*, Daisy braced in anticipation of a scathing reprimand.

Instead, she received a smile. "Oh, worry not." The recently wedded young lady waved a hand "It certainly would not have been the first time I'd toppled myself over."

She'd spent the better part of three weeks resenting this woman. Daisy *wanted* to hate her, *wanted* to despise her for having had everything Daisy herself desired. But she couldn't. Not with her smile and humility. "That is kind of you to say, my lady," she said pragmatically. "But it was entirely my fault." She'd always had a rather unfortunate tendency of knocking objects over. It would seem she'd now add people to that rather bothersome habit.

"Hardly," Lady Stanhope assured her. She motioned to her frayed hem. "I tore my gown and sought a moment of privacy." A pretty blush stained her cheeks and Daisy knew nothing about matters of stolen interludes and clandestine meetings, but she knew the countess waited for someone.

Envy, dark and ugly, twisted inside Daisy, as she considered whom the countess had stolen away to meet. Surely the proper, polite Duke of Crawford didn't dally with wedded ladies? Except on the heel of that was the ugly niggling thought of him dallying with any woman. Jealousy tightened her stomach into pained knots and she clasped her hands close to her waist in an attempt to dull the sensation. "My lady," she began. "I am Lady Daisy Meadows." Horrid name. Couldn't have had been given a light, feminine name such as Anne or a regal, stately name such as Katherine.

The countess' smile widened, the warmth of it sparkled in her blue eyes. Blue. Not brown. "Please, no need for such formality. It is just Anne."

A woman of her beauty, with her husky, melodic tone, could never be just anything. Which brought her back to the matter of this orchestrated exchange. To calm her trembling fingers, Daisy smoothed her palms over her pale yellow skirts. "My lady...Anne," she amended. She took a deep breath and then looked around. When she returned her attention to the countess, she found the other woman studying her, head cocked at a slight angle.

"Is there something I might help you with, Lady Daisy?"

"Daisy," she corrected. "Please, just Daisy." No other lady, certainly not any of Daisy's acquaintance anyway, would offer assistance with such sincerity. Which made it vastly easier to continue. "I heard tell of a necklace," she said softly. Even as the words left her mouth the inherent silliness in believing in such a talisman struck.

Lady Stanhope stared, unblinking. "A necklace?" The question came haltingly.

Daisy nodded. She touched her neck. "A heart pendant, to be precise. I heard it had been worn by you and your sister and...and others. That whoever wears this pendant will possess the heart of a duke." As soon as the words left her mouth, she bit the inside of her cheek. Cool practicality reared its head once more and the shame of both her boldness and foolishness in believing in enchanted objects. "Er, forgive me," she said hurriedly. "I..." *am a fool.* She turned to go.

"Wait," the woman's exclamation stayed her movement.

Daisy forced her legs to move and slowly faced Lady Anne once more. Pained embarrassment coursed through her being. It curled her toes and burned her cheeks.

"Oh," the countess said. A smile played about her bow-shaped lips. "You've heard of the pendant."

A thrill of hope drove back all previous shame. "It is true, then." The words escaped her on a breathy whisper. She'd learned long ago that all tales spread by gossips only contained the tiniest shreds of truth, if any, and had suspected the legend of the heart was nothing more than fool's gossip.

Lady Stanhope stood and wandered closer to the massive worktable, littered in pink peonies and crimson roses, and two flutes filled to the brim with bubbling champagne. The fragrant scent of spring wafted about the glass conservatory, at odds with the crisp, cool of the unseasonable late spring night. "It is true."

Hope flared in Daisy's breast. "I knew it," she whispered, more to herself. She'd ceased believing in magic and fate seven years ago, but in this, this she'd dared hope. Because the *emotion*, though buried, somehow nudged part of her heart, reminding her that it still dwelt inside her. Real and…there. Even as she denied it to herself. "May—" Daisy wet her lips, quelling the forward question she longed to ask. She was nothing more than a stranger to this woman and had no right to ask this horribly intimate favor. The woman stared on encouragingly and before courage deserted her, she blurted, "I would be eternally grateful if you would be willing to share your necklace with me." She winced at how very pathetic that entreaty emerged. Desperate. Hopeless. A lady willing to humble herself before a stranger for the dream of a certain gentleman's hand.

The countess studied her a long while, head tipped to the side, as though she examined an oddity just unearthed. Then a slow, dawning of understanding lit the woman's eyes. "Why, you desire the heart of a duke."

"No!" The exclamation bounced mockingly off the crystal windows. Another wave of heat slapped at her cheeks. "No," she said, this time in a far steadier tone. Except, that wasn't altogether true. "Well, yes." Daisy clamped her lips together, eyeing the glass door leading out to the Marquess of Harrison's enclosed garden and momentarily contemplated escape. "Not per se. Rather…" For, the truth was, she didn't want the heart of just *any* duke.

She wanted *Auric's* heart. Wanted it even though he still saw her as nothing more than Lionel's sister. Wanted it even as she'd bumbled and fumbled her way through not quite one, but somehow almost three, London Seasons, with the always-polite Auric there visiting or partnering her in the requisite dances, but never a waltz.

"Daisy?"

The gentle prodding jerked her from her woeful musings. "Forgive me," she murmured. "I was woolgathering." She'd been brave enough to humble herself thus far by orchestrating this meeting. Daisy squared her shoulders and pressed ahead. "I need the pendant, my lady." The fabled necklace represented the last sliver of innocence and hope—the hope of Auric, and more, Daisy's hope for them.

"Oh, Daisy." Sympathy flared in the countess' expression. "I am so sorry."

No! She didn't want the words she knew were coming. She wanted her hope and her sliver of gypsy's magic and lore. Her life was full of enough sad truths.

"After I wed Lord Stanhope, I had no further need of the pendant. I'd claimed the heart of the only man I'd ever wanted and gave the necklace to another young lady." Hope flared again in her breast. The countess knew who possessed the heart pendant—"Lady Imogen has since married." Daisy's mind raced. She had a name. A twinkle lit Lady Stanhope's eyes. "Not to a duke, but she found love, which is what matters most." All Daisy must do was approach Lady Imogen and humble herself before yet another stranger. Auric was worth the sacrifice. "We've since returned it to the care of the rightful owner."

Daisy's heart sank. Of course, Lady Stanhope recently wed, and her twin sister, the Duchess of Bainbridge, both possessed what all young ladies dared dream of—a happy, loving match; bits of fairytales that Daisy had ceased believing in.

Only now, with the truth of how very close she'd come to possessing that pendant, she was confronted again by the mocking truth of her own silliness for hoping and believing in fairytales and chasing rainbows when life had already shown her the gloom of rain. She swallowed. Gone. She'd lost her sole hope. Her only opportunity. Daisy dropped her gaze to the floor, managing a polite curtsy. "Forgive me for intruding on you, my lady. I shall allow you," Emotion lodged in her throat as she confronted once more the ugly possibility of whose company the countess even now awaited. She coughed into her hand. "I shall allow you your privacy," she repeated. She turned to go.

"Daisy."

She froze and looked back at Lady Stanhope questioningly.

"When I first discovered the existence of the Heart of a Duke pendant, I believed it would bring me the heart of a duke."

And it had. Even if the fool woman had chosen another over the Duke of Crawford, Lady Stanhope had earned Auric's heart. "Didn't it, my lady?" she asked quietly. "The papers purported that Aur…" She curled her toes with embarrassment at that telling revelation. "*The Duke of Crawford*," she amended, "made you an offer." Daisy knew. She knew because she'd lashed herself with each torturous word in the scandal sheets. Knew because she'd observed Auric as he publicly courted the golden beauty. Needle-like pain pricked her heart.

Understanding flashed in the woman's eyes. "You care for him."

"No," she said quickly. Because she didn't *really* care for him. She loved him. And love, this deep, abiding, twisting, aching sentiment that wreaked havoc on one's thoughts, was far greater than merely caring for a person. "I've known him for my whole life," she murmured into the damning silence. And she'd loved him since the picnic at her parents' country seat when he'd promised to make her his duchess and saved her fingers from being burned. Daisy slid her gaze away, unable to bare her greatest hopes and desires to this woman. No one knew of her love for Auric. Mostly because Daisy Meadows had ceased to exist for the past seven years, since her brother Lionel's death.

Anne claimed her fingers and she started at that unexpected boldness. "Do you know, the pendant worn by my eldest sister, Aldora, was lost. Given back to the gypsy woman who entrusted it to the care of her and her friends."

No, she'd not known the piece had left the Adamson sisters' care, until now.

"It always finds its way into the hands of the lady who needs it, Daisy." A wistful smile pulled at Anne's lips. "For me, the pendant represented," her gaze took on a faraway quality. "Well, it represented a good deal to me. When I discovered it gone, I pledged to find it. I dragged my sister Katherine along to the Frost Fair in search of it." The Frost Fair. That inane event held on the frozen Thames nearly two winters ago. Anne laughed, the sound clear like bells. "All on the word of a gypsy and maid who indicated that is where it could be found."

She pierced Daisy with her gaze. "Do you know why I'm telling you this?"

Daisy shook her head. The other woman spoke with a hope and optimism Daisy had not known in seven years. A stab of envy struck her for altogether different reasons.

"You see, Daisy, I wanted that necklace with a desperation. I was not willing to relinquish my hopes merely because of the inconvenience of not being able to find it. I set out in search." Her smile widened. "Of course, Katherine discovered it at the Frost Fair."

All Society knew the romantic story. A broken-hearted duke plucked the then Lady Katherine Adamson from the frozen Thames and now they had a grand love, the kind of which had debutantes and dowagers sighing with envy.

"Sometimes, Daisy," the woman said, interrupting her thoughts. "Sometimes you might have to look more or try harder, but if you do, ultimately you'll find the heart of a duke."

When you love something enough as you do, it will come. A cool wind slapped against the windows. Daisy folded her arms across her chest and rubbed, as Lionel's voice echoed around her mind.

Footsteps sounded in the hall and, in unison, they swung their gazes to the entrance of Lord Harrison's conservatory. A tall, golden-haired gentleman stepped inside.

"Hullo, lo—" The Earl of Stanhope's words trailed off as he moved his stare between his wife and Daisy.

It was the Earl of Stanhope! A giddy breathlessness filled Daisy's chest, threatening to lift her up and carry her from the room on the brusque breeze battering the glass panes of the conservatory. Why, it was the lady's husband. The countess had stolen away from the ballroom to meet her husband. Not Auric. But rather, her own husband.

Suddenly feeling like the veriest worst sort of interloper, Daisy dipped a curtsy. "Forgive me," she murmured. She should be properly scandalized at having interrupted the stolen interlude between two lovers. Except, relief dulled any other sentiment.

Anne shot a hand out. Daisy started as the countess captured her fingers. "The woman we returned it to is an old gypsy by the name of

24

Bunică. I cannot tell you where she will be." The countess squeezed Daisy's hands. "But if it is meant to be, you will find her."

Frustration warred with hope. The gypsy, Bunică, had been found at the heart of the frozen Thames, along the streets of Gipsy Hill, the English countryside. Why, the woman might as well be anywhere. Daisy squared her shoulders. And yet, the heart was out there. It had been handed off to the woman, Bunică, after seeing more than three ladies wedded and, more importantly, in love. A slow smile turned Daisy's lips. Lady Stanhope was indeed, correct. Some young ladies, well, the fortunate ones, they found love without the benefit of baubles and talismans. The others, the Daisy Meadows of the world, with their ridiculous names and freckled cheeks, they had to look more and work harder for happiness, for the gentleman who'd love them. Some men were worth looking for—and Auric was indeed one of them.

Even if he'd been an absolute lout through the years. Not all the years. Just seven of them. The most important seven of them. "Thank you so much, my lady," Daisy said softly. She dropped another curtsy, hurried to the door, and then paused a moment beside the handsome earl.

He sketched a bow and stepped aside, but Daisy paused in the doorway and spun back around. "My lady?"

"Yes?"

"You are so very fortunate."

The sparkle of happiness in the woman's eyes indicated she knew as much. "And you will be, too."

Having already stolen enough of the couple's time, Daisy slipped from the conservatory and closed the door behind her. She started down the long corridor, retracing her steps to the noisy din of the crowded, overheated ballroom. As each step brought her closer, the strands of the orchestra's waltz and trill of laughter from Lady Harrison's guests grew increasingly in volume.

Daisy paused at the fringe of the ballroom entrance and scanned the twirling couples, bathed in the soft glow from the chandelier ablaze with candles. She leaned against the column and took in the unadulterated smiles, the exultant laughs. Had she ever been that happy? Shoving aside the familiar melancholy, she scanned the hall. Daisy searched for and then found her mother staring sadly out at the dancers.

Just then a buzz filled the ballroom like a million swarming bees. Daisy followed the rabid stares and whispers and she stilled.

Auric stood at the entrance of the ballroom. Her heart quickened at his broad, powerful figure towering above the crowded room; a king amongst mere mortals. And she wished she could look away, wished she could be different than every other hopeful and equally *hopeless* young lady present. Alas, she'd lost her heart to him early on. The whispers became murmurs from eager mamas desperate to make a match between their daughters and the mighty duke, who'd proven with his courtship of Lady Stanhope he was, in fact, in the market for a wife.

"He is here. Pretty face, dear," one eager mama whispered to her golden haired, just out that Season, daughter.

The young lady puffed her chest out and tipped her chin up in an attempt to capture Auric's notice.

Daisy resisted the urge to point her gaze to the ceiling. Not that anyone would have noticed if she *were*, in fact, pointing her gaze any-where, or hopping on one foot, or spinning in a circle. Least of all, Auric. Only she seemed to suspect the truth. The Duke of Crawford wasn't just in the market for a wife. He'd been in the market for a *par-ticular* wife. Two vastly different things. He'd selected Lady Stanhope and, following Daisy's meeting with the woman in the conservatory, she could hardly blame him for the wise decision.

She claimed a spot beside the white, Scamozzi column and used the moment to study him. How effortlessly he moved through the throng of guests, with a casual grace most men could strive to emu-late and never hope to master. Gentlemen dropped deep, deferential bows. Ladies dipped their eyes and touched a hand to their surely fluttering hearts.

While other ladies wanted Auric for his title, Daisy didn't give a fig about the title of duchess. She wanted him to be the man she'd once known him to be. She wanted that man, who'd rescued a girl in need of frequent rescuing. After Lionel's death, however, Auric had become a stiff, somber figure. The *ton*, who didn't truly know him, attributed his austereness to that title of duke. She knew the truth. He'd been forever changed by the loss they'd both suffered. Now, Auric was the one desperately requiring saving and foolish Daisy had, of course, set her sights upon being that person. Whether he wanted it or not.

Auric paused beside the host and hostess. His hard lips moved, the words lost to the distance between them. She searched for a hint of the grinning young man he'd once been. Years had added depth and strength to his features and form. The harsh, angular planes of his face, the aquiline nose may as well have been chiseled in stone. His fashionably cropped chestnut hair with the slightest tendency to curl, the same rich, brown hue she'd once envied him for. Gone was the lean, narrow frame, instead replaced with whip-chord muscles. He shifted and the black fabric of his evening coat pulled over the taut muscle of his triceps. Her heart kicked up a beat.

Why couldn't he be one of those doddering, old, monocle-wearing dukes? It would be vastly easier to hate him—the polite, remote man she barely recognized.

As though he felt her stare upon him, he stiffened. With his cold, aloof gaze, he skimmed the ballroom. The distant glint in his eyes hinted at his boredom over the inane amusements. Then his stare collided with Daisy's. The ghost of a smile played on Auric's lips and her heart sped up. She returned his grin. Just then, their host and hostess said something to their revered guest which called his attention away from Daisy. The hard mask was firmly back in place. Had she merely imagined the slight softening when he'd found her in the crowd?

Perhaps those years of laughter and teasing she remembered spent with him and Lionel had been merely conjurings of a lonely, sad, little girl. Except, there had been a smile. Though faint and quick, it had been, at least, *real.* Though logic and propriety told her to look away and allow him to carry on as he did at these stiff, stodgy soirees, she caught his eye across the heads of the twirling dancers and winked twice, in rapid succession—their silent, unspoken secret shared between them.

He hesitated a moment. His gaze lingered on the top of her head and then he looked away.

Embarrassment slapped her cheeks. Of course, one would have to notice Daisy Meadows to have recognized the lady had been given the cut directly. By Auric. And Society paid little notice of the shelf wallflower. She folded her arms across her chest and tightened her mouth into a mutinous line. He thought to ignore her. Avoid her as though he'd not tugged at her curls when she'd been but a child and promised to make her his duchess. Granted she'd been but eleven years old. Still, a promise was a promise.

With determination in her step, she started across the ballroom.

Auric might see her as nothing more than Lionel's younger sister, but he should have a care. For she intended to hunt down that blasted pendant, and by God, when she did, she was going to have his damned heart.

THREE

C hrist. She'd winked twice.

It had been…Auric's mind raced…some seven years or so since either of them had winked at each other. So long, in fact, that he'd nearly forgotten that secret code only they two had known.

"You are to wink once if you're having a splendid time."

Twelve-year-old Daisy had snorted. "And what if I'm having a deuced, awful time?"

He tweaked her nose. "Two winks."

He'd not remembered, until this very moment.

Auric retrieved a glass of champagne from a liveried servant and carried it to the far corner of the ballroom. Or, to be more precise, the farthest corner away from the freckled, plump, young woman still staring openly at him. He glowered into the contents of his glass. *Do not look. Do not look. Do not look.*

He'd taken good care to relegate Lady Daisy Meadows and her floral name to the role of unaging child and yet at each ball, dinner, or soiree attended where she was present, he was jeered with the truth that she was no longer a child. All the innocence they'd once known, the ease in one another's company had been shattered. No. To see her merely reminded him of his greatest failings toward a friend he'd loved like a brother.

The sight of her never ceased to riddle him with guilt and regret for all his sins, for all he'd not done. Too often she stood forgotten on the sidelines of the hall and he'd have to make his way through the crowd and offer her his arm, in an attempt to erase the frequent sadness that lined her face.

Auric growled and took a long swallow of his champagne, and shoved aside thoughts of Daisy. Instead, he focused on the purpose of his attendance this evening. Practical and long driven by logic, it was time to do his requisite duty by the title. He required a wife, an heir, and a spare. That lesson had been impressed upon him early on by his parents, tutors, and Society. With that purpose in mind, he surveyed the crowd, deliberately avoiding sight of a certain mischievous miss with her bow-shaped lips. The only lady in the whole of the crowded hall who dared frown at him. The rest of the marriage-minded misses wore practiced smiles and fluttered their lashes when he caught their eyes. All of them with one, single aspiration—to become his duchess. For all his practicality these many years later, he aspired to be seen as more than a duke. He took another sip of his champagne and frowned over the rim of his glass. And he'd set his sights upon his perfect duchess, the lady, Lady Anne Adamson, now the Countess of Stanhope. Blonde, trim, with ample hips and a lovely singing voice, and wholly *unimpressed* by his title, she would have made him a fine wife. She, however, had gone and foolishly accepted the Earl of Stanhope's suit over his clearly superior, more advantageous offer. Which had thrust him back into the marriage mart, in search of an alternate duchess.

And there wasn't a single lady who'd attracted his notice since. As a result, he'd resumed his search for a wife with a renewed vigor and very specific expectations. She would need to be at least passably pretty, refined, a proper, English miss. What he did *not* need was a troublesome vixen, in frequent need of rescuing with too many freckles and a constant frown for him. He'd long ago sworn off troublesome vixens with freckles. Though, she'd not always been frowning. Once upon a lifetime ago she'd always had a smile for Auric.

He knew what had killed the girlish innocence. Through his negligence and influence, he was to blame. The sight of her was always like a lash of guilt being applied to his skin. Auric downed the contents of his glass and cradled the empty glass. A servant rushed forward to relieve him of the crystal flute.

Unwittingly, Auric's gaze wandered back over to the tall column Daisy hovered beside. He jerked his stare away. A frown formed on his lips. Furthermore, what was a young, unwed lady doing—alone, *sans* chaperone? Where was the lady's notoriously proper mother? Then his intent stare landed upon the somber Marchioness of Roxbury. A close friend of his late parents, the once vivacious woman was now a mere shell of the person she'd been before the death of her son, the late marquess' heir.

A loud humming filled his ears as Lionel's grinning visage flitted to his mind. Auric grabbed another champagne flute and took a long swallow, trying to drive back the memory of his friend. He directed his attention to where it should reside—on finding his duchess because the thought of that didn't suck the breath from his lungs and hammer his mind with guilt—

"Your Grace."

"Bloody hell." The startled curse escaped him at the stealthy Daisy's unexpected appearance.

She widened her eyes. "Did you just curse?"

"Did I curse?" he repeated blankly. He was nothing if not in control. In fact, he'd prided himself on his ability to not be roused to emotion since that night seven years ago. "I don't know what you're—" The twinkle in her brown eyes called him a liar when her words did not. A grin pulled his lips at the corners. "Lady Daisy Meadows." The lady who refused to stay buried in the proper chambers of his mind. "I imagined you'd know it is improper to speak without introduction."

She snorted. "I daresay cursing in Lady Harrison's ball is a good deal more inappropriate." Daisy waggled her eyebrows. "Even for a duke, I suspect." Her smile widened. "And considering our families' long connection, I'm permitted a mere hello."

He really needn't bait her. It merely encouraged her insolence. "There wasn't one." Alas, he'd always been hopeless where Daisy was concerned.

She tipped her head.

"A mere hello," he pointed out. "You issued a simple 'Your Grace', devoid of a curtsy." She'd been the only woman in the course of his life who'd been more put out with his title than impressed. His baiting words had the desired effect.

She stitched her eyebrows together into a single line "I beg your pardon?"

"A curtsy, my lady." He motioned to her legs. That impolite gesture one more freedom permitted him as duke. "A general expression practiced upon a polite greeting." He paused, drawing out the moment. "And you're forgiven."

Daisy opened her mouth to likely deliver a stinging rebuke to singe his ears and he blinked once, confounding her into silence. She scratched at her furrowed brow. Had she truly believed he'd forgotten the secret, unspoken language only they had shared? His was an unwillingness to use it, but he remembered everything and anything where Daisy was concerned. She'd been the sister he'd never had.

Then she gave a flounce of her brown curls, that familiar twinkle lighting her eyes. "Ah, yes, the curtsy." She tapped her fingers against the front of her forehead. "How could I ever forget, the ever important curtsy usually preceded by a polite *bow*." He'd have to be without hearing to fail to note the heavy sarcasm underscoring her subtle admonishment. She'd always possessed an indomitable spirit, his Daisy. He remembered her earlier claim to being a wallflower. How odd that not a single English gentleman had the good sense to appreciate the lady. Fools, all of them.

Which reminded him of his own purpose in being here this evening. With no little reluctance, he set aside the easy exchange with her and redirected his attention back to the ballroom floor, renewing his quest for a duchess.

Daisy cleared her throat.

Surely it was not such a difficult task to find an adequate duchess.

She coughed.

There certainly was no shortage of woman clamoring for the revered role.

Daisy coughed again.

With the exception of Lady Stanhope, who'd thrown him over for the Earl of—

"I said, 'ahem'."

For the love of all that was holy. "Is there something in your throat, madam?" From the corner of his eye he detected the slight tilt of her head. "Perhaps you should have punch, or champagne, or a bit of wine to clear whatever affliction bothers you."

"I was not apologizing."

He stared unblinking at her.

"Earlier," she went on to explain. "For the lack of curtsy. That wasn't an apology. I just thought you should know that, Your Grace."

Ah, she was "Your Gracing" him. She always did that when she was displeased with him. Even when he'd been a mere marquess. Had she always been this vexing? The chords of the waltz drew to a close and the collection of dancers upon the floor politely clapped. Then, arm in arm, the couples filed off the dance floor. Yes, yes he remembered now that she had been. And mischievous. And prone to prattling on which she'd since managed to cease. Auric took a sip of champagne.

"I gather you're looking for your duchess."

He choked.

The gold flecks in Daisy's eyes danced with amusement and she made to pat him on the back.

"Do not," he squeezed out.

She sighed. "Oh, you used to be so much more fun than this cold, curt, and crusty duke." Daisy waggled her eyebrows. "Well, then?"

Do not indulge her. "Well, what?" he gritted out, because he'd never been able to not indulge her. Not since she'd been a small girl with too many freckles and not since she'd grown into this woman with...well, still too many freckles.

"Who is she?"

Auric stole a glance about to gather whether or not some hopeful miss had heard those dangerous words uttered by the hoyden at his side. "Remember yourself, Daisy." He gave her a quelling look. This

33

was a dangerous game that really was no game at all, she played in public. His interest in the now wedded Lady Stanhope had only encouraged the matchmaking mamas and scheming title-hunters.

Daisy pointed her eyes to the ceiling. "Bah, you sound like my mother."

And because he'd known the marchioness since he'd been a squalling babe in the nursery, he knew precisely what she meant by that, and it was in no way a compliment.

Only the lady forgot he knew her as well as she knew him. "And I gather you're in the market for a husband." Her cheeks pinkened and she immediately clamped her full lips closed. Hmm. So this is all it would have taken to silence her. Except now, he eyed her with a renewed interest. This was interesting. The Daisy he did know, however, never did something as telling as blush. "Ah, come now, Daisy, are you shy all of a sudden? I would wager there is a certain gentleman who has captured your notice." Her color deepened a ripe red, swallowing up her freckles.

"Er, if you'll excuse me. My mama is motioning to me."

Auric stepped into her path, blocking her escape. "You can't know that."

"Of course I should know that." She bristled her shoulders with indignation. "She is, after all, *my* mother."

"Yes," He leaned down and murmured close to her ear. "But she also happens to be positioned *behind* you."

Daisy whipped around and found the marchioness and then swung her attention back to him. "Oh." If her cheeks turned any redder, they would catch fire.

"Yes. Oh." In spite of himself, Auric grinned. He'd forgotten what it was to tease and be teased. Granted this teasing business was a good deal more enjoyable when it was he that was doing the teasing and not being teased.

She dropped a hasty curtsy. "If you'll excuse me, I should allow you to return to your duchess hunting and I—"

"Never tell me." He lifted a single eyebrow. "Your mother is motioning to you?"

Daisy pointed her eyes to the ceiling once more. "You're insufferable," she muttered. With that, she spun on her heel and left him laughing in her wake.

Oh, the great big lummox.

Daisy stomped away and sought out the precise row of seven chairs tucked at the back, central portion of Lord and Lady Harrison's ballroom.

They were either completely devoid of logic or deliberately cruel to place the partnerless ladies at the center of the ballroom, in the exact spot every bored lord and lady's eyes were inevitably drawn to, if for no other reason than because of its obvious location.

She claimed an empty seat and glanced down the empty row. It was a lonely night for wallflowers.

She tapped her canary yellow slipper upon the marble floor. And that was another thing altogether. There really should never be such an inglorious class as wallflowers. Why, as long as gentlemen existed, every young lady should be partnered in at least one set. Then considering the Duke of Crawford's rather mocking dismissal, perhaps the dream of chivalry had been dealt the death knell.

Daisy glanced down at the very empty card dangling from her wrist. That was not to say she craved just any partner. She didn't want just any gentleman. Quite the opposite. She wanted a certain one. The great big lummox who really didn't deserve her regard—and yet had it anyway, because of the man he once was, and the man she knew he could be.

The man who now searched the crowded ballroom.

"Probably for his next duchess," she muttered under her breath. He'd not confirmed her supposition, but he hadn't had to. She'd well known that Auric, a man who so valued responsibility and honor as to visit almost weekly the family of his late friend, would, of course, see to his ducal obligations. He'd wed a proper blonde miss, have an heir and then a spare, and live his perfectly boring ducal life.

With another woman.

Absently, she touched a finger to her bare neck. It spoke to her desperation that she'd hang her hope of Auric, Duke of Crawford, upon the charm given out by a gypsy. Why, the gypsy probably had all number of heart pendants she gave to silly, romantic, young ladies in the market for a husband who also happened to be dreaming of love. She suspected the madness in pinning her happiness to that bauble, all to win Auric's heart, stemmed from a desire to return to a time when she had known happiness. Since Lionel's limp body had been returned to them, forever silenced, a perpetual cloud had followed her family. The kind of thick sadness that no smile or silly jest could cut through.

She scanned the crowd and found her mother precisely where Auric had last motioned. The marchioness stood off to the right side of the room with a blank-eyed stare as Lady Marlborough prattled on at her side. She didn't remember the last time Mother had smiled. Daisy sighed, not giving in to the wave of self-pity that threatened to consume her. She was best to focus her attention on where it belonged.

Auric.

…Who now stood conversing with Lady Windermere and her pretty blonde, blue-eyed daughter, Lady Leticia.

Daisy wrinkled her nose. Really, did every young English lady possess golden ringlets and those pale blue eyes? Auric bent over Lady Leticia's hand and dashed his name upon her card. "Humph," she mumbled.

And that was quite another thing. He well knew Daisy loved to dance the waltz. He had, in fact, served as de facto tutor when the miserable French bugger hired by her parents had boxed her ears for possessing not even a smidgeon of talent. Auric and Lionel had fashioned themselves as her dance instructors and had taken turns waltzing her about the room until she no longer stomped all over their toes. Yet, he'd reserve the dull minuets and reels for Daisy and one of those outrageously wonderful waltzes for those other ladies.

Did he not care that every other young woman would settle for the miserable Duke of Crawford for the sole reason that he was a step away from royalty? Whereas Daisy wanted him for the man he was. No, those young ladies likely didn't care that Auric was serious and hardly ever laugh—

He tossed his head back and laughed at something Lady Leticia and her mother said. The deep rumble echoed through the ballroom. "Humph," she mumbled again. If she were to do anything as outrageous as laugh in that belting, unrestrained way, she'd have garnered all manner of nasty stares. But he, as a duke, was permitted such freedoms as great big laughs.

Even if it was a fake laugh.

Unlike Lady Leticia and any of the other duchess-minded ladies, Daisy remembered the deep, alluring sound of it. Slow and quiet as though he weighed what he'd heard and gave it his special attention.

The orchestra plucked the beginning strands of a quadrille. She picked up her fan and tapped her arm in rhythm to the beat of the lively dance.

"I have been searching for you, Daisy."

She started at the unexpected appearance of her mother. "I tore my hem," she lied. Though she strongly suspected her perpetually sad mother lied as well. She'd not been searching her out. She no longer seemed to remember that she'd had a second child. Her heart had died with Lionel.

"Are you enjoying yourself?" she asked, her words eerily devoid of inflection.

"Oh, indeed." The lie came easy. Daisy didn't begrudge her mother the aching sorrow she cloaked herself in. First, she'd lost her only son and then her husband just a few years later. She understood loss perhaps better than anyone. Daisy darted her gaze about the room and found Auric, alone once more, his remote stare trained on some unknown spot in the vast ballroom.

Well, except for Auric. He and Lionel had been thick as thieves with their hands in the vicar's Sunday collection basket. Born but a few months apart, they'd been inseparable, attending Eton together, and then going off to university. Only one boy had made it out of university to see the world with a man's eyes.

She returned her gaze to her mother. For the first time, an uncharacteristic spark flashed to life in her deadened eyes. "It is Auric." Her throat worked with emotion. She yanked Daisy up by the hand.

Daisy grunted. "Mother—"

"Come along, Daisy. Surely you'd not be so rude as to avoid Auric."

No. Quite the opposite. If her mother had opened her eyes and truly seen her a short while ago, she'd have noticed that she'd quite embarrassed herself before the gentleman in question. "I just spoke to him, Mama." And teased him and was teased by him. Her heart fluttered wildly in her chest. *Get control of yourself, Daisy Laurel Meadows.* He'd since shifted his focus to Lady Leticia and the other golden-haired creatures he preferred.

Her mother ignored her protestations and continued dragging her along. "Surely not."

Daisy gave a juddering nod that dislodged an errant curl. It tumbled over her brow. "Surely."

Which apparently mattered not at all. With a single-minded purpose, her mother all but dragged Daisy through the crush of guests. She waved her free hand about. "Hullo, Your Grace?"

"Mother, please," she squeezed out through tight lips.

"Auric?" her mother continued, ignoring Daisy as was her usual. *Oh, bloody hell.* Heat burned her entire body as people peered down their noses at the Marchioness of Roxbury's bold pursuit of the sought-after duke. The *ton* failed to realize that this single-minded push for the Duke of Crawford was not born of a matchmaking mama, but of a mother who longed for whatever trace reminder she could steal of a beloved, long departed child.

Several inches past six-feet, Auric's imposing frame towered over the lesser people scattered around him. The duke stiffened. He turned his focus in on her mother.

"Auric!" Mother cried again.

And for one horrifying, painfully agonizing moment she thought Auric would turn and give them both the cut direct. She could forgive the miserableness he'd cloaked himself in. She could not forgive any cruelty toward her grieving mother. Mother staggered to a halt before

38

him. Then he smiled and the tension left Daisy's body on a slow exhale. It may be the same empty, cool grin he offered to members of Society, but the effort was there to spare the woman hurt and embarrassment, and for that goodness, he would always own a piece of her heart. The rest of it had always been his anyway. What was the remaining sliver?

"Lady Roxbury, a pleasure," he inclined his head, ever polite and kind to her mama. "Forgive me for not having paid a visit recently." He may as well have finished that off with, *I've been busy duchess-hunting.*

Her mother released Daisy's hands and raised trembling fingers to her lips. "Oh, Auric, it is so, so very wonderful to see you. We do not see enough of you. I am forever saying that." She briefly attended Daisy. "Aren't I, Daisy?"

Auric slid a glance over in her direction.

"Indeed." Another handful of lies by all. By all of them. The duke for saying it was a pleasure. Mother for suggesting she said anything at all to Daisy. And her for supporting the lie. She touched gentle fingers to her mother's forearm. "Mother, come, the duke is quite busy."

Mother's eyes went wide. "Do not be silly. We would never be an imposition. Not to Auric. Isn't that true, Auric. Assure Daisy she's merely being silly and impolite."

Daisy curled her toes so tight the arch of her foot ached. It didn't escape her notice that he failed to acknowledge her mother's request. Instead, the usually laconic marchioness launched into a flurry of questions and comments, as she always did around Auric. For him, Mother somehow found a way to be the lively woman she'd once been.

With agonized embarrassment, Daisy blew back the stray strand of hair over her eye and doggedly avoided Auric's attention, though it was difficult to ignore such a commanding figure of a man. With his intent, ice blue stare he could command the room with a single glance. She'd never before truly appreciated the masculine perfection he evinced, the—

"...must dance with Daisy."

Two pairs of eyes landed on Daisy. Her mother frowned, urging Daisy with her eyes to say something, and Auric, entirely too amused by her mother's urgings. "That won't be necessary. I'm certain the duke already has a partner for this set." All the sets. There was, after all, a sea of elegant, perfectly blonde, English creatures, hoping for a duke.

Her mother glared. "Of course he will dance with you. Isn't that right, Auric?"

He hesitated. "It would be a pleasure." As he was nothing, if not well-mannered, he reached for Daisy's dance card.

Daisy yanked her card close to her chest. "What are you doing?" She'd detected his slight, almost imperceptible, pause following her mother's request.

He froze.

After Lionel, Daisy had become nothing more than a young lady Society felt sympathy for. Well, she was tired of being pitied. She would not dance with Auric because he felt badly for her nor because he'd been bullied into it.

"Daisy!" Her mother glared at her with far more life than she'd shown in weeks.

Daisy tipped her chin at a mutinous angle. Nor did she want another of Auric's polite country reels. She loved performing the steps of any and every dance but she'd had enough of those dratted polite sets with him.

With the same boldness he'd evinced as a young lad, Auric made another attempt for her wrist. "I'm marking your card."

Daisy held the offending object close to her breast. She wanted him, but not like this. Not partnering her at the bequest of her mother, a pitying favor from a magnanimous duke. His gaze followed that damning card and lingered. Some hot emotion flared in his eyes. For one slight moment she imagined he noted her bosom, which was first silly because Auric noticed nothing of her and second, humiliating to imagine he'd stare at her *there*. Humiliating mounds of flesh. That is what they were. She really wished she had a trim waist and small bosom. Not the too-rounded figure that would never fit with the *ton's* dictates for a beauty.

In the end, the marchioness settled the dispute between them much the way she had when they'd been squabbling children.

Invariably, Auric had always been in the right. "Don't be ridiculous, Daisy," her mother snapped as she took Daisy's wrist and extended it toward Auric.

Daisy's pulse jumped wildly as his fingers brushed the sensitive skin of her wrist. A touch shouldn't elicit these shivery thrills of awareness, the kind that…She bit the inside of her cheek as Auric scanned the card.

The empty card. As in devoid of partners. As in utterly humiliating. As in she wanted the ballroom floor to swallow both her and her miserable card up, whole. Or in the very least that program upon her wrist.

Giving no indication that he'd noticed her remarkable lack of partners, he penciled his name for a set, as he sometimes did and then sketched a respectful bow—as he *always* did. "If you'll excuse me. Lady Roxbury, a pleasure as unusual. Lady Daisy," he murmured, his low baritone washed over her like warmed satin.

As he wandered off, she fiddled with the card dangling from her wrist.

"How could you be so rude to Auric, Daisy?" her mother chided. "He is a dear friend of this family."

He *had* been a dear friend. Now he was more a polite gentleman who paid frequent visits to her and her always-sad mother.

Then, with an uncharacteristic energy in her step, her mother turned away and returned to the spot she'd previously occupied at the side of the ballroom. What the other woman failed to realize was that Auric had merely been forced into partnering her. Nothing more than her mother's needling and his dratted sense of obligation had driven his offer.

Absently, Daisy glanced down at her card—and her heart paused. A waltz. She whipped her gaze up and passed it through the crowded room, and then located him in conversation with another golden-haired, marriage-minded miss and the lady's mama. She looked past the young woman. If Auric had wanted to avoid contact with her, he'd surely have claimed an available quadrille or country reel. But he hadn't. He'd claimed her waltz. A waltz, when he never before dared partner her in that most intimate, still slightly scandalous of the sets.

A small smile played about her lips as she sought out her previous seat. If he'd claimed her waltz without even the benefit of the heart pendant, the Duke of Crawford stood little chance when she had that bauble clasped about her neck. Enlivened, Daisy sat and tapped her feet to the orchestra's lively country reel. As much as she detested the crowds of London and the mindless amusements of balls and soirees, she really *did* quite enjoy dancing.

It really was quite a shame she didn't have more opportunities to practice the intricate steps of the quadrille or the forbidden movements or the waltz. Why, she'd settle for even the out of mode minuet. And, she wouldn't even be particular with her dance partner. She frowned and again located Auric amidst the sea of dancers. That is, assuming the gentleman hadn't been forced into said set by Daisy's adamant mama.

Her frown deepened. Auric moved with graceful precision through the motions of the dance. His partner was none other than Lady Leticia, golden-haired and black-hearted and utterly vile—all the necessary criteria for a lofty duchess. Daisy curled her fingers around the edge of her seat. He deserved more than an empty, emotionless entanglement.

What if it is not emotionless? What if he carries the same aching desire for Lady Leticia that I carry for—?

"Daisy Meadows, the girl of the flowers."

A small shriek escaped her, earning her the curious stares of those around her. She flushed and, with a hand at her fast-beating heart, surged to her feet. An unwitting smile turned her lips. "Marcus," she greeted warmly. Lord Wessex and Auric had both been fast and loyal friends to her brother and would therefore always hold a special place in her broken heart. She ignored the outraged gasp from lone wallflower seated just a handful of seats down.

Daisy and Marcus and Auric, they three shared a bond that defied societal norms and matters of propriety. Their relationship had been forever cemented by the unfortunate bond they shared in the great loss of their friend, her brother.

Marcus, the Viscount Wessex bowed over her hand. "Hullo, Daisy." Where Auric had been something of a fixture through the years at her home, the viscount had made himself scarce. Then, according to the papers, Marcus had long been the unrepentant rogue, living for his own pleasures, and certainly without time for the former girl he'd found underfoot. "Good evening, my lord."

"My, how very formal you are." He wagged a blond eyebrow. "Should I expect you to begin prattling on about what fine weather we've been enjoying?"

She inclined her head and donned her most proper-hostess expression. "Splendid spring weather we're having, wouldn't you say, my lord?" Thunder rumbled and shook the foundations of the elegant townhouse, as though in appreciation of her wry attempt at humor.

He chuckled. "Indeed." Then Marcus did a quick, detached up and down of her person. "You look lovely as usual."

She snorted. "It seems you've grown into one of those compliment spouting, polite gentleman."

His grin widened, and then a mask of seriousness replaced his earlier mirth. "How are you, Daisy?" He searched her face with his blue gaze.

She pasted a smile to her lips. "I'm well."

Marcus cleared his throat. "I should have come around."

She waved a hand. "It is fine." It hadn't been for very many years. Eventually, she'd learned to breathe again, and laugh again, on her own without the support of those who'd mattered to Lionel.

He shook his head. "It's not."

They seemed to realize as one that he still held her hand. Daisy yanked her fingers back. Not one to attract frequent notice, it still wouldn't do for her to be seen holding a gentleman's hand overly long, even if it was just Marcus. The *ton* didn't care how long a lady knew a respectable gentleman or the familial connections shared but rather the juicy morsel of gossip they might represent to the *haute ton*. She smoothed her palms over her skirts and returned her attention to the ballroom floor.

"Did you just dismiss me, Daisy?" he drawled and gone was the somber figure of a man, in his place, the notorious rogue.

"Er...no." Though she could certainly see how it appeared that way.

Marcus stood shoulder to shoulder beside her, and then with a deliberate slowness, folded his arms across his chest.

She stole a sideways peek up at him. His gaze remained fixed on the crowded dance floor. "What are you doing?"

His lips pulled up at the corners. "Trying to gather just who has earned your attention."

Heat burned her cheeks and she jerked her attention back to the neat rows of clapping dancers.

"Ah, you won't tell me, then?"

No, she would not. She clamped her lips into a tight, determined line. She'd sooner pluck each too-curly strand of hair from her head than ever acknowledge to him, Auric, or anyone that the sole gentleman whose attention she longed for was, in fact, the proper Duke of Crawford.

"I take that as a no," Marcus murmured.

She gave a firm nod. "That is a no."

He pounced faster than Cook's cat on the kitchen mice. "Which means there *is* some certain gentleman who has ensnared your attention."

She pointed her eyes to the ceiling. "I didn't say that, Marcus." He was worse than Lady Jersey with her desire for gossip.

"You didn't need to."

The repartee, the teasing, but hard, protective edge underscoring his words seemed so very similar to her brother's vexing treatment that her heart tugged with the pained reminder and, for a moment, she forgot that she sought to bury the truth from him, forgot she'd gone and fallen in love with a gentleman who seemed to have forgotten she even existed.

Then Marcus pulled her back from her musings. "Who is he, Daisy?"

The orchestra's tune reached a lively crescendo and the stomping feet and clapping hands threatened to drown out his words. She cupped a hand around her ear. "What was that you said?" Daisy shook her head. "I could not hear you," she mouthed.

He folded his hands around his mouth. "I said—"

And when it seemed he'd shout his suspicions before a room full of witnesses, she mouthed, "Don't you dare."

Marcus blinked in feigned innocence. "But you indicated you were unable to hear…"

She swatted him with her dance card. "Oh, do hush. You know I was being deliberately difficult to match your deliberate difficultness."

They shared a smile. A companionable silence descended as they stared back out at the ballroom floor. "So you'll not tell me." From the corner of her eye, she detected the hard, determined set of his jaw. "Very well. I'll be forced to guess," he said, his sudden concern at odds with the indifferent, young boy and then man, she'd known through the years. Even as a friend to her late brother, hers and Marcus' relationship had never been a close one. Unlike her relationship with the duke, who, if he'd seen her as bothersome had certainly never indicated such sentiments. If he had, mayhap she'd not have thought of him with such fondness through the years "Is he present this evening?"

In spite of herself, she located Auric with her gaze. His large hand intertwined with Lady Leticia, they made quite the striking couple. "Hmm?" She gritted her teeth in annoyance, detesting the image presented to Society. Nothing plump or freckled about Lady Leticia.

"Daisy?"

She started at Marcus' gentle prodding and gave her head a shake. "No. I'll not tell you."

He sighed. "You'll force me to guess the unworthy blighter's identity."

Daisy bit back a smile. "I'd rather you not spend any efforts guessing the er…gentleman's identity."

Marcus captured his chin between his thumb and forefinger and rubbed. "Hmm, then answer me this. Is he a good man, because I'll not allow you to ensnare the attention of a rogue like myself?"

She'd not earned anyone's notice, and most certainly not the gentleman she'd hoped to, as Marcus put it, *ensnare*. "He is, honorable," she said softly.

"Well, then. I'll be left to guess."

"Yes, I believe we've already surmised as much," she said dryly.

"Humph," he muttered.

She bit the inside of her cheek to keep from smiling, refusing to give in to his baiting. She'd wager the use of her right hand he'd never guess the identity of the gentleman in question. Neither Auric nor Marcus had ever truly seen her as anything more than a sisterly extension of Lionel. Yet, for the bother Marcus now made of himself, it felt so very nice to be teased. For too many years, with servants and polite Society alike, she'd become accustomed to being tiptoed around, whispered about pityingly. Lady Daisy Meadows, the poor, young lady, whose family had crumbled, first with the loss of Lionel and then with Papa.

The orchestra's frantic playing drew to a cessation and the crowd erupted into a bevy of applause. The violins plucked the opening strands of the next set.

Marcus held his elbow out.

She eyed it. "What are you doing?"

"Dancing with you."

She folded her arms and took a step away from him. "Are you asking or ordering?"

He leaned close and again waggled an eyebrow. "Have a pity, Daisygirl. However am I to gather the identity of the gent who's captured your notice if I don't do a bit of investigating?"

A strangled laugh worked its way up her throat. "Well, then in the name of your research, I suppose I should allow you this set." She placed her fingertips upon his coat sleeve and allowed him to guide her toward the dance floor.

He maneuvered her expertly through the crowd. "Lord Darbyshire?" he whispered close to her ear.

She looked around. "Where?"

"Is it Lord Darbyshire who has caught your fancy?"

She pinched his arm. "Lord Darbyshire is sixty if he's a day."

"Even older gentlemen require the love of a good, kind lady."

"Ideally from a good, kind lady closer in years to his own," she said, her tone droll.

They took their places alongside the other couples lining the floor. She curtsied with the row of ladies. Marcus dropped a bow. They walked down the center of the line. "Lord Willoughby, then?"

They switched partners. She gave her head a little shake and moved through the steps of the quadrille until she and Marcus were brought together. They raised their palms and performed the next motions of the dance. "I daresay a waltz would be more conducive to finding out your secret, Daisy Meadows," he said under his breath.

"You should have better strategized before hastily requesting the quadrille." She laughed, earning disapproving stares from the other dancers. "We're attracting notice, my lord."

He winked. "Which would make it in your best interest to share the name of your suitor."

Some of her amusement died. She'd the same chance of calling Auric her suitor as she did in being named the Queen's favorite. Both about as likely as a rainbow without the rain. "I don't have a suitor," she muttered.

The dance saw them separated yet again.

When the steps brought them back together, he took her hand and gently twirled her. "You do know you'll leave me little choice but to enlist Auric's support."

Daisy stumbled.

Marcus' teasing grin faded and he righted her.

"I'm sorry," she said hurriedly, grateful when the dance saw them separated once more. She glanced around in search of Auric and located him at the opposite end of the ballroom floor where he now stood, a glass of champagne dangling carelessly between his elegant fingers. With an almost detached interest, he surveyed the ballroom. She frowned. No, it wouldn't do for Marcus to discover she'd gone and done something so foolhardy as to fall in love with the unattainable duke.

The steps of the dance brought her together with Marcus once more. Gone was the teasing light in his pale blue eyes. Her stomach clenched as she braced against the dawning awareness in his intelligent gaze.

"You do know I was merely teasing. I'd not dare enlist Crawford's stuffy support."

The tension drained from her and an almost giddy sense of relief filled her. "Oh, is he stuffy?" Marcus didn't realize the gentleman who she'd gone and fallen hopelessly and helplessly in love with many years ago was, in fact, his best friend.

Lord Marcus' response was automatic. "Certainly. Hopelessly stuffy and seems more so in the years since he became duke."

They went through the delicate, circle steps of the quadrille.

Auric's parents had died a number of years ago in a tragic carriage accident. Not long after Lionel's death. Pain pricked her heart. Selfishly, she'd been besieged by the agony of her own loss that she'd never really stopped to consider the great heartbreak he had known in such a short span of time. She sought him out in the crowd once more and again stumbled.

His coolly detached gaze took in her graceless movement, Marcus' quick rescue, and then he glanced back out across the floor, promptly dismissing her.

He'd not always been so *ducal*. Not to her. Never with her. She wanted him the way she remembered him to be, and she was prepared to fight for that man. Whether he wanted her to, or not.

FOUR

For the better part of the evening, Daisy had been seated at that ignoble place at the back, central portion of the vast ballroom relegated to the fate of wallflower. What hostess set up a neat, little row of chairs in that area for all those to see, gawking and gaping at the poor, partnerless creatures? Of which, there happened to be but one for the better part of the evening. One he cared very much about. He'd spent the night studying her, fuming with the realization that Daisy was, in fact, one of those poor, partnerless creatures. How had he failed to realize as much? Perhaps because he didn't see her as a young lady in the market of a husband but rather the small girl sprinting through the grounds of her family's country estate.

Now, he studied her for altogether different reasons.

He took in the sight of her graceful, elegant steps as the Viscount Wessex—his sole remaining friend in the world—led her through the movements of the quadrille. At that moment, Wessex touched his hand to the curve of Daisy's lower back and said something close to her ear. A crimson blush stained her cheeks and she faltered. Auric narrowed his eyes. A dark haze of red descended over his vision. He blinked it back. Wessex wouldn't dare betray Lionel's memory by turning his roguish charm upon Daisy. Not that his annoyance with Marcus mattered for any reason other than to honor Lionel's memory. This seething rage had absolutely nothing to do with the lady herself. Nothing, at all.

Auric continued to study her and Wessex as they stepped a deliberate circle about one another. Did the other man have to clasp her waist in that manner? She was not one of the viscount's many lightskirts. His fingers twitched with the sudden urge to plant a facer on the other man, and to keep from doing as much, Auric drummed his fingertips on the edge of his thigh while eyeing her objectively, seeing her as the foolish young swains who'd relegated her to the role of wallflower, saw her. There were her brown curls and the shock of freckles. Then, it was hard to see the lady and *not* see those very unique features that set her apart from the other ladies. Now, however, he forced himself to peer past the curls and the freckles—and then he widened his eyes, swallowing back a curse.

Daisy Meadows had grown from troublesome child to voluptuous woman. Vastly different than the lean, delicate, golden creatures he generally preferred, she possessed rich, brown tresses that gleamed in the candlelight. Her heart-shaped face would never be considered characteristically beautiful like that of a delicate, English lady and yet, her large, brown eyes and bow-shaped lips were enough to make a man dream of all manner of wicked thoughts involving those lips. A surge of awareness coursed through him.

Thunder rumbled outside, shaking the walls of the ballroom. The earth's way of telling him he would be spending the end of his days in hell for lusting after Daisy Meadows. Not that he was lusting after her per se, because he had sense enough, *honor* enough, to not ogle Daisy. Any more than he already had, that was. He'd merely noted her lush form the way any other gentleman might. Such as Wessex. He jerked his attention back to the charming viscount.

His friend, on the other hand, was less than discreet in his appreciation. Auric glowered as Wessex's gaze dipped overly long to the generous swell of her bosom. By God, surely the man had sense enough to not long after Lionel's sister. Auric finished the contents of his champagne and placed the glass down on a passing tray.

This mind-numbing, black rage that clouded his vision stemmed from a desire to protect Daisy from hurt. That was all. A mere obligatory reaction. Regardless, she would never harbor romantic sentiments for Wessex. Why, the idea was as ludicrous as the lady developing a *tendre* for Auric's miserable self. He fixed his gaze on the pair. Just then the other man, who could charm the proper out of matrons and young misses alike, said something Daisy seemed to find of extreme hilarity. Her laughter earned disapproving stares from nearby matrons.

Auric sucked in a breath, as Daisy was temporarily transformed from someone unremarkable into someone really quite captivating. Her hips were generous, her waist well curved, her breasts…He winked. Twice. The one-two wink that, had she been looking, would have suggested immediate help was needed. And perhaps it was. For he had no place appreciating Daisy Meadows' lush breasts.

Egads, she'd become a woman in need of a husband. With the same methodical precision he applied to all aspects of life, Auric turned his attention to the crowded ballroom, taking in the gentlemen assembled. By her admission that morning, the lady sought…he shuddered, romance. He resisted the urge to tug at his suddenly too tight cravat, not at all welcoming the idea of thinking of Daisy as a romantic lady, seeking love.

Who of the lot here would Lionel have approved of? With the man's devotion to his younger sister, the obvious answer was, in fact, no one. Daisy's greatest defender, her most ardent champion, Lionel would have scoffed at the prospect of nearly any one of these gentlemen present courting or wedding his sister.

Restiveness stirred to life in his breast. He didn't want this responsibility. The task was too great. The risk of failure not to be contemplated. He registered the orchestra concluding the lively quadrille.

Except, at the very least, he owed Lionel this much. The details of that night remained cloaked in a black shroud. He could not sort through the memories but for a disjointed collection of experiences that belonged to another. He and Lionel, who'd never argued, had quarreled—but about what? Ultimately, Auric had encouraged the other man to join him at the club, Auric had paid the coin for the woman who'd taken Lionel to another room, and it had been Lionel, who'd ultimately paid—with his life.

He pressed his eyes closed as a sickening wave of dizziness struck.

The orchestra plucked the haunting strands of a waltz, the discordant tune eerily suited to the dark memories. He forced his eyes open and there, across the dance floor where even now dancers assembled, his gaze collided with Daisy beside that same Scamozzi column. Only now, she was not alone. She was with Wessex. The other man had also been more of a brother to her than anything else through the years, treating her as a bothersome, younger sister.

At seeing the wide, unfettered smile that was patently Daisy turned up at the other man, an odd pressure tightened in Auric's chest. He scoffed. Why should it matter if she was with Wessex? The viscount's presence relieved him of responsibility. Except, there was nothing at all brotherly in Wessex's attention now, and annoyance rolled through Auric at the truth of it.

With a determined step, Auric strode across the ballroom, bypassing marriage-minded misses and their hopeful mamas. He stopped before Daisy and Wessex. "Wessex," he drawled in the indolent tone he'd perfected as a young boy who'd known he'd ascend to the role of duke. He ignored the narrowing of his friend's gaze and shifted his attention to the young lady on his arm. "Hello, Daisy."

She frowned. "Hullo, Your Grace."

Frowned. When she'd been all smiles and boisterous laughs for Wessex, which only mattered because this was Lionel's sister. He extended his elbow. "I believe this is my set."

Daisy hesitated a moment and then placed her fingertips along his coat sleeve.

Wessex spread his arms and bowed. "I bid thee good evening, lady of the flowers." That endearment set Auric's teeth on edge. With a wink, the viscount took himself off.

Without another glance for the other man, Auric guided Daisy onto the dance floor. Friendship or not, it wouldn't do for Wessex to go winking at the young lady in public.

"Oh, Auric, it is merely Marcus," she said as though gently scolding a small child.

"I didn't say anything."

The lady's smile was back in place. "You didn't have to." She gave him a wink. A single wink.

*You are to wink once if you're having a splendid time...*His heart kicked up a rhythm. On the heel of the damned lightness in his chest was a surge of annoyance with himself.

"Will you slow down?" Daisy muttered at his side.

Immediately repentant, he adjusted his stride and guided them to the edge of the ballroom floor. They took their place alongside the other couples. "Wessex, is it?" he asked, placing her hand upon his shoulder and his own along her waist. The orchestra struck the chords of the bold, still frowned upon, dance.

Another red blush stained her freckled cheeks. "Wessex is what?"

A muscle ticked at the corner of his mouth. Was the blush because he'd ascertained her interest in Lord Wessex? "Never tell me the romantic hopes you carry for a love match reside with Wessex?"

A laugh escaped her full, bow-shaped lips. "I don't imagine that is your business, Auric."

He lifted a single eyebrow. "Everything you do is my business, Daisy." He'd made that pledge over Lionel's lifeless body.

A snorting laugh burst from her. "Why, I believe in all your ducal arrogance you actually believe that." Then, this was Daisy and she'd never been impressed by his title as marquess and the promise of him becoming a future duke. She patted him on the arm. "I'll assure you, as I assured Lord Wessex, I don't require additional mothering." He told himself the rush of relief had more to do with the fact that Wessex had like honorable intentions to see her cared for, and yet, why did that feel like a lie?

"What if I were to tell you it is because I care, Daisy?"

What if I were to tell you it is because I care...

Daisy's heart sped up with that question, an admission more than anything else. If she were to answer truthfully, her response would be *"I've been waiting for you to notice me, forever..."*

Except, his words were not born of a man who carried a love for a woman. He didn't love her. Not in the way she desperately wanted him to. She knew he cared. He'd likely lay down his life to protect her because of the connection shared between their families. But she wanted more of him than that.

He applied a gentle pressure to her waist and warmth radiated out at the point of his touch. Thrills of awareness coursed through her. His firm caress invoked a familiarity that defied the mere bonds of their familial ties and spoke to her awareness of him as a man.

Daisy wet her lips and dragged forth a suitable response. "I would say thank you," she said simply. For even as he didn't care for her in the way she wished, it mattered that he still remembered her existence when her own mother had forgotten.

Auric searched her face. "I do care, Daisy. I've been deplorably remiss these past four weeks." *Three weeks and six days.*

The earlier warmth faded. She'd never been anything more than a responsibility. With his misplaced sense of obligation to her and her family, he'd insert himself into her life as another brother, failing to realize that his constancy would never replace Lionel. She tipped her chin up. "I appreciate that you visit my mother," she began, because she did. His presence, though obligatory, brought much joy to the grief-stricken marchioness. "But you have duties that extend beyond my family." The muscles of her throat worked. "In your effort to be loyal and devoted to Lionel's memory, you fail to realize that you have to live your life for you, first." And *that* is the only crime he'd been guilty of in the weeks he'd courted Lady Anne and committed himself to finding a duchess.

Well, that and the crime of breaking her heart.

The strong muscles of his arm twitched under her fingers, hinting at the tension in his frame. It did not, however, escape her notice that he didn't issue any false protest to her words.

She slid her gaze off to the dancers twirling about her. Her eyes collided with the grinning Lady Stanhope and her husband. The tall, blond gentleman whispered something that raised a blush on the lady's cheeks. Even over the thrum of the orchestra and the buzz of conversation throughout the ballroom, she detected the woman's husky laugh blended with the earl's chuckle. Envy tugged at her breast. That is what she craved for herself, and yet studying the other woman in her golden glory, who was so perfectly pleasant and kind and warm, was it any wonder Auric had wanted her for his duchess?

Auric followed her gaze.

"She's lovely," she murmured.

He did not pretend to misunderstand. "She's married."

"Are you still hurt by her rejection of your suit?" She immediately wanted to call the words back. "Not that it is my business." Then she gave him a dry smile. "After all, I'm not a duke and don't have the right to ask such intimate questions," she added in an attempt to divert him away from that immediate question that exposed her before him.

A half-grin turned his lips at the corner and her breath caught. "What you are and are not supposed to do have never stopped you before." His smiles, once so easily given, were now mere fleeting glimpses of mirth he then buried under his practiced ducal expression and aloofness. This brought her back to the young man who'd willingly schemed with her as a girl.

She found herself smiling. "No, this is true." Daisy wanted their waltz to go on forever and steal more time with Auric, and yet the closing strands of the orchestra indicated the end of the set. The dancers drew to a stop, clapping politely about them as they shuffled from the floor.

They lingered a moment, studying one another, and then remembered themselves at the same time. She dropped a hasty curtsy and allowed him to guide her from the dance floor over to her mother's side.

As they stopped beside her melancholy mama, the woman's eyes lit with eagerness. "Auric."

He smiled. "Lady Roxbury."

Her heart pulled. He was ever so patient with her mother's humbling displays of emotion. For a moment, a glimpse of the teasing, vivacious hostess from their youth was restored. She clasped Daisy's hand

and gave a squeeze. "I told my Daisy you didn't merely feel a sense of obligation to her, isn't that right Auric?"

Oh, God.

The ghost of a smile hovered on his lips. "Indeed, not. It is, of course, an estimable pleasure to claim a dance with Daisy." Any other lady would surely be simpering and swooning at such high praise from the young duke.

Then, she'd never been just any lady where Auric was concerned. She winked twice. For, if this didn't merit some manner of salvation, she couldn't determine what else would.

He laughed and then buried that sound behind a cough. "If you'll excuse me," he said once more.

Mother shot a bold hand out and wrapped it about his forearm. "Do promise you'll come 'round more frequently, Auric. We do so miss your presence."

Ashamed of her mother humbling herself so, Daisy gently chided her. "Mama, please." She stole a glance about at the curious lords and ladies taking in the marchioness' audacious gesture.

Auric caught Daisy's eye, both a gentle reassurance and an understanding in his warm, blue gaze. "I pledge to visit more frequently," he murmured.

And she remembered all the reasons she'd fallen in love with him in the first place. He sketched another bow and made his excuses once more, before taking himself off to the opposite side of the ballroom. To Lady Leticia. She frowned. Daisy openly studied the couple they presented with the same interest as the members of the *ton* present. Society had begun taking wagers the moment she'd made her Come Out that Daisy Meadows would find herself the Duchess of Crawford. They'd based that fool, erroneous decision off those faithful visits and his loyal attendance at Almack's and every other event she was unfortunate enough to attend. All such rumors were quashed when she'd come out of mourning two years ago, with no offer forthcoming from the Duke of Crawford. *That* had, in fact, proven there was nothing remotely romantic about the duke's relationship with Daisy. Nothing at all.

Now, the busybodies of London wondered who would be the duchess in waiting, since it would not be Lady Stanhope.

Auric guided Lady Cordelia, another golden haired, flawless, English beauty, upon the dance floor and another fool sliver of her heart cracked. She curled her hands into tight fists. Even through the fabric of her fine gloves, her nails marred her flesh.

"He will realize you're there, Daisy."

She stilled, staring wide-eyed out at the couples performing the intricate steps of a country reel. For a moment she imagined she'd merely thought those words in her head, or worse spoken her private thoughts aloud as she too often did.

Her mother settled a hand at her waist and gave a gentle squeeze. "He will," she repeated, soft, for her ears alone.

She wanted to remind her mother that this certainly wasn't the place, and assuredly not the time, to discuss her hopes, dreams, and love of Auric, the Duke of Crawford. And yet…she removed her gaze from the perfect tableau presented by the dancing couple and shifted it to her mother. How did she know? How, when she'd ceased to see Daisy these past seven years now?

The older woman gave her a knowing look. "Mothers know everything, Daisy." She gave one slow, deliberate *wink*. "Someday you'll discover that on your own. Lady Harrison is motioning to me." Tension settled in the lines of her mouth. At one point, once upon a lifetime ago, Mama would have eagerly trotted off to gossip and titter like so many of the other matrons present. Now, she moved painfully and awkwardly through most exchanges. "Would you mind if I went and spoke with her?" For a moment, Daisy suspected her mother secretly longed for her daughter to issue some form of protest.

"Not at all," she said softly. However, she would not truly be helping if she allowed her mother to remain inside the shell of a person she'd become. The marchioness hesitated and then, with a sigh, sailed off in a sea of sapphire blue skirts, the closest, appropriate color to the black mourning attire she adopted at home. Daisy stared contemplatively after her. How much her mother had seen through the years and how little credit Daisy had given her. There was something painfully exposing in discovering before an entire crowded ballroom that she was not as invisible as she'd believed all these years.

She looked out at the dancers once again, scanning the crowd, but only caring about one—a tall, powerful gentleman and his unworthy dance partner. Daisy found him with her gaze, all the while thinking on her mother's handful of words that had, in effect, tossed everything Daisy had believed for seven years into upheaval. She'd believed herself invisible. Convinced herself that her mother and father didn't see her or the hopes she carried of her very much alive soul. She had been so wrong about her mother failing to see her. If she'd been wrong of that, perhaps she'd also been wrong where Auric was concerned. Mayhap he, in fact, saw more of her than she truly believed.

Just then, he glanced over the tops of the heads of the dancers performing the steps of the country reel. Their gazes collided.

And he gave her two, slow winks.

FIVE

The next morning, Daisy peered out the carriage window at the passing London streets. The fashionable streets gave way to the crowded shopping district of North Bond Street and continued rolling past the fashionable lords and ladies on toward Gipsy Hill. Auric, as he'd been last evening, grinning and winking and so kind to her mother, was the sole focus of her thoughts.

She released the curtain. Since Lionel's passing, which was the only way in which she allowed herself to think of his death, the grinning Auric, thoughtful young man of their youth had been replaced by a more somber...well, *duke*. She drummed her fingertips on the comfortable leather squabs of the carriage. He'd grown into the role of duke and it suited him to perfection.

Not in a good way.

Sometimes, she allowed herself to believe the man she loved was nothing more than a memory, but then when he visited and when he winked twice as he'd done last evening, she caught glimpses of the true man buried beneath propriety and proper, ducal obligations. She didn't love Auric for the title he possessed. She loved him for a million different reasons—the least of which had to do with the silly, blasted title.

She sought the pendant, which would earn her Auric's heart. The tiny pings of rain struck the carriage windows and made a mockery of her efforts this day. She'd not allow gray skies to deter her on this day.

"My lady, perhaps this might not be the best day for us to shop."

"Oh fiddle." Daisy peeled back the curtain and peered out at the dark sky. Thick gray-white rain clouds rolled overhead. "Why, it is a perfectly splendid day to shop," she assured the nervous maid. Rainy streets meant empty streets. Blessed solitude was just what she required. Solitude and a lack of notice from polite Society. Not that Daisy was frequenting the fashionable North Bond Street shops where she'd be more likely to be viewed by said polite Society members.

The carriage lurched to a halt. In a bid to stem the reservations on her maid's parted lips, Daisy shoved the carriage door open then hopped to the ground. Her slippered feet sank into a deep puddle. With a sigh, Daisy drew her foot out of the murky waters and shook it off. Slippers had been a deuced, bad idea. Without waiting to see if Agnes followed, Daisy hurried down the streets lined with gypsies hawking their wares.

In spite of her earlier dismissal of the rain, cold wracked her frame and she drew her cloak close to shield herself from the chilly, spring day. She weaved between various passersby while picking her way through the cobbled streets littered with refuse and touched a scented kerchief to her nose, as the smell of rotted vegetables and sugared treats melded into a sickening blend. *The things a lady will do for love.* She edged out of the way just as a shopkeeper hurled a bucket of slop water from the doorway of his shop. Brown water sprayed the cobblestones and marred her skirts.

With a gasp Daisy yanked back her already hopelessly sullied hem. Alas, irreparable damage had already been done to her green muslin cloak. She drew the garment closer about her and continued, each step being fueled by the memory of those two winks last evening and her and Auric's dance. Oh, he'd asked her to dance any number of quadrilles and polite, country reels but never a waltz—until last evening. Granted, with her mother's insistence, Auric couldn't very well have not asked her to dance. However, he could have chosen a more polite, less intimate dance. And yet, he'd chosen a waltz. Surely, that signified something where the duke was concerned? Sporadic raindrops touched her skin. She brushed away a bead of moisture from the tip of her nose.

"My lady," her maid called after her, her tone fairly pleading.

She paused and spun back around. The wind tugged at Daisy's skirts. "Agnes, we have a good number of shops and carts to search. I'll not be out of your sight, but if I'm to have any hope in finding this particular necklace, I require your help."

Agnes sighed. "My lady, the marchioness will sack me if she discovers I've left your side." She skimmed her troubled gaze over the cobbled roads of Gipsy Hill. "In these streets of London, no less."

Daisy patted the girl comfortingly on the shoulder. "Oh, Agnes, she wouldn't. I promise," she added, in some attempt to mollify the young woman's worries.

When mother was in one of her moods, which was more often than not, she wouldn't notice if Daisy hiked her skirts above her knees and hopped on one foot through the corridors calling out her name. After Lady Harrison's ball last evening, the marchioness had withdrawn into her chambers and retreated with one of her familiar megrims. Though Daisy had long suspected there were really no headaches and more a desire for solitude so she could be alone with the memory of the son she'd lost. No, indisposed as she was, mother wouldn't know, nor likely care, if Daisy was only a handful of carts away from her maid while shopping on Bond Street. Even if it was the unfashionable parts of Gipsy Hill.

Agnes studied her and then sighed. "Very well. It is a heart, you say?"

Pleased to at last have some help in this madcap scheme she'd crafted, Daisy nodded excitedly. "Yes. A heart. I've been told it is this big," she gestured with her fingers. "And gold with faint etchings." Troubling her lower lip, she glanced up and down the street littered with vendors peddling their wares. "I imagine we'll be more effective if we move on the opposite sides of the street." She took Agnes gently by the shoulders and steered her toward the column of carts. "Now, off you go."

Agnes hesitated a long moment and then, muttering under her breath, allowed herself to be propelled gently forward.

Not wishing to risk that Agnes changed her mind and clung uselessly to her side as a rather weak chaperone, Daisy lifted her hem a bit, keeping the fabric from the thick, muddied puddle and stepped over the murky water. As she made her way to the gypsy carts, she recalled Lady Stanhope's words last evening of an old woman by the name of Bunică. The gypsy with graying hair was, in fact, the rightful owner and the last to hold the heart pendant. What were the chances that some young woman had already found the gypsy and been given the heart pendant? Furthermore, what lady would even be in search of that bauble?

She came to a stop on the busy sidewalk. "Every woman in the blasted kingdom," she mumbled to herself.

A nearby vendor, an older man with a shock of white hair tugged a black cap from his head. "Beg yer pardon, ma'am?"

Heat slapped her cheeks. "Er, nothing." Bothersome business of speaking to herself. She really required a confidante or friend. There was nothing else for it. She gave her head a clearing shake, coming back to her purpose in being here this day—and it wasn't to wax melancholy about her circumstances. The gypsy turned to his cart littered with fabric and an array of small fripperies, drawing her attention to his goods. She wandered closer and ran her fingers along the edge of the large, wooden wagon with heavy nicks and dents. The wind carried the gentle sprinkling of rain and splashed her cheek. With the tips of her glove-encased fingertips, Daisy wiped away a drop and moved slowly around the side of his cart.

A small, round piece of glass, smattered with raindrops caught her eye. The delicate piece gleamed from the beads of moisture giving Daisy pause. Leaning across his eclectic array of items, she picked up the small, glass piece and with the tip of her finger, brushed the rain off the smooth glass.

Granted when you make your Come Out, Auric will be one of those old dukes with a quizzing glass to his eye...

A wistful smile played about her lips at Lionel's voice, as clear as the day he'd uttered those words, rang in the bustling streets. She hopelessly glanced about for her oft-smiling brother. Yet, there was not a familiar face or friendly smile within the crowds of strangers. Alone. Just as she'd been these seven years now. Her smile dipped.

"Ye be wontin' to buy that, moi lady?" The gypsy's words brought her back from her sad musings.

"No. I…" She ran her finger down the frame and then froze at the slight, silver ornament at the center. *A daisy*. The wind tugged at her hair, freeing a curl. The quizzing glass was perfect. "Yes. I believe I do." She reached into the reticule that hung from her wrist and fished about the bottom of the satin sack. Daisy withdrew a sovereign and held it out to the man who eyed the coin in wide-eyed wonder.

His rheumy eyes went wide and he doffed his hat once again. "Thank ye, so much. Is there anythin' else Oi might 'elp ye te foind?"

Daisy gave him a smile. "No, thank you." She dropped the quizzing glass inside her reticule. "This will do perfectly."

He pocketed the generous payment and dipped a bow.

With a spritely step, Daisy started across the street. Why, every duke eventually required a quizzing glass. Particularly dukes who were approaching their thirtieth year. Perhaps it might serve to remind Auric that he needed to wed. And soon. Wind tugged at her cloak and she ran her palms over the front, smoothing out the fabric. Granted, he'd already seemed to realize that important piece of his ducal responsibility. He'd just not seen her as fitting into his ducal obligations.

She stepped out into the street just as another gust of wind, more fierce and biting, whipped her hood over her eyes. Daisy shoved it back and a scream lodged in her throat as a gentleman riding his horse at a quick gallop cut across her path. She stumbled. Her foot turned on the uneven cobbles and she tumbled backward, crashing hard onto her bottom. Daisy grunted as her palms scraped the rocks and dirt-packed road, shredding her thin gloves. She grimaced at the pain radiating up her back. The wind whipped about, tugging free several more strands of hair and the long curls slapped her cheeks. Sputtering around a mouthful of hair, she pulled out several dampened tresses then tucked them behind her ear, grimacing at the foul stench of her fingers. She stole a glance about and a relieved sigh escaped her at finding her maid across the street, wholly engrossed in her search. Daisy carefully pulled her gloves off and inspected the damage done to her palms. The poor girl would suffer an apoplexy were she to discover her mistress in this moment, as she was sprawled on the ground. Daisy shoved herself up to her feet and dusted off the pebbles and dirt flaking her hands.

She rather hoped this was not fate's opinion on her search for the Heart of a Duke pendant.

Then it began to pour.

Auric stared out at the rainy London streets from within the confines of his carriage. Following his visit with Daisy yesterday, where she'd pointed out his absence these past weeks, he'd been shamed by his neglect of both the young lady and her mother. So it was, with guilt driving his motives, as it so often did, he found himself on his way to the Marchioness of Roxbury's townhouse to pay his requisite visit. The familiar front façade of the ladies' residence drew into focus, and then moments later, his carriage rocked to a slow stop before their townhouse. A liveried footman drew the door open and cool wind filtered into the carriage, ruffling his hair. Smoothing his hands over the front of his cloak, Auric stepped down. The black fabric whipped angrily at his ankles, as thunder rumbled ominously in the distance.

In five long strides he reached the familiar front door. A door he'd entered more scores of times than he could count; as a child at his father's side, as a young man visiting his closest friend, and as a gentleman seeking absolution for a sin that could never be forgiven. He rapped once.

Almost immediately the door was drawn open. The butler, as familiar as that front door stepped back, admitting him.

"Good afternoon, Frederick."

"Your Grace," the ancient servant said, sketching a deep, respectful bow. He cleared his throat, correctly interpreting the reason for Auric's visit. "The marchioness is indisposed."

Again, guilt sat like a stone in his belly. The woman frequently took to her chambers during the day. Grief had made her despondent, a mere empty shell of the refined hostess she'd once been. He inclined

LOVED BY A DUKE

his head in understanding. "Please tell Lady Daisy I've come to call." Odd, how Daisy, the girl who'd abhorred all social events hosted by her parents, had stepped in as hostess to receive him when her mother was indisposed. But then, they'd all grown up. They'd not been children for a very long time. Regret tugged at him for the simplicity of the life they'd once known, now lost.

"Lady Daisy is not here, Your Grace," the old servant murmured.

Auric frowned. "Not here?"

"Not here," the man echoed. A flash of concern filled the man's rheumy eyes. "She's gone," he coughed into his hand, "shopping."

"Shopping," he repeated dumbly, knowing he must sound the total lackwit and yet, as long as he'd known Daisy Laurel Meadows, which was, the entire course of her existence, the lady had long detested shopping.

"Yes, Your Grace," Frederick confirmed with a nod. "Shopping."

Auric furrowed his brow. The only enjoyment she'd found in it as a girl was when he and Lionel had taken her to the bazaar and purchased a collection of small soldiers for the small girl forced to secretly play with the little figures, after her proper mama had denied her the pleasure.

Frederick cast a glance about and then returned his attention to Auric. "If I may be so bold, Your Grace—"

"You may," he said briskly.

"The lady has gone off."

"Gone off." He knew he sounded like one of those parrots so favored by the bored ladies and gentlemen of the *ton*. "I believe you said the lady had gone shopping." But Daisy didn't *shop*.

"But she did go shopping, Your Grace." Concern roughened the man's tone. "She's gone to Gipsy Hill."

Unease filled his belly and Auric opened his mouth, but then promptly closed it lest he repeat the servant's words once again. Gipsy Hill, on the outskirts of the fashionable part of London, Daisy had no place being there. He tamped down a curse. "Has she brought a chaperone?" he bit out, because God help her if she didn't, he would blister her ears when he found her.

65

"She brought her maid."

Her maid? Yes, he would do a good deal more than blister the lady's ears for such recklessness. "Thank you, Frederick," he said curtly.

The servant drew the door open. A blast of wind blew through the entranceway, slapping Auric's face with drops of rain. "Thank you, Your Grace," the butler said quietly.

He paused and looked questioningly back at him.

"For watching after her," he clarified. "Lord Lionel would have been grateful," Frederick said and then closed the door.

With furious steps, Auric stormed toward the street, the man's flawed words trailing after him. Lionel would not have been grateful. Why, in death, Lionel surely loathed Auric for having brought him to that sin and not being the one to care after Daisy, as she should be cared for.

"Gipsy Hill," he ordered as he reached his carriage. The liveried driver pulled the door open and Auric climbed inside. What business did the lady have in that unfashionable part of London? He searched his mind, thinking of the girl he'd known these years. He'd not believed Daisy motivated by the frills and fripperies that drove the ladies of the *ton*, and yet how well did he truly know her, now? The soldiers she'd once played with had since been replaced with an embroidery frame. All these years he'd come calling, he'd gone through the motions of a visit but not once had he noted the truth—Daisy was getting older. His frown deepened. No, she was no longer a girl and he no longer knew the lady's interests. With the exception of that embroidering business.

The driver flicked the reins of the conveyance and it lurched forward. As Auric's carriage rumbled through the crowded London streets, he peered out at the thick, gray clouds and small beads of rain which beat against the windows. The weather perfectly suited his mood and only reinforced the absolute madness in the lady being out with nothing more than a maid's escort for protection. A growl built low in his chest, filled by a fast-moving fear of the implications of her being at Gipsy Hill, unprotected.

Despite the chilled air and his gloved hands, his palms dampened as he was thrust back into the horrors of his past. At one point in time, Auric had been a self-absorbed bastard who'd sought the thrill of dancing on the edge of respectability. He'd forced Lionel into the underbelly of London, and for Auric's selfishness, that one faulty decision had cost Lionel his life, dead in a whore's bed with a worthless street thief's blade buried in his belly.

It had also cost Daisy her one and only brother. All the implications of her being out alone slipped into his mind, chilling him with the prospect of a wide-smiling, freckled Daisy cut down in an equally vicious fashion. Nausea churned in his gut. If anything were to happen to her, he would not forgive himself. It would be the ultimate betrayal, which could never be atoned for.

The memories now came hard and fast—of Lionel, lying in a pool of blood, staring sightlessly up at the water-stained ceiling. Except, the image shifted and it was Daisy alone in that room with some faceless stranger. An agonized groan worked its way up his throat, nearly choking him. He banged hard on the ceiling. "Faster, man," he thundered. The carriage increased its pace, barreling down the cobbled streets. Onward.

He stared blankly at the occasional rider passing by and the wagons and carts lining the cobbled road of Gipsy Hill while he searched for Daisy.

The sharp whinny of a horse jerked his attention across the street. As his carriage rattled along, he peered outside, squinting into the distance, just as the wind whipped a young woman's hood from her head. Auric narrowed his eyes on the riot of brown tresses and a shock of freckles. He pressed his forehead against the crystal windowpane and knocked once on the roof. The conveyance rocked to an immediate and jarring stop. He braced his feet upon the floor and then shoved the door open and leaped from the carriage. A loud screech split the noise of the busy streets and howling wind. An eerie chill snaked down his spine, sucking the life from him. Time froze in an agonizing moment, his world stilled as Daisy barely escaped being trampled under the enormous hooves of some fool's black mare.

His pulse pounding hard in his ears, Auric raced down the cobbled road. He dodged between carts and carriages while blood pumped furiously through his body. Distantly, he registered the icy cool of the thick puddles penetrating the heels of his boots and the now blinding drive of rain. "Daisy," he barked, the call lost to the furious wind battering his cloak. The young lady blinked several times as though dazed. By God, he'd never forgive himself if she were hurt. His life would be eternally dark without her in it.

Auric closed the distance between them in just a handful of strides.

Rain matted her hair and ran in steady rivulets down her pale cheeks. She glanced up and then stared at him. With her brow furrowed in consternation, she tipped her head as though trying to place him, which was of course foolish. He'd known her since she'd been a babe and carried her throughout the marquess' estate atop his shoulders. "Auric," she greeted with a smile.

At that easy grin, a confirmation that she was unhurt, his heart resumed a normal beat.

He fed his annoyance, preferring that sentiment to the cloying fear at discovering her here, alone in the streets. *Auric, she said?* As though they were meeting amidst a ballroom or in a drawing room and not in the muddied, dangerous streets of London. Fury replaced the mind-numbing fear from moments ago and he stalked the remaining distance to her. Her eyes widened, perhaps in fear? Good, she should be fearful. He fed his ire. "What are you doing out here in this weather, unchaperoned, in this part of London, my lady?" Rain blurred his vision and he angrily swiped away the drops.

"I'm shopping." She planted her arms akimbo. "The better question would be, what are you doing here, Auric?"

"Returning you home."

"Oh, no you're not." She winked once.

She was having a splendid time, was she? "This is not a game," he gritted out. The lady didn't realize she risked life and limb coming here.

"I never said it was," she said on a beleaguered sigh. She narrowed her eyes. A suspicious glint lit their brown depths. "And for that matter, Your Grace, how did you find me here?" Daisy wrinkled her nose. "Are you spying on me?" Which suggested the lady was engaging in activities that merited him spying on her. He swiped a hand over his face. God help him. He could manage his estates in a way that saw his coffers abundantly full. He could command a room of peers to silence with a single look. He was *not*, however, equipped to handle this older brother business. "Well?" she prodded, annoyance in her tone.

Auric lowered his arm to his side. "Frederick was very enlightening." Because the old servant clearly had more sense than Daisy and her mother combined.

"Traitor," she mumbled. Then, she gave a toss of her damp curls. "Regardless, I've important business to see to." With that, she turned on her muddied heel and started down the road.

Auric remained fixed to the spot, blinking several times in rapid succession. By God, had she just wandered away from him? In this weather? Unchaperoned? In this part of London? With a growl, he stalked after her. "Lady Daisy Meadows, by God if you do not stop I will toss you over my shoulder and remove you to my carriage." He planted himself in front of her and halted her forward movement.

She stopped. Which was good. Because he really didn't want to do anything as barbaric as tossing her over his shoulder. Which he would do if he needed. But he'd still rather not. Not with Daisy. Nor any young lady for that matter. But especially not Daisy. For all the sins he was guilty of, he cared to leave off any further ones that involved Daisy and, most especially, any outrageous acts that involved his hands upon her person.

Rain ran in a steady stream around them, like crystal teardrops upon her cheeks. But then she smiled, the one splash of joy in an otherwise cheerless world, and for a brief moment, he forgot the terror that had dogged him since Frederick had announced the lady's plans to visit Gipsy Hill and any annoyance. "What were you thinking going out without an escort?" he asked, when he at last managed to form words.

"I have an escort." Daisy looked around. A frown tugged her lips downward and then she lifted a finger up. "Ah, here she is."

As if on cue a young woman in a serviceable, brown cloak came tearing down the street. "My lady, we need to go. It is—" She skidded to a halt at the sight of Auric and fell silent.

He returned his attention to Daisy. "That is not an escort, my lady."

She folded her arms across her chest. "Indeed, *she* is."

Auric took a slow, steadying breath and counted to five. "No. No, she is not." She was a young maid who didn't look strong enough to stand upright in the howling wind knocking into them now.

A chill stole through him at the idea of all manner of danger that could have befallen her.

"What manner of madness has befallen you to come here alone, Daisy?" he asked, slipping with formality. Her mother would do to not let her from her sight for the rest of the Season, or better yet, until she was wed and firmly enfolded in some gentleman's protection.

Except, then he imagined her with some bastard of a husband who didn't deserve her, and then he would feel a whole new onset of guilt for the absence of her brother who'd have seen to the very important detail of securing a match for his...for his...

Daisy muttered and proceeded to rifle through her reticule.

He furrowed his brow. "What are you doing?"

She continued to dig around the inside of her pale yellow satin bag.

"Daisy, I asked what you are—?"

Her head shot up and her smile widened. "Here." She handed a small silver object over to him.

Auric accepted the delicate piece. "A quizzing glass?" He alternated his gaze between Daisy and the fragile item.

She pointed to the quizzing glass. "I imagine if you can't see Agnes standing right before you to know I'm not, in fact, alone, well then you need this even earlier than I'd imagined you would."

He scrubbed a hand over his face. "Daisy?"

"Yes, Auric?"

"Get in your damned carriage. Now."

Daisy opened her mouth to protest when thunder rumbled in the distance. She jumped. Unfortunately, landing her slippered feet into the fast rising puddle between them. She glanced forlornly down at her soaked hemline. "You know, this is really all your fault."

If he weren't so concerned with getting her safely ensconced within her carriage he'd have dearly loved to hear an elaboration on her reasoning behind *that*. "I assure you, for all the power I do possess, I cannot make the skies thunder."

Her mouth formed a small moue of surprise.

He leaned down, so close he detected the hint of honey and lavender that clung to her. "Did you imagine I forgot your fear of thunder and lightning?"

She wrinkled her pert nose. "I am not still afraid of thunder and lightning." As if to prove her as a liar, lightning cracked the thick, gray sky and a little shriek escaped her.

He grinned, tucking her gift into his pocket. A *real* smile, the first he'd managed in more years than he could remember. It was hardly appropriate for an unwed young lady to give an unwed gentleman, who was not a relation, a gift. But this was Daisy. "Liar."

"That didn't startle me," she said, wrinkling her brow. "It…" He arched an eyebrow. "It…" She sighed. "Very well, I may be still just a slight bit frightened. A very slight bit," she added when his smile deepened. "But more than anything else I was startled by the lightning. As most people would be. Startled by lightning," she added as though he were a total lackwit who couldn't have pieced together what she'd suggested. A damp, brown tress fell over her eye and she blew at the strand. Alas, the sopping lock remained plastered to her forehead.

His hand shot out of its own volition and he brushed the lock behind her ear. "There," he murmured.

"What are you doing?"

"I'm escorting you to your carriage."

"Oh, that won't be necessary. Isn't that right, Agnes?" she directed toward her maid.

The wise maid had the good sense to remain silent.

With a silent curse, Auric reached for Daisy's wrist and placed her fingers on his sleeve. The maid, Agnes muttered a quiet prayer of thanks and started toward their carriage. "I expect your mother will be furious," he said out the corner of his mouth. Daisy of years ago would have had proper fear of her mother's admonition.

"You would be wrong," she muttered.

He snorted. Young Daisy Meadows had seemed to be the bane of her mother's existence. The poor marchioness had shaken her head in lamentation so many times, he and Lionel had jested that the woman surely walked around in a perpetual state of dizziness from the movement.

He recognized Daisy's black carriage. The driver hopped down from the top of his perch and pulled the door open. Auric looked down at Daisy. "I expect you to use more common sense, my lady, than to go out shopping in this Godforsaken weather. I can't imagine some frippery is worth risking your life for."

"You're wrong." Something flared in her eyes. "It was important. *Is* important," she amended. "And I'll not make apologies to you for being out in the rain, Auric. I'm no longer a child, nor am I a woman who answers to you." Her chest rose and fell with the force of her emotion, drawing his gaze downward to the generous swells of her breasts crushed beneath the rain-dampened fabric of her cloak.

No. At some point, these past seven years, Daisy had become a woman. A beautiful woman. Auric swallowed hard and forced his gaze to her face.

"Is there anything else you'd say, Your Grace?"

Ah, so she was Your-Gracing him now? Good, this was safe. He could deal with tart charges and angry "Your Graces" a good deal better than he could Daisy's abundant breasts and generous hips. "I caution you to use better judgment, my lady." He took her hand to help her into the carriage.

Her lips pulled in a grimace of discomfort.

Auric looked down. He turned her hand over and, with a curse, gently tugged off her delicate, now shredded, kidskin gloves. An angry, red bruise stood vivid, a small scrape with a thin line of blood intersected her palm. Nausea turned in his gut and he closed his eyes a moment counting to three to drive back the horror of the past that converged with the present. The sight of blood did and, he suspected, forever would, transport him to that horrific day.

"Auric?" Her tentative questioning pulled him back to the moment.

72

He swallowed back the bile in his throat. "Bloody hell, Daisy," he growled. He yanked a kerchief from the front of his coat. "Why didn't you say you'd been hurt?"

"It is just a scrape," she said softly.

Most other young ladies would have dissolved into histrionics at the sight of blood and bruises. Not Daisy. Then, the girl who used to bait her own hooks when fishing her father's well-stocked lake had never been squeamish. He used the edge of the fabric to wipe free the dirt and tiny shards of pebbles lodged in the delicate lines of her palm. She gasped. "I'm sorry," he apologized. He'd rather lob off his right arm than cause her any more pain. He froze mid-movement, guilt ravaging his conscience as he considered the greatest agony he'd already caused her.

"What is it?" Her whisper-soft question jerked him from his reverie. "You've gone all serious."

His expression grew shuttered. "I'm always serious." He'd not always been.

"Yes." She shook her head. "But this is different. Your lips are—"

"Here." He hastily wrapped the cloth about her hand. It wouldn't do for them to be discovered in the streets of Gipsy Hill with Daisy talking about his mouth, or any part of his person. "Now, take yourself home, Daisy, and have more of a care in the future."

"But—"

He tossed her up into the carriage.

She peeked her head out. "Auric—"

He closed the door.

Daisy jerked the red velvet curtains back and glared at him.

And, if the driver hadn't just then slapped the reins and set the horses into motion, he didn't doubt that Daisy Meadows would have climbed right back down and told him exactly what she thought of his high-handedness. His lips pulled up in a slow, unfamiliar grin. He stood there, as her carriage disappeared down the road, a faint, black mark in the gray horizon, his cloak soaked from the unrelenting rain.

He'd not realized until this moment just how much he'd missed smiling.

SIX

Seated on the robin's egg blue sofa in the Blue Parlor, Daisy made quick work of her embroidery. She jerked the crimson thread through the fabric. Well, she made *work* of it anyway. With a sigh, she paused to assess her sixth attempt at a heart that week. There was some improvement. This one rather resembled conjoined teardrops, which was a good deal better than a dejected circle with a droop in the middle.

She tossed the frame down and came to her feet. The sun's rays filtered through the opened curtains and illuminated the room in a soft, ethereal glow. Drawn to the warmth, she wandered over to the window and drew the curtain back even further, welcoming the soothing caress of the sun on her cheeks. After days of rain, the thick clouds overhead broke to allow a trace glimpse of sun. Daisy studied the bustling streets below. She'd not found the heart pendant. Of course she'd not been so naïve to believe she'd manage to find the old gypsy, amidst a sea of gypsies after one rather unproductive afternoon.

Not altogether unproductive. A smile pulled at her lips, while her heart thumped wildly. For yesterday, in the cold, dreary London morn she'd come to a staggering revelation. As much as she'd believed Auric had failed to see her all these years, she was not invisible to him, either. If his connection to her was strictly one of obligation, the moment he'd called and found Mother indisposed and Daisy out, he could have turned on his heel and sought out his clubs or done whatever it was gentlemen did. Instead, he'd set out after her.

74

Nay, he'd pressed Frederick for details of her whereabouts and then set out after her. If she were being truthful, after years of not being seen, heard, or noticed by anyone, there was something enlivening in the discovery that to those who mattered, she'd not ceased to exist, as she'd believed for so long. Granted he'd been brusque and rude and dukelike, but there had also been those traces of gentleness. Her still-sore hands thrummed with the memory of his fingers upon the soft skin of her palm. Her grinning visage reflected back in the crystal pane.

She spun to face her maid Agnes in the corner. "We're returning to Gipsy Hill."

The young woman hesitated. "Are you certain, my lady? His Grace—"

"Come, Agnes," She didn't want to hear a word about Auric's high-handed opinion of her excursions. "The sun is shining." Out. Shining. It was all really the same. "Gipsy Hill is far more enticing in the sun than a dreary, cold, rainy day."

"As you say." Which of course meant Agnes heartily disagreed but was too polite to say as much. With all the enthusiasm of one being marched to the gallows, she climbed to her feet. She cast a dubious glance at the open curtains "I'll have the carriage readied, my lady," she announced.

A short while later, Daisy made her way from the parlor to the foyer. Frederick stood in wait, her green muslin cloak in his hands. She eyed him cautiously. "Frederick," she greeted as she shrugged into her cloak. "I intend to go shopping once more." She gave him a frown. "To Gipsy Hill." At one and twenty she'd enjoy the freedom to shop where she would.

The ghost of a smile played on his lips. "Very well, my lady."

"If a certain...gentle *person*," duke "should happen to come by inquiring as to my whereabouts," which she certainly didn't anticipate as Auric had put in his requisite visit. "Would you be so good as to not mention where I've gone off to?" After all, she'd hardly manage to find the pendant if her efforts were thwarted by both a protective butler and a stubborn fool, too blind to see she was hopelessly in love with him.

"As you wish, my lady." Frederick inclined his head. He pressed a hand against his heart. "You have my assurance that I shall not breathe a word of your whereabouts to His...er...some gentleman."

Daisy eyed him a moment in an attempt to gauge his veracity. Frederick had been quite loyal to her through the years. He'd never betrayed her whereabouts to stern governesses, and even, in some instances, when Mother had been in one of her tempers, to the mistress of the house.

He arched a bushy, white eyebrow. "Is there anything else you require, Lady Daisy?"

Just his discretion. "No, that is all." With a nod, she sailed through the open door and down the handful of steps to the waiting carriage. She accepted the waiting coachman's assistance into the carriage and settled into the seat across from her maid.

The servant closed the door behind her and then the carriage dipped as he climbed atop his perch. Daisy settled into her seat with a renewed vigor. All these years she'd believed Auric failed to see her. And yet, their last exchange revealed he, in fact, saw her. Mayhap not in the light she hoped. But according to Lady Stanhope, all Daisy required was that pendant. Her lips turned up in a smile. How wonderful it felt to turn herself over to hope. She'd lamented her mother and Auric's perpetual state of seriousness all these years, but had Daisy truly been any different? With her sad thoughts and agonized regrets, she really wasn't unlike either of the two remaining people left to her.

Well, no more. The time for sadness and frowns and regrets was at an end. Lionel would not have wanted any one of them to move through life in a constant gloom. She stared out at the passing streets. The sun peaked through the dark, gray skies, and then was swallowed by the fast moving storm clouds. No, Lionel would have likely committed himself to eliciting smiles and laughter, because that had been the kind of man he'd been.

It was time to honor his memory—by living.

Thunder rumbled overhead—and by setting her fears free.

...Bah, afraid of thunder? Why, merely imagine all of Mother and Father's stuffy guests playing a raucous match of Bowls...

"My lady, perhaps we should turn back?" Agnes questioned from the opposite bench. "The weather is threatening."

She leaned across the bench and patted the other woman's hands. "Bah, it is just a bit of thunder." Her smile deepened. She'd no intention of giving up her search over a little rain. No, free of Auric's austere presence this day, she would make good use of her search. Thunder or no thunder.

Thunder shook the foundations of his townhouse and Auric froze, his pen poised mid-movement, and his gaze fixed on the handful of words written.

Dear Lionel,
I've failed you again...

He tapped the edge of his pen on those handful of words marked upon his opened journal in a deliberate, staccato rhythm. Taking pen to paper and committing words to his friend had brought him back from the edge of madness, early on. When sleep eluded him, or the amorphous memories crept in, he wrote to his friend. He found a soothing peace in being honest—if at the very least with the pages in a black leather volume.

Except, he stopped mid-tap and stared at those six words. Today he was preoccupied. He held his pen up and fixated on the sharp tip. With two meetings this week, he'd paid *more* than his requisite visit to the Marchioness of Roxbury's home. The familiar niggling of guilt he carried, a debt he could never repay those broken people, the dearest friends of his now departed parents, still unassuaged.

He released a pent up sigh. There was the matter of the still troublesome Daisy. Annoyance roused in his chest. Nay, this was something far more gripping and potent. It sucked at his breath until his fingers itched for the reassuring presence of his black leather book. He drew in several breaths. What madness had possessed her to go off on her own to Gipsy Hill? Did she not have a care for the perils that could befall a young woman venturing beyond the fashionable end of London?

Auric tossed aside his pen. He fished around the inside of his jacket and withdrew the small, silver token given him yesterday. A ray of sunlight filtered through the curtains, a splash of cheer amidst the overcast skies. The hint of sun reflected off the shiny metal and sent beams of light radiating out upon the walls. Odd how, even amidst such thick gloom and darkness, there should be a hint of lightness. He passed the quizzing glass back and forth between his hands, his mind drawn once more to Daisy.

She was still a cheeky, insolent miss. And infuriating. And bothersome. And beautiful. He frowned. Where in blazes had *that* bit of madness come from?

A knock sounded at the door.

Grateful for the interruption, Auric closed his journal and set it aside. "Enter." A footman entered, carrying a small, silver salver with a note atop it. The young man rushed forward and held out the missive. With a murmured thanks, Auric accepted the folded piece of velum, written in an unfamiliar scrawl. "That will be all," he said dismissively, unfolding the page.

It felt essential that I inform His Grace of a certain lady's return to Gipsy Hill—

"Wait!" Auric leapt to his feet with such alacrity his winged back chair tumbled backward.

The liveried servant froze on the threshold.

"My horse," he barked. "Have my horse readied instantly."

The young man nodded and sprinted off to see to Auric's bidding. With a dark curse, he reread the handful of sentences on the unmarked missive and then stuffed it into the front of his jacket. In loping strides, he made his way from his office to the foyer.

What madness possessed the lady? There was no accounting for her ill judgment in going out not once, but *twice* to Gipsy Hill. And when he found the worthless gentlemen responsible for those ill-thought out trips, by God he would stuff the man's teeth down the back of his throat.

His butler stood in wait, Auric's cloak held out in his old, gnarled fingers. "When did that recent missive arrive?" He shrugged into the thick, black garment.

"Just a short while ago, Your Grace," the servant said, entirely too calm.

Minutes? Seconds? Hours? "When?" he bit out. For every unaccounted moment was another blasted moment the lady was out on her own, unchaperoned with some shiftless bounder…A deep growl stuck in his chest.

"Six minutes and a handful of seconds, Your Grace." Had anyone else uttered those words, they'd have hinted at sarcasm. However, the precise, masterful servant, Justin, attended his duties with a military like precision. He pulled the door open and Auric swept through the doorway then bounded down the steps to his waiting mount, a black gelding named Valiant. "Gipsy Hill," he muttered. The horse whinnied in like displeasure. Even his blasted horse knew better. What in blazes was the lady doing in that unfashionable end of London? Again.

The servant handed the reins over to Auric. "My lord?" he asked, with a furrowed brow.

Could she not stay on North Bond Street with every other sensible lady? "Nothing," he bit out and then issued a belated thanks. He climbed astride and nudged Valiant forward. Then, Daisy had never been anything like every other English lady. She'd been unashamedly bold and proud and…he gritted his teeth, fearless. Such a thing had amused him at one time. Now, with her a lady grown, it was a good deal less entertaining. He squared his jaw. In fact, there was nothing the slightest bit funny about Daisy visiting Gipsy Hill. Again. After he'd expressly forbidden it. Auric urged his horse faster through the thankfully quiet London streets, onward to Gipsy Hill. With each moment, he was humbled more and more by the depths in which he'd failed Lionel, *and* Daisy.

He'd been of the erroneous assumption that the attention he'd paid Daisy and the marchioness over the years was sufficient. He'd carved time out of his schedule to regularly visit mother and daughter. He'd made sure to be present for her Come Out, those years ago, throwing his support as the Duke of Crawford. The pain of that, serving as the *de facto* protector to a then wide-eyed, young lady in too many white ruffles, standing beside her when the responsibility had belonged to another, would always be with him. It should have been Lionel.

Auric stroked Valiant on the withers and nudged him along. The faithful creature reveled in the freedom and quickened his strides. In Auric's devotion to Lionel's family, he'd believed such attention would lessen his sense of guilt over the loss of his friend. Time had shown him, however, that he'd never be free of those sentiments. Not a single day passed or a night was slept where Lionel's last night alive didn't creep in and hold on. This moment was no exception. Auric flayed himself with the guilt of his own doing.

Young, still in university he and Lionel had been rash and reckless, living in a world where their status as noblemen had made them immune to the harsh realities of life. At Auric's urging, they'd visited a disreputable hell in the Seven Dials. Bile burned like acid in his throat. Lionel had wanted to return to the comfortable clean and *safe* end of the fashionable parts of London. And how had Auric responded to the other man's unease? With mocking laughter and an offer to pay for some comely light of love. He'd sent Lionel above stairs with some scantily clad creature.

Lionel had never come back down. Not alive.

He absently scanned the shop front windows and wooden carts lining the streets and slowed Valiant's strides. The possibility of failing both Daisy and Lionel ran him ragged. If she were hurt here in her naïve trustingness in visiting places such as Gipsy Hill, the guilt of that would destroy him.

Auric scanned the crowded streets and then his gaze collided with a riot of dark brown curls and a familiar cloak. The vibrant, green fabric served as a bright splash of color amidst the rainy day. With a black curse, he wheeled his mount to a halt, and then leapt to the ground. He motioned a young boy over, all the while keeping his gaze on Daisy.

The boy sprinted over. "Guv'nor?"

"Watch after him for me," he instructed. He withdrew a purse of coins and tossed it to the lad who caught it with an effortless grab. "There will be more when I return."

The young boy puffed his chest out and stood in wait with Auric's horse.

Auric started after Daisy. He frowned as she carefully stepped over a particularly substantial puddle and looked about for a tall, powerful footman. He growled. Bloody hell, she'd not even had the sense to add a servant for protection. Did she not realize a coachman left at the lady's carriage served her little good? Not when there were vicious, unscrupulous bastards about.

Just then, Daisy paused beside an enormous wagon and gestured to her neck. An old gypsy woman with stringy hair shook her head once and Daisy moved on. This time, she stopped at a cart belonging to a man of nondescript years.

With a growing rage, Auric lengthened his stride. He'd grown so accustomed to people taking his words as a ducal command that when he'd handed Daisy up into her carriage yesterday, he'd not even considered the fact she'd disobey his order—an order he'd made, intending to protect her. He quickened his stride as she continued. "I should have spoken with her mother," he muttered under his breath, earning curious stares from the men and women hawking their goods. His boot sank into a dank puddle and he ignored the chill seeping through the leather of his once gleaming Hessians.

Because if he'd spoken to the marchioness, Daisy would be safely ensconced away within the security of her home or, at the very least, in the presence of a chaperone who'd have sense enough to bring the lady to North Bond Street where all young ladies shopped. He stopped at the opposite side of the street, directly across from Daisy. Well, not all young ladies, as Daisy's presence indicated. The sensible young ladies, anyhow.

Auric stepped onto the cobbled road just as Daisy shoved back her hood. He froze as a beam of sunlight stole through the bilious grayish-white clouds. The ray of sun kissed her creamy skin and touched on her silken, brown tresses loosely arranged at the base of her neck. A gust of wind tugged a strand free and it slapped her cheek. She laughed at something the vendor said and brushed the tress behind her ear. His breath stuck in his chest. And he, who'd only before seen blonde saw the world in shades of russet.

Henceforth my wooing mind shall be express'd
In russet yeas and honest kersey noes.

Another threatening storm cloud swallowed the sun, just as a carriage passed by, and yanked Auric from the momentary spell she'd cast. The world resumed spinning. And with it, annoyance, a far safer sentiment for Lionel's sister, chased away his momentary lapse in sanity. Auric glanced left and then hurried across the street.

Daisy tugged her cloak closer and then continued on. He started after her, quickening his stride. She stopped alongside another large, wooden cart littered with fabrics and fripperies and said something to the vendor, an old woman with white hair. With crooked, wrinkled fingers the gypsy sifted through some of her wares. Daisy's brow creased and she shook her head.

Then the old woman shifted items around the top of her small cart. She held up a necklace. Daisy took the gold chain. She turned it over in her hands and then shook her head, handing it back to the woman. What was the reason for that forlorn little shake? Did she not have enough funds? Did she seek something more extravagant? Neither of those suppositions fit with all he knew about her.

He folded his arms and drummed his fingertips over his forearms. Perhaps he knew her a good deal less than he'd thought. For the spirited, young girl he'd once known would not have risked all for a piece of jewelry. The romantic woman who believed—He stilled, as his thoughts churned along with infinite slowness and then sped up with a frantic speed he tried to sort through. A romantic woman, who believed in love, however, would risk her safety and come out alone without the benefit of a chaperone.

With the distance between them, he still managed to detect those lush, red lips turning up in a smile. An insidious thought slipped into his mind—of some bounder, the gentleman she likely even now came to meet, claiming that mouth, exploring it…

Rage that felt very much like jealousy coursed through him, licked away rational thought, until he saw, felt, and breathed green. He grappled for control. The idea of him being jealous over Lady Daisy Meadows was preposterous. Auric had an obligation to Lionel and that was the sole reason for this mind-numbing fury. Daisy clearly had little care for her safety, but Auric owed this much to Lionel. Yet, why did the desire to take apart the nameless suitor with his bare hands remain? With fury in his steps, he strode over to her, closing the remaining distance between them. He planted himself behind her. "What have we here?"

A startled shriek escaped Daisy as she spun around. She shot a fist out, connecting with a solid punch to his nose.

He blinked as blood trailed a path down his lips. By God, she'd punched him. His stomach pitched while the thick, sticky blood seeped from his nose.

"Auric!" The horrified shock stamped on Daisy's face drove back all remembrances of that gruesome night. "My goodness, you startled me."

And he knew he must look like the very biggest lackwit, but standing there, blood pouring from his nose, Auric grinned.

Oh, blast!

Daisy slapped a hand over her mouth. Her heart still hammered from the shock of Auric's sudden, unexpected appearance. "I punched you," she blurted. And then registered the crimson drops staining his fingers.

Auric fumbled around the inside of his cloak and withdrew a kerchief. He pressed it to his nose and flinched. "Indeed," he drawled, sounding far more humorous than the situation warranted.

The old vendor held out a small scrap of fabric. Daisy collected the cloth from the old woman. She caught her lower lip between her teeth as a wave of guilt flooded her. "I'm so sorry," she said on a rush. And she was. But still…"You startled me." A man hadn't any business going about sneaking up on a lady, either.

He continued to hold his embroidered kerchief to his injury. "You deliver quite the punch, my lady. Gentleman Jackson himself would be impressed by your efforts."

Daisy plucked the bloodstained kerchief from his fingers and stuffed it into her reticule. She handed him the one given her by the gypsy. "Lionel," Daisy supplied. She fished around her reticule and handed several coins over to the old woman who took the small fortune with wide-eyes. When Auric's eyebrows dipped, she clarified, "Lionel taught me. He said all ladies should know how to properly defend themselves." As though he'd somehow known he'd not be there to see to that role himself.

"I do not believe Lionel imagined you requiring such skills while shopping." He dipped his head close to hers. "Without a chaperone. Again." His breath fanned her lips with a delicious scent of brandy and mint. The sensual masculinity of him washed over her and warmed her through.

Her lids fluttered as, for one span of a heartbeat, she imagined he intended to kiss her, here, in the muddied streets of London for all to see. Which was really rather foolish because the proper, powerful Duke of Crawford would never do something as scandalously wonderful as kissing her, Daisy Meadows, in the streets of London, for all to—

"Daisy?"

"Hmm?"

"Do you have something in your eye?"

Her eyes flew open and her skin burned at the odd tilt to Auric's head as he studied her. The vendor held over another cloth. "Er…" She waved off the gesture. "No."

His chestnut eyebrows dipped further.

"Er…that is…I do not have anything in my eye." Only, how else to explain the silly fluttering of her lashes. "Or I may have," she said on a rush, her mouth moving faster than her mind. "But no longer. I think I quite managed to…" *Stop talking, Daisy Meadows. Stop talking.* Her words trailed off as he continued to study her around the stained fabric of his cloth. "I'm all right," she said on a sigh. The wind tugged at her cloak and she pulled it close.

"What are you doing?" he asked somberly.

She lifted her shoulders in a small shrug. "I'm shopping." It was true. Granted, it was no mere frippery she sought.

"The Daisy I remember loved riding astride and spitting and cursing. She detested shopping."

She bit the inside of her cheek. Is that how he still saw her? As the small, bothersome child who'd dogged his and Lionel's every step. And yet, he was right. A woman grown now, she still detested going shopping. With her plump frame, she'd tired of the modiste's tsking about her generous proportions.

"What is so important that you'd come out without an escort, Daisy?" His low baritone rumbled from his chest.

Had his tone been disapproving and condescending, she'd have turned on her heel and ignored his question. But it wasn't. Instead, it was gentle and insistent all at the same time. "I'm looking for a necklace." After years of being relegated to the role of the forgotten, surviving child, there was something warm in knowing someone cared and was concerned.

He stuffed the bloodstained yellow fabric inside his cloak. "A particular style of necklace?"

She'd learned long ago to be suspicious of too many questions from Auric. Daisy eyed him cautiously. "Perhaps," she said noncommittally. She braced for his stern ducal displeasure.

His lips twitched in a manner reminiscent of the teasing young man she remembered. "That is vague." He folded his arms at his chest. And waited. And because she'd witnessed firsthand the strength of his obstinacy over the years perhaps better than anyone else, she also knew he'd stand there until the night sky slipped across the horizon many hours from now.

"Very well." Daisy rocked back on her heels. "It is a heart pendant." She put her fingers together. "About this big, and gold with slight etchings upon it."

Auric glanced up and down the street at the endless rows of wagons and carts littered with peddlers' wares. "And you expect to find this heart?"

"I do," she said softly. She *had* to find this heart. For, according to Lady Anne and the lady's sisters, to find it would mean Auric's heart. The foolishness of such thoughts did not escape her, and yet...she still needed to believe, in something: a pendant, Auric, the dream of them. To not have this small hope she would find herself empty, with nothing. She braced for his cool grin and mocking words. He said nothing for a long while and she shuffled back and forth on her feet. She really wished he'd say something—even if it was a coolly mocking response about the futility of her search. Anything to this silence. She cast a glance about and located her maid. Agnes moved quickly among a row of carts, dutiful in her search. Daisy looked once more to Auric.

He held out his elbow.

Daisy tightened her jaw. She folded her arms across her chest. "I'm not leaving, Auric. I'll not allow you to hand me into the carriage like I'm a recalcitrant child. I'm a grown woman and—"

"Daisy?"

"Yes?"

"Take my arm." His smooth, refined tones gave no indication as to his thoughts.

She eyed him warily. For surely he was as perturbed with her this day as he so often was. "Why?" She'd not be tossed unceremoniously into her carriage as he'd done yesterday.

The ghost of a smile played on his lips. "You'll need help looking for this necklace."

Her heart paused. "What?" She hated the breathless quality to her voice.

Auric motioned to the wagons along the edge of the cobbled road. "I'd not forgive myself if I left you to your own devices hunting for a floral pendant amongst the endless number of carts."

He wanted to join her. "It's a heart," she whispered. Surely it was an obligatory protectiveness on his part toward her and yet, he did not rush her back to her carriage as he'd done at their previous meeting. Instead, he remained.

He waved his elbow.

With a smile, Daisy placed her fingertips upon his coat sleeve. They continued down the street.

"A heart, you say?"

She nodded.

"What is so special about this particular necklace?"

Everything was special about the Heart of a Duke pendant. Her fingers tightened reflexively about his sleeve. She kept her gaze trained forward, lifting her hem as they stepped around a particularly deep puddle. "Well, it is…" She searched for words. "Beautiful." As she'd never before seen the necklace she couldn't say that with any real certainty. However, she knew what it foretold and for the fable surrounding the famed necklace, that in itself made it beautiful.

He stopped beside a cart. Daisy disentangled her arm from his and walked the perimeter of the wagon scanning the assortment of items. "Alas, I don't see your heart pendant."

She picked up a small quizzing glass and peered into the delicate lens. "Perhaps you've forgotten your quizzing glass, Your Grace?" Auric's visage blurred before her single eye, his crooked grin moving in and out of focus.

"Can oi 'elp ye foind anythin' fer yer lady, yer lordship?"

The quizzing glass slipped from her fingers with a soft thunk. "Oh, no. I…"

Auric sifted through the man's goods. He held up a pair of hair combs, with a red, filigree heart etched at their center. "We shall take these." He retrieved a sovereign and tossed it to the wide-eyed vendor. He grinned, which displayed an uneven row of stained and cracked teeth. The duke handed over the combs. She eyed them studiously, wetting her lips. The impropriety of even being discovered here with him, alone, would be ruinous, to be seen accepting a gift would be disastrous. "Take them, Daisy," he urged.

She took them, trailing her finger over the heart ornamentation at the center of each intricate piece. *A heart.* Not the fabled piece whispered about by ladies eager for the title of duchess. This great symbol that revealed itself time and time and time again, a necklace, her horrendous embroidery frames, and now...Auric's gift.

He stuck his elbow out once more. "Now, on to find the necklace to match your hair combs."

Daisy fiddled with her reticule and dropped them inside. As she took his arm once more, the skies opened up, pouring rain down. *Blast, damn, and double damn.* She stole a glance up at the bilious clouds overhead.

Auric leaned down. Her heart started as he pulled the hood of her cloak back into place. "I'm afraid the weather does not intend to cooperate with your efforts to find this particular necklace."

She glanced across the street toward where her maid hurried toward them. With a sigh, she allowed Auric to guide her back to her carriage. They moved quickly through the street.

Her coachman waited with the door opened. Agnes scrambled inside the carriage.

Daisy lingered, loathe for the moment to end. "Thank you, Auric," she purred.

He inclined his head. The steady rain soaked his chestnut hair and proceeded to run in rivulets down his eyes, his aquiline cheeks, and hard mouth. And yet, despite that, he remained wholly elegant, coolly beautiful. This is what Poseidon, that great and powerful Greek God of the sea, would look like when he emerged from the underwater depths. She sighed.

"Daisy?"

He really was quite magnificent. "Yes, Auric?" More than any man had a right to be.

"Unless you care to die of chill, I suggest you get inside the carriage, my lady." With that, he all but tossed her inside.

As the driver closed the door behind her, she peered out at his retreating frame as he made his way across the street to his own waiting horse. Daisy rested her chin in her hand and smiled.

SEVEN

Daisy ran her fingers along the edge of the wrinkled, crimson stained handkerchief she'd stuffed into her reticule earlier that day. She studied the initials stitched in gold upon the fabric. In her first quest to locate the Heart of a Duke pendant, she'd instead found herself with injured palms, a red nose, and a handkerchief belonging to Auric, but no necklace. Seated at the edge of the bed, she stared wistfully down at the slip of cloth in her hands. Though not the fabled bauble, the embroidered cloth belonged to Auric and for that, it mattered. Daisy raised his kerchief to her nose and froze mid-motion. She groaned and dropped her head back. "I am a pathetic miss." She'd gone and become one of those mooning sorts.

A knock sounded at the door. She yanked her head up swiftly. "Yes?"

Her maid poked her head inside the room. "The marchioness is awaiting you in the foyer, my lady."

With a sigh, she stuffed the cloth under her pillow. "Thank you, Agnes."

The maid nodded and ducked back out of the room.

Daisy rose from the edge of her bed in a flutter of green satin skirts. She'd been dreading Lord and Lady Windermere's casual dinner party since *last* year's dinner party and the year before it. Come to think of it, she'd always hated those intimate gatherings with her parents' stiffly proper friends.

Yet, for the manner in which the marchioness had retreated from the living, she somehow roused herself for her small, intimate circle of distinguished friends. Perhaps she felt closer to her past that way?

89

Those friends, however, either failed to see or care that the smile worn by the marchioness was, in fact, false.

Daisy moved quietly down the hall, her footsteps muffled by the thin, mauve carpet. Shortly after Lionel's death, when she couldn't manage another teardrop, she'd wondered how many days would need to pass before she felt like she could breathe again. Wondering if she'd ever be able to laugh or smile, or move again without feeling like she would splinter into a thousand million shards of broken pain.

Daisy paused beside an always-closed door. She touched her hand to the wood panel.

"Rap three times when you need me…"

She flung her arms about her brother's waist. "But what if you're not here?"

"I'll always be here, Daisy girl…"

The hall still echoed with the laughter following those boastful words of a young gentleman and older brother who'd believed himself invincible.

She tapped the door three times. No matter how hard she knocked or how many times, he was never coming back. When her brother had died, she'd thought herself incapable of ever smiling again. Yet, despite the grief that still had the power to suck the air from her lungs, in time, she did again smile.

Daisy let her hand fall back to her side and continued the long, slow walk down the corridor. In the blackest moments, when the night-mares came, she ached for Auric's reassuring presence. For he was the only one who shared this ugly, unbreakable bond. When her world had collapsed about her, she'd known if anyone could teach her to laugh and smile again, it would be Auric; who as a young man had welcomed an awkward, friendless girl into his fold, who'd teased her as though she'd belonged to a special club of which only he, Lionel, and Marcus were members. Except after Lionel's services, Auric, too, had been forever changed. That grinning, affable boy was replaced by the somber, oft-scowling duke.

Then how could he not be? As a lady, she'd been carefully sheltered from the truths of that night and, as a result, she'd been able to resume some sense of normalcy. Auric, however, as the last person to have ever seen, spoken to, or laughed with Lionel would not be so fortunate. Until this very moment she'd not considered how greatly that had affected him and how that had surely changed him.

She continued down the corridor, toward the sweeping staircase that spilled out into the foyer. Her mother stood silently at the base of the stairs, her blank gaze trained on the wall. Daisy had learned to smile. Her mother, however, had not. She took the steps quickly. "Hullo, Mother."

Her mother started. "Daisy," she murmured.

Odd, Daisy had spent the first thirteen years of her life wishing her mother could have been someone other than the consummate hostess who relished any and every *ton* function. Now, she'd trade her right hand to have that familiar, now missed, woman back.

The butler gave Daisy a quick, supportive smile and then pulled the door open. Her mother stepped outside. Daisy trailed behind to the carriage. She accepted the footman's assistance with a murmur of thanks. He closed the door behind her and then the spacious conveyance rattled onward toward Lord and Lady Windermere's townhouse.

"I expect Auric will be there."

Long accustomed to only her own thoughts and words for company, Daisy's body went taut. She glanced around a moment.

Then, her mother spoke once more. "It was so wonderful seeing him again. He is always such a dear boy," Mother continued in a wistful, faraway tone.

Yes. Yes, that was her mother talking. Emotion clogged Daisy's throat and just then she dared believe that maybe her mother could live again, finding some reason to once again smile. Even if it was for the memory of Lionel's friendship with the duke. That could be enough, *would* be enough. For this whispering soft woman was vastly preferable to a silent ghost. "Yes, he is."

Then her mother shook her head and the blankness fell across her expression, erasing the hint of life.

Daisy shifted her attention out the window at the passing streets. Yes, her life had resumed spinning on its slow, predictable axis but still, for that, she wanted more. She wanted to reclaim Auric, the memory of him anyway. The dream he represented.

Lord and Lady Windermere's townhouse pulled into focus. Candlelight set the impressive, white stucco structure awash in a soft orange glow. She dropped the curtain back into place when the driver pulled the door open. Her mother made her way out and to the townhouse, with Daisy trailing along behind her.

Daisy picked over the puddles and climbed the handful of steps to the townhouse. A butler pulled the door open and accepted their cloaks. He proceeded to lead them up to the first floor sitting room.

Ten or so of Lady Windermere's guests had arrived. The woman rushed over to greet the marchioness. While the two exchanged pleasantries, Daisy scanned the opulent space. Her gaze landed on Lady Leticia seated in a neat, little row alongside Daisy's childhood nemesis, the sisters, Ladies Caroline and Amelia Davidson. Leticia said something that set the other girls giggling.

She sighed. For all the great many aspects of life that changed, the mundane matters continued to march on with a tedious predictableness.

At that moment, Viscount Wessex appeared at Daisy's side. "Lady Daisy Meadows. It is a pleasure seeing you once again," he said, ever the charmer.

Daisy smiled. "If your younger self could hear you this moment, he'd be calling you the worst sort of liar."

His lips tugged at the corners. "But then, we all grow up, don't we? Life shows us the errors we've made and the mistakes."

"Yes. I suppose that is true." Unbidden, her gaze wandered off in search of the viscount's childhood friend.

"I daresay that wistful expression belongs to a lady seeking out a particular gentleman," the viscount drawled, jerking her attention back. He quirked an eyebrow. "Mayhap the same gentleman you were searching for at the Harrison ball, hmm?"

Heat flooded Daisy's cheeks. "No." She gave her head a hard shake. "I wasn't. That is to say…" His soft, blue eyes glinted with warmth. "Oh, you're teasing me," she finished, realizing too late that she'd confirmed a supposition that hadn't really been any kind of supposition, but rather good-natured teasing merely continued from their last repartee.

"I *was* teasing you," he added quietly. "Now I'm asking for altogether different reasons."

Daisy shifted on her feet. "I don't prefer you serious and protective. I prefer you—"

"Self-absorbed and uncaring?"

"I was going to say smiling and carefree," she added dryly.

Lord Wessex lowered his voice. "In this case, it would seem carefree has, in fact, been careless."

Daisy made a sound of protest. "Do not be silly." She gave a wave of her hand. "You've responsibilities enough of your own with your sister and mother and—"

"And I could certainly have taken some care to note that some bounder had captured your attention."

"He's not a bounder." The look in his eyes indicated she'd stepped very neatly into his trap. "He's not even real," she mumbled under her breath, which wasn't altogether a lie. She may as well be invisible, in the ways that mattered, to Auric.

"Call me a fool," he whispered. "But do not think me a lackwit who'd believe that weak lie."

Daisy sighed. She should be grateful for both his and Auric's concern and, with the rather solitary existence she'd lived since Lionel's passing, should relish any and every bit of attention thrown her way… and yet, she didn't want either him *or* Auric to act out of some misbegotten sense of obligation to her brother. Neither of them would replace him, nor did she want them, too. Particularly not Auric, whose heart she'd decided long ago she must possess.

A flurry of excited whispers cut into their exchange, saving her from responding.

Her heart quickened as Auric's tall, imposing frame filled the doorway. Lord and Lady Windermere rushed over to greet him even as Auric surveyed the room, as though searching for someone. Most likely one of the golden-tressed trio clustered together on the sofa, sighing and ahhing in his general direction.

"It is moments such as this that I'm glad to be a mere viscount."

An unexpected laugh spilled past her lips at Marcus' teasing words, grateful that he was no longer the stern, disapproving brotherly type. That Marcus was foreign. This man she was accustomed to and comfortable with.

She sought out Auric once again. He stood conversing with her mother. Whatever he said remained lost to the size of the room. The marchioness, every so often, nodded. How devoted Auric was to her family. Through the gossip and the sorrow and the whispers, he'd been there. He'd been there, yet all the while failed to truly see her—just as the rest of Society.

Just then, Daisy's skin pricked with the familiar stares. She stiffened and looked up in time. Two of Lady Windermere's guests stared blatantly at her and gave their heads pitying shakes. Her gut tightened and she wrenched her stare away.

There they were. Those pitying, sympathetic stares reserved for her and the Marchioness of Roxbury. Daisy bit the inside of her cheek, as that potent desire coursed through her—a desire to be noticed, not for the tragedy surrounding her family, or for her relationship to Lionel, but because someone noticed that there was a young woman by the name of Daisy Meadows…a woman worthy of notice and love. Her gaze strayed once more to Auric. He remained engrossed in conversation, unaware as he invariably was that Daisy stood in wait.

"You're quieter than I remember, Daisy."

Marcus' observation pulled her to the present. She forced her attention away from Auric. "It's as you've said. I've grown up."

The viscount opened his mouth to say something, but then he looked to a point beyond her shoulder.

"Wessex," a bored, *familiar* voice drawled.

A thrill of awareness coursed through her and Daisy straightened, turning to greet Auric. Goodness, with his long-legged stride he moved quickly.

Marcus bowed, returning the greeting and then froze. "What in blazes happened to your eye, Crawford?"

A mottled flush marred Auric's cheeks. "Nothing," he bit out.

Amusement flecked in Marcus' eyes that could only come from a familiarity shared these many years that defied Auric's lofty title. "It certainly does not appear as though noth—"

"Shove off," Auric snapped in an entirely un-dukelike way. Not for the first time, a wave of remorse slapped at her for his injured face. The heated intensity of his gaze never left her and she swallowed. "Your Grace." She dropped a curtsy. "I hope you are well."

She hoped he was well? By God, would she offer him tea and biscuits, next? She'd reserve a carefree smile for Wessex and to him, dip an insolent curtsy and a two-word utterance in the form of his title?

"Undoubtedly," he said in his most clipped, ducal tone that a frown came to her lips. Yet, he was not undoubtedly well. He was…He didn't know what he was. Annoyed, perhaps. Outraged? Furious? Perhaps a combination of the three. For some, unknown reason her familiarity with Wessex rankled. Which really made little sense. Drawing on the years of polished, ducal politeness drilled into him, he managed to bite out, "You're well, Wessex?"

"Was that a question or a statement, Crawford?" Droll humor underscored the viscount's question.

"Oh, it was *undoubtedly* a statement," Daisy said with entirely too much amusement in her words.

At their amusement at his expense, Auric gritted his teeth so tight, pain shot up his jawline. Alas, the two appeared either unaware of or unfazed by his displeasure. By the mischievous look that passed between Daisy and Wessex, it was likely the latter.

Then Marcus lifted his head. "I, too, am well." Then a half-grin formed on his lips. "We've now ascertained we are all three," he waggled his eyebrows, "well."

A sharp bark of laughter escaped Daisy and Wessex joined in. Auric wanted to bury his fist in the other man's belly for being so blasted entertaining and charming and a blasted paragon to make Daisy smile. Which shouldn't matter. He should just be bloody happy that the lady was smiling. But he wasn't. He was enraged and seething with a lifelike fury.

He was never more grateful for the interruption of the servant who entered the room to announce dinner. With respect for the commitment to rank, the hostess, Lady Windermere, came over. With a final look at Daisy, he held his arm out, damning the silly pomposity of a mere meal. Hating that she placed her arm upon her partner, Wessex's, sleeve and filed along behind Auric.

As the couples took their respective seats at the vast table that was covered in a stark, white tablecloth and awash in the soft glow from the four evenly distributed, silver candelabras, Auric stole a sideways glance at Daisy seated to his left. Wessex engaged the young lady at his right in conversation. The host and hostess' daughter, Lady Leticia, blushed and tittered at the attention. Daisy, however, sat in silence, staring at the silver candelabra and he was brought back to a different table, to a different time, he'd not remembered until this very moment. A Daisy of ten or eleven years with her elbows propped forlornly on the tabletop.

The memory slipped free as he considered the woman she'd become. The candle's glow bathed her cheeks in a gentle softness and he started. She really was quite lovely and yet, despite that fresh, uncommon beauty, there was something so very wistful, so sad about her. A viselike pressure tightened about his heart, as a familiar guilt crept in. Through his self-centeredness on that horrific night, he'd reduced her to this and...He glanced momentarily at her laconic mother, he'd reduced the older woman to the wan, somber creature she'd become.

As if feeling his gaze on her, Daisy looked up at him, a question in her eyes.

Auric leaned down and whispered close to her ear. "Is the tureen too far from your reach, Daisy? I'd not have you knocking down the candelabra and setting the table afire."

Surprise lit her eyes. "You remember?"

"How could I forget?" He chuckled. "Certainly the most memorable of all the picnics enjoyed by our families."

A wistful glimmer lit her eyes, transforming them from a simple brown to a rich, chocolate hue that put him in mind of the warmed beverage on a cold day and…He gave his head a hard shake, dispelling the maddening direction his thoughts had traversed. All of which involved the young lady beside him and her full breasts exposed for his worship.

If it hadn't been decided years ago, he was going to Hell. For only a bounder would dream scandalous dreams about his best friend's sister. Auric grabbed his glass of wine and took a long swallow.

A footman hurried over and served first Auric and then Daisy a bowl of turtle soup. She picked up her spoon and gingerly stirred the contents of her porcelain, white bowl. The delicate movement drew his eyes down to her slight palms. Did she know that she'd set his world into tumult?

Auric broke the silence. "I trust you are well?" He silently cursed the pathetic attempt at conversation and wished, not for the first time, that he possessed a hint of Wessex's ease with the ladies.

Daisy's lips twitched.

God, he detested the need for banal, polite conversation "That is, I trust you are well following your fall?" Then, talk of the weather and other topics deemed polite were far safer than the wicked thoughts racing through his mind, even now.

She paused mid-stir. "I am." She raised a spoonful of broth to her mouth and his eyes were drawn inexplicably to her full, red, bow-shaped lips as they parted.

Auric fought back a groan and took another sip of wine. He stared into the contents of his glass unwilling to look at her, lest the madness overtake his senses and reason. Lusting after Daisy Meadows was the ultimate betrayal of Lionel's memory.

"Oh, dear," Daisy said. She made a tsking sound.

He'd known the imp well enough through the years that the very last thing he should do was rise to her baiting.

Then she sighed.

"What is it?"

"I fear your vision is a good deal worse off than even I'd imagined." She motioned to his partially empty wine glass. "You seem quite fixed on the contents and I can only imagine that is because of your declining ducal vision."

He bristled and set the crystal glass down. "I'm hardly at an advanced age to be needing a quizzing glass." Though for some reason he'd tucked the silly gift she'd given him inside his coat and continued to carry it there. Not because he required the fool thing. His vision was quite fine and should be for another thirty years or so.

"Auric, all dukes require a quizzing glass." She dropped her voice to a conspiratorial whisper. "Especially the aging dukes, such as yourself."

"I'm only a few months past nine and twenty," he said, a touch of defensiveness underscored his words.

Daisy gave a decisive nod. "Certainly old enough to require a monocle." She winked and then returned her attention to her soup.

She'd winked at him. Winked. In the midst of an intimate dinner party, and more, she'd dismissed him. He opened his mouth but then Wessex said something at her opposite side, calling her attention away. A haze of outrage momentarily clouded his vision, which had nothing, absolutely nothing, to do with Daisy dismissing him to speak with the viscount. After all, the viscount had been like a second brother to her, just as Auric had.

Only, his unwitting attention to her lush figure, better suited for bedrooms than ballrooms, did not feel in the least brotherly. He grabbed his wine and took another long swallow, eventually draining the contents of his glass. If it hadn't been decided seven years ago, it was certainly decided now—with his lustful thoughts, Auric was going to hell.

A footman removed his untouched soup.

"Your Grace?" His hostess, Lady Windermere, looked at the bowl almost questioningly, but too unfailingly polite to dare ask a duke as to whether he'd found something unfavorable she instead offered him a tight smile. "I am most sorry to have learned of Lady Anne's decision to wed the Earl of Stanhope." She shook her head. "These are sad days indeed, Your Grace, when young ladies would choose the marital offer of an earl over an esteemed duke." But not too impolite it would seem to make such a gauche statement over his courtship of the now Lady Stanhope. "Perfectly lovely, the countess is with her golden ringlets and pleasing smile."

The servants rushed forward to set out the trays of duckling, Plover's eggs in aspic jelly, a macedoine of fruit, and various other servings.

Lady Windermere angled closer. "Though my daughter, she too has lovely golden ringlets and the papers, of course, say you'd not ever have a lady with brown hair for your duchess. Though who can blame you?" she prattled on.

A loud clattering of silver meeting porcelain resonated through the dining room. From the corner of his eye, he detected the blush in Daisy's cheeks, as she hastened to pick up her utensil. He was again brought back to a different table with a younger, belligerent Daisy and himself. Had the lady always had to confront the condescending sneers and snide remarks? How could members of polite Society not see with her freckled cheeks and tight brown curls, there was a uniqueness that made all other ladies pale beside her? Auric rested his arms upon the mahogany dining chair. He kept his face a cool mask. "One should take care to not rely on the gossip to be had in the scandal sheets, Lady Windermere." Familial friendships be damned. He'd not see Daisy shamed or humiliated before anyone.

A dull flush stained her cheeks at his curt reprimand.

"And Lady Windermere?"

"Yes?" she squawked.

"Do you not believe there is something pleasing to be found in the color brown?"

She gulped loudly. "Er, uh-why y-yes, undoubtedly," she stammered and then promptly shifted her attention back to her husband who sat at the head of the table, opposite from her.

Though he'd courted Lady Anne with intentions of offering marriage, it had been clear her feelings had been otherwise engaged. His interest had been stirred by the unconventional miss, but there had never been anything more there than a proper duchess for his position as duke.

A small elbow nudged his, knocking his forearm from its place upon the arm of the chair. Flecks of gold danced in Daisy's eyes. "That was well-done of you, Auric."

They shared a smile. Just like that, with one gentle nudge and an effortless smile, they became simply Auric and Daisy. And if he was being truthful with just himself, he could admit to how right that was.

EIGHT

The following evening, seated at the private table at the back of his club, Auric stared into the contents of his brandy. He took a slow sip and acknowledged the great shift that had occurred in him, with Daisy, with *them*. At some point he'd seen the world in those shades of russet and he could no longer cease to notice. He swirled the glass in a small circle and then took a long sip. More specifically, he could not ignore that Daisy had grown up. And more, the young lady with romantic intentions who took herself off on her own to Gipsy Hill, unchaperoned, his best friend's sister needed caring for. His lips pulled in a grimace and he took another swallow of his drink. That rather made the lady sound like a favored hunting dog. Except, with her generous mouth, lush figure, and husky laugh, she assuredly was no hunting dog.

With a silent curse he downed the remaining contents of his drink. He'd no business thinking of Daisy's glorious form. He glanced up from his empty glass. From the entrance of White's, the Viscount Wessex strode through the hallowed club. He moved with a single-minded purpose. The usually affable gentleman ignored the greetings called out. He came to a stop before Auric's table and looked more serious than he had in seven…. He thrust back the memory of Lionel.

"Wessex," he greeted. They two shared a bond that no man would want, having together discovered Lionel's lifeless body.

The viscount didn't waste time with pleasantries. He pulled out a seat. A servant hurried forward with an empty glass. Wordlessly, the other man accepted it and waved off the offer of assistance. He proceeded to pour himself a tall glass of brandy and then set the bottle

101

down hard. It thunked loudly on the table. The other man picked up his drink and downed it in a long, slow swallow. He grimaced and then reached for the bottle again. He sloshed several fingersful in the glass.

Auric frowned. Wessex had long ago earned a reputation as an indolent rogue and reprobate. However, the *ton* failed to look close enough at the true image before them to recognize the viscount hadn't touched another drop after Lionel's death.

Until now. This shaken gentleman before him was not someone he recognized. Wessex raised the glass to his lips and this time took a more leisurely sip. He broke the silence. "Daisy Meadows."

Auric's frown deepened. "Daisy—?"

"Lionel's sister," he said, as though there was another Daisy that mattered to the both of them. Wessex waved his hand about and several droplets splashed Auric's immaculate table. He looked about, ascertaining there were no eavesdroppers close by, and then returned his attention to Auric. "There is a gentleman."

What was the other man on about? He looked around for the gentleman referenced by his friend.

"You misunderstand," Wessex hissed. He strained to lean over the table. "A gentleman has captured Daisy's affections."

Auric opened his mouth, but no words came out. A haze descended over his vision. It had been one thing when those very worries had belonged to him alone. Then, they had been unfounded fears about Daisy. It was quite another when the viscount breathed life and truth to them.

The other man leaned back in his seat. "It should come as no surprise. She's no longer a girl, even though that is the way you will forever see her."

Guilt pebbled in his belly. For where Wessex took him as the honorable gentleman and loyal friend, Auric had noticed her mouth. And her breasts. And her—

"Crawford?"

He gave his head a clearing shake. "What have you based your…?" Daisy, as she'd been at Gipsy Hill, moving between gypsy carts, flitted through his mind. "…your…" The air left him on a slow exhale. He'd shoved aside the idea of Daisy with another gentleman when he'd first discovered her in the unfashionable end of London. Only now, her outrageous actions coupled with Wessex's words painted the possibility in a greater light.

"What?"

He rubbed a hand over his mouth. "I discovered her at Gipsy Hill." Twice. "Unchaperoned." She'd claimed to be in search of a necklace. But of course a woman of Daisy's sense and romantic spirit would not venture into that end of London just to look for an inexpensive bauble. No, what else would cause a lady to do something so insensible, *other* than a clandestine meeting between two lovers? Auric's knee jumped reflexively, knocking the table. By God, he would kill the man dead.

"Gipsy Hill?"

Auric gave a terse nod.

The viscount sank back in his seat, flummoxed. He stroked his chin. "There was also the Harrison's ball," he declared, more to himself.

Tension coursed through Auric's frame. His thoughts and emotions were blending and blurring in a mass of confusion. "What of it?" With Wessex's confirmation of his own earlier suspicions, he was forced to consider all manner of things he'd rather not—about Daisy, her future, his obligation to see to that future.

Wessex swiped his glass off the table once again and took a sip. He set it down hard and, for a long while, said nothing so that Auric believed he didn't intend to speak. Then, "She was studying a gentleman."

"Who?" he bit out.

"Oh, I'd merely teased her, not believing, not thinking that she was in fact—"

"Who?" he said loud enough to earn curious stares from those around them. He waited until the nosy noblemen nearby returned their attention to their own drink and company.

"That is the problem, Crawford. I've questioned the lady several times in search of the bounder's identity. To no avail." Wessex lifted his shoulders in a slight shrug. "But if he were honorable..."

Daisy would not be running off to meet him on the streets of London and his identity would not be a secret.

Wessex set his glass down. He turned his hands over and made a show of studying his palms. "She's unwed. Do you know how many Seasons she's had?"

"Two." They both responded simultaneously.

"That is correct." The viscount nodded. After the marquess' passing, Daisy had disappeared and, unfortunately, when she'd reentered Society almost two years later, the dandies in the market for a wife didn't realize the rareness of Daisy. She was the hidden pendant amidst the other baubles—only no one had bothered to see what was right before them. Her unwedded state and romantic spirit accounted for why a romantic young woman such as Daisy would throw away logic and reason to pursue a worthless bounder in the rainy streets of London.

Wessex held his gaze, intruding on his turbulent thoughts. "The marchioness has forgotten her existence."

"That is preposterous," Auric scoffed. He remembered the older woman tugging Daisy behind her at Lord and Lady Harrison's ball. "Her mother has always paid a good deal of attention to Daisy."

"Perhaps at one time, but not since..." His blue eyes darkened a shade nearly black. "Not since...By the way, what the hell *did* happen to your eye?"

Ah, yes, the impressive purplish black bruise he now wore, a credit to Daisy's efforts on Gipsy Hill. Auric waved his hand. "It matters not."

Fortunately, Wessex was content to let his question rest, rightfully focusing on Daisy. "It occurred to me last evening, at Lord and Lady Windermere's, we had an obligation to see after her, Crawford, and we failed."

The blade of guilt twisted all the more at Marcus' reminder of another wrong Auric had committed. First, in bringing Lionel to that hell and costing the man his life, and his parents their future, and now...Daisy. They'd both had an obligation to protect and defend her.

Wessex seemed to agree for he continued. "We've not only failed Daisy, we've failed Lionel. It occurs to me that one of us," he sucked in an audible breath, "must do right by her." He gripped his crystal glass so tight his knuckles whitened. "We owe that much to Lionel."

The other man's meaning was clear. They should find her a husband. Auric's hands tightened reflexively over the arms of his chair. He didn't know why he should care if Daisy Meadows wed, as long as she was wed to a decent enough chap who'd care for her and mayhap gave her a handful of children. Yet he cared. Very much. Something fiery and hot licked at his insides, something that felt very much like jealousy…which was, of course, rather ridiculous, he'd no right to be jealous and certainly not over—

"Crawford? Are you listening to me?"

He cleared his throat. "You were saying?" He picked up his brandy, suddenly appreciating the need for fine, French spirits at a time like this.

He could no longer be the coward. He told himself it had been a sense of pity. He'd seen the card devoid of gentleman's names and something had stirred in his breast. Perhaps it was guilt. For if Lionel had lived, he'd surely have managed to bring some deserving gentleman up to scratch to not only partner young Daisy, but wed her.

"She needs a husband," Wessex said bluntly.

An image flooded his mind. Daisy, in all her lush glory, spread out upon soft, satin sheets while he covered her with his body. "Surely, you don't propose one of us wed her?" he asked, his voice hoarse.

The viscount scratched his brow. "Egads, no, man." He gave a mock shudder.

Auric tightened his jaw. What did the other man find so objectionable about the young lady? She was perfectly lovely and far more clever and spirited than any other member of the peerage.

"Not that I find anything objectionable with the lady," Wessex carried on, having no idea how very close to Auric burying his fist in his face he was. "She's…"

He quirked an icy eyebrow.

"She's Lionel's sister," the viscount finished solemnly. "And we have to present her suitable, *honorable*," he amended, "gentlemen who'd make her a good husband." A red haze descended over his vision, momentarily blinding him. What was this odd pressure in his chest? "With your influence you can likely bring any number of good gentlemen up to scratch."

Those words somehow managed to sink in and reclaim control of his inexplicable, not at all brotherly, interest in Daisy. "You are correct," he said with the cool, flat, emotionless logic that had shaped him all these years. Why yes, his friend was correct. They owed this not only to Lionel but also to Daisy. "What do you suggest?" He hardly recognized the garbled tone as his own.

Wessex held his gaze. "We present her with options. We…" Auric shoved back his chair and stood. "Where are you going?" he called after him.

"I've a matter of business to attend."

Mayhap his friend had the right of it. Mayhap this sudden, untoward interest he had in the lady stemmed from a sense of remorse. Daisy required a husband and he would see her properly wed. He ignored those raising their hands in greeting and continued on to the front of White's.

Perhaps then, when she was comfortably wed, then he could live his life feeling that, at least in this regard, he'd not failed Lionel.

Seated on the blue upholstered sofa, Daisy held up the embroidery frame for her maid's inspection.

The young woman's lips twitched. "Uh…a…"

"Do not say a circle with a dip in the center," she implored.

Agnes promptly closed her mouth and then leaned forward to better analyze Daisy's latest work. It was never a good thing when one's work required this level of scrutiny. "A teardrop?" she ventured.

Yes, never a good thing at all. She tossed aside the frame. "Will you be so good as to collect," another, "the embroidery I left in my chambers?"

Agnes hopped to her feet, dropped a curtsy and shuffled off. Daisy scooped up the rather pathetic and, in fact, the seventh attempt at her heart. She angled her head studying it objectively. A sigh slipped past her lips. Yes, there was no helping it. She really was quite awful. So, practice did *not* always make mastery, now she knew. All too well.

Footsteps sounded in the hall. She looked up as the butler admitted Auric. Her heart did an odd little flutter. He eyed her in that nondescript way, both of them silent, studying one another. Frederick cleared his throat. "My lady, His Grace, the Duke of Crawford."

She scrambled to her feet. "Frederick, will you have refreshments—?"

"That will not be necessary," Auric interrupted.

She furrowed her brow. He'd adopted an I'm-here-on-serious-ducal-business-tone. Daisy motioned him forward. He strode over in a handful of long, powerful strides and as Frederick backed out of the room, she swore she saw the ghost of a smile on his lips. She sank onto the edge of her seat and stared up at him expectantly.

Auric clasped his hands behind him and rocked back on his heels…and remained standing.

"Would you care to sit, Auric? Or do you intend to hover over me like a too-stern governess?"

Instead of any hint of a smile, his frown deepened. Oh, this was quite serious business. Auric did, however, flick out his coattails and sit. With all the boldness afforded him as a duke, he reached for her embroidery frame and perused her work. "A cloud?"

"A red cloud?" she scoffed. Surely, if she'd been intending a cloud it would have been gray or white. Well, that wouldn't work. The white would quite get lost within the equally white background. "Have you come to assess my needlepoint skills?" Or had he come with the sole intention of seeing her? She certainly preferred the latter. An excited thrill coursed through her.

He set her frame down. "You're unwed."

Daisy choked on her swallow as her earlier jubilation died. She coughed into her hand and waved off the concerned question forming on his lips. "I-I beg your pardon?" It had sounded as though he'd said—

"You're unwed." Auric drummed his fingertips on the arm of his chair. "Surely, you've given some consideration to whom it is you'll wed?"

"Undoubtedly," she said with dry humor he either failed to detect or cared for. "After all that is certainly how every single, young, unwed lady spends her day."

"Of course." Oh, the lout. "And?" he pressed.

Her heart picked up a funny rhythm. What grounds did he have to discuss marriage with her unless he himself had considered that very possibility? "And are you here presenting me an offer?"

Auric recoiled in such horror that would have stung painfully if his reaction weren't so very un-Auric-like. "God, no."

Well, so much for that particular wish. She tamped down a sigh and, lest he look too close and see the hope she carried in her heart etched upon her face, she leaned over and patted his knee. "Rest assured, Auric. I was merely teasing." He stiffened. At her words? The boldness of her touch? Regardless, she lied to him. She'd take him as her husband under any circumstance, if he simply uttered those three words.

He slashed a hand through the air. "I'm here to discuss the matter of your husband."

"I don't have a husband," she couldn't resist teasing. But she had a particular duke who would do splendidly. If the foolish man would but open his eyes and see.

*When you love something enough as you do, it will come...*Lionel's whispered words wrapped about her, comforting for their familiarity and truth—and because they belonged to him.

Auric leapt to his feet. "That is precisely why I've come." He began to pace a quick path upon the Aubusson carpet.

She eyed his restless movements. "To marry me?" she asked, her words threaded with her consternation. "You're really not making much sense, Aur—"

"I have come with the intention of helping you find a husband."

Daisy stilled, her gaze fixed upon his well-muscled legs clad in those midnight black breeches. He spoke as casually as if he mentioned retrieving her forgotten kerchief and not a man she'd be forever tied to. A humming filled her ears like a thousand buzzing bees circling close to her head. She curled her hands into tight fists, welcoming the sting of her nails biting into her palm. With a slow awareness that caused her heart to sink into the soles of her slippers, she faced the ugly truth—"You'd find me a husband." Her words, a barely there whisper, brought him to an immediate stop.

Auric drove his fist into his palm and came to an abrupt halt in front of her. "Precisely, Daisy. An honorable gentleman, and," his mouth tightened, "and whatever requirements you find essential in a husband."

Daisy craned her neck at an awkward angle to look up at him. "He should not be a great, big dunderhead," she snapped, because that was precisely what *His Grace* was being.

"Of course not," he said brusquely. He nodded. "You'll require an intelligent gentleman."

"If there is such a thing," she mumbled, because surely an intelligent duke could see the perfect woman for him sitting right there before his still too-young-for-a-quizzing glass-eyes.

"What was that?"

Daisy shoved to her feet, a mere hairsbreadth from his tall, powerful frame. Her breath caught raggedly at the heat of him pouring into her and she damned her body for reacting as it did when he should not even garner a hint of her heart's desire. "Do you know what *I* want?"

Auric leaned his head down and the scent of him, sandalwood and coffee and the faintest hint of brandy, danced about her, intoxicating. "Wh...?" That question trailed off as his gaze dipped and fixed on her lips.

Did she imagine the audible inhalation of breath? She slid her tongue over her bottom lip. "I want—" He claimed her lips under his. He moved his mouth over hers demanding and seeking all at the same time.

Auric wrapped a hand about her waist and drew her close, angling his head to deepen the kiss. Even through the fabric of her gown, her skin burned with the hot heaviness of his touch and she moaned, pressing herself to him. He wrenched his head away, setting her from him with such alacrity she stumbled against the mahogany table. The duke backed away, his face wreathed in a mask of horror. "I...I..."

"I wanted you to," she said on a breathless rush, because she could not bear the shock and disgust to follow that stammered response.

Usually unflappable, the stoic duke dragged a trembling hand through his hair. "You need a husband." He would speak as though with a joining of their lips he'd not shaken her world and breathed a hope of them as a couple into her. "What do you desire," a dull flush climbed up his neck and splashed his cheeks, "in a husband?" he squeezed out, his words sounding pained.

You. I desire you. Daisy smoothed her palms over the front of her skirts. "He must be devoted to me. He must care for my well-being and happiness." *And see me as more than a mere obligation.*

"Devoted. Caring." Auric gave a brusque nod and with that handful of wishes from her, took his leave.

NINE

Dear Lionel,
God forgive me. I kissed your sister…

With a groan, Auric tossed his pen aside and stared at the damning pages of his journal, feeling no better for putting the truth down onto the empty sheet. He'd kissed Daisy Laurel Meadows. Nor had that kiss been a polite, meaningless gesture upon her gloved fingers or even a gentle meeting of mere lips. Rather, theirs had been an explosive, passionate exploration of two people learning one another, hungering for more.

She'd tasted of springtime and life and innocence and he'd wanted to drown himself in the sweetness of her. The nine words inked in black, glared back at him in silent recrimination. "I know it was unpardonable," he acknowledged.

Since he'd taken his hasty leave of Daisy, he'd been unable to purge the memory of her lips or the curve of her hip from his thoughts. With a groan, Auric dropped his head onto those damning words. He knocked his forehead against the opened journal, hopelessly wrinkling the page.

What manner of madness had possessed him to kiss her? For God's sake, he had no right desiring her as he did. She was the sister of a man he'd gotten killed and a girl he'd never before seen as anything more than a vexing, spirited child, and then an equally vexing, spirited young lady.

Only now he knew she tasted like warmed chocolate and honey with the hint of lavender water on her person and, God forgive him, he'd wanted to search out the spot she'd dabbed that intoxicating fragrance.

"I'm going to hell," he mumbled into the leather volume. He opened his eyes and stared at the ivory pages. "It was just a kiss," he bit out and with determination sat back in his seat. Just a kiss. Taking a deep, calming breath, he smoothed his hands over the wrinkled page trying to put some order to his turbulent thoughts. Of course he would react as he had to Daisy. As Wessex had so *un*helpfully pointed out, she was no longer a small child who dogged his footsteps and winked once when things were splendid or twice when she required rescuing. No, instead she was the troublesome vixen who wandered through the streets of London unchaperoned and winked once when things were splendid and twice in need of rescuing. With one more slow, deliberate breath, he evaluated the handful of words he'd penned just moments before he'd been consumed by the memory of how right it had felt to hold Daisy in his arms.

He flipped through the pages of his book, pausing on yesterday evening's entry.

Dear Lionel,
It is my intention to find a devoted, caring gentleman for your sister…

He drummed his fingertips over the now dried ink. He'd long known Daisy possessed a romantic heart. Now he knew she sought a husband who would be devoted, as she certainly deserved nothing less. Auric firmed his lips into a hard, furious line and continued turning pages to the most recently completed entry.

Dear Lionel,
I've compiled a list of the following gentlemen who might make Daisy a respectable match…

By the king and all his men, he'd ruin the man who failed to give her his fidelity. Though, with the amount of rogues, cads, and bastards in London who took their pleasures where they would and carried on with whores and mistresses and widows, which gentleman had proven he'd be worthy of her? Auric searched his mind of all the gentlemen he'd known through the years.

There was the Marquess of Fenworth. With two younger sisters already out in London, the young marquess had proven himself a devoted brother, standing at their side for any number of soirees and balls. Auric dipped his pen in ink and added the man's name to Daisy's list.

"*You'll become a duchess someday when all those other, unkind girls find themselves with mere future marquesses such as myself...*" Lionel's words to his sister all those years ago at the Marchioness of Roxbury's summer party echoed so clear in his mind. A chill stole down Auric's spine.

He drew a dark, hard mark through that name. No marquess. A marquess would forever remind her of the role Lionel had been intended to fill and she did not deserve that sadness. With a small, contemplative frown, Auric drummed the tip of his pen back and forth.

The Earl of Coventry. He marked the man's name down. The dark-haired, tall gentleman, quite impressive with Gentleman Jackson was diligent in his daily routine. His prowess in the ring and his commitment spoke to his devotion. Except, it also served to conjure an image of the muscular gentleman paired with Daisy, kissing her lips in the way Auric longed to. With a growl he dragged the tip of his pen across Coventry's name. The man was too handsome, and handsome gentlemen were invariably rogues who *inevitably* led to broken hearts. He'd not allow Daisy to wed a rogue.

Bloody hell. Who was there? Of course! The Baron Winterhaven. Ah, yes. Winterhaven would make her a perfect match. The bookish gentleman from his days at Oxford had been so very dedicated to his studies he'd been reputed to not miss a single class in any of his days at university. An educated, bookish man would be faithful. Such a man also lacked Daisy's fire and passion which perfectly suited Auric—He gave his head a clearing shake. Daisy. A passionless, safe match would suit *Daisy*, because—well, it just would. He eyed the list coming along with a pleased nod.

A knock sounded at the door. He didn't pick his attention up from the leather volume. "Enter," he called out, contemplating which other devoted gentleman might make Daisy an acceptable match. It would need to be a man whose happiness would be intertwined with the lady's, who'd see her—

"The Viscount Wessex," his butler announced.

Abandoning his efforts, he looked up as Wessex entered the room. The other man strode over, appearing entirely too bored and disinterested for one who'd identified their obligation to Daisy. With a yawn, he sank into one of two leather chairs opposite Auric's desk. "Well?"

"Well?" he asked impatiently. Did the man believe him a mind reader?

"Knowing you and your fixation on that journal," he jerked his chin toward the opened book. "you've already lined up at least three possible suitors for the lady on those pages. Well, then, who are they?" Without allowing Auric an opportunity to respond, he leaned over and swiped the book off his desk. Wessex skimmed his gaze over the page. "Hmm."

Cross at the other man's audacity, Auric glowered. Then, Wessex would have to one, look up to note his displeasure and two, care. Their friendship went back far enough that he'd never intimidated easily. Auric's curiosity got the better of him. "What is it?"

"I'd considered Fenworth as well." His friend, however, said nothing else about his ultimate decision on that gentleman's suitability. "Coventry," he murmured in a contemplative tone. He picked his head up and gave him a questioning stare. "What is wrong with Coventry?"

"He's…" *Too handsome.* "He's…" He waved a hand and partially wished he could pluck the appropriate words from the air. "A rogue," he managed.

"*Ohh,*" That single syllable utterance drawn out, hinted at a differing of opinion. "Is he?"

"He is," he said tersely.

The viscount returned his attention to the page. "Winterhaven?" By the incredulity underscoring that particular name, Auric gathered they were of opposite views on this prospective suitor as well.

Tamping down his annoyance, he stood. "I gather you've prepared a list of possible gentlemen as well?" he asked, highly doubting Wessex had given Daisy and her future bridegroom another thought. Auric leaned across the table and collected his journal from the other man's fingers. When he had committed himself to looking after Lionel's family, Wessex had spent the past seven years devoted to his own happiness and pursuits. He'd likely not given a thought as to who might make Daisy a—

His friend reached into his jacket front and pulled out a folded sheet. "Well, have a look." He set it down on Auric's desk.

Blinking back a moment of shock, he reached for Wessex's list. His very *full* list. The viscount had managed to identify, one-two-three, he jabbed his finger at each name, four-five-six, he continued counting. "Ten names?" he charged.

Wessex rolled his shoulders. "Certainly a better showing than your meager collection," he drawled, mistaking the reason for Auric's questioning. "You've but Winterhaven and Danport."

This was not the time to mention that he'd intended to ink Danport's name from the sheet. The Earl of Danport wasn't a rogue, but he was too charming. That would never do.

"The list," his friend drawled, effectively jerking him to the moment.

Irritation stuck in his chest as he returned his attention to the potential husbands selected by the viscount. Surely, Wessex didn't believe there were *this* many men worthy of Daisy? No, unlike Auric, he had not taken time to inquire as to Daisy's expectations and requirements for the man she'd take for her husband, which likely accounted for that very full list.

Coventry was there. Fenworth, as well. Winterhaven...? He picked his gaze up.

"Winterhaven is not on there," Wessex confirmed, anticipating his unspoken question.

He tossed the sheet back and it fluttered in the air. The other man caught it reflexively, rumpling the sheet.

Auric scowled. Friend or not, what did the roguish viscount know about who would suit Daisy? "And what rationale went into your selection of the respective gentlemen?" he asked, unable to keep the annoyance from his tone.

115

Singularly unaffected by Auric's displeasure, Wessex smiled. "I sought a respectful gentleman, free of scandal, for the lady."

He dug his elbows into the edge of the table. "*That* is your main criteria for the lady?" When it should be her happiness and making sure there was a man who not only desired her heart, but also, more importantly, cared for it.

Wessex snorted. "Oh, and I expect you, in all your ducal arrogance, have quite determined the *correct* criteria?"

Auric frowned. He'd not thought much beyond Daisy's own desires and the immediacy of *his* own passionate sentiments. No handsome gentlemen. No rogues. No man who'd worship that mouth as he'd done yesterday afternoon. He gave his head a shake.

His friend squinted, peering closely at him through thin slits. "What is that?"

Auric looked about. "What is—?"

"On your brow." He motioned to Auric's forehead. "It appears as though you've ink just above your eyebrow."

Likely from slamming his forehead into that page. He fished around the front of his jacket and withdrew an embroidered kerchief. Remembering too late—The small quizzing glass etched in daisies slipped from the folds of the white fabric and clattered to his desk. He instantly scooped it up.

Wessex followed his gaze. He widened his eyes. A sharp bark of laughter escaped him. "By God, what the hell is that, man?" Deep, bellowing guffaws bubbled from his lips and he slapped his knee. "Never tell me in your advancing ducal years you've need of a quizzing glass."

"Shove off," he ordered, except he knew the other man well enough through the years to trust Wessex would not so readily relinquish the matter.

Tears of mirth seeped from the corner of his eyes, as he snorted with amusement. "Th-the alternative i-is that you've further protected your s-starchy, frowning r-role to perfection."

At the other man's words, Auric scowled. Is that how the world saw him? As this miserable, unpleasant, disapproving fellow who'd never have his name scratched upon a list of one such as Daisy's?

"…You used to be so much more fun than this cold, curt, and crusty duke…"

Not that he wanted to be on Daisy's list. Nor did she have a list. But if she did, he'd not want his name on there. Because…"Go to hell," he growled to a still chuckling Wessex. He didn't like the idea of him having fun at his expense.

Wessex stood. He tugged out his own handkerchief and, with the edge of the fabric, brushed the moisture from his cheeks. "I have it on authority that the first three gentlemen upon that list are in the market for a wife."

Auric took in Coventry, Fenworth, and the Viscount Marsdale's names. Gentlemen who were in the market for a wife were generally seeking a match for a reason. No man would have her for her dowry. He'd see to that. "Their finances—?"

"There is no debt. I've made specific inquiries."

He looked up with no little surprise.

A flash of annoyance lit the other man's eyes. "Come, did you believe I'd be dishonorable to Daisy and in so doing, the memory of Lionel?"

"No," he replied instantly, and a wave of guilt struck him for his friend's unerring accuracy with that leveled charge.

He yanked on the lapels of his jacket. "Regardless, I'd recommend Astor."

The obscenely wealthy Earl of Astor didn't sit down at the gaming tables. He was rumored to keep a single mistress and never did anything so outrageous as visiting those infamous sins. In short, the man was a bloody paragon. He'd always detested Astor.

"Crawford?"

"Er, right. I'll pay the gentleman a visit." After all, what was the likelihood that Astor was in the market for a wife with too full lips and generous hips, and—?

"And?" Wessex prodded.

He spoke through gritted teeth. "And I'll bring him 'round for a visit with Daisy."

Another sharp bark of laughter burst from the viscount's lips and Auric grew increasingly annoyed with the other man's enjoyment at his expense.

"*That* is your plan?" The viscount shook his head. "Do tell me how Daisy responds to your, er…visit with the earl." He sketched a bow. With another round of laughter trailing in his wake, Wessex took his leave.

Directing a frown at the now empty doorway, he looked once more to the two very different lists comprised of two very different sets of names of gentlemen.

Daisy's carriage rolled up to the front of her townhouse and rocked to a slow, effortless stop. She pursed her lips. Another dratted outing and another failed attempt. Though she appreciated Lady Stanhope's optimism that Daisy would, in fact, manage to find the Heart of a Duke pendant if she but looked, it was more like finding a needle in the streets of London.

A footman pulled the door open and handed her down. She flashed the young liveried footman—Thomas—a smile. "Thank you," she murmured and started for the entrance of her home.

Yes, she appreciated the lady's optimism, but she was also…Daisy paused at the base of the stairs and frowned. Well, hell and bloody hell, she was frustrated because she'd taken herself to Gipsy Hill three times without a hint of the gypsy Bunică. Of all the gypsies she'd asked, not a single one had guided her to the woman's whereabouts. And that was assuming the old gypsy and her pendant were even there. Instead, Daisy's inquiries had been met with stony silence and wary eyes. She stomped up the handful of steps and Frederick, as uncanny as he'd been since she'd been a girl tearing through the halls of the then joyous townhouse, drew the door open.

"Lady Daisy," he greeted.

"Frederick." A servant rushed over and she shrugged out of her cloak. The winning of Auric's heart resided in that pendant and, though she'd ceased to believe in magic and fairytales of happily ever after's many years ago, she allowed herself this last dream. Daisy started up the stairs. Frederick cleared his throat. Though it was foolish to hang her every remaining hope upon a gypsy's bauble, this was the last dream she carried, and to give up on that dream would represent the last shred of joy left inside her soul.

Frederick gave another subtle cough. She glanced over her shoulder. "I took the liberty of showing His Grace, Duke of Crawford to the drawing room, as well as—"

"Thank you, Frederick!" Her heart sped up and she bounded back down the steps in a way that would have made her mother of old cringe. Following his visit yesterday when he'd spoken to her of making a match with another—a man who was not him—she'd been besieged by alternating feelings of outrage, hurt, and annoyance. She reached the end of the corridor and slowed to a quick, jerky halt. Daisy smoothed her hands over her cheeks and then ran her palms down the front of her skirts, composing herself. Through the years, she'd believed his frequent visits a mere obligatory social call paid her mother, and yet, with the marchioness so often indisposed, why, why would Auric return day after day if not some small part didn't long to see her? Daisy turned down the hall. Why, unless…She stepped into the room.

Her gaze locked on Auric, standing at the hearth, arms clasped behind his back. And then she became aware of another gentleman, seated on the King Louis XIV chair looking about as put out with Auric as Daisy herself. The tall, lean, dark-haired gentleman, the Earl of Astor. She'd not met the man beyond an introduction and two or three sets in total at a variety functions. It was certainly not enough to merit an unexpected afternoon call. Unless—

Her mind spun rapidly. Then the truth settled around her brain and Daisy slowly narrowed her eyes. By God, she would bloody Auric's nose for this, she would. And if he were lucky, that was all she would do.

Lord Astor tugged out his watch fob, happening to glance up at her silent figure in the doorway. He sprang to his feet. "My lady," he greeted, in a not at all displeasing baritone.

Auric stiffened and then turned around slowly, coolly unaffected as he so often was. Tamping down her annoyance, she shifted her attention from him to the smiling Lord Astor. "My lord," she greeted. She dipped a curtsy and then entered further into the room. Her maid, Agnes, bustled in behind her and set up sentry in her usual seat at the blue arm chair in the far right corner of the room. Forcefully thrusting aside the urge to throttle Auric, Daisy drew on years of good breeding and motioned to his chair. "Would you care to sit?" The young earl with his chiseled features and hard, square jaw hesitated a moment and then reclaimed his seat. She claimed the nearest chair opposite him.

The dunderhead in the corner crossed over in three formidable strides. With a glower, Auric sat on the blue sofa, making the elegant piece of furniture appear hopelessly delicate with his broad, powerful frame.

Daisy folded her hands primly on her lap. "Would you care for refreshments?"

"No," Auric snapped.

She arched an eyebrow and then looked pointedly at the earl.

He grinned. "No, refreshments, thank you, my lady."

The gentleman had manners, which was a good deal more than she could say for certain boorish dukes who took it upon themselves to go and select men she might take for her husband. Fury stirred in her belly once again. She forced her features into a pleasant, unruffled mask.

An awkward pall of silence descended over the room, made all the more glaring for the incessant tick-tocking of the loud clock.

Pleasant discourse. Pleasant discourse. She ran through years of proper lessons on deportment. Weather. She discarded that inane, dull topic cared about by none. After all, maybe one needed only to direct their stare to the window to ascertain as much.

The earl's gaze skittered about the room.

"Lady Daisy quite enjoys music," Auric supplied, unhelpfully.

She pressed her lips into a tight line to keep from telling him what she thought of his pronouncement. Would he have her show her teeth next?

"Indeed?" Lord Astor inquired, his expression fairly pained, and she appreciated the honesty of that reaction.

"She does." Is that what Auric thought he knew of her after a lifetime of friendship? She'd kick him in the shins if there weren't an additional guest present.

Daisy shook her head. "No, I don't."

Both men startled at her contradiction. She grinned. "I enjoy dancing to music." She wrinkled her brow. "I detest the pianoforte, as I'm quite deplorable at it."

Lord Astor made a gentlemanly sound of protest.

She gave a flick of a hand. "Oh, you needn't defend on my account." Daisy lowered her voice to a none-too-quiet whisper. "I'm really quite horrid. My mother despaired of my nonexistent skills through the years."

The first real grin turned the gentleman's hard lips upward and some of the stiffness in his shoulders eased. He placed his hands on his knees and leaned forward, shrinking the space between them. "Your secret is safe with me," he whispered back.

Auric coughed quite noisily.

Daisy looked away from the earl. "Are you unwell?"

He gave his head a jerky shake. "Fine," he grit out between clenched lips.

"I daresay a woman of your grace is not deplorable at anything," Lord Astor said in somber tones. All the right words that should rouse a sense of romance in her breast, and yet...She preferred his earlier honest reaction to any feigned response. "Quite the opposite," he said confidently.

"Th—"

"Astor was just taking his leave," Auric snapped, rising suddenly.

The man angled his head. "I was?" The black glower fixed on him by the powerful duke brought him swiftly to his feet. "Er, right, uh yes." He bent low at the waist. "My lady, if I may be so bold as to request the opportunity to call on you in the future?"

She inclined her head and gave him a smile. "Of course," she said, as she stood.

He opened his mouth to say something more, but Auric glared him into silence. With that, Lord Astor spun on his heel and made a hasty retreat.

What was that about? "Why did you run off Lord Astor?" The gentleman he'd brought 'round? Daisy took a step toward Auric and jabbed a finger in his direction before he could speak. "And firstly, why was Lord Astor here? With you?"

A mottled flush stained his rugged cheeks. "Astor is a perfectly agreeable gentleman."

Not that she'd had time to notice in the earl's brief, *very* brief, visit. "So friendly you ran him off?" Her words instantly silenced him. That was an impressive feat considering no one servant, peer, or Prinny himself could silence the powerful, austere Duke of Crawford. "Why was he here?" she repeated, her tone firm, even as she knew the answer.

"Courting you."

Courting her? "Courting me?" she blurted. Then a sharp bark of laughter escaped her. Daisy gave a sad shake of her head. "That was most certainly not a gentleman courting me." Of his own volition, anyway. She widened her eyes. He wouldn't. He had. She groaned and covered her eyes.

"What is it?" Auric bristled.

"You forced him here."

He hesitated. "I hardly forced him."

And she *hardly* believed him. Daisy closed her eyes, not knowing whether to laugh or cry at the idea of the man she loved going to such lengths to arrange a match between her and another gentleman. She opened her eyes. "Agnes, will you see to refreshments?" she asked, not taking her gaze from him.

Agnes hopped up and hurried to the door.

"I do not require refreshments."

The maid froze with one foot over the threshold. She looked expectantly at her mistress.

He'd come into her home and play *matchmaker*? "I believe you do," Daisy bit out. For she'd known him the whole of her life to know he'd not care to have his ears blistered before her maid.

Agnes completed her step.

Auric furrowed his brow in consternation. "I assure you, I do not." He turned to her maid.

By God, if he gave directives to her maid, she'd have him tossed on his pompous, ducal arse before the whole of London Society. "Agnes, refreshments." Auric might be an all-powerful duke who could command a room with his stare alone, but she would not be cowed by him. Nor would her maid.

The relieved young woman all but sprinted from the room.

Silence filled the parlor. Auric broke it. "Did you not care for Lord Astor?" He spoke as though selecting a potential bridegroom in the same way as choosing a chocolate biscuit over a sweet, fig pudding for dessert.

Daisy counted to five for patience. "I don't know, Auric," she said in calm, quiet tones. "Beyond his opinion about me not being horrid and a possible suggestion of my being graceful, he said all of two statements." Excluding his greeting and hasty goodbye.

Auric gave a curt nod of agreement. "I quite agree. He'd make you a deplorable husband."

Despite outrage over his highhandedness, Daisy's lips twitched and the blistering words on her lips died. He'd determined all of that with but a handful of exchanges? Even as a boy he'd possessed the same arrogance. Then, when one was born heir to one of the oldest, most respected dukedoms, such bumptiousness was inevitable.

He took a step toward her, and then another, and another, until only a hairsbreadth separated them. Heat spilled off his muscle-hewn frame and her pulse quickened at his body's nearness. Struggling to rein in the warring annoyance and almost pained amusement thrumming through her, she tipped her head back and held his stare.

A tight curl slipped from her chignon and almost in a reflexive movement, Auric captured the strand between his thumb and forefinger. He studied the dark tress as though he'd never before seen a single lock of hair before this one. "What else do you require in a husband, Daisy?" His voice, a deep, husky whisper washed over her and her brain had to remind her lungs to draw in air and release it once more. "Tell me and I'll find him for you."

She'd already found him. Only he was too blind to see *her*. She wetted her lips and his gaze dipped lower, following that subtle movement. "Confidence," she managed to force the single word out.

His thick lashes swept down.

"I'd want him to be resolute." So that a mere glower from another man, even if that other man happened to be a duke, didn't send him fleeing with wan cheeks. Auric the boy and now Auric the man was fearless and bold in all matters.

He released her strand of hair, as though burned and then took a step away. Then another. "Resolute," he repeated, as though to himself.

"In all matters." Of the heart, in his beliefs, in his hopes and dreams. Just as Auric would be.

With another bow, he turned on his heel and wordlessly took his leave.

Her shoulders sank and she wandered over to the window. She peeled back the curtain and stared down into the street. The front door opened and Auric stepped outside. He paused on the top step and surveyed the street. Then, as though feeling her gaze upon him, he looked up. With a gasp, she released the curtain and let it fall back into place.

"Daisy?"

She spun around, slapping a hand to her breast. "Mother." Whatever was her mother doing from her chambers? She so very rarely took herself from her rooms.

"He's left, Mother," she informed the lady. Or rather, he'd run off. *The coward.*

A wistful expression stole over her face. "I believe he's courting you," she whispered, the faintest hint of joy underscoring those words. Odd, how any and every other Society mama would be fixed upon that link to the Duke of Crawford for his title, and yet her own mother craved that connection for altogether very different reasons. Reasons that were not at all material.

Daisy loathed robbing her sad parent of the one hint of something that brought her a remote bit of happiness. "He's not courting me, Mama," she said gently. She could not, however, allow her to hang upon false hope.

Mother walked over in a flurry of black, bombazine skirts. She came to a stop in front of Daisy. "He visits *you.*"

"He arrived with the Earl of Astor."

"The Earl of Astor?" Lines of concern creased her brow. "Is he friendly with the earl?"

She didn't believe Auric to be friendly with anyone beyond Marcus. As she saw no other way to gently let the other woman down, she said, "He's playing matchmaker, Mama."

"He's matchmaking for you?" Her mother pursed her lips. "Do not be silly. Why would Auric play matchmaker?"

Likely because he felt some form of brotherly obligation to her. *Except, there was nothing brotherly in his kiss.* "Perhaps from some misbe-gotten sense of loyalty to Lionel." Auric's devotion to Lionel through the years in life and in death had been steadfast.

Daisy may as well have thrust a dagger into her mother's chest. Those words, the mere mention of Lionel jerked the other woman erect. "Don't be silly."

She didn't doubt, even with his death, that Auric carried a commit-ment to his best friend's family. "That is all we are," she said, needing the words more for herself. "An obligation, Mama. He must live his life."

Her mother swirled away. "Cease this instant," she cried, clamping her hands over her ears. "This is not about…about…"

"Lionel," Daisy supplied, feeling a needle of guilt as her mother went wan. "And it *is* about Lionel, for there is no other accounting for his frequent visits." Even as she wished there was more, he'd proven with his interest in seeing her wed that there was not more.

There is the kiss…

Agnes entered the room, bearing a tray of refreshments. She looked between mother and daughter and then hurried to set her burden down. Daisy expected her mother to touch her hands to her temples, plead a megrim, and rush out, as she was wont to do. Instead, she claimed a seat on the sofa and proceeded to pour herself a cup of tea. "Sit down, Daisy."

Daisy blinked and then automatically slid into the chair across from her mother. The other woman added sugar and milk and then took a sip. "How long have you loved him?"

She choked. "How long have I—?"

"Loved him. Thirteen years? Fourteen?" Twelve. "I daresay you'd not be so dismissive of Auric if you'd have his heart." She gave her a knowing, motherly look from over the rim of her cup.

Unaccustomed to communicating with her mother in not only this way, but also any way, Daisy glanced down at her lap. "He doesn't know I exist." After so many years with no one to talk to and confide in, there was something sweet and wonderful in hearing her own voice and knowing someone else heard it, too.

Mother snorted. "If that was the case, then he'd not come week after week, even when I'm not receiving callers."

"What of the suitors he's trying to foist me off on?" Pain pressed on her heart. Why would he do that if he truly cared for her in the way she wished him to care?

"Oh, I never claimed he was smart. He is, after all, a gentleman and would no sooner know his own feelings than he'd spot the sun falling from the sky."

A startled bark of laughter bubbled past Daisy's lips and she delighted in a glimpse of her mother's former verve.

Her mother gave her a smile. "Now, my dear, instead of all this wounded hurt at his presenting you with possible suitors, I suggest you do something a good deal better."

Daisy tipped her head.

Her mother took another sip and then lowered the delicate, porcelain piece to her lap. "Why, you make him jealous."

There was a greater likelihood of the sun falling from the sky as her mother had earlier commented than in Auric being jealous over her. Daisy made a sound of impatience and hopped to her feet. "Make him jealous?" A humorless laugh escaped her. "I do love you

Mother, but you do not see…" She let the words trail off. For the same woman who'd ceased to remember her daughter's existence these years, now looked at her through the lens of a proud mama, her judgment skewed.

"See what, Daisy?" her mother called up from her seat. "You've lovely hair."

"It is brown," she complained. Lady Stanhope and Lady Leticia and all their gloriously golden, loose curls slipped into her mind. "And tightly curled." When every other sought after lady had those flowing, loose curls.

"It is unique. Just as your freckles."

Unique, which was really just a polite way of saying deuced odd. Daisy wandered over to the ornate, gold-framed mirror. She studied herself with a critical eye. She was seeing those brown curls and freckles and trying, desperately trying, to see a hint of truth to her mother's prideful words. With a disgusted shake of her head, she shifted her attention to her form. "And I'm plump," she pointed out, not taking her gaze from the not-at-all slender, lithe figure appreciated by gentlemen. Or rather, appreciated by the only gentleman that mattered.

Her mother came to her feet and sailed over. "You are indeed plump."

Daisy's lips pulled up at one corner in a wry smile. "Thank you." She wasn't insulted. She appreciated that honesty.

Her mother rapped her on the knuckles. "Do hush, I was not finished." She gripped Daisy's shoulders and forced her gaze to the plump, freckled woman reflected back at them. "You have a form that any sensible gentleman would admire." The marchioness ignored Daisy's snort. She took her by the hands.

"What are you doing?" Daisy asked, shifting awkwardly on her feet, as her mother turned her about, eyeing her the way Cook might assess a corner hock of beef.

"Shh," her mother urged. Mama released her suddenly and raised a hand to her chin. "Hmm." She tapped the tip of her finger against her lower lip and, but for that meditative glimmer in her eyes, said nothing. For a long while.

Daisy shifted on her feet, in that moment finding she might prefer the lack of notice to this contemplative study. She'd become so accustomed to being invisible where her mother was concerned, that she didn't know what to do with this scrutiny.

Then her mother took a step backward, shaking her head. "Oh, Daisy, how remiss I've been." She eyed Daisy's mauve skirts, shame fairly bleeding from her eyes.

Smoothing her palms over the front of her dress, she looked down and attempted to see what had earned the regretful look from her mother.

"I've failed to see you for too long, my dear."

A swell of emotion balled in Daisy's throat. "It is fine," she managed, wishing her words came out clear and full of conviction.

"No. It is not all right."

Yet, selfishly a part of her had wished to have some guidance on those inane matters that, well, *mattered* to other ladies. A lovely gown. A proper coiffure. Only she'd known in the scheme of what her family had lost, how trivial, how nonsensical those wishes had been.

Then her mother's lips turned up in the first real smile she remembered since Lionel's death. She took Daisy by the hand and wordlessly began pulling her to the door.

"Where are we going?"

Mama shot a glance back over her shoulder, a twinkle in her eyes. "Why, we are going to visit the modiste, my dear. It is time to capture the heart of a duke."

TEN

Auric had not heard a hint or whisper of Daisy in three days. Not since he'd taken his leave of her, which was certainly not for a lack of effort. He'd attempted to visit the lady three times.

He gave his head a shake. The ladies. He'd intended to visit with the *marchioness* and her daughter. Each time they had been indisposed. At first he'd been filled by panic. As long as he'd known Daisy she'd been lively and healthy and possessed of a strong constitution. On the second day, he'd begun to believe he'd inadvertently offended her with the gentleman he'd put before her. After all, Astor was not resolute and…Well, not resolute, and Auric was certain there was a host of other grievances he could level against the other man if he was inclined.

On the third day, he was forced to accept that Lady Daisy Laurel Meadows, who'd dogged his footsteps, not once fawned over his title, and teased him mercilessly, was avoiding him and he missed her. He'd convinced himself these past years that she was nothing more than an obligation, a debt he owed Lionel paid with weekly visits. Yet, some shift had occurred in him, between them, and the need to see her was a physical ache.

He passed a deliberate gaze throughout Lord and Lady Ellis' crowded ballroom, and looked for Daisy. Where in hell was she? He had it on the authority of his butler, who had it on the authority of the Marchioness of Roxbury's butler, that the lady was, in fact, the model of health and planned to attend Lady Ellis' annual ball. These were sorry days indeed when the Duke of Crawford was reduced to putting

129

inquiries to his servants and relying on the discretion and inquiries of another man's servants.

Surely, Daisy recognized he intended to help her make a match. Nay, not just any match, but one with a devoted, caring, and now, resolute gentleman. Auric curled his hands into balls at his sides only now recognizing he couldn't identify a single man present who'd fit the lady's requirements, because not a single gentleman deserved her. And more, it would shred him if he were to choose anyone that was not him…

The air burst from his lungs on a hiss. God help him. He—

"Are you looking for someone in particular, Crawford?" the Viscount Wessex drawled as he came to a stop at his shoulder.

Auric startled at the other man's unexpected appearance. He swallowed a curse and pointedly ignored him.

"Perhaps someone who fits with your strict, unrealistic expectations for a certain lady?" Again, jealousy built in his chest.

"They are not my expectations," he bit out. Rather, they'd been Daisy's. He'd not betray her confidence. Not even to one of their closest friends. "What brings you here, Wessex?" Every last lord and lady in London knew that the viscount studiously avoided polite Society functions. Yet, just this Season he'd taken to attending dinner parties and balls. "Never tell me you're in the market for a wife?" he asked in an attempt to shift attention away from talks of Daisy and all the men Wessex would pair the lady with.

"Don't be ridiculous," the viscount scoffed. Something in the dull flush on his cheeks, however, told a different tale. "Regardless." Yes, it would seem there was more there. His friend neatly turned the conversation to that dangerous, undesirable topic. "Rumors have circulated that Lord Astor paid a visit to Daisy?"

He swung his attention to Wessex. A dark, unpleasant sensation swirled in his chest. "When?" The question burst from him. She'd turned *him* away but was receiving the earl?

A servant stopped before them with a tray of champagne. With a murmur of thanks, the viscount accepted one of the flutes. "I daresay you should remember," he said when the footman continued on.

"You did after all, join the gentleman there." Some of the tension seeped from Auric's frame. "I expect you had something to do with Astor?"

His shoulders sagged in relief. There had been just that visit, then. Not another. Only…He reflected on the flash of appreciation in the man's interested gaze. And his fawning. And nauseating compliments. What a bloody damned fool he'd been all but serving the lady to him upon a silver tray. "I merely coordinated a meeting with," the unoriginal bastard, "the earl and Daisy." Any subsequent visit was a product of Daisy's allure and charm. The lady deserved a good deal more than Astor. A resolute gentleman wouldn't have been run off by a duke's displeasure, or anyone's displeasure. "Astor will not suffice," he said at last, out the corner of his mouth.

Wessex was determined to make a bother of himself. "Ahh, I expected you'd say as much." He inclined his head. "I've composed another list."

How many men did the lackwit truly believe he could drum up that might make Daisy an appropriate match?

"A mere three names this time."

"That is all?" he said, forcing a droll tone when he'd really stake the blasted list and stuff it down his friend's throat.

Wessex continued as though he'd not spoken. "The Earl of Warwick."

"Too fond of the faro tables."

"Baron Wright," he returned.

"A mother's boy." Daisy deserved far more than a gentleman who was devoted, caring, and resolute to his mother and not one person more.

"The Viscount Reddingbrooke."

Auric frowned. Reddingbrooke was…And then there was…His frown deepened. "He's too old," he said at last. Why, the man must be…?

Wessex laughed, attracting unwanted notice. "He's a year younger than your miserable self, Crawford, which I suppose explains your need for the quizzing glass." His laughter redoubled.

131

The delicate piece he carried at the front of his jacket pocket, a gift given him by Daisy, lent a silent mockery to Wessex's words. "Shove off," he bit out. "I…"

Wessex's merriment faded, and he looked to the doorway, unblinking. "Here." He thrust his crystal flute in Auric's hands.

"What?" Perplexed, Auric glanced between the glass and his friend.

"Take a drink," Marcus advised.

A flurry of activity at the entrance of the ballroom captured Auric's notice. The hum of noisy whispers flooded the room, as ladies and gentlemen strained their attention to the front of the hall.

Auric didn't give a jot about Society gossips and their latest *on-dit*. There was the matter of Daisy to attend. When she set aside her not at all Daisy-like temper and admitted him once more.

Wessex made a strangled sound in his throat.

Auric eyed him, concerned, and made to slap him on the back. "What—?" Then, he followed the other man's shocked stare to the front of the receiving line. The air left Auric on a swift exhale. There was something familiar in the heart-shaped planes of her face, and yet somehow altogether different. By the splash of color on her freckled cheeks and tightly coiled, dark brown curls, he recognized Daisy's visage with the same certainty of recognizing his own. And yet the voluptuous woman in ice blue satin, with the fabric clinging to generous hips and bountiful breasts, was a siren.

Wessex let out a soft whistle. "By God, the duck becomes a swan."

No, the lady was no swan. His mouth went dry as a wave of longing so deep and powerful threatened to consume him there before all of Society. She carried herself with the same comfort and ease, a smile on her plump lips, a sparkle of excitement in her eyes. His Daisy. His girl of the flowers. Their host and hostess, Lord and Lady Ellis, said something to her. She nodded and then, with her mother at her side, moved to take their spot at the side of the ballroom.

Then, her fool mother stepped away to converse with Lord and Lady Ingold. What manner of parent would leave her unattended so any worthless, shiftless bounder could—?

A rush of gentlemen converged upon her. "Bloody hell," he bit out. Something primal stirred to life inside him. A seething fury that boiled hot and threatened to burn him with his own rage at the sight of the unworthy bastards scribbling their names onto that delicate card upon her wrist.

"Indeed," Wessex muttered.

"Bloody hell," he cursed once more, ignoring Wessex's startled look.

The viscount jerked his chin in her direction. "This will pose a problem in singling out the best match for the lady." Despite the flippant deliverance of those words, the hard set to his mouth indicated Wessex's concern with the transformation of Lady Daisy Meadows.

Auric downed the viscount's champagne. Indeed it did. He took in this new figure being ogled by any manner of lascivious, undeserving rogues. With another curse, he set the glass down hard on a nearby tray then started after Daisy. He'd be damned if he would sit by while those *gentlemen* removed her silken gown with their rakish eyes.

"Where are you off to, man?" Wessex called behind him.

Auric ignored him, moving with a single-minded intent, narrowing his gaze as the Marquess of Rutland, a notorious reprobate and black-hearted scoundrel, whispered something close to the lady's ear that raised a blush on her cheeks. He quickened his step and cut a path through the collection of dandies and fops fawning over Daisy. With a black, long-ago practiced, ducal stare, he sent a number of the men scurrying off in fear of earning his ducal disapproval. "Rutland," he bit out.

Daisy started, the color rising in her cheeks. Annoyance stirred. Surely, the lady was wise enough to not fall prey for a predator such as Rutland.

The marquess stiffened and, straightening his shoulders, partially turned. "Crawford," he said on an almost lethal whisper.

Auric's desire to have Rutland away from Daisy had nothing to do with the title of marquess that would forever remind him of Lionel and everything to do with the lascivious leer in the man's eyes as he ogled her breasts.

Daisy frowned and looked between them, a question in a gaze too innocent for the likes of Rutland.

"Lady Daisy," Auric sketched a quick bow and then reached for her dance card and froze. He took in the filled program and then his head shot up. By God, how quickly had the vultures swooped in and claimed all but…he looked down at the card once more. A quadrille.

"A bit late," Rutland said mockingly. The orchestra thrummed the beginning strands of a waltz. He held a hand out to Daisy.

Fury tightened Auric's belly. By God, he'd sooner deliver Rutland to the devil than allow him to put his filthy hands upon her person. With fury coursing through his being, Auric stepped between them. "I am claiming this set."

"Are you?" Rutland drew those two syllables out in a mocking fashion. He held a hand out to Daisy once more. "I believe you aren't, Crawford."

Daisy stared bewildered between the gentlemen. The mottled flush on Auric's cheeks, the muscle ticking at the corner of his right eye, uncharacteristic for one so composed, so austere, and so perfectly ducal. And yet, the icy fury emanating from his frame hinted at a man about to come to blows with the marquess. She cleared her throat. "My lord," she said, calling the marquess' attention. "I had forgotten my promise to reserve this set for the duke," she lied. A chill raced along her spine, at the dark glint in the man's eyes.

Auric took a step closer and extended his elbow. She placed her fingertips upon his coat sleeve and allowed him to guide her onto the dance floor where the dancers were assembling for the next set. Daisy raised her hand to his shoulder and a thrill shot through her as he settled his large, warm palm at her waist.

The haunting, slightly discordant hum of a waltz filled the ballroom Auric and Daisy moved in a strained, tense silence. They, who through the years had never been without words or jests or even insults, now had no words. When her mother had proposed assembling a new wardrobe, Daisy had recognized the futility of the woman's goals. Even as the ice blue satin creation was by far the grandest, most luxuriant, if daring, piece she'd ever donned. Yet, she'd not roused anything more than a dark glower from Auric.

He'd say nothing to her?

"I don't want you near Rutland."

She looked at him through the thin slits of her eyes. *That* is what he'd say? "I beg your pardon?" He'd order her about as though he were nothing more than a protective brother. Jagged pain ripped through her at the remembrance of Lionel.

Auric angled her closer, dipping his head lower. "This is not a game, Daisy." Her breath caught at the nearness of his lips, remembering his mouth upon hers and shamefully longing for the heady passion she'd known in that all too brief embrace. "Rutland is a dark, vile reprobate." His mouth hardened. "And he is assuredly not the devoted, caring, and resolute gentleman you spoke of."

She jerked. Did he dare throw her longings back in her face? Daisy spoke in hushed tones. "You've spent so many years being the Duke of Crawford, ordering others about and coming to expect blind subservience, that you've forgotten how to speak to a friend," she chided. His frown deepened. "You took it upon yourself, Your Grace, to decide I required a husband and even were so bold as to drum up a suitor." With each word, the implications of his actions these past days filled her with a hot rage. She continued, speaking through gritted teeth. "You would find me a husband. For what end, Auric?"

He opened his mouth to speak, but she spoke over him. "To absolve yourself of a guilt for Lionel's death."

He went white and a momentary wave of remorse slapped her for throwing that charge at him in this public manner. If only, perhaps, had he truly seen her and heard her through the years, he'd have heard her need for more from him. "I would see you happy, Daisy."

"Why?" she demanded.

Auric hesitated. *Tell me it is because you care for me in the way a man cares for a woman. Tell me because you've at last looked within your heart and realized it's complete because of me.* "You are my friend," he spoke in flat, empty tones somehow more painful than any of that icy ducal annoyance she'd come to expect of him.

I don't want to be your friend. That was no longer enough. "You always saw me as a sister, didn't you?" she whispered the question more to herself.

An almost wistful smile hovered on his lips. "You always dogged our footsteps, didn't you?" he said in a reflective manner of the past, not hearing the pained words truly spoken to him. "At one point I found you underfoot, and that changed. Do you know when that was?"

A bond of their past tugged at her, where even in this moment, that was enough. The link to the times they'd once shared. "When I put ink in your tea?"

His grin widened. It was the real, uncomplicated smile of a man who did, in fact, remember that simple expression of mirth. "Ink intended for Lionel."

She giggled at the remembrance of the young marquess and his ink-stained teeth. "Yes, yes it was. I was quite put out from being excluded from your fishing excursion." And with this memory there was no agony at the loss of her brother, but rather the joy to be found in those too short memories of him.

"It was not the tea incident."

Daisy winked up at him. "There really are surely too many incidents to recall, aren't there? Was it when I snipped up the fabric of your and Lionel's jackets to be turned into garments for my doll?"

"She did look rather splendid in her midnight black gown, but no, that was not it."

She discreetly pinched his arm. "Do stop being deliberately va—?"

"Your parents' annual summer picnic. You stared down your bullies and set the table ablaze with great strength."

Her heart started funnily in her breast. Then she drew in a breath in an attempt to calm the fluttering in her belly. "Of course you recall that day," she muttered. "Who wouldn't remember a table fire?" And yet, this was now the second time he'd recalled the memory. So perhaps it meant more to him, as well?

His lopsided grin fit with the gentleman who'd glowered at the Lady Leticia bullies of the world. "Yes, it is rather hard to forget the shouts and screams of some of Society's leading peers as the fire licked at the tablecloth. Except that isn't what I remember of that day, Daisy." He stared at a point over her head. "You were the only one not shouting," he said softly to himself. "You had this faraway expression."

Because, it was the moment she'd fallen in love with him, and even though it should surely bring her some hurt that all the years she'd joined him and Lionel, Auric had, in fact, found her a bothersome bit of baggage…until that much later day when she'd hovered on the cusp of girlhood and womanhood.

The set drew to a close. They glided to a gentle stop. As the couples about them politely clapped and then shuffled from the dance floor, they stood locked in a silent, intense scrutiny of one another. Daisy dropped a curtsy and allowed him to lead her back to the edge of the ballroom. It did not escape her notice that instead of returning her to the earlier spot she'd occupied, he sought out her mother.

"Where is your mother?" he searched the crowd. It was no secret to anyone, with the exception of Auric it seemed, that her mother hovered on the fringe of activity, wan and hopelessly withdrawn. Daisy gave a little shrug. "Ah, I see her," he noted.

She pursed her lips. He was likely eager to be free of her. Daisy said nothing, instead allowed him to escort her to the white, Doric column where her mother stood.

The marchioness' usually lifeless eyes lit. "My dear boy, how lovely it is to see you." She gave them such a pointedly knowing look that Daisy shifted on her feet praying that subtle movement would some-how cause a shift in the floor and in turn swallow her whole.

"The pleasure is mine, Lady Roxbury," he responded, flawless, proper, and always respectful.

"I gather you've quite enjoyed your visits with Daisy?"

She swallowed a groan, her skin prickling with the ghost of a smile on Auric's lips. The great lout was having a good deal of fun at her expense. "Undoubtedly," Daisy muttered. "Or, you can surely say, indeed," she supplied for him. His smile widened and her heart raced all the faster.

Lord Astor chose that precise moment to stride over, coming to a stop before them. The easy camaraderie between her and Auric was gone as he turned once more into the remote, polished duke. The two men eyed each other a long moment, their gazes doing a form of inventory of the other. "Crawford," the earl said hastily, breaking the silence. They exchanged stiff, polite pleasantries and then Astor turned his attention to Daisy's mother. "Good evening, my lady."

A small moue of displeasure formed on the older woman's lips. "Lord Astor, a pleasure." Though by the obvious disappointment underscoring her tone, those words sounded anything but. "I trust your mother is well?"

"Indeed well," he said quickly. He held out his elbow for Daisy.

She stared at his arm for a long moment. The strains of the quadrille filled her mind as she tried to sort out why he had his arm extended. "Our dance," she blurted. Her skin warmed. "Er, uh, yes, very well," she said, hastily placing her fingers upon his sleeve.

As the earl guided her onto the dance floor, her neck prickled with the heated intensity of Auric's stare. Odd, until this moment she'd not given much thought to needing that heart pendant worn by the Lady Stanhope.

Another visit to Gipsy Hill would be in order, and most especially after Auric's admissions this night.

ELEVEN

T he tick tock of the long-case clock filled the quiet, punctuated by the rapidity of Auric's hand as he frantically wrote on the empty page of his journal.

Dear Lionel,
I have seen your sister as an obligation and nothing more than a sister
for the whole of my life. My debt to you is great and for having been the
reason you lost your life. I promise to see her wedded.

Those cathartic words continued to fill the pages and he found a sense of freedom in giving this, his apology for having long neglected Daisy, and more, for having desired her as he did.

Auric finished his entry and then set down his pen. He blew upon the page, drying the ink, and then a moment later, closed the book with a firm *thud*. With a sigh, he sat back in his seat. Since he'd taken his leave of Daisy, he'd been unable to rid himself of thoughts of her, as she'd been, and all those bastards who'd eyed her, seeing the woman transformed. He should feel an overwhelming sense of relief in knowing it wouldn't be long for some gentleman to be brought up to scratch. He scrubbed his hand over his face.

They had not, however, appreciated her as she'd always been. They'd not seen her smile and bold spirit or infuriating cheekiness—not in the way he had. *Except, have you truly seen her? Or* had he relegated her to Lady Daisy Laurel Meadows, his unaging girl of the flowers? In that, he was really no different than all those other foolish fops who'd failed to see the complexly unique soul that made up Daisy. With a growl, he shoved back such nonsensical musings not liking that he'd fallen into a category with every last lord. "Do not be ridiculous," he muttered under his breath. Furthermore, he wasn't altogether certain why it should matter that the lords in the market for a wife had finally taken note, only that they had.

Auric drummed his fingertips along his journal. It would be more important than ever to pay careful attention to those men courting her and, most importantly, the men she considered as prospective bridegrooms. This responsibility to see Daisy happy and cared for was a debt owed to Lionel. It had nothing, absolutely nothing to do with Daisy Meadows, herself.

Surely it didn't.

He glanced across the room, his gaze alighting on the case clock. He'd not paid the Marchioness of Roxbury a visit in several days now. How could he have been so remiss? Auric tucked his journal into his top drawer and shoved it closed. Yes, a visit to the lady, and her daughter, just by nature of her position in the household, was certainty in order. Coming to his feet, he started for the door and made his way out of his office.

Why did it feel as though he lied to himself?

A short while later, Auric stood at the front of the Marchioness of Roxbury's townhouse. He rapped once and waited. And continued to wait. With a frown, he peered out at the busy street. His presence had ceased to attract notice some years ago. Society had long known the close familial connection between his late parents and the Marchioness of Roxbury and her now departed husband. He impatiently beat his hand against his thigh. Yet in all his years knowing the butler, he'd never known him to keep a visitor waiting.

Auric raised his hand to knock, just as a slightly winded Frederick pulled the door open. "Frederick, how—?" The congenial greeting died on his lips at the beleaguered white-haired servant and *Baron Winterhaven*, in all his cool arrogance. The other man started.

The baron remembered himself first. "Crawford," he greeted, sketching a bow.

He must appear the lackwit with his mouth agape. Auric snapped his lips shut. "Winterhaven," he returned the greeting.

"Good day." The other man settled his hat upon his head and then slipped by Auric.

He stared after the man a moment, and then stepped inside the familiar doors. Winterhaven? Had he truly put the man's name down as a suitable suitor for Daisy? Surely not. The man was too damned aloof and laconic for the garrulous Daisy. He looked to the old servant. "What is the meaning of that?" he asked, shrugging out of his cloak.

The other man's lips twitched. "I daresay I do not know what you refer to you, Your Grace," he remarked, accepting the cloak and passing it off to a waiting footman.

Auric remembered himself and fell silently into step beside the faithful servant, walking the familiar corridors to the Blue Parlor. As the Duke of Crawford, he held himself to certain standards and expectations. It was one thing putting inquiries to the servant about Daisy's well-being. It was quite another to boldly inquire as to the unexpected appearance of a bounder who had no business with the two ladies here. He scoffed. Had he truly considered Winterhaven bookish and boring? No, the man was likely a rogue, wholly undeserving of Daisy. Auric furrowed his brow. Surely he recalled *some* mention of Winterhaven in the gossip columns. Not that Auric put much stock in the gossip sheets—

They stopped outside the parlor. A husky laugh spilled from the open door and into the hall, the sound of Daisy's unrestrained mirth so vibrant it momentarily froze him to the floor. Desire coursed through him. How had he failed to note the captivating quality of her laugh? He registered Frederick's curious stare. What manner of madness had she weaved upon him these past days? He gave a tug of his lapels.

Auric stepped into the room and found Daisy with his gaze seated on the robin's egg blue sofa—with a gentleman entirely too close. He narrowed his eyes. Daisy and the Earl of Danport sat engrossed in conversation. By God, he'd known he'd been correct to silently ink the man's name from that blasted list. With his knee pressed against her skirts, Danport ogled Daisy's generous bosom as though she were a ripe berry he'd like to pluck. A primitive growl rumbled in Auric's chest and the couple looked as one to where he stood framed in the doorway. Did he imagine the guilty flush on Daisy's cheeks?

"His Grace, the Duke of Crawford," Frederick belatedly announced and then wisely took his leave.

A pall of silence fell over the room. Annoyance burned in his chest. Where was Daisy's earlier laughter or unfettered smile? Instead, she studied him with a pensive expression.

Auric shifted his gaze and it landed on a bouquet of daisies in a crystal vase. He narrowed his eyes.

Sensing his focus, Daisy cleared her throat. "Aren't they lovely? The earl," she motioned to Danport, "brought them." The other man had brought her flowers. He swung his attention back to the earl who slowly came to his feet, and in Auric's estimation dropped an insolent bow. "Crawford," the too charming by half gentleman drawled.

Urbane, possessed of all the right words, and a carefree attitude, the earl was everything that Auric had never been. Nor had he minded it. "Danport," he said stiffly. Until now. Then turning his attention to Daisy, he instantly dismissed the other man.

She fiddled with her pale pink skirts, fisting the fabric in a way he'd come to recognize as nervousness. He narrowed his eyes. Nervous? Around him? Annoyance rolled through him and he strode over, stopping before her. The silence stretched on and he gave her an expectant look.

"A seat," she blurted. He quirked an eyebrow. "That is, would you care to sit?" Her cheeks pinked.

"Indeed," he replied in the indolent, ducal tone he'd practiced as a child.

Her full lips formed a small moue of displeasure and he'd wager all his landholdings that if Danport wasn't present, she'd have given him quite the dressing down for his high-handedness. As it was, she reclaimed her seat.

He and Danport followed suit. Auric rapped his fingertips on the arm of the narrow shell chair he occupied.

Daisy cleared her throat. "Would you care for—?"

"No."

"But I didn't even finish my—"

"You intended to ask whether I required refreshments?"

Danport looked back and forth between them with a deepening frown. He slowly came to his feet. Daisy shifted her attention to the tall, too charming gentleman. "If you'll excuse me," he offered, pointedly giving Auric his shoulder. "I have matters to see to." The coward would run. Yes, Daisy deserved far more than this one. "I shall leave you and His Grace to your visit."

Daisy hopped to her feet, with Auric reluctantly following suit. "Thank you for the daisies," she said softly and God, if Auric didn't want to kiss her into silence and be gone with Danport so he might have her to himself.

She gave him a pointed look. Auric remembered the years of politeness ingrained into him by too many tutors and sketched a bow. "Danport, a pleasure as usual," he lied.

"Crawford." The other man's narrowed eyes indicated he detected that untruth, but with a curt bow, took his leave.

After the earl had gone, Auric glared at the crystal vase. "Daisies?" He knew he was being boorish and rude and surly. But daisies?

Daisy spun to face him. "Yes. What is wrong with that?"

He clenched his teeth to keep from listing all number of things wrong with the earl's gift. The unoriginal bastard had given her daisies. "Furthermore—"

"You didn't provide a reason, Auric."

"Didn't I?" He shifted as some of the jealous fury left him, leaving in its wake a healthy dose of embarrassment.

"No. You didn't." Daisy propped her hands on her hips. "What was that about?" she charged.

He blinked several times. "What was what about?" Though he knew very well the precise *that* she referred to.

They'd always possessed an uncanny ability to know what the other was thinking. "Oh, you know precisely what that I refer to." Deuced bothersome, it was.

In several steps, he closed the distance between them. He lowered his head close to hers, detecting the slight audible intake of her breath. "What if I say it is because I despise Danport?" he whispered.

She tipped her head back to meet his eyes; emotion filled the piercing brown irises. "Why?" she demanded.

He gave her the only answer he had—the truth. "I do not know," he said quietly. Auric cupped her cheek in his hand. "All I know is the sight of Danport near you, beside you, or with you in anyway, eats at me like a poison." These were not the sentiments of a man who saw in her a mere sister.

She widened her eyes until they formed round moons in her face. "He doesn't deserve you, Daisy."

She trailed her tongue over her lips, wetting them. "And who does?" she asked, unabashedly bold in her questioning.

Her words drew him up short. Certainly not *him*. He dropped his hand to his side. With something akin to horror Auric took a quick step backward and another. His mind raced out of control like a speeding phaeton. His legs knocked into the rose-inlaid, mahogany table, rattling the tea service from her previous guest's visit.

"What is it?" she asked, extending a palm toward him.

Auric stood stock still as with dawning horror, he confronted the truth of his emotions. *He* wanted her.

During one of her parents' annual summer parties, Daisy, had come upon Auric, alone at the edge of her father's lake. The victim of a plate of rancid kippers, his face had been gray, a sheen of perspiration had dotted his brow. In this moment, he bore a strong likeness to that young man of long ago.

"Are you all right?" she asked tentatively.

He gave a jerky nod but remained silent.

Daisy took a few steps closer, expecting him to retreat as he had moments ago, but his gaze remained locked on a point beyond her shoulder. For the span of a heartbeat, when he'd cupped her cheek and studied her through his thick, chestnut lashes, she'd dared to believe he was here because he'd looked inside his own heart and found his love for her.

Pain knifed through her. She'd never have his love. "Have you had a plate of kippers?" But she'd always have his friendship. Had she ever truly believed that would be enough? She wanted all of him, in every way and any way a woman could truly possess a man.

"Have I…?" His words trailed off, and then a slow, half-grin turned his lips upward. Ah God, how she wanted more of him. "No, I've not had kippers in ten years."

Nine years. It would be ten this summer. To point out the specifics of the date however would only humble her before him, as the pathetic creature who'd longed for him on the sidelines of life since she'd been just a girl. "Why are you here, Auric?" she asked with a boldness borne of their lifelong connection.

A muscle leapt at the corner of his eye, but still he said nothing.

"You come here day in and day out—"

"Hardly day in and day out," he said curtly. Yes, he was indeed correct.

"Very well, then, you come here every week." Every Wednesday to be precise, as had been the case for nearly seven years now. But for the days in which he'd courted Lady Anne, he'd become a fixture in this household. She'd tired of it. "Agnes," she called to the maid at the back corner of the parlor.

The young woman knew Daisy so well that she sprang to her feet then dashed out of the room, partially closing the door behind her. Not even the servants feared the two of them being alone. The obvious truth only fueled her rapidly increasing annoyance.

"You shouldn't send away your maid."

She widened her eyes. He'd chide her? "I hardly believe my reputation is at risk around you," she said. His eyes darkened. "You speak of finding me a suitor." His lips compressed into a hard line. "You bring Astor and then hurry him out." She motioned to the door. "You run off Lord Danport—"

"He is a rogue."

Daisy pointed her eyes to the ceiling. "He is not a rogue." Quite respected by the lords and ladies, Lord Danport had hardly earned the black reputations as some of the more scandalous, outrageous rakes and scoundrels. For reasons likely connected to a familial obligation, Auric had taken it upon himself to find her suitors and judge their worthiness. All these years she'd spent loving him, and he'd devote his energies to finding her a husband. Her patience snapped. She jabbed her finger in his chest. "I do not need *you* to find me a husband." Not when she'd already found one, but the stubborn lout was too blind to see her—truly see her.

He eyed her hand as though she'd jabbed him in the heart with a dull blade.

She stuck her finger into his chest once again. "I do not need," *another brother.* "Your interference," she substituted.

With an effortless grace, he captured her hand in his broad, strong hand. "Is that what I am?" he asked. "An interference?" He drew her wrist close to his mouth, and her breath caught, as for one infinitesimal beat of a heart, she believed he intended to put his lips to the sensitive skin there.

Daisy struggled to call forth words, wishing she had some flippant response that would give little indication to how desperately she longed for more of him and from him.

He ran his gaze over her face and then he fixed his unreadable stare upon her lips. In the flecks of emotion sparking in his blue eyes, she detected the same hint of desire from the moment he'd first kissed her. She tipped her head back, closing the distance between their lips, wanting his kiss, needing him in every way. Auric dipped his head lower.

Footsteps sounded in the hall and he rushed to place the sofa between them.

Frederick reappeared with another caller. "The Earl of Astor," he announced.

Her heart dropped somewhere to the vicinity of her toes as disappointment filled her. She dropped a curtsy, aware of the young earl's suspicious stare alternating between her and Auric. "My lady," he greeted. "Crawford," he said, the grudging words emerged as more of an afterthought.

"My lord," she murmured.

Auric remained coolly silent, peering down the length of his aquiline nose at the earl—the gentleman he'd first brought by four days prior.

Lord Astor shifted, as though unnerved by the commanding duke. He did a quick survey of the room, clearly noting the absent maid.

Daisy's skin heated as the suspicion in his gaze grew. She gave silent thanks as Agnes rushed into the room bearing a tray of tea. Or rather, *another* tray of tea.

"As you requested, my lady," Agnes assured, setting her burden down on the table between Daisy and Auric. She stole a peek upward and gave a conspiratorial wink.

Auric sketched a stiff, polite bow. "I shall leave you two to your visit," he said, his voice flat of emotion.

A protest sprang to her lips, but she swallowed it down and followed his movements as he strode from the room. Reluctantly, Daisy returned her attention to the gentleman who, by his visits, gave every indication that he'd have her for his wife. She waited for her heart to race, or for a thrill of excitement at the prospect of it.

Yet, as she slid into the seat across from the handsome, young earl, she acknowledged just how much she longed for another man, who but for that one unexpected kiss would never see her as anything more than the girl he once knew. With a forced smile, Daisy shoved aside thoughts of Auric and entertained her suitor.

TWELVE

The following morning, seated in his breakfast room, Auric's plate of cold ham and biscuits sat before him untouched. He scanned the pages of *The Times,* and he, a man who'd never before relied on gossips, read the scandal sheets. This is what he'd been reduced to. Rather, this is what she'd reduced him to. He passed the other *on-dits* about lords and ladies who meant nothing to him, instead focusing on one particularly lady.

> *The Lady DM has quite taken the* ton *by storm...being courted by the Earl of D.*

With a curse he threw aside the page and reached for his black coffee. He blew upon the steaming hot mug and then took a tentative sip, grimacing at the bitterness of the brew, his mind in tumult over his meeting with Daisy. For some time, he'd relegated Daisy to the role of unaging child, seeing her as nothing more than the same girl he and Lionel had teased and defended with equal intensity. No more. The girl had been replaced by a tempting siren. Still, for the absence of golden ringlets and blue eyes, Daisy Laurel Meadows, his girl of the flowers, was captivating, and now every damned dandy knew as much, too.

Auric ran through all the *gentlemen* who'd looked upon Daisy. Astor and Danport, even Rutland at that blasted ball two nights ago. Every one of those men had lust in their eyes. Auric tightened his grip reflexively upon his cup, nearly shattering the porcelain.

Footsteps sounded in the hall and he glanced up as his butler presented Wessex. The other man's face was set in a serious mask. "Crawford," he greeted, his gaze taking in the scandal sheets littered about the table. When he returned his attention to Auric, there was shrewdness in his far too perceptive eyes.

A dull flush climbed up Auric's neck. He motioned the other man over.

Wessex bypassed the sideboard. "I see you've taken to reading the gossip columns," he said with more than a hint of knowing as he slid into the chair on Auric's right.

"Go to hell," he gritted out, taking another sip of his coffee.

A footman rushed over with a steaming cup for the young viscount who accepted it with a word of thanks, before returning his focus to Auric. "She must wed," he said without preamble.

The muscles of Auric's chest tightened painfully. "I know that." Only, now he thought of the woman Daisy with some undeserving cad like Rutland, and the man learning each lush contour of her body, something dark and primal roared to life inside his breast until he wanted to toss his head back and howl like a primitive beast. Nor was there anything remotely brother-like in this desire to crush all those unworthy men who dared to look upon her.

When it became apparent he didn't intend to speak, Wessex set his cup down and leaned forward in his seat. "We, together, have come up with twenty," seventeen, "names of prospective suitors."

"None of the gentlemen would make her an adequate match," he said, annoyance making his tone sharp. "I've no names," he said when the viscount continued to look upon him in a recriminating silence.

"We owe it to Lionel to see her wed." Wessex was tireless. He propped his elbows upon the table. "If it had been one of us…" He swallowed loudly. "If it had been one of us," he repeated, "who'd left behind a younger sister to care for, he undoubtedly would have seen at least one decent gentleman was brought up to scratch." With each of the words tumbling from Wessex's lips, his guilt doubled.

For Lionel had been that sort of devoted, loyal person. Always more adult than child, he'd had a unique ability to laugh while studying the world through a lens belonging to a much older, mature soul.

Auric set his coffee down hard and surged to his feet. "He would not however have seen Daisy wed to just anyone." And certainly he'd not have approved of the roguish Danport or the Earl of Astor.

Wessex sank back in his seat. The lines of his face settled into an angry mask. "I'd hardly say I've tried to wed her to merely anyone. What fault do you find with Astor?"

Astor, who'd caressed her waist and guided her about the steps of the waltz. "There is everything wrong with him." The protestation exploded from him. He began to pace. "He...and..." With a black curse, he increased his frantic back and forth movement. Bloody hell he detested when he was in the wrong, and yet...Auric came to an abrupt stop. "He stomped all over her feet two nights ago." Even as the flimsy excuse slipped from his lips, he recognized how pathetic that sounded.

The ghost of a smile hovered on Wessex's lips and then quickly faded.

Balling his hands into tight fists, Auric reclaimed his seat feeling exposed before the other man in ways he did not understand, nor cared to explore just then. Mayhap ever. He reached for his now tepid coffee and took a sip of the horrid stuff. All the while his skin pricked under the viscount's scrutiny.

Wessex cleared his throat. He set down his glass and then fished around the front of his jacket. "I have one final name," the viscount murmured. "There is but one gentleman we've not considered; a man who is worthy of her." He placed his list on the table.

Auric downed the remaining contents of his coffee. He placed the cup upon the table and cast an annoyed glance over another one of his friend's masterful lists. He didn't want to see another damned name of a potential husband for Daisy. In fact, he wanted to set it to the lit candelabras upon the table. Which only served to remind him of eleven-year-old Daisy and the laughter he'd known with her, before he'd gone and stolen all traces of true happiness from her. He swiped the folded sheet off the table and unfolded it.

The Duke of Crawford.

He stared unblinking down at the lone name marked upon the page. His fingers shook ever so slightly and he jerked his head upright. "What is the meaning of this?" he demanded, his tone harsh. Auric waved the page. "Is this some manner of jest? For if it is, I assure you, it is not in the least funny." His pulse pounded so loudly in his ears, the steady staccato rhythm threatened to drown out Wessex's response.

The viscount shook his head and when he spoke, did so in solemn tones. "This is no game." Wessex leaned back in his seat and rested his arms upon the sides of his armchair. "Two evenings ago, after I'd taken my leave of Lady Ellis' ball, I reflected on Daisy's magnificent transformation. I spent the better part of that night contemplating who might be worthy of Lionel's sister. Who would he have trusted with her happiness?" *Don't.* "Who would he have trusted with her heart?"

"No," he rasped.

"Who would care for her in a way that she'd never want for anything and be protected and cherished?" Wessex held his gaze. "It is you," he said softly. "You are meant to wed her. It is why you cannot accept a name. It is why—"

"Stop," he barked. The sharp command bounced off the walls and that explosion of emotion only further exposed him to his friend's potent deduction. "You do not know what you say. This is *Daisy.*" Lionel's sister. The girl he'd seen as a sister. Nay, the woman he'd once seen as a sister. Except, from the moment he'd taken her in his arms and explored the lush contours of her plump lips, everything he'd once believed had ceased to be, throwing him into a world he no longer understood.

"Marry her."

Did those words belong to him? Or were they Wessex's in his relentlessness?

Auric looked down at the sheet and then raised his eye, uncomprehendingly. "You're mad."

A chuckle rumbled up from the other man's throat. "Yes, there is truth to that." He tipped his chin toward the note clenched in Auric's grip. "There is, however, also truth to my words."

He stared blankly down at his friend's familiar scrawl. The name carefully etched upon the page. His own. "I can't." His voice came as though down a long corridor. His palms dampened, the room spun as it always did when remorse licked at him.

"You can." Wessex leaned forward and the wooden chair creaked in protest. "And you should." He held Auric's gaze. "The lady loves you."

Auric's mouth went dry. "Don't be a fool. She—"

"Loves you," he repeated.

And God help him for being the worst sort of bastard. He wanted to seize upon Wessex's suggestion and make Daisy his, for reasons that had nothing to do with honor and loyalty and everything to do with a newfound desire for the spirited vixen. "I…" *want her. Even as I have no right to her. Anything between Daisy and me, the man responsible for her brother's murder, was the kind of tragic tale captured by The Bard himself.* Auric studied the list handed him moments ago. "Even if I desired more from the lady, which I do not," he said when his friend arched an eyebrow. "There is…" Lionel. There would always be Lionel between them. There was a bond sealed by their loss.

"It was not your fault."

The same bond that prevented any possible union between them. For despite Wessex's insistence, the truth was, Auric had been to blame.

"Did you hear me?" Wessex persisted with the same temerity shown by a matchmaking mama.

Lionel's' death may as well have been upon Auric's hands as though he himself had gutted him in the belly that night. "I heard you," he said, his tone deliberately wooden. That one transformative moment of his life had shaped the whole course he'd chart from then on. It also served as the reason he could not do as his friend suggested and take Daisy as his wife. She could never forgive his role in Lionel's death, nor did he deserve her forgiveness.

*Even though I want her...*He thrust aside the thought. She was still Daisy, the girl he'd taught to bait her fishing rod. Only now, she possessed luscious lips and a generously curved figure that had haunted his waking and sleeping moments for days.

"Marry her," Wessex urged once more.

He couldn't. Auric pressed his fingers against his temples and jammed them into the sensitive flesh, in a desperate bid to thrust aside this slow, dawning realization. *I want her.* And this was not the sentiment of a man who merely hungered for her body. He wanted all of Daisy—her smile and her sauciness and her spirit.

With a slow, knowing grin, Wessex confirmed, "At last you realize it."

"I can't." Even as he wished to know her in every way. There would always be Lionel between them.

Whatever his friend intended to say was interrupted by the appearance of Auric's butler. The servant carried a silver tray bearing a missive. Auric took it, recognizing a certain butler's scrawl. He frowned and ignored Wessex's curious stare, instead directing his attention to the note. Even as he unfolded the ivory vellum, he knew what those damn words would say.

The lady has returned to Gipsy Hill.
Your Faithful servant

With a curse, he crumpled the ivory velum in his hands and jumped to his feet. His heart climbed into his throat, threatening to choke him with his own fear. *The fool. The bloody fool.* He started for the door.

"What is it?" Wessex called out.

"I've a matter of importance to see to," he returned, not breaking his stride to deliver those words. He shouted for his horse.

By God, the lady was vexing and infuriating and with each reckless action placed herself in danger. As he moved with long, purposeful strides through the corridors, his heart climbed into his throat and threatened to choke him. Daisy required a husband and for all the reasons a union between them was wrong, he could name the singular, most important reason it was right. It was not the truth that he wanted her—which he did.

She required protection. *His* protection. His pulse loud in his ears, he all but sprinted into the foyer, nearly colliding with his butler. "My hor—?"

"The horse has been readied, Your Grace."

A footman rushed forward with his hat and cloak. Auric shrugged into it and then slammed his hat atop his head. He bounded down the handful of steps and, ignoring the stares teeming with curiosity turned on him by passing lords and ladies, he raced to collect Valiant's reins.

He climbed astride and then quickly nudged the horse into motion. With a single-minded purpose, he guided Valiant down the fashionable end of the Mayfair District to the less popular, seedier parts of London. A mind-numbing panic clutched at his throat. Even with the loss of Lionel, Daisy had retained her innocence. She didn't understand the depths of man's depravity and vileness. Yet, she'd take herself to the outskirts of London, jeopardizing her safety.

Auric tightened his grip on the reins. If anything were to happen to her, he'd not forgive himself. This wrong would be the manner of which would destroy him. He pressed his eyes closed as the familiar terror crept in. She, just as so many of the fashionable lords and ladies of London, craved the romantic excitement to be found outside the glittering world of the *ton*. Auric knew because there had been a time when he'd exulted in the freedom and hint of danger in stepping away from the rights and responsibilities and into something more raw.

He concentrated on the slow rise and fall of his chest otherwise he'd drown under the weight of remorse. In one night, every illusion he'd carried had been shattered at the expense of Lionel's life. Never more did he truly see the accuracy in Wessex's words—Daisy was in desperate need of a husband, for then she'd not take it upon her fool head to…to…he growled. Do whatever it is she was doing at Gipsy Hill.

And if it was a man she met, Astor, Danport, or anyone else, by God he'd meet him by pistols at dawn and end the man for daring to encroach on that which belonged to him.

THIRTEEN

Daisy's carriage rocked to a stop in the bustling streets of Gipsy Hill. The coachman pulled the door open. She gave him a smile and allowed him to hand her down. Daisy paused and turned her face up to the sky. She savored the splash of the sun's rays bathing her face in warmth. "It is a sign."

"What is a sign, my lady?" her maid asked, as she came to a stop beside her.

Daisy started. She gave the young woman a smile. "Why, the weather, of course."

Agnes wrinkled her brow and stole a glance up at the clear, blue sky as though seeking some literal sign within the passing white clouds.

Not allowing the young woman's skepticism to dampen her spirits, Daisy started down the street toward the colorful tents and caravans lining the road.

"My lady, please you mustn't go off…" Agnes called out, all but sprinting after her.

Daisy paused and faced the woman. "Agnes, the sun is shining, we are out at Gipsy Hill. Enjoy the day."

The young woman looked about. "But, my lady, His Grace was quite clear in your last meeting—"

"Agnes?"

"Yes?"

She spoke to her as though speaking to a fractious mare. "I've only come in search of a heart pendant sold by an old gypsy woman." The maid set her jaw at a mutinous angle but Daisy launched into the most convincing argument she might put to the maid. "The sooner we find the necklace, the sooner we may leave and never return." Agnes seemed to consider the words. "You begin there." Daisy pointed to a crimson red tent with a gypsy peddling his wares. "And I shall be just over there." She pointed to the sapphire covered wagon.

"Very well, my lady," the maid said on a beleaguered sigh. She set out to do her mistress' bidding.

A smidgeon of guilt filled her at distressing her maid by forcing her to abandon her post as companion, and yet...She took in the bustling street activity. The aromatic scent of mace lingered in the air. It blended with the smell of the salop being sold by an old gypsy. Exhilaration coursed through Daisy, an excitement at being here and taking part in mundane activities that most took for granted.

With energy in her steps, she eagerly picked her way along the cobbled streets, bypassing those vendors she recognized from her previous two visits to Gipsy Hill. As she made her way along the street to the sapphire tent, she reflected on how these stolen outings served as a reminder of life. Daisy paused beside a large wagon and touched her hands to the edge of the coarse, wooden frame. She closed her eyes and lost herself in the sounds and scents that came from simply being alive.

A powerful hand shot around her wrist. "Are you out of your bloody mind?"

Daisy shrieked and drew her fist back. She punched the tall, commanding figure square in his aquiline nose. Auric released her and for a second time, yanked out his embroidered handkerchief and held it to his nose. He applied slight pressure to stem the blood flow. From over the edge of that fabric, he glowered at her.

She clamped her fingers over her mouth. "Auric. I didn't realize it was you." Oh, dear. She'd whacked him. Again. Well, *that* would never win her the duke's heart.

The deep blue of his eyes were lost to the ever-narrowing slit through which he gazed at her.

Daisy let her arms fall to her side. "You startled me." She supposed faintly accusatory was hardly the tone to take when he was in one of his ducal tempers.

"I startled you," he whispered, taking a step toward her.

She retreated and stole a glance about. Alas, passersby moved about their daily business, flitting from vendor to vendor, unaware that she'd unleashed a powerful beast.

"Are you afraid, Daisy?" Even through the noise of the mundane streets sounds, his hard whisper reached her ears.

"D-don't be silly" she scoffed. "Afraid of you." Her words ended on a gasp as he wrapped his fingers loosely about her wrist. Her skin warmed with the heat of his touch and she alternated her gaze between his gloved hand upon her person and his snapping eyes. She moistened her lips, seeking to calm the wild fluttering in her belly.

"You should be afraid, madam." Auric lowered his head. His breath fanned her ear. "Very afraid."

Daisy tugged her hand free. She'd not been cowed by him as a girl and she'd not allow him to intimidate her in all his snarling fury now. Sometime between his damned list of suitors and this high-handed showing, she'd tired of this brotherly-like position he'd assumed. "I'm not a child in need of protection." She jutted her chin out. "I am a woman, Auric." A woman who'd wanted him for longer than she could remember. "And I needn't answer to you."

He ran his gaze over her face. "Do you believe I do not know you are a woman?" There was a husky quality to his tone that wrapped about those words and sucked the breath from her lungs. For this man, who stood tall, his eyes veiled, his mouth hardened, bore no hint of the proper, polite Auric, Duke of Crawford. This figure was that of a man who desired a woman. "My girl of the flowers has bloomed into something quite splendid and captivating."

And the hope that she'd kicked ash upon long ago, the hope that he would someday see her, stirred to life once more. For with his words, he'd revealed that he saw her as more than just Lionel's sister. He saw *her*.

There amidst the bustling street sounds, with gypsies peddling their wares, uncaring who watched, she tipped her head back her lids fluttering closed, craving his kiss. Needing it.

His low, mellifluous baritone brought her eyes open. "What brings you here?" He doffed his hat and gestured to the busy cobbled roads.

A gentle breeze tugged at his hair, tumbling a chestnut strand over his eye giving him an almost boy-like look, when there had been nothing boy-like of the austere, aloof duke since that tragic day. Auric didn't wait for her answer, instead perused the area with a black frown on his lips as though searching for someone.

"The heart of a duke," she whispered.

He snapped his attention back to her.

She curled her feet into the soles of her slippers in abject mortification.

"Beg pardon?" Auric asked, standing there immobile.

"That is to say, the heart necklace, duke," she amended feigning a nonchalance she did not feel.

"You've never addressed me as duke."

Must he be so astute as to catch even those humiliating, inadvertent words from her lips? "Er, when you're highhanded I do." Which wasn't true. If that were the case, she'd be "duking" him until the end of eternity. She waved a hand about in a breezy manner. "And it is quite highhanded of you to come here and forbid me from going out—"

"Where is your chaperone?" he asked between gritted teeth.

"With my maid as a chaperone," she continued over him. "Now, if you'll pardon me." Then with braveness she didn't feel, she marched off, leaving him standing there.

Auric's long strides immediately ate up the distance between them.

She stole a sideways glance up at him and swallowed hard. The muscle ticking at the corner of his right eye and the tenseness of his mouth indicated his displeasure. He really was quite an imposing figure when mad. "What are you doing?" Had she not known him since she'd been in leading strings, she supposed she'd be terrified by the glowering duke.

"Accompanying you."

Which, by his aggrieved tone, was not something he sounded altogether thrilled with. The lout. As they moved through the throngs of shoppers, he angled his body close to hers in an almost protective manner.

An old gypsy woman called out. "Would you care to have your fortune read, my lady?"

Daisy stopped beside a colorful wagon belonging to the aged woman with graying, thick hair. Some inexplicable energy radiated throughout her person, a sense of familiarity. Of course she did not know the woman. She'd been to Gipsy Hill but three times before this. "Have we met?" she blurted, Auric momentarily forgotten.

The woman's mysterious grin widened. She beckoned her over. "Come, I shall tell you your future. A beautiful lady such as you surely dreams of love? Do you not wonder if the man whose heart you wish for will be yours?" *Every day.* Daisy was saved from replying. The gypsy's gaze shifted, to the gentleman who'd positioned himself at Daisy's side, eyeing him curiously. The old woman widened her eyes. "Ah, forgive me. I was mistaken. You already have love."

Daisy and Auric exclaimed in unison. "No!"

Daisy's cheeks burned at Auric's volatile response. She cleared her throat. "You are mistaken." *I want love. His love.*

The woman gave her a knowing look. "I've just the thing for you, my lady." She hurried around to the other side of her massive wagon and sifted through the goods she had laid out, muttering to herself, periodically glancing up at Daisy, looking to Auric with a frown, and then returning her attention to her colorful collection of items.

"Your being here is madness, Daisy."

"Perhaps." Only, she'd spent the past years not truly living or being seen, that stolen moments such as these served to remind her that she lived. "But tell me there is not something invigorating in seeing places you don't normally see and exploring a side of the world you'd not otherwise know."

"You'd make the world to which you don't belong something it's not," he snapped. The gypsy glanced up from the items she sifted through, curiosity teeming from her eyes. Auric lowered his voice. "You believe it is romantic and—" A coarse-looking man with pock-marked skin, in homespun garments knocked into Daisy. Auric cursed and caught her to him, righting her. He fixed his black glower upon the man. The stranger gulped and then spun around and headed in the opposite direction.

When had he become this stiffly disapproving gentleman? She planted her arms akimbo. "You needn't be so rude and condescending, Auric."

"Would you have had me invite him for tea?"

"Well, not tea," she said, wrinkling her nose, and then registered his faintly mocking tone.

Auric closed his eyes and his lips moved as if in a silent prayer. When he opened them, they were the hard, commanding eyes of a man accustomed to having his every wish obeyed. "This is not a game, Daisy."

"I never said it was," she snapped.

"Ah, here it is," the old gypsy said with a pleased nod.

Auric glanced at the woman as though she were a Bedlamite who'd wrestled her way free of the hospital and set up her cart here on Gipsy Hill. With another curse, he took Daisy by the wrist.

As Auric dragged her off, Daisy cast an apologetic glance back at the old gypsy. "What are you doing?"

"Leaving. *We're* leaving," he amended. "I do not want you here." His words were a bold command that stirred annoyance in her belly. "I do not want you near anyone in this part of London."

A gasp escaped her and she wrenched her hand free, forcing him to stop. "Whatever has happened to you? You'd be unpleasant to men and women merely for the station of their birth?" She gave her head a sad, little shake. "The Auric I knew would never be so coolly arrogant." Nor did she like the glimpses of this dark, unfamiliar side of him.

"And you know me so well?" he taunted.

Perhaps not, because neither had she ever known this condescending man. "I do," she angled her head back, holding his gaze square on.

He passed a hard, furious stare over her face and then in an un-Auric-like manner, cursed.

She widened her eyes. What else did she not know of him?

Auric jammed his hat on his head. "It is not safe for you, Daisy," he hissed. "Surely Li—?" She sucked in a breath, clasping and unclasping her hands against her chest. A mottled flush stained his cheeks.

"Surely life has taught you to be wary of venturing out into places no polite lady should be?"

His chest moved forcefully with the harsh, angry breaths he drew. Daisy widened her eyes. At last his almost panicked urgency to remove her from Gipsy Hill made sense. "Oh, Auric," she whispered. How could she have failed to realize? What an utter fool she'd been. Many of the details surrounding her brother's murder had been carefully kept from her. Even the most shocking aspects of his death, by the very gruesome nature of them had not been bandied about the *ton*, as was the case with nearly all gossip. But Auric knew all the details. Knew, because he'd been there. The air around them filled with Auric's angry, rasping breaths.

"I'll not come to harm," she said gently.

A bitter laugh, devoid of all humor escaped his lips. "How naïve you are to believe that you could prevent such a thing." There was no heated charge in those words. He clenched and unclenched his hands at his side, hinting at the thin level of control he had over his emotions.

"Auric," she spoke in hushed tones, wanting to take him in her arms and erase the horror of the past from the both of their memories. "I—"

"Marry me."

She blinked. Surely, in her own desperate yearnings she'd drummed up the request she'd carried in her heart.

He took a step closer and claimed her hands, raising her knuckles to his mouth. "I said, marry me."

What in hell had he done?

Daisy undoubtedly required a husband. She did not, however, deserve a husband who'd consigned her brother to the grave. *Wouldn't Lionel want you to care for her…?* Auric gave his head a shake. He'd proven himself incapable the night he'd found his pleasure in some whore's arms, putting his own baser needs before the lives of his friends.

The tremble on her tempting lips and the wistful glimmer in her piercing eyes indicated what a bloody, dangerous folly he'd committed.

For Daisy dreamed of romance and fairytales and longed for love—and he could never be more removed from those whimsical sentiments.

Auric released her hands quickly and doffed his hat once more, beating it against his leg. He cleared his throat as the silence stretched on. Perhaps she'd failed to hear his offer…but no, there was the tremble on her lips, lips he longed to capture under his, and the hope in her eyes that spoke to all number of damning truths and troubles.

"Yes," she whispered.

Yes. "Yes," he said dumbly. His heart shifted oddly in his chest.

A smile played about her lips.

He jammed his hat atop his head and gave a tug at his lapels and with no ready words on his lips, said, "Er, yes, well then."

Some of the light in her eyes dimmed and for the length of a heartbeat, one infernally long moment he thought she intended to change her mind. And for an equally long moment, anxiety turned inside him. Then her smile was firmly in place.

Unable to meet her gaze and all the pressure that went with the expectations he saw there, he perused the streets. "You were here searching for something again," he murmured. Anything but speaking on the offer he'd put to her that would make her forever his. "A necklace, wasn't it?" She'd spoken of a heart pendant.

Daisy gave her head a slight shake. "It turns out I require that pendant a good deal less than I'd imagined."

Eager to put this end of London behind them and remove Daisy to the safer, more well-traveled parts of North Bond Street or Mayfair, he held out his elbow. "Then, allow me to see you to your carriage."

She placed her fingertips along his sleeve and then wordlessly he guided her to the waiting carriage at the opposite end of the street, a ways ahead. Her maid hurried along behind.

And as Auric handed her up into her conveyance, he thought for all that had initially appeared correct with Wessex's argument, now seemed the very worst mistake. He could not be for Daisy the man she deserved.

God help him, he wanted her anyway.

FOURTEEN

The first meeting had been the easiest.

Auric had paid the requisite visit to Daisy's first guardian, the Marchioness of Roxbury's brother. The older, kind-eyed gentleman had asked all the appropriate questions and displayed a genuine concern for his niece's happiness.

The second meeting was the one he had been dreading since he'd asked Daisy to marry him. A now imminent meeting.

Auric found himself following the current Marquess of Roxbury's butler down familiar corridors in a familiar home. Their steps fell in a matched rhythm. The bewigged man of indeterminate years kept his gaze trained forward, his face set in a proper mask.

They moved past portrait after portrait of former marquesses lining the plaster walls, the men who'd come before this current interloper. The stares of those long gone forever memorialized Roxbury ancestry, faintly accusatory in nature. The inanimate figures even recognized the one responsible for the loss of the rightful Roxbury heir being here this day. Guilt pricked his skin as he passed Lionel and Daisy's father, and he gave silent thanks as they reached the end of the blasted hall lined with the portraits. The tread of his bootsteps were quiet in the foreign corridors as he moved past additional family portraits of other wigged and powdered ancestors.

One particular painting halted his forward movement. The lone figure of a man committed to the canvas forever smiling, forever young, but never a marquess. The butler looked questioningly back at him and Auric lifted his hand in a staying movement. He wandered closer and then stopped beside the painting wedged unceremoniously between a lady in a wimple and a mother with two children at her feet. His chest tightened as he looked on the last painting done of Lionel. This should not have been his last. His likeness belonged in the previous hall, beside the other rightful heirs and marquesses.

Emotion threatened to choke him and he momentarily pressed his eyes closed. *Egads, man. My parents will have me sit for another blasted painting. I intend to smile my way through the whole sitting. That should please my dear mama...*The walls even now echoed with Lionel's bellowing laugh.

The butler coughed discreetly into his hand and Auric shook his head once and resumed walking. With each step, the weight of guilt became all the heavier. How could he in good conscience wed Daisy? A woman of her keen wit and spirit deserved far more in the man she'd call husband. Certainly more than mere protection and the security of a title. She should have love and happiness, and a gentleman who smiled. And Auric, well he no longer remembered what it was to freely grin. Not in the way that he once had and not in the way she deserved.

They stopped before the current marquess' office and a chill stole through him. The butler rapped once and then threw the door open. "His Grace, the Duke of Crawford."

The slender gentleman seated behind his desk glanced up from the open ledgers upon his desk and then stood. After Lionel's father had died two years ago, Auric had studiously avoided the distant cousin who'd stepped into the role of marquess. He took this stranger in. With clever eyes and sharp features, the marquess was likely no more than a year younger or older than Auric himself.

Auric broke the silence "Roxbury," he murmured as he entered the doorway. The butler closed the door behind him.

"Your Grace," the man said, his tone modulated and kind. He spread his arms wide, motioning him forward. "I gather by the contents of your missive, you've come to speak on the matter of my ward."

Odd to think of the lush, clever Daisy, a woman of one and twenty years referred to as a ward. Wards were young children with parents gone too soon and young ladies about to make their debut. "Yes," he replied, moving deeper into the room. Alas, that is what she was. With his selfishness seven years ago, he'd turned her into that ward.

With an assessing eye, the marquess evaluated him. Then in one effortless move, strode out from behind his desk and crossed to the sideboard. He held a crystal decanter aloft. "A drink, Your Grace?"

Auric waved off the offer as Roxbury filled his own glass. He carried it back over to his desk. "Sit, sit, please," he encouraged, as he slid into the folds of his seat.

Tension thrumming through his frame, Auric claimed the seat opposite him, still taking stock of the man. Roxbury swirled the contents of his glass in a slow circle and then took a small sip. Then, glass cradled in his fingers, he eyed Auric over the rim of his snifter. An irrational resentment for this young gentleman filled him, even as he recognized the wrongness of those sentiments. Roxbury shifted back into the folds of his leather, winged back chair. And waited.

Eager to be free of this man and this place, he said in cool, clipped tones, "I would like to wed Lady Daisy Meadows." He didn't know what he expected the other man to say.

Roxbury smiled over the top of his brandy. "Of course."

That however was not it. He frowned. "Of course?" he repeated. Fury rolled off his person in waves. Odd, he'd never known one could taste, see, and breathe rage. It was volatile and potent, and threatened to consume him. He took several slow, calming breaths. They had little effect to stem his anger.

"Yes." A wry grin turned the other man's lips and he likely had no idea how close to a vicious thrashing he was. "Of course."

He gritted his teeth, glad at last to have more solid grounds with which to hate the marquess on. "You do not even know me." Daisy's smiling visage flitted through his mind.

"You're a duke, Crawford." Roxbury motioned to him, waving his drink in his direction. "You're obscenely wealthy and you have a familial connection to the lady's family. I think your suitability has been aptly gauged."

Auric tightened his hands upon the arms of his seat as he considered the handful of dukes of his acquaintance. A combination of aged, lecherous, and widowered, not a single one of them would have been fit to scrape the hem of Daisy's skirt with their gloved fingertips, let alone wed her and bed her. By Roxbury's standards, then, any one of those dukes with their fat purses would have been hastily accepted whether the lady willed it or not.

Roxbury cleared his throat. "Would you have me tell you no?" he asked, consternation underlining that question.

Yes, yes if Auric was undeserving of her, then that is precisely what he'd have the man do. "No." *Yes.* How could an answer be both? And yet, it was. He'd have the man at least allow him to present his offer and determine his worth as a man. Swallowing a curse, he slid his gaze away. An uncomfortable pall of silence descended upon the room, punctuated by the ticking clock at the back corner of the room.

This untenable existence Daisy had known through the years, with a stranger responsible for her care, shook him. How wrong he and Wessex had been. The lady's need for protection defied a mere marital connection. She'd needed saving from her lonely world where the man charged with her care was nothing more than a stranger, the late Roxbury's only male cousin, who'd slipped into the role of marquess following the older man's passing. Guilt balled in his throat, nearly choking him. He loathed the idea of her dependent on one such as this for her care. He shifted his attention back to Roxbury, holding his stare. "No, I would not have you reject my suit." He proceeded to lay out the generous terms of the contract that raised the other man's eyebrows nearly to his hairline.

The absolute rightness of being here filled Auric. He had little right to her, yet he would care for her and see she didn't dwell in this uncertain, dark existence she now did. He shoved himself to his feet. "I'll procure a special license. We'll be wed within the week."

That, in itself, should have roused the gentleman's concern as a guardian. Instead, Roxbury continued to sip away at that damned brandy, as casual as he'd been the whole damned exchange. "Of course," he said, uttering another one of those damned "of courses".

166

No concern for Daisy forthcoming. Roxbury set down his glass and stood. "Is there anything else you require?"

Just Daisy. "No. That will be all." With stiff movements, he started for the door and then stopped at the entrance, as a thought came to him. "Actually, I do require something, Roxbury." The man listened while Auric spoke, nodding at all the appropriate places. With that, he took his leave of Roxbury. Auric needed to see Daisy.

Daisy sat at the window seat and through the slight gap in the ivory satin curtains, stared down into the London streets. She pulled her knees close to her chest and a little sigh escaped her. He'd asked to wed her. An almost giddy excitement bubbled up in her chest and spilled past her lips. She buried her head into her skirts and laughed. The sound was unrestrained and free and real.

She'd spent the better part of the last few years believing he didn't see her—not in the way she longed for him to notice her. Yet, his presence at Gipsy Hill not once, not twice, but a third time were not the actions of an uninterested gentleman who failed to register her existence. Nor were they merely the actions of a man with an obligation to her brother, as was evidenced in his proposal. And his kiss. And the heated manner in which he'd studied her through thick-hooded lids. Suddenly, the gypsy's bauble worn by Lady Stanhope and her sisters no longer mattered. The talisman Daisy had hung her hopes upon, was now unnecessary and unneeded as something proved far greater than magic—the love she carried for Auric.

Daisy furrowed her brow. And whatever it was Auric felt for her. Did he love her? Her mind danced around the truth of that question. Of course he loved her. He'd not have asked to marry her if he did not. *Why, Daisy?* Aren't most marriages based on powerful connections and a general fondness between two people and not much more? She thrust aside the niggling of doubt peppering her mind.

She raised her head and inched the curtain back, expanding her view of the activity below. After Auric had handed her into her carriage

167

yesterday morn, he'd not said another word about his offer. He'd not indicated when he would call upon her guardian, father's second cousin, who'd been charged with her care. She contemplatively chewed her lower lip. Part of her had believed he would arrive first thing that morning to speak with the new marquess and then come immediately after their meeting. She stole a glance across the room at the ormolu clock.

Once again, her own misgivings swirled in her belly. In all the dreams she'd carried of the moment Auric at last realized his love for her, that offer would have looked so very different than that almost hastily spoken question that hadn't really been a question in the middle of Gipsy Lane. She'd not ever needed anything of the material such as flowers or sonnets from him. There would, however, have been his grand declaration of unwavering love.

In the crystal windowpane, her frowning visage reflected back. "Don't be silly," she muttered. In the same way in which life had changed her, Auric too had been changed from smiling, garrulous boy to this oft somber, laconic fellow revered by all, feared by most. He would never be one of those gentlemen to wax poetic, nor did she crave those empty words. Rather, she'd have his heart and the man he'd become with time's passage.

A black carriage with the familiar crest of a roaring lion interrupted her musings. She swung her legs over the side of the bench. Her skirts settled around her ankles with a soft rustle. A servant pulled the door open and Auric stepped down. The wind whipped his cloak and it swirled about his thick, well-muscled legs clad in immaculate, black breeches.

Her mouth went dry and with him unaware of her presence above, she studied him, frozen in the streets below. She touched a finger to her lips remembering his kiss. Her *first* kiss. She burned with a hunger for more of him, wanted to know in his arms, all the intimate secrets shared between a man and woman. Auric gave his head a shake and yanked at his lapels. The tick-tock of the ormolu clock and the sound of her own breath filled her ears as he remained fixed to his spot in the street. Then with a pained expression stamped on his face, he started toward the front door. Her heart started. His was not the look of a man eager to see his betrothed.

"What are you looking at Daisy?"

She gasped and the curtain slipped from her fingers. "Mother," she greeted, springing to her feet.

Her mother wore her perpetual frown and black bombazine skirts. "It won't do to be seen gawking out the window." Ah, this reprimanding, propriety driven lady bore hint to the person she used to be. Some of the blankness to her stare that she'd affected these seven years had lifted, though Daisy suspected part of that great heartache would always remain. Then, how could a woman recover from the loss that her mother had known?

"It is Auric," Daisy said at last, knowing if anything could dispel her mother's displeasure or disappointment, it was mention of the duke.

"How lovely! He's come to visit." She made to ring for a servant.

Daisy called out, halting her. "I don't believe he is here on a social call." She folded her hands together and studied their interlocked digits.

"What are you—?"

She raised her head. "I believe he's just come from speaking with my guardians."

"Speaking with your guardians?" her mother parroted. "Whatever about?"

She hesitated. The tension in Auric's mouth and his wan complexion hadn't hinted at an eager bridegroom, rushing over after securing the appropriate permission from her guardians. "I…" she hesitated. She thrust aside her misgivings. "He asked that I marry him." Nothing could compel Auric to do something he didn't wish. He wanted to marry her. Otherwise, he'd not have asked.

Silence met her pronouncement. Then a cry escaped her mother's lips and she buried the expression of joy in her fingers. Even in her happiness, ascribing to societal dictates for appropriate behavior. "Oh, Daisy, how could you not have said anything?" She sailed over in a flurry of black skirts and captured her daughter's hands. There was a gentle reproach in her eyes.

"I—" Hadn't been completely certain that she'd not dreamed the entire exchange. Nor could she be certain that between their meeting yesterday morn to this moment that he hadn't regretted his request. "I thought it would be best to wait until he'd spoken to the marquess and Uncle," she settled for.

Tears filled Mama's haunting, blue eyes and slipped down her cheeks in a graceful display of quiet happiness. "I always knew he cared for you."

As had Daisy. She'd merely thought his feelings were those reserved for a younger sister. Where she had loved him with a woman's heart.

"We shall have a grand ceremony—"

A sound of protest escaped her. "No, Mama, please." She'd become accustomed to the introvert who avoided any and all conversations, that she'd not anticipated her mother wanting to put her and Auric on display for all of polite Society. "I would prefer a small, intimate gathering." There was a faintly pleading tone to her words. She loathed the attention. Through the years she'd been invisible to the *ton* and, as such, she'd never quite managed to move with the grace and assurance evinced by Auric.

"Bah, of course there is to be a grand ceremony. Why, we must invite Lady Jersey," Daisy groaned, "and I daresay Prinny himself will come," her mother continued over her. "After all, it is not every day that a duke weds."

Daisy buried her head in her hands and shook it back and forth. Mama might not give two jots of whether her daughter was pleased. She would, however, care a good deal of Auric's wishes. "Auric will not welcome a lavish event, Mama. I'm certain of it." The man of his youth would have. Whereas Daisy had always been hopelessly gauche and bumbling at the summer parties thrown by her parents, Auric had moved with the same effortless grace he possessed, even to this day.

"Hmm." Her mother tapped a finger against her lips. "Do you believe so?"

"Oh, I'm certain of it."

"We shall, of course, defer to the duke's desires in the matter." She threw her arms around Daisy.

"Oomph!" She staggered under the weight of her mother's unexpected frame and she stiffened as Mama ran her palm up and down her back the way she had when Daisy had been a small girl who'd stumbled or fallen. Daisy held her body taut with the unfamiliarity of this embrace. Too many years had passed where her mother hadn't managed to look at her surviving child, let alone hold her.

"I am so very happy," her mother said, her voice clogged with emotion.

Daisy closed her eyes and accepted her mother's affection. The same way she'd missed Auric's teasing, smiling presence was the same way she'd longed to return to the simpler times when Mama had been stern and disapproving and Papa jovial, and Lionel—just being Lionel. There had been a void and Auric had been the one to fill it, and in so doing had healed some part of her shattered mother.

The marchioness seemed to remember herself. She released Daisy and stepped back. "Well," she said, smoothing her palms along the front of her skirts. A pink blush stained her cheeks. "If you'll excuse me?" With that, her mother turned on her heel and left Daisy—alone.

Her lips curved upward in an unrestrained smile. Now, she'd never be alone again. Daisy reclaimed her seat and picked up her embroidery frame once more, periodically shifting her attention from the scrap of fabric to the ormolu clock, ticking away on the mantel. A little frown played on her lips. Where in blazes was he? He'd stepped down from the carriage…and she stole a glance at the clock, several minutes ago. Perhaps he wished to speak to her mama first?

She stilled, feeling his presence. Then, they'd always shared a unique connection, one that defied Lionel's passing. Frederick appeared at the entrance of the room.

"His Grace, the Duke of Crawford," he boomed and then backed out, allowing them their privacy.

Quiet echoed in the still of the Blue Parlor and Daisy climbed to her feet. "Hullo," she offered belatedly.

"Daisy," he murmured. Thick lashes that no gentleman had a right to possess swept low as he peered at her.

When he'd arrived a short while ago, she'd detected a flash of panic and horror on his face, and he'd then disappeared inside, so that she was left to wonder if she'd imagined his inexplicable reaction. With the manner in which his hot gaze lingered upon the swell of her décolletage, all her misgivings lifted when presented instead with his masculine appreciation. She fiddled with the embroidery frame, grateful for its comforting presence in her hands. "Hullo," she said. Again. Twice now. Or perhaps she hadn't? "Mayhap I'd only thought it in my head?" Which would, of course, be the preferable, less humiliating—

A half grin pulled at his lips as he strode over, coming to a stop just several feet away. "No, you did indeed greet me twice."

Daisy bit the inside of her cheek. "Oh." Bothersome habit to have. "Would you care to sit?" she asked, motioning to the collection of seats about the room.

Wordlessly, he inclined his head and waited until she'd reclaimed her spot, perched upon the edge of the sofa. Auric took the seat beside her. His broad, powerful frame filled the King Louis XIV mahogany chair. She rested her embroidery on her lap.

"I spoke with your g…" Auric dropped a contemplative gaze to her lap.

She held it up for his perusal.

"A teardrop?"

Daisy shook her head. "Why ever would I want to capture a teardrop upon a handkerchief?"

Auric grinned. "You are correct." He leaned over and in a very undukelike manner, plucked it from her fingers.

"Well?" she prodded.

With the tip of his index finger, he trailed it over the crimson red threads, outlined in gold. His creased brow spoke to his concentration, which was undoubtedly never a promising sign of one's embroidering prowess, or rather lack therefore of. She sighed and took it from his fingers. "Oh, do give me that."

"Do *you* know what it is?" he teased.

Daisy pointed her eyes to the ceiling. "Of course I do." She kicked at his foot with the tip of her slippers. "Do hush." Yet, secretly at his teasing, she trilled with happiness; the kind of uncomplicated joy she'd never thought to know and most certainly never again from him, the stoic, somber Duke of Crawford. She proceeded to pull her threaded needle through the fabric with deliberate care.

"I spoke to your guardians."

She paused, not taking her gaze from the indecipherable heart she worked on. "Did you?" Her heart thumped wildly in her chest.

"I asked for your hand."

Daisy jammed the tip of her needle into the pad of her thumb. Reflexively, her fingers opened and the frame slipped from her fingers.

Auric tugged off his gloves and tossed them on the rose-inlaid, mahogany table, all the while watching her with an inscrutable expression.

He'd not changed his mind. "D-did you?" A giddy sensation replaced the tension in her chest.

He shot a hand out and laid claim to her fingers, his gaze holding hers. "I did," he confessed. The vital strength of his olive-hued fingers burned her skin. "Did you believe I would change my mind?" Then with a wickedly delicious slowness, he ran the pad of his thumb over the palm of her hand.

Well, the idea *had* entered her thoughts. She swallowed hard, a warm sensation fluttered in her belly. "No," she managed, her voice breathy as Auric's expert touch sent all manner of delicious shivers spiraling through her being. The fear that he'd recognized the folly in wedding plump, freckled Daisy Meadows hadn't entered her thoughts—until, he'd paused on the cobbled streets a short while ago, his expression pained. Since then, she'd been consumed by a niggling fear that with the morn he'd come to his senses and recall that he could have any glorious, golden creature, which he surely favored, as evidenced by his courtship of the Lady Anne Stanhope.

Her lashes drifted closed as he dragged the tip of his index finger over the intersecting lines of her palm. How was it possible for a mere touch to affect her so? Daisy dropped her gaze and studied that seductively innocent caress. All the while her heart danced a funny rhythm in her chest. "You're quiet. I never remember you to be quiet."

She couldn't very well admit that the hard, heavy assurance of his hand robbed her of coherent thought, made it nigh impossible to string words together. "I'm not the same woman I was." Except, with those words, inadvertently she'd roused the ghost that would always be between them and part of their lives. She'd not shatter this moment with the ugliness that would forever unite them.

His gaze grew shuttered and his finger resumed its slow, explorative movement. "Yes, you've said as much, haven't you?" He now ran his thumb up her palm and back and forth over her wrist.

Her mouth went dry and all thoughts fled as he slowly brought her hand to his mouth. His lips caressed the spot where her heartbeat pulsed madly for him. Only him. It had only ever been him. Her lids fluttered closed as he continued to worship the skin with his kiss.

"I'll be obtaining a special license so we may wed within the week." His pronouncement penetrated the thick haze of desire roused by his touch.

Warmth fanned her heart once more. "A special license?" The speed with which he'd wed her hinted at his eagerness to take her as his bride and it would spare Daisy from her mother's grand plans for the blessed day.

Auric raised her other hand to his mouth and dropped a kiss on her knuckles. "Will you regret not having a proper ceremony and—?"

"No." She drew in a shuddery breath. "None of that matters to me, Auric." It never had. "I've never longed for an elaborate affair before a sea of lords and ladies who do not matter."

He released her hands and she mourned the loss of that simple, yet enticing, caress. "What do you desire?" There was an earnestness to his tone. As though should she call for the stars, he'd capture her the moon. "What do you want, Daisy?"

When was the last time anyone had wondered as to her wishes or desires?

She stood, her gaze fixed on the blood-red, distorted heart she attempted to capture on the fabric in her embroidery frame. She picked it up and ran her finger absently over the gold thread stitched crookedly onto the fabric. "I want a family, Auric." Something she'd once had, but lost. Daisy looked at him once more. "I want to love and be loved." Did his cheeks go waxen? The frissons of unease worked down her spine. *Not once has he spoken to you of love, Daisy*, a dark voice niggled. But then, neither had she. "That is all," she finished lamely.

FIFTEEN

That is all.

She may as well have asked for the moon and the stars, and where he would have sought to climb into the sky and gather her a handful, could he love her, as she deserved? For with her seemingly innocent words of children between them, she roused images of his and Daisy's bodies moving as one in a beautiful, synchronized rhythm. And he wanted her and those children belonging to her. His body ached with the desire to explore her and brand the silken softness of her skin in his palms, cupping her generous breasts and—

A garbled groan lodged in his throat.

Daisy fiddled with that silly frame. Wordlessly, she carried it over to the window and stared out into the streets below. Then she angled her body back to face him. "It occurs to me, for everything we know of each other, we don't truly know each other, do we?"

"Of course we do," he said, frowning at her words. But for himself, he knew her better than anyone. "Your favorite color is blue."

She widened her eyes with surprise. "You remember that?"

His silent, cowardly self still fearful of the implications of her own admission moments ago, urged him to lie. "Of course I remember that, Daisy," he said gruffly. There was not a single detail he did not recall where she was concerned. Society would have deemed her a horrid painter.

"My mother said it was merely paint splattered upon the canvas," she said more to herself.

Auric, however, had only seen the stunning mastery of color. The masterpieces she'd turned out for his and Lionel's inspection had captured more shades of blue than he'd ever known existed. "I admired that you weren't restrained by Society's dictates." With the memories of their past unraveling between them, he wandered down a more and more irreversible path, cementing this new relationship in which they were more strangers than not.

"But that isn't truly knowing someone," she said softly. "The color I like or the colors I hate—"

"Orange and purple," he supplied automatically.

"—do not speak to the dreams I carry in my heart."

He fell silent. For in this, she spoke true. Beyond that shockingly intimate desire she'd shared of love and a family, he didn't truly know Daisy's interests. He knew sometime in the recent years she'd taken up embroidering, but didn't know why or if she'd been made to or whether she merely challenged herself with the tedious task, and God help him, he longed to know all those pieces of her. Auric drew in a slow, staggering breath as he realized—he wanted to know everything there was to know about Daisy. He wanted to know the things that made her smile now as a woman, the tasks she enjoyed and, more importantly, he had a desire to know why she enjoyed them.

"For everything we've shared, and as long as we've known each other, there is so much we do not know of each other, even so." Her words served as an echo to his tumultuous thoughts.

Drawn to her like the siren, Calypso, his legs of their own volition carried him closer and closer until a mere hairsbreadth separated them. "What do you wish to know?" His words emerged husky.

She tipped her head back. "What do you desire, Auric?"

You. The word hung, unspoken on his lips. *I desire you.* Since that fateful night seven years ago, he'd not taken another woman into his bed. He hungered for her the way a starving man longed for food. And yet, this force of emotion that gripped him defied a mere physical awareness. "Peace." The word danced in the air between them. "I desire peace." And escape from the hellish memories he carried, memories he likely always would.

Daisy slipped her hand into his and raised their interlocked fingers. This again, that bond shared by only them who'd known this tragic loss. "Then we shall know peace together."

Warmth slipped inside his heart. The cold and hollow organ stirred to life.

She studied their joined hands. "Surely, you desire more than peace." Daisy raised her gaze. "Your courtship of Lady Stanhope was not borne of a hope for peace alone."

There had been a great appeal in the lovely, young, blonde woman who'd not fawned over his title as every other lady of marriageable age. Yet, a good deal of that had stemmed from her absolute disconnect from the darkest part of his life. The countess did not know the shameful details of his youth, or the horrors of that night. Daisy, on the other hand, would be forever intrinsically connected to the whole of his past.

After a long stretch of silence, Daisy let her arm fall back to her side and his hand went cold at the loss of her reassuring touch.

Auric brushed his knuckles under her chin, tipping her gaze back to his. "Come, surely you'd not have me speak of my previous courtship?"

"Yes, yes I would," she said with the same boldness he'd come to expect of Lady Daisy Meadows through the years. She pinked, as though embarrassed by such an admission, but she stared on relentlessly. "Did you care for her?"

Some, powerfully intense emotion in her eyes gave him pause. It was something that indicated his response was an important one and the wrong response would prove disastrous in ways he didn't fully understand. "The lady didn't fawn over my title," he said, picking his way carefully through this exchange.

"And you'd have wed the lady for that reason alone?"

"I would say that it speaks to the lady's honor." He dropped his brow to hers. "I'd not speak of my courtship of another. Not today." Not when he'd so recently offered for her. The mention of Lady Stanhope or any other sullied whatever this indefinable pull was between them. He curved his hand around the graceful lines of her long neck.

Her lower lip quivered as he angled her close "I'd only speak of you, Daisy." He took her mouth under his as he'd longed to since he'd first tasted the sweetness of her kiss and the passion on her lips, that yearning made only stronger when she'd sailed into Lady Ellis' ballroom, a voluptuous angel sent to torment. Auric slanted his mouth over hers again and again until she sagged. He easily caught her to him and drew her against his frame. His body roared to life with a hot, primitive awareness of a man who'd not given himself to another and now only wished to learn her and no other. He slipped his tongue inside her mouth.

She moaned and, at first, tentatively touched her tongue to his and then shamelessly met his in an age-old dance. What once had been wrong because she was Daisy of his past now became right in every way. He drew back and she tangled her fingers in his hair, attempting to draw him close, but he merely continued his tireless exploration. Afire with a need to explore all of her, he trailed a path of kisses over her freckled cheeks.

"Beautiful," he whispered.

Daisy's head pitched back, a whimpering moan slipped past her lips as he moved his lips to the corner of her mouth and lower to the place where her pulse throbbed wildly in her neck. The scent of lavender clung to her skin and he drew an intoxicating breath that sucked him into the past—visiting her family, a family he'd forever destroyed.

He wrenched away, his chest heaved in agonized, shuddering breaths.

Her lashes fluttered wildly and she blinked several times as though she sought to clear the haze of passion that had enveloped her. "What—?"

"Forgive me," he said gruffly, guilt ravaging his conscience.

"There is nothing to forgive."

Only, there was everything to forgive. Guilt churned in his belly.

She held her palms up misinterpreting the reason for his regret. "We are to be married." Emotion filled her eyes. "And I love you."

A dull buzzing filled his ears with her words coming as though down a long corridor. He gave a brusque shake of his head. The implications of this admission so much greater than the amorphous wish she'd spoken of earlier to love and be loved. Now, she spoke of him and yearnings for his heart, when she didn't know the dark lie he'd kept from her. Once because the words of his shameful past would never be fit for a respectable lady's ears, now because he was a coward. She was deserving of the truth even as it would kill all the warmth in her eyes, leaving him dark and empty. But he could not enter into a union with this between them. He swiped a hand over his eyes and turned on wooden legs, needing to put distance between them, too much of a coward to witness the moment all her love for him was replaced with that deserved loathing.

Daisy rushed around him in a flurry of blue skirts and planted herself in front of him. "Do you intend to leave?" Incredulity underscored her question. She settled her hands upon her hips, her eyebrows dipped.

But for the details of one night he kept to himself, he had always chosen forthrightness. He lowered his voice, speaking in hushed tones. "Surely, you know I care about you?" He'd have lobbed off his left arm if it would bring her happiness. "There is something I would have you—"

The lines of her face gentled. "Oh, Auric," she whispered, caressing his cheek.

He flinched. He'd never been worthy of her affections. She'd made him, with his visits through the years, into someone honorable and good, when in truth there was none more complicit than he. "Daisy," he began once more, his voice gruff. He captured her wrist in his hand, intending to remove it from his person so he could at last give her the truth.

Footsteps sounded in the hall. Their gazes swung as one to the doorway where the Marchioness of Roxbury stood framed in the entrance, a wider smile than he remembered of the lady these years wreathed her aged face. She clapped her hands together. "Oh, Auric, I have heard the splendid news."

He dropped a bow. The woman's enthusiasm stabbed him with more of the agonized guilt. He'd bungled this all up. Daisy should have been given the truth before he'd rushed over with an offer for her hand. "Lady Roxbury, it is a pleasure." Only, deep inside where truths dwelled, he'd recognized this was the only way he might have her. Panic climbed up his throat, threatening to choke him. "If you'll excuse me? As much as I'd enjoy visiting, there are matters to see to."

"Of course, of course there are," she exclaimed. She captured Daisy's hand and locked their fingers together. "I do not remember when I last knew this happiness," she said softly.

Would the woman feel that way if she were to know that he was not the honorable, devoted man she'd taken him as through the years? He spun on his heel and fled as though the hounds of hell nipped at his heels.

And if there had ever been a doubt these years, his hasty retreat only proved something he'd long known—he was a bloody coward.

SIXTEEN

When she'd been a girl, Lionel had teased Daisy about her remarkable ability to slumber through anything and everything, from the volatile summer storms to their mother's loud rapping on Daisy's chamber doors. The only time in Daisy's life she'd struggled to sleep had been the evening of Lionel's death. She'd lain abed and stared up at the ceiling. She'd flipped onto her side, back and forth, all night, until ultimately flopping onto her back again to stare at the canopy over her head. Anxiety had turned in her belly and ran down her back, and she'd not known how to make sense of the inexplicable misgivings.

Much the same way she'd had an innate sense of hovering darkness, so did she after Auric had beat his swift retreat three days earlier. She'd not seen him since that hasty flight. *His are not the actions of a gentleman in love.* Then, he'd never spoken of love, or even affection. Yet no one could or would ever make Auric do something he'd not want to. His life stood as testament to that. Surely, he'd not wed her if he didn't love her with at least some sliver of his heart. No, a man who remembered such details as her favorite color and her least favorite colors and the foods she enjoyed proved that he felt at least *something* where she was concerned.

A shadow fell over her and she started. "You are quiet, Daisy."

She cast an upward glance. "Mother," she answered. "I did not hear you enter." For somehow, with an offer of marriage from Auric, Mother had become the invisible one and Daisy the one lost in her own world—a world that made so very little sense.

Mother sank into the seat alongside her on the blue satin upholstered sofa. "I daresay you'd have more of a smile. This is to be after
all, your wedding day."

Daisy forced a smile.

If the marchioness detected the lack of sincerity to that expression
of happiness, she gave no indication. "I always dreamed of a union
between you and Auric," she spoke in those deeply introspective tones.

As had she. Since she'd nearly burned down her parents' table
during a summer picnic. She'd just not allowed herself the real hope
of that in these recent years, as with a woman's jaded maturity she
saw his interest reserved for another. *Surely, you know I care about you…*
Whatever other words he'd have uttered had been cut into by her
mother's ill-timed appearance.

Daisy gave her head a clearing shake, shoving aside any misgivings.
He'd not said as much with her mother's sudden appearance, but she
could not doubt that love would have driven his offer. She glanced over
at the long-case clock, her stomach fluttering with excitement. Filled with
a restless energy, she wandered over to the window and pulled back the
curtain. She peered down into the quiet streets. He would arrive soon. In
a short while, they would wed and all her hopes would be realized, and
she'd no longer be invisible or lonely. They would have each other.

From the crystal pane of the window, she looked at her mother.
The older-than-her-years marchioness cast an empty gaze about the
room and then the ghost of a smile hovered on her lips as she confronted the dreams she'd once carried. "I imagined a grand ceremony
for you and an extravagant breakfast with all the leading lords and
ladies of Society present." A prospect Daisy had shuddered with. "What
are those?"

Daisy looked over her shoulder. "What is what?"

With a flick of her hand, Mother motioned to the butterfly combs
artfully woven through Daisy's dull, brown tresses that morning. "They
are hair combs," she said patiently, pretending to misunderstand.

"I see that." Her mother wrinkled her nose. "I'd always imagined
you in something a good deal more extravagant with diamonds and
rubies."

The earliest memories Daisy had of her mother, were of the woman resplendent in impeccable and expensive French fabrics, her neck dripping in glittering gemstones. How different she'd always been than her mother. "I adore these," she said softly. They were not the grand pieces donned by those diamonds of the first water, but for what they represented—the first gift given her by Auric amidst the streets of London that had brought them together in the most meaningful ways—and for that they were more priceless than the Queen's crown.

Her mother let out a little sigh. "I was so certain you were wrong and that Auric would desire a lavish ceremony befitting his rank."

Then her mother didn't know Auric in the intimate way Daisy had over the years. The man he'd become would have glowered away every last guest to assure his privacy.

A lone carriage rolled down the street and then that familiar, black conveyance rocked to a halt in front of her townhouse. "He is here."

Her mother raced over to the window. "He is here?"

Daisy started not realizing she'd spoken aloud but remained with her gaze fixed upon Auric as he descended from the carriage.

"Release the curtain," her mother admonished. "It will not do to be discovered studying him so brazenly."

How many times had she been cowed by that stern frown? There had been a time Daisy would have lowered her head, humbled at those chiding words. Not any longer.

"Did you hear me, Daisy?"

Daisy ignored her. She trailed the tips of her fingertips over the glass, looking for the hint of hesitation she'd spied days ago in Auric's ruggedly beautiful face. "I heard you, Mother." There was none. His face was set in a hard mask. "A young lady would be granted such boldness upon her wedding day, surely." He said something to his driver. The man nodded and rushed back to the carriage.

"Surely not," her mother said with the shocked indignation of the proper lady she'd been. "Standing in the window, gaping down at him with anyone to see?" She launched into a diatribe about proper behavior and decorum. All in all, seven years too late. In the wake of Lionel's death, her mother and father had ceased to see her, and their influence in her life had therefore ceased to matter. It had been no deliberate insult, merely her attempt at an emotional survival.

Daisy continued to watch him. He started forward, but then, as though he felt her stare upon him, froze mid-step. Auric glanced up and scanned the handful of windows of the townhouse, until his gaze found hers. Her heart started. She'd never been one of those ladies to fawn over fashion and yet, now wished she was draped in one of those elaborate satin gowns and not this modest blue dress selected for her wedding day. He squinted, peering up through eyes narrowed into thin slits and she fisted her blue satin skirts. What did he see when he looked at her? Then he shifted his attention to his cloak. She furrowed her brow in consternation as he rummaged through the front of his jacket and then he withdrew something. Warmth spiraled through her and a bark of laughter escaped her as he pressed a quizzing glass, *the* quizzing glass she'd given him, to his eye.

And she fell in love with him all over again.

She shook her head, laughter spilling past her lips. "You are incorrigible," she mouthed.

With two winks, he touched the brim of his hat, startling another sharp bark of laughter from her lips.

"Please remember yourself, Daisy. It is impolite to laugh."

She returned his greeting with an eager wave that caused her mother to cry out. "Come, Mother. I rather think it is preferable to go through life laughing than with a stern frown."

Her mother either failed to hear or appreciate the reproach there. "Oh, Daisy, do come away from that window."

Daisy returned her gaze to the cobblestones below, locating Auric just as he stepped through the open doorway. She released the fabric and it fluttered back into place. "Surely, a bride is allowed some excitement on her wedding day?" Improper thoughts no true lady should dare have, wandered down the path of her wedding night. Nervousness warred with a scandalous eagerness that burned her cheeks.

"There is never a place for such unrestrained excitement in a polite, respectable lady's life," her mother replied.

Her mother certainly believed as much. Daisy gave silent thanks that the proper marchioness couldn't glean the true musings traipsing through Daisy's head even now.

Her lips pulled at the corners.

Silence. It filled the Blue Parlor—thick, uncomfortable, and tense. But for the rustle of Daisy's blue satin gown as she occasionally shifted back and forth on her feet and breaths of the handful of guests present, the room was otherwise silent. As it had been since the butler had shown Auric inside a short while ago.

The lady's guardians were quiet. The marchioness was beaming. And Daisy was, well bloody hell, he couldn't tell precisely what the lady was. The smiling vixen waving boldly from her place at the window had become this subdued stranger the moment he'd entered the parlor.

Did she sense that she had bound herself to the veriest bastard? A vile monster who, in his silence, would take choice from her hands? The muscles of his stomach clenched. *I love you...*God help him for being selfish and self-serving, but he wanted her even with the lies between them. Odd, he should have lived the better part of their lives failing to see her as anyone but Daisy, his small girl of the flowers; an obligation he had a responsibility to. Now, she was a woman he ached to possess in every and any way—body, mind, and soul. She deserved more than a marriage constructed from lies. He thrust aside the thick fingers of guilt clutching at him. He would be good to her. He would protect her and make her smile. In time he would tell her and then, perhaps, she could forgive him, even as he could never forgive himself.

"You owe the lady at least some words. It is, after all, your wedding day," the Viscount Wessex, friend, witness, and sharer of this sad collection of peoples' dark past, whispered at his side.

He glared at him. Except, Daisy chose that inopportune moment to glance up from her position at the floor-length window. She frowned at him in return and then shifted her attention to the streets below.

"The very least you can do is stop glowering at the poor lady," Wessex persisted.

Heart pounding loudly in his ears, Auric took her in, framed as she was by the white damask curtain. God help him. "I cannot do this," he whispered. Not with the lies between them. He took a step toward her.

Wessex shot out a hand, gripping Auric by the forearm, halting his movement. He looked blankly down at the hard, gloved fingers. "You've moved well past that," he gritted out the corner of his mouth, his hushed tone barely reached Auric's ears. "If you do not do this, you will ruin her."

Not if Daisy herself was to call it off at this moment. The scandal would, of course, attract gossip, but her reputation would not be devastated. She'd find a gentleman worthy of her. A man Auric would hate with every fiber of his being until the moment he drew his last breath. But then, when you loved someone, you put them first. He started, staring at the graceful curve of her neck, the simple butterfly combs he'd gifted her six days? A lifetime ago? How could he have failed to realize until this moment, when he'd lose her, that she owned him in every way and that his heart beat for her and only her.

"Do not." There was something faintly pleading in Wessex's entreaty. "Do not for the both of you."

He shrugged him off and started forward. Just then, a glint of silver caught his eye. Auric turned, taking in the wan, oft indisposed, Marchioness of Roxbury. Today, however, an uncharacteristic smile lined the woman's lips. Yet for that smile, the same sadness that clung to her hovered about the woman's narrow frame and even filled this room, on her daughter's wedding day. Auric pulled his gaze away and looked to Daisy. She rocked back and forth on the balls of her feet the way she'd done as a child, as though excitement thrummed through her being and sought an outlet. A woman of her spirit would ultimately be smothered here. No, he could not allow her to remain the lone, forgotten child of the late Lord Roxbury. Daisy deserved more. Even as he believed he would never be the more she deserved, he could not go through life knowing she was the lonely daughter of an oft-depressed mother.

The vicar cleared his throat and the decision was made. "Shall we proceed?"

It was a decision Auric would likely go to hell for, if he'd not already earned a spot in the devil's flaming lair seven years ago.

Daisy hovered at the window and for a too-long moment his heart hung suspended with the fear that she'd come to her senses and did not intend to move forward with her intention to wed him. Then, she crossed over and came to a stop beside him. The other guests took their places in the various seats scattered about the room. Auric fixed his attention on the vicar, who turned the pages in his Book of Common Prayer, all the while Auric's skin burned with Daisy's stare fixed on his person.

The older man opened his mouth to speak, when Daisy spoke, her question carrying up to his ears. "Have you changed your mind?"

He blinked.

The vicar promptly closed his mouth.

Auric swung his attention to Daisy.

"For if you did, if you realized you do not love me," *I love you in every way a man can love a woman.* She continued on a rush, her cheeks red. "If you realized that, then I'd set you free so you can find the woman whose heart you'd have."

Ah, God, she was far more honorable and good than he ever could be. Even loving him as she did, she would still set him away. Then, with the decisions he'd made in life, he'd long proven himself selfish and self-serving.

The vicar removed his spectacles and made a show of cleaning them, making a concerted effort to studiously ignore the bridegroom and bride-to-be's exchange.

"How can you not know I love you?" he asked her softly.

She sucked in an audible breath. "I—"

He lowered his brow close to hers. "I've known you nearly all my life, and yet I failed to see that which was truly before me. I was incomplete in ways I didn't know until I opened my eyes and at last saw you." Just like that, the protective walls he'd constructed about his heart, the protective veneer of icy duke, lifted, as this truth freed him.

Her lips parted.

"Shall we proceed?" the vicar said politely, and their gazes swung as one to the smiling servant of God. As though he feared the couple would alter their decision to wed, he launched into verse. "Dearly beloved, we are gathered together here in the sight of God, to join together this Man and this Woman in Holy Matrimony; which is an honorable estate, instituted of God..."

His reservations and fears lifted. For there, with Daisy in her blue satin skirts patterned in delicate daisies, Auric knew the bond between them was too great, their love strong enough that they would not be destroyed by the past.

"*...and therefore is not by any to be enterprised, nor taken in hand, unadvisedly, lightly, or wantonly, to satisfy men's carnal lusts and appetites, like brute beasts that have no understanding; but reverently, discreetly...*" The vicar's words cut across Auric's silent musings. His verses a taunting reminder of the lies and futility in his deliberately naïve hopes for him and Daisy. He studied her openly. Her gaze fixed forward on the vicar, a wistful expression on her face.

Feeling his stare on her person, Daisy looked at him questioningly.

"*Therefore, if any man can show any just cause, why they may not lawfully be joined together, let him now speak, or else hereafter forever hold his peace...*"

"*I don't see why I can't join your conversation...*" Daisy's child's voice filled the corners of his memories.

The room echoed with the distant remembered sound of Lionel's laughter. "*Come, Daisy girl, stop prattling on, let Auric speak.*" Auric opened his mouth to be the sole, sensible voice of protest, but then the ghost of his closest friend slipped from the room and the ceremony continued.

SEVENTEEN

Through the years, Daisy had all but forgotten what it was to dine at a lively, energized table. There had been a time when the dining room had peeled with laughter, hers and Lionel's, while her mother moaned and lamented her hopelessly ill-behaved children. Since her father's passing, breaking her fast and all other meals for that matter had been something of a solitary experience. When her mother was not indisposed, she was otherwise laconic and selfishly the weight of her mother's misery had become so much that Daisy had deliberately avoided partaking in those meals.

This meal should be different. A wedding feast was supposed to be a celebratory affair and yet it wasn't. For all the joy of this day, her wedding day to Auric, his admission of love, and the promise of their future together, there was something quite humbling and painful in this breakfast with Auric, Marcus, and these other outside observers to her family's private grief.

Feeling a stare upon her person, she glanced up from her plate and found her uncle Charles and the current Marquess of Roxbury studying her with regretful expressions. She quickly returned her attention to her untouched dish. She'd long ago accepted that the curious stares and the whispers would forever be part of her life. Daisy and her mother and, when he'd been living, father had become something of an oddity. After all, it was not every day that a nobleman was knifed to death by a stranger in the street. Or, at least that was what she'd pieced together from whispers she'd once heard between her parents.

Such crimes didn't happen to members of polite Society. Or that was what the *ton* erroneously believed. Daisy however, had learned the truth. Dark, ugly things happened to *all* people. Being born of wealth and status did not make one immune to pain. Regardless of station or lot in life, you ached and bled and cried. In short, you suffered.

Daisy picked up her fork and shoved around the untouched eggs on her dish. She made the mistake of glancing over in time to catch Marcus' concerned stare. Her fork slipped from her fingers and clattered noisily upon her plate. She'd come to detest those pitying looks and regretful words whispered about her and her shattered family. She hid her hands under the table, folding them in her lap, fixing her attention back to the fare of eggs and cold ham and salmon upon her plate. Couldn't this day be different? Couldn't this small collection of guests smile and celebrate the way she wished? Perhaps it spoke to Daisy's selfishness for on this day, the day she'd bound herself to Auric, she'd bury the memories of Lionel and loss and that long ago, dark night.

When she'd been a girl, she'd longed for glorious, golden curls and a trim waist and *something* to set her apart, more than the odd freckles upon her cheeks. Now, she longed to be no different than any other woman. When she'd made her debut, she'd not aspired to the status of diamond of the first water. Rather, she just wanted to be ordinary and normal. Plain Daisy with her nondescript looks and her perfectly proper, polite mother.

A large, warm hand settled over hers and she started. She swung her gaze up to Auric who, under the table's concealment, stroked his heavy, reassuring fingers over hers. He held her stare a long moment and then, too quickly, the touch was gone and he drew his hand back. However, he only reached into the front of his jacket and withdrew the small daisy-etched quizzing glass. "Here," he whispered against her ear. Under the table he pressed the delicate piece into her palm. Her skin warmed at the heat of his touch. "It seems your marriage to a dod-dering, old duke has quite turned you into a doddering duchess." He tweaked her nose. "Your new rank appears to have affected your vision and you need some assistance seeing the contents upon your plate," a gentle teasing humor threaded his words, and with that, a small laugh escaped her. A lightness buoyed her heart with the reminder that the person he'd been, a man who teased and jested and smiled—remained. He'd not died that night alongside Lionel. As though sensing her thoughts, he gave her hand a gentle squeeze.

From Auric's other side, Mother said something demanding his attention. He gave Daisy's hand one more squeeze and then shifted his attention to the marchioness.

"He's not the same teasing, charming young man you recall of your past," Marcus murmured.

Daisy frowned and looked to the young viscount, seated on the left of her not knowing how to make sense of his cryptic words. "Perhaps," she said noncommittal in her reply. Though in truth, just as she saw traces of the new man he'd become that her mother failed to see, so did she see glimpses of the grinning boy he'd been, a figure Marcus no longer saw. She absently toyed with the delicate, daisy-encrusted eyepiece Auric had pressed into her hand. "I think it is important to find the happiness we all carried, the uncomplicatedness of who we once were," she said for his ears.

Marcus settled his hands before him on the tablecloth. "I fear if you go through believing the simplicity of that thought, you'll enter into your marriage to Auric idolizing the boy he'd been and failing to realize the honorable, devoted man he's become."

The same stirrings of unease from three days past when Auric had strode up the steps to her townhouse, his expression curiously blank, rolled through her. "You think I'm wrong because I choose to see light and happiness?" she asked, unable to keep the thread of defensiveness from her tone.

He lowered his voice. "I believe you're wrong because you'll never truly love the man he's become if you continue to see him with the eyes of your past." Marcus picked up his champagne flute and took a long, slow swallow.

Daisy's frown deepened as she tried to sort through that cryptic warning. "Is there something you'd say to me?" She'd never appreciated the veiled comments and innuendos favored by the *ton*, preferring instead stark honesty.

The handsome young viscount inclined his head. "It is not my place to say." He looked into the contents of his nearly emptied glass, seeming lost in thought. "It is my place, however to apologize to you."

She furrowed her brow. "Apologize to me?" Marcus had been about as interested in her as a young girl as a sinner showed interest in attending Sunday sermon. That disinterest had carried into her adult years. But for that he'd never wronged her. "You've committed no wrong," she said quietly.

A muscle jumped at the corner of his eye and he appeared ready to say something, but then the rakish, charming grin that had set too many hearts aflutter turned his lips at the corners. "Perhaps you know me a good deal less than you imagine." His was a deliberate ploy to shift the conversation to something safer than the veiled warning he'd issued moments ago.

Never one to take part in his flirtatious repartee, she only had a small smile for him. An inexplicable relief filled her when he turned his attention to neatly dicing up his cold salmon. His words and warnings of Auric and that faintly accusatory tone he'd taken in mentioning her naiveté clouded her thoughts, stealing altogether her ability to eat.

She trailed her fingertip over Auric's quizzing glass, running it over the rounded lens and the cold, firm, daisy-etched handle. She'd spent so many years believing herself jaded and cynical and world-wary. The loss of a sibling would do all those things to a person. So there was something humbling and almost embarrassing to be accused of looking at the world through the lens of an innocent who only saw sunshine in life.

"What has you so uncharacteristically silent?" Auric murmured against her ear, calling her attention back.

She wet her lips and thrust Marcus' dark, cryptic warning to the distant corners of her mind. "I was just thinking how much I l—"

Auric leapt to his feet so quickly, his chair scraped noisily along the wood floor. "A toast," his deep, commanding baritone bounced off the walls, as he held his glass aloft.

Daisy furrowed her brow. If she didn't know better, she'd believe he deliberately tried to stifle the declaration on her lips. But then

Auric glanced down at her, holding her gaze. "To my wife. May she always know peace and happiness."

The other guests raised their glasses in salute.

She swallowed back a wave of emotion as the last of her reservations slipped away. Through the years, she'd grown to depend on no one and rely on only herself. With the loss of her brother and father and the misery of her mother, Daisy had found herself alone. For so long she'd believed herself mature and capable, not needing any help from anyone. Yet, with Auric's brief but telling toast, he'd reminded her—everyone, at some point or another, needed someone. And now she had him.

Never before had Auric been more grateful for the end of a meal, than this his wedding breakfast. He and Daisy stood in the foyer amidst the smattering of guests. Servants bustled back and forth with the remaining items belonging to her.

Frederick rushed forward with Daisy's green cloak and helped her as she shrugged into it with a murmur of thanks.

Tears flooded the old servant's eyes and it occurred to Auric that since Lionel's passing, the butler had become more of a devoted family member than perhaps Daisy's own mother.

The marchioness swept over and took Daisy's cheeks between her palms. She managed a watery smile but no words. Instead, she patted her daughter gently on the cheek before turning to Auric. She captured his hands in hers.

He stiffened at the warmth seeping from gray-blue eyes—Lionel's eyes. "I've always loved you like a son, Auric."

The pit that had formed in his belly since he'd registered the implications in wedding Daisy despite the secrets between them grew to the size of a boulder. He was undeserving of the marchioness' warmth and affection. He cleared his throat, uncomfortable with the show of emotion.

As though remembering herself, the marchioness drew her hands back and let her arms fall to her side.

"I will care for her," he said quietly. Care for her when he'd not cared for the woman's other cherished child.

The muscles of Lady Roxbury's throat moved. "I trust you," she said quietly, unknowingly twisting that blade of guilt all the deeper.

He needed to be free from here. Auric reached for Daisy and she boldly placed her fingertips in his. A charge of awareness shot between them and he guided her hand to his sleeve. Frederick rushed over to pull the door open. The wrinkled lines of his face conveyed the man's regret. Auric suspected the one splash of joy that had remained these years had been in the lady's presence here. What remained when Daisy was gone?

Daisy gave a smile to the old servant. "I shall miss you, Frederick." Was there another lady in the whole of the kingdom so unabashedly good and kind to her servants?

The older man blinked rapidly in an attempt to keep the sheen of tears in his eyes from falling.

"Thank you," Auric said quietly. For caring for her when her parents did not. *For caring for her when I failed her and Lionel.* The words went unspoken.

The servant nodded. "It has been an honor, Your Grace," he said, proudly straightening his shoulders.

With that, Auric and Daisy stepped out of a townhouse they'd taken their leave of countless times through the years, and into the blindingly bright, spring day. The large, white clouds filling the blue sky rolled over the sun, blotting the bright rays. They moved in a companionable silence down the pavement and paused beside Auric's carriage. A handsome footman held a hand out to assist Daisy into the carriage, but with a frown, Auric reached past the young man and helped her in himself, uncomprehending this possessive, primitive desire to keep her only for him.

Since his great folly, he'd prided himself on practicality and composure. With Daisy, he forgot the years of carefully ingrained decorum he'd drummed into himself. The clouds shifted overhead and a ray of sun beamed into the carriage, momentarily freezing him. He could be happy. *They* could be happy. Perhaps she didn't ever need to know the truth of Lionel's death. The horrors of that night, the shame he carried, they were too ugly and deserved to be buried.

Daisy peeked her head out of the carriage. "Well, are you coming?"

A half-grin pulled at his lips and he climbed inside, claiming the opposite bench. The footman closed the door behind him. A moment later the carriage rocked into motion. They sat there, two people who'd known each other the length of their lives, once friends, now wed. His gaze went to the butterfly combs artfully arranged within her curly, brown tresses. He leaned over and lifted her atop his lap. The abrupt movement loosened several silken curls. They tumbled over her brow.

A startled shriek escaped her. "What are you—?"

Auric placed a kiss at the corner of her ear. "How did I fail to see that which was right before me?" he whispered to himself. He captured one of the silken curls and rubbed it between his thumb and forefinger, marveling at the silken texture.

She held his gaze, a tremulous smile on her lips. "Perhaps because you required your quizzing glass," she whispered.

"Ah, yes." He tucked one of the tresses into the butterfly comb. "Because I'm an old, doddering duke?"

She giggled. "Well, not *doddering*, perhaps."

Auric claimed her lips, exploring the feel of her. A breathy sigh escaped her and he swallowed that sound. His tongue found hers. Daisy wrapped her hands about his neck and angled her head, as though she sought to better avail herself to his mouth. He drew back and a sound of protest bubbled up her throat and spilled past her lips. He turned his attention to her neck, moving his lips over her wildly fluttering pulse. He shoved open her cloak and through the fabric of her dress cupped her breast.

Daisy's head fell back and she moaned. "Auric," she pleaded.

He teased the tip to awareness until she emitted desperate, panting gasps of air. The carriage hit a large bump and their heads knocked painfully together. They startled apart and then looked at each other, her soft laugh blended with his. Auric held her close and dropped his chin atop her brown curls. He rubbed it back and forth. He didn't deserve this level of happiness.

As though sensing his thoughts, Daisy drew back. "What are you thinking?" She worked her gaze over his face. Before he could respond, she asked, "Are you regretful that you didn't marry your Lady Anne?"

The greatest mistake he'd made in his life had been that reckless night with Marcus and Lionel. He took her face between his palms, forcing her gaze to his. "I love you," he said simply. Wedding Lady Anne instead, and failing to see that which his heart had always known, would have been the second greatest mistake. "If I was one of those charming gentlemen, I would have the words and sonnets you deserve." But he'd never been one of those affable gentlemen. Mayhap had life moved along differently?

"I don't need pretty words and sonnets, Auric," she said, pointing her eyes skyward. "How could you not realize what I wanted?"

"What was that?" he asked, his tone gruff.

She tweaked his nose. "Why, your heart, you silly duke."

The carriage rocked to a stop before his—*their*—townhouse. The driver opened the front door and helped Daisy down. Auric lingered. Would she truly feel that way if she knew the truth?

Daisy cast a glance back at him. Her smile dipped and she cocked her head in that inquisitive way he'd come to know through the years. "What?"

He shook his head and jumped out of the carriage. "Nothing at all, Your Grace." And placing his hand on the small of her back, he guided her to their home where they could together find the peace and happiness they'd both yearned for these years.

EIGHTEEN

Daisy sat at the edge of the bed. Nay, *her* bed. Her *new* bed, she amended once again. Staring as she'd been for the better part of the night at the wood panel of the door. She wasn't altogether certain about this whole bridal bed business. Her mother hadn't spoken to her much through the years and she certainly hadn't spoken of such personal matters. But Daisy rather suspected that on a lady's wedding night that the bridegroom wouldn't do something as rude as to keep his lady waiting nervously since she'd retired for the evening.

The moment they'd arrived, a servant had rushed forward to show Daisy abovestairs to her chambers. Auric however had not climbed the grand, sweeping, Italian marble staircase to the living quarters. Instead, he'd stood at the foot of the stairs a moment, with that unnervingly distant expression in his eyes, before he'd quickly spun on his heel and continued down the corridor to…to…wherever it was bridegrooms went on their wedding days.

She folded her arms and a bothersome curl fell over her eye. Daisy blew it back. At the very least, she'd have expected he'd take the evening meal with her. Particularly as a tray had been sent to her chambers. Not that she had much felt like food. Her stomach still churned with nervousness and all the questions she had, questions that would be answered this night.

"Or questions that should be answered this night," she muttered under her breath. With a growl of annoyance she shoved herself to her feet and began to pace a path upon the cold, hardwood floor. Surely, he intended to…to…well, visit her. By his kiss in the carriage, she'd expected he would, her skin warmed, at the *very* least be eager to see to the bridegroom business.

Daisy stomped over to the embroidery frame she'd abandoned sometime into hour one of being so forgotten by Auric. She swiped it off the vanity and studied the now tenth attempt on this particular piece. The red threads may as well have been an indecipherable, crimson blob. She'd worked on the dratted thing and *she* could barely tell what the blasted rendering was.

With another growl, she marched over to the door and yanked it open. She needed to be free of her new chambers for if she stayed here in silent wait for Auric, with only herself for company, she'd go mad. Daisy strode down the eerily silent corridors. The gold sconces upon the walls cast an eerie glow upon the mauve carpet. A shiver stole down her spine and she gave her head a shake. She'd never before feared ghosts and she'd not begin now. Daisy made her way down the stairs, holding the embroidery frame in one hand, trailing the other over the bannister.

How many times had she visited this very townhouse? As a young girl she'd delighted in escaping the not-watchful-enough eye of her nursemaids and sprinting through the long corridors in search of the trio of boys. Eventually, her proper mother had quelled such outward displays of enthusiasm. Daisy had instead taken care to sprint, just not with a watchful mama nearby.

She stopped at the base of the stairs and looked about the soaring foyer to the mural painted at the central part of the ceiling. She'd dreamed of becoming mistress of this grand home for reasons that had nothing to do with the lavish opulence and the revered title of duchess. She'd simply wanted Auric.

Now she had him. Not in this precise moment, necessarily, as she'd quite misplaced her husband. On her wedding night. Her lips pulled in a grimace. Well, misplaced might not be the correct choice. Abandoned. She'd been *abandoned* on her wedding night.

Daisy resumed walking down the corridor to the library. With the towering shelves and massive collection, it had long been one of her favorite rooms in the Duke and Duchess of Crawford's home. She paused outside the closed door and a thrill of awareness ran through her. She pressed the handle. The door swung open silently. "Auric?" she called quietly. She blinked several time as her eyes adjusted to the dimly lit space. *Empty.* A swell of disappointment filled her. Daisy cast a glance over her shoulder, considering seeking him out. Except, she'd not be the bride who hunted for her just-wedded husband in the dead of night. Faced with the alternative of running abovestairs to her infuriatingly quiet chambers, she opted for the still of this room full of cheerful memories.

Daisy stepped inside the room and wandered a path about the perimeter. She trailed her embroidery frame over the volumes of leather books. Perhaps he had business to see to. Important business. All evening. Business that would preclude him from dining with her. His wife. "Bloody unlikely," she muttered. Daisy turned on a huff and marched over to the leather button sofa then sank into the aged fabric. She eyed the pathetic attempt at a heart upon the stark, white cloth in her hands. The crimson blob served as a taunting reminder of a certain duke's heart.

She drew the needle through the fabric. No matter how she turned Auric's actions this past fortnight over in her mind, she could not sort through his conflicting moods. One moment he spoke to her of love and kissed her until she couldn't so much as remember her name. The next he hid from her with an ease that would have impressed their younger selves all those years ago. She continued to work her needle through the embroidery fabric with a speed borne of the need for distraction. There was a somberness to him and had been for the past seven years. She paused and studied the red distorted heart a moment while reflecting on Marcus' words at the wedding breakfast. At the time, she'd been insulted that he should suggest she was innocent and naïve of all that had come to pass in Auric's life—shaping him into that somber man.

She knew better than most how life and its tragedies changed a person. Yet, now in the quiet of the library with no one but her own thoughts for company, she acknowledged the obvious truth—she'd not truly considered how Auric had been forever changed by that dark night. Daisy ran the pad of her thumb over the fabric. Both Auric and Marcus had been with Lionel that last night, and when she'd been a young girl of thirteen, listening outside her father's office, her ear pressed to the wood panel of the door, she'd heard enough of the muffled words to know they had discovered Lionel's body. Her heart wrenched. How that would forever shape a person. Is it a wonder that Auric had become the stern, aloof, oft-bitter seeming man seen by Society?

Daisy slowly tugged her needle through the fabric once more. Only, she'd allowed herself to hold onto the glimpses of the teasing, devoted, and caring boy she'd once known. Until Marcus' words, she'd not realized the immaturity in relegating him to an unchanged man.

Regardless of what life had made of him, she'd love him. He'd always had her heart. And he always would.

Seated at the edge of the leather, winged back chair in his office, Auric glanced across the dimly lit room to the long-case clock. Midnight. He dropped his head into his hands and pressed the heels of his palms into his eyes.

She should be sleeping now. She, as in Daisy. His wife and duchess. Not that he preferred her to be sleeping. He didn't. He preferred her awake. In his arms, under him, beside him. He braced for the familiar rush of terror that such an admission had wrought mere days ago when he'd acknowledged that he'd fallen in love with Daisy. Except, the terror did not come. Nor did the guilt or regret for all the wrongs he'd committed. Oh, in time he suspected the familiar sentiments would slap at his conscience once more. Today, he could only see and feel his love for her.

That, as well as his own damned nervousness. He felt that, as well. It twisted his stomach into vise-like knots and had made movement difficult for the better part of the day. Since the moment he'd spied Daisy across the street in Gipsy Hill, with the wind whipping at her russet curls, he'd ached with a desire to know her in all the ways a man could know a woman.

And he, who'd prided himself on his unwavering courage and confidence sat alone in his office, on his wedding night, forced to acknowledge the truth to himself—he was bloody terrified to make love to his wife. After he'd been rash in seeking out his pleasures in that notorious hell with his friends as his companions that long ago evening, he'd never taken another woman to his bed. It had been a small sacrifice to make for the sins of his youth. Now, he wished he knew more so that he could be, even in this physical union of him and Daisy, all she deserved.

With a growl of frustration, Auric surged to his feet and began to pace. Yet, even in wishing he could come to her as one of those proficient lovers, part of this felt somehow right—the knowing that, but for a one exchange born of a young man's lust seven years ago, Daisy would forever be the only woman he'd take to his bed. He paused mid-stride and glanced at the closed door. That is, if he sought out her bed.

The blade of guilt twisted all the deeper. He'd little doubt that the ever inquisitive, always bold Daisy would have waited for him and, with each passing moment, had surely had questions for her largely inexperienced, in matters of the bedroom, husband. If he knew Daisy, even now she'd be filled with a burning annoyance that he'd not come for her.

Auric drew in a slow, deep breath. He wanted her and all the questions and confusion and uncertainty could be sorted out later. With a determined step, he started for the door. He pulled it open and then strode down the thin-carpeted corridor. His bootsteps fell quietly in the hum of midnight silence. He moved past the closed parlor doors and the formal drawing room and then paused beside one slightly ajar wood panel.

"*Bloody unlikely…*" The muttered words drifted from inside the library, out into the corridor. His lips twitched and he readjusted his earlier intentions of seeking a certain lady's chambers and wandered over to that partially opened door. He peered through the slight gap and squinted into the dark space. It took a moment for his eyes to adjust and when they did, he easily found her.

From her seat upon the leather sofa, Daisy squinted down at the fine muslin. With little regard for the dark, she jabbed her needle viciously into the expensive fabric. He winced, feeling a sense of guilt for that particular inanimate object that was likely bearing the lady's displeasure with her new bridegroom. She worked her long fingers in a quick, jerky rhythm. Not for the first time he wondered when she'd taken up the ladylike pastime.

Regardless of when, how, or why, there really was only one certainty at this moment—Daisy had no place spending her wedding night alone in the darkened library, brutalizing the stark, white fabric. Shoving aside the self-doubt and anxiety he'd carried from the moment they'd arrived that afternoon as newly wedded man and wife, he pushed the door open and stepped inside. "You're not sleeping."

Daisy shrieked and leaped to her feet. The wood frame tumbled to the floor with a soft thump. "Auric," she breathed. She pressed a hand to her heart. "You startled me."

The moon's soft, white light splashed through the floor-length windows and bathed her in an ethereal glow. "Forgive me," he apologized. He stepped deeper into the room. Her modest, white, night wrapper drew him like a moth to the flame.

She wet her lips. "Should I be sleeping?"

He arched a single eyebrow. Surely, she didn't mean what he believed she…

"Of course I should be sleeping at this hour," she said on a rush. "After all, I cannot imagine a single thing we should be doing other than sleeping." Then she widened her eyes and she clamped her lips into a firm line. If her cheeks became any redder, the lady's face would catch fire.

He would very gladly now show her the alternative to the question on her lips. Auric stopped beside her. "Oh?" he drawled. He bent and retrieved her forgotten frame, studying it a moment. The object in gold and red stitch was still indefinable and he was at a loss for just what his wife sought to capture with those same threads.

"Indeed," she said with a toss of her dark brown curls and then her eyes flew wide. "We," she blurted.

A smile tugged at his lips.

"That is, what I'd intended to say is I cannot imagine a single thing I should be doing other than sleeping. Not sleeping with you," she added, prattling on.

He bit down hard on the inside of his cheek to keep from laughing, knowing she'd believe he was laughing at her.

Alas, Daisy had often known him better than he knew himself. She narrowed her eyes. "Are you laughing at me?"

Auric schooled his features and spread out his hands. "I know you well enough never to do something as outrageous," he said neatly.

Daisy plucked the frame from his fingers. "Something outrageous?" She settled one hand upon her hip. "Such as, avoid one's wife. On your wedding night, no less?" Then, a very determined, angry glint flickered in her eyes and sent warning bells clamoring.

Only Daisy would be so bold as to speak so candidly about his lack of attentions this evening. And once again, he wished he was one of those charming rogues with a million words on the ready. "I take it you are angry with me?" he asked, in a placating tone.

That merely served to lower his wife's eyebrows altogether. "Do you know, Auric?" Oh, Christ, the placating tone had never been the one to adopt with her. "I am rather angry with you." She took a furious step toward him and he retreated. "I've been alone. In my chambers. By myself." Yes, that rather was the meaning of the word alone. It would not however do to point such a thing out. More precisely, not at this particular moment.

She really deserved an explanation. His neck heated with embarrassment. "Daisy," he began. He fumbled for words but came up empty with the embarrassing truth. For all the women she imagined he'd taken to his bed, but for one nameless woman in his youth, there had never been another.

"Yes?" she whispered.

Nor would there ever *be* another, but her. He tugged at his lapels. "I…" Certainly couldn't say "oh, you see I've only been with one other woman in my life and she'd been a lightskirt, and not you, the woman who captured my heart between one unchaperoned venture to Gipsy Hill and an afternoon visit in that Blue Parlor."

"That is not all, husband." That word wrapped around him, enveloping him with the absolute rightness of it. She slapped her embroidery frame into his chest. "Are you listening to me?"

He grunted. *No.* "Yes," he lied.

"We should not simply be sleeping either, Auric." He stilled. What did she know about what they should be doing? "Did you hear me?" Daisy jabbed him again with the wood frame. The needle dangling from the fabric speared the fabric of his jacket. "I don't know all the details," she said the way a Bow Street Runner might in discussing the terms of a case. "But I certainly have gleaned enough."

"The details," he echoed back. Which only conjured all manner of details that ended with Daisy upon her back on the leather button sofa with her skirts rucked up about her waist. A groan rumbled up from his chest.

"Yes." She gave a flounce of her curls. "The details."

He shouldn't ask. He really shouldn't. The years in knowing her had taught him as much. "And just...uh, where did you come by these details?"

A becoming blush stained her cheeks. "It really matters naught," she said quickly. Too quickly. In a way that suggested the lessons and details imparted had come by no proper mama, as they should have.

By God, he'd kill the bounder who'd filled her ears with words of seduction and dared put his hands upon that which belonged to him. She'd always belonged to him, even as he'd denied it to himself. "Daisy," he gritted out. He counted silently to five for patience.

She lifted her shoulders in a little shrug. "Oh, very well. Mr. Fenerson's Lessons of Livestock and Procreation."

Surely, she hadn't said...? Oh, God, to laugh would be the greatest folly. He fixed on the crown of her dark curls to keep from looking at her with her face scrunched up in deep seriousness and concentrated on his breathing. "Mr. Fenerson's—"

"Lessons of Livestock and Procreations," she interrupted, her head bobbing up and down with a quick nod. "Yes. And it was very enlightening."

It would likely prove perfectly enlightening for sheep and cows and horses. "Was it?" he asked, unable to squelch the drollness of his tone. It would assuredly not prove helpful on matters of lovemaking between creatures of the *two-legged* sort.

"Oh, undoubtedly," she said with another little nod. A dark strand of hair tumbled over her brow. She blew it back.

She really needn't expand. They'd both be a good deal better if she...

Expanded. "It explained about the necessary instruments—"

"Instruments?" his voice emerged garbled from pained laughter.

She widened her eyes. "Auric Kinsley Richards, you *are* laughing at me." Not at her per se, but he suspected that slight distinction wouldn't make much of a difference to his fiery wife. By the fury snapping in the brown irises, the lady quite took offense at his lack of protestations.

"Not at all," he said, belatedly and entirely too late.

"Humph," Daisy marched around him, her miserable embroidery work in her hand.

Auric closed the space between them in two long strides. He folded his hand gently about her forearm, staying her forward movement. Through widened eyes, she looked to his fingers wrapped about her person with a frown, then the little indication of her displeasure lifted as her lips parted ever so slightly. With nothing but silence about them, the rapid intake of her breath echoed in the stillness.

He tossed aside her embroidery frame then cupped his other hand about her neck. "I was not laughing," he purred, placing a kiss against the side of her mouth. Her lids fluttered wildly. "Well, perhaps I was laughing." He moved his lips to the opposite corner of her mouth. "But not at you." Their mouths met in a probing, explorative kiss. "Never at you, Daisy."

Her lips trembled under his. "My lack of experience then," she whispered when he moved his lips down her neck. He parted her modest wrapper and placed a kiss to the swell of her breasts. She moaned.

"Never that. I'd have you innocent and untouched." He'd have had her any way he could have her, but it would have destroyed part of him to know another had known the perfect contours of her generously curved frame. Auric drew her against the vee of his thighs, bringing her close to his hard, aching flesh. He palmed her breast through the fabric of her nightshift, toying with the nub. It pebbled under his ministrations.

A little, breathless moan slipped past her lips and she layered herself to him. "I-I imagine a man such as you has limitless e-experience." He nibbled gently at her neck. "W-with…"

She thought wrong. "With?" he breathed against the place where her pulse pounded its awareness of him.

"I-I cannot think when you…" A sound, half-groan, half-moan, killed the remainder of her words. She pressed herself against him as though attempting to meld their flesh together.

Auric swept her into his arms as he'd longed to do but had denied himself. What had once been wrong for who she was and everything between them, became right for every reason that mattered. "I love you," he whispered as he carried her through the threshold of the door and down the quiet corridors.

She cupped his cheek. "I love you, too." Daisy captured her lower lip between her teeth. "You really should set me down." He'd sooner run through the streets of London, bellowing like a madman. She nudged him in the side. "I said—"

He grunted as her sharp elbow collided with his ribs but continued his forward path through the halls. "No."

As they reached the base of the staircase, she wiggled in his arms until he was forced with either stopping or risk dropping her. Auric stopped, one foot on the bottom of the stairs. "Yes?" he asked with far less patience than he felt.

"You *really* should set me down." Wiggling her hips back and forth, she continued to shift in his arms.

He gritted his teeth. "Blast it, I'm trying to be romantic." And now he'd gone and said blast it. "Bloody hell," he muttered. And now he'd gone and said bloody hell.

Her lips parted on a moue of surprise.

"Now, if I may continue carrying you up the stairs?" He'd made it no further than three steps.

"No," she shook her head against his chest. "No, you may not."

Auric pressed his eyes closed a moment. "For the love of—"

"I'm too plump," she blurted and then promptly fell silent. Daisy, who was never short of words, who prattled on when she was nervous, was of a sudden quiet. Ah, God. Is that how she saw herself? How could she not realize with her form and freckles she was more captivating than any of those damned statues created for the Greek goddess Athena herself? He caressed her cheek and turned her face up to his. "Daisy?"

She studiously avoided his eyes. "Yes, Auric?"

"You are perfect in every way." And not for the first time, he wished he was capable of all the words she was deserving of. "You are—"

"Not blonde," she cut in, tipping her chin up in a bold challenge.

He wrinkled his brow. What was she on about?

"I'm not blonde and I don't have gold ringlets and I cannot stitch and I'm quite horrid at the pianoforte."

Ahh. At last, it made sense. Lady Anne Stanhope. How could Daisy not see he wanted her and only her? Auric said nothing for a long while. Instead, he carried her up the remainder of the stairs and down the hall to their rooms. He paused beside his chamber doors and then moved on to her bedroom.

"You really needn't say anything, you know," she assured him as he shoved the door open and then pushed it closed with the heel of his boot. He carried her to the bed then let her go, falling onto the plush, feathered mattress. "Oomph." Another brown curl fell over her eye.

Auric stood over her. "I have never desired another the way I've desired you." And it was true. For his celibacy these many years, not once had he hungered for a woman the way he did Daisy. He claimed a spot beside her and brushed the recalcitrant strand behind her ear. "I never loved Lady Anne," he said quietly. Nor did he care to discuss a woman who never could, nor ever would, rival Daisy in beauty and courage.

Daisy plucked at the silk coverlet with her fingers. She studied her own distracted movements as though she worked a masterpiece upon the pale blue fabric. "I must confess I am a rather nervous about you..." She colored. "Using some manner of instrument, as the manual mentioned."

A wave of tenderness slammed into him. God, how he loved her. Auric drew her stiff form against him and then gently guided her upon the bed. He rolled onto his side and brushed his knuckles along the satiny soft skin of her cheek. She leaned into his touch like a kitten seeking warmth from its master. "We shall learn together, Daisy," he said, in quiet hushed tones.

His words brought her lashes drifting open. She looked up at him, a thousand questions in her brown eyes. Auric dropped a kiss atop her brow, drawing in the hint of lavender water that clung to her, the scent intoxicating. Holding her gaze, he tugged off his cravat and then removed his waistcoat. Through his disrobing, in all her boldness, Daisy took in his every movement. Desire coursed through him. A hungering need to make her his, now. He leaned up and shrugged out of his jacket, and then tossed it aside. His shirt followed suit. With a slow breath, he lowered himself above her, effectively framing her between his arms. "I," he cleared his throat. "I've been with but one other woman." He braced for the shock in her eyes.

Instead, she tipped her head at an endearing angle and looked at him. A smile quivered on her lips. She opened her mouth to speak and then her contented grin dipped. "Did you love her?" Her question emerged on a hesitant whisper.

Her words had the same effect as though he'd been doused in a bucket of freezing water from the Thames. The innocent question, the most likely supposition from his wife. He rolled onto his back and stared up at the mural of a bucolic country setting painted in pale blues, greens, and pinks at the center of the ceiling. Auric fixed on the patch of white. How could he speak to Daisy of any part of that night? A woman he'd paid coins to for the opportunity to lie in her arms and lose himself in the pleasures of her body. He flung an arm over his eyes. How very much that entire night had cost him…and so many others.

The sheets rustled as she moved closer to him. Her feather soft touch landed upon him. "Auric?" He stiffened at the gentleness of her touch, undeserving of that warming caress.

He lowered his arm to his side. "She was a light of love," he said at last. A dull flush climbed from his chest, up his neck, and then his face. He scrubbed a hand over his eyes. Surely, they were the only wedded couple in the entire bloody kingdom to be speaking of lightskirts on their wedding night.

"I see." But her tone and the manner in which she scrunched her mouth up contemplatively indicated she did not at all see.

Knowing he'd not squelch the remainder of her questions unless he was forthright, Auric said, "Daisy, I've known but one woman before you. If I'd known there would be you, and," he motioned between them, "this. Us," he corrected. "I would have never sought her out. But I cannot undo that night." A swell of emotion lodged in his throat and he coughed in a bid to drive back the guilt and pain and instead focus on the rightness of him and Daisy. The mattress dipped as she came up on her knees beside him and then she slipped her hand into his. He stared at their interlocked fingers, her smaller, delicate palm against his larger one. So very different and yet perfectly paired. "All I know is that I love you and want you and I'd not spend the night speaking of other w—"

Daisy leaned down and kissed him.

NINETEEN

As Daisy kissed Auric, an airy lightness filled her chest. There had only been one other woman before her. And though she abhorred the faceless, nameless stranger, she reveled in the knowledge that but for that one other, he would belong to her in this most intimate of ways.

He wrapped his arms about her and as he drew her close to his chest, he slipped his tongue inside and mated with hers in a sweetly erotic rhythm. Daisy boldly met his movements. A moan worked up her throat and he took that desperate sound of desire into his mouth.

Daisy reached between them and fumbled about for his hand, and finding his fingers, she raised them to her breast as she'd longed for him to touch her since the library only moments ago. With a little moan, she let her head fell back as the heavy warmth of his palm radiated through the thin slip of fabric.

He stilled. His blue eyes clouded and he peered at her with an inscrutable expression.

Daisy burned red with sudden embarrassment at her boldness. "Should I not? I should not—?"

Auric touched a finger to her lips, silencing her words. "You should." Then, with swift, sure movements, he divested her of her night wrapper. He tossed it aside where it landed in a fluttery wave of white atop his pile of garments. "Anything between us is right, Daisy." His deep, mellifluous baritone cascaded over her and all earlier vestiges of fleeting embarrassment lifted. He slowly drew her nightshift overhead, but the row of buttons along the back of the modest garment snagged in her hair.

Daisy's gasp was swallowed by Auric's curse. A smile tickled her lips as he set to work disentangling her loose curls from the buttons. She winced as he tugged a bit too hard. "Allow me," she said and reached up. Their fingers brushed.

"I have it," he murmured, and then a moment later the pressure eased as he freed the strands. With more precise movements, he carefully undid the endless row of buttons. His long fingers trembled along her skin hinting at his nervousness, and all of her heart fell into his hands. "I am making a rather pathetic show of this," he whispered against her lips as he claimed her mouth in another kiss.

Daisy angled her head to better receive him. "You're…" He lowered his lips to her neck. "N-not."

"I wish I came to you with the grace and assurance you deserve, Daisy," he said softly, lowering her onto the mattress. He shifted over her once more.

She preferred he came to her as he was. "I love you as you are," she mewed. Her fingers twitched with an urge to touch his powerfully muscular chest, grazed with a dusting of tightly coiled curls. Daisy stroked the flat disc of his nipple. "How very different," she marveled. Where he was hard, she was soft.

Auric lowered his head and captured the tip of her breast between his lips. Daisy gasped. She fisted her hands in his chestnut locks and held him close to her chest so he'd not stop worshiping her as he did. Desire licked at her senses, driving back logical thought, so all she was capable of was feeling. Her body burned from the inside out in a scorching heat. He teased at the nub until the warmth settled, hot and heavy, between her legs.

"Au-Auric," she moaned as he shifted his attention to her other breast, laving the neglected tip with his tender attention. Daisy thrashed her head upon the mattress, hopelessly wrinkling the fabric of the coverlet, and uncaring about anything and everything but her body's hungering for him.

He shifted away from her and she cried out, scraping her fingers along his back in an attempt to draw him close, but he resisted. Except, he only yanked off his boots and threw them to the floor where they landed with a loud thump. Daisy shoved herself up onto her elbows and watched him with wide eyes when his fingers went to his breeches. Their gazes caught and held as he shoved them down.

Her mouth went dry as some of her earlier desire was replaced by a sudden nervousness. She stole a peek down for a hint of his instrument…and promptly choked. He was enormous. The angry, red flesh sprang proudly from a thatch of chestnut curls. And he was also not at all what Mr. Fenerson's manual had suggested. "You're going to do what with that?" Her question emerged garbled. It would seem livestock and men were different—*very, very* different. Blasted Mr. Fenerson and his quite misleading manual.

Auric crawled over to her on the bed. "All will be well," he murmured, and kissed the corner of her lips. "Trust that I won't hurt you." He lowered his head to her breast once more and then tugged at the swollen tip until some of the anxiety seeped from her frame. Then he palmed the curls that concealed her womanhood and her hips shot off the bed. The air left her on a hiss as he slipped a finger into her moist heat. She splayed her legs open, allowing him better access to her throbbing center.

He slipped another inside, and a hot, heavy need burned at her core, a desire to know the feel of him. She bit down hard on her lower lip, her lashes fluttering closed as he worked her with his sure fingers. Pleasure built from that intimate part of her he now caressed, except like a conflagration, the ache of desire so intense that pleasure blurred with pain, spread throughout every corner of her being until she feared she'd splinter into a million tiny pieces that would never be able to be put back together.

Daisy dimly registered him shifting his tall, powerful frame over her. He removed his fingers. She moaned at the loss, her body crying out for a surcease that had felt so very close. He settled himself between her legs and rested his large shaft against the moist curls that concealed her womanhood. She expected she should feel some maidenly modesty or shame at her body's unabashed response to him. For ladies surely did not cry out and moan with this wanton desire, and yet she could no sooner cease responding to his touch than she could stop breathing.

The muscles of his throat moved, that subtle up and down movement hinted at the thin thread of control he retained. She raised her
hooded gaze higher and took in the rugged planes of his hard, chiseled cheeks. Beads of perspiration dotted his brow. Auric clenched
his eyes so tight, a muscle ticked in the corner of his right eye. His
taut face etched in that same blend of pleasure-pain, she herself knew.
Daisy stiffened as he pressed into her, reflexively tightening.

His eyes flew open. "I don't want to hurt you," he said, his voice
hoarse with emotion as he continued moving deeper.

Her body took him slowly into her tight channel. "Th-that is good,"
she managed a smile. "Because I d-don't want you to h-hurt me, either."

A grin tugged at one corner of his lips and just then he was transformed into the easy, carefree, young man she'd once known, and she
turned over nervousness and simply felt.

She closed her eyes as he reached between them and found the
slick nub at her center, toying with it. The room resonated with their
rapid breaths joined in a loud, harsh rhythm. Daisy moved against his
hand, desperate to be closer, which sent him deeper.

"Stop," he ordered gruffly. A single bead of sweat ran down his
cheek.

Except, her body ached with a throbbing awareness of his hard-
ness, inside her tight heat, and she continued undulating against him.
She soared higher and higher, nearing a dangerous crest that she both
feared and hungered for—

Auric flexed his hips.

A cry tore from her lips at the sudden, unexpectedness of him
completely filling her. She pressed her eyes closed, fixing on the lingering remnants of that near glory she'd been so very close to.

"I'm so sorry, Daisy." That hoarse apology came as though ripped
from somewhere deep inside.

"It is all right," she assured him, lying through her gritted teeth.
He was hard and throbbing and too enormous for her. She'd known
Mr. Fenerson had been incorrect. None of those instruments he'd
written of could possibly fit in the manner in which he'd suggested.
Now she knew.

Auric captured her lips under his and she kissed him back. He slid his tongue in and the tendrils of warmth unfurled in her belly once more. All the while he continued to work her with his hand as he'd done earlier, when she'd been so very close to some kind of masterful explosion she'd not understood. Then he began to move. She braced, but some of the discomfort receded, and a growing ache of desire fanned out, filling her once again. Daisy arched her hips, but this time there was no pain, just a hint of discomfort that was rapidly replaced by the pleasurable sensation of him moving inside her. She looked up at him. His eyes were tightly clenched as though in concentration. Sweat beaded his brow. At the evidence of his tightly restrained control, a quivering smile turned her lips up. Auric, with his title, power, and wealth could have chosen any lady in the whole of the kingdom and yet he'd chosen her. He belonged to her. And she him. At last. In every way, in all ways—forever. Her heart swelled with love and she stroked his tense jaw.

Her gentle caress brought his eyes open. "I love you," he said hoarsely.

He gave her the words she'd longed to hear from him, for the past ten years. For a moment, a wave of emotion rolled through her, consuming in its intensity. "I love you, too," she whispered and then matched his slow, deep thrusts, and everything fell away but the sensation of them united as one in ways she'd never imagined two souls could be joined. He closed his mouth over the peak of her breast and a whimpering cry slipped past her lips.

She was close. So close. And then she shattered into a million tiny shards and ecstasy swept through her as she rode crest after crest of a mind-numbing explosion of sensation and feeling. Auric stiffened above her and then with a final flex of his hips, he spilled himself, filling her with his seed.

With a groan, he collapsed atop her. She brought her arms about him and stroked her fingers up and down the broad expanse of his back. A contented little smile played on her lips. Auric shoved himself off her and then rolled onto his side. She mourned the loss of his body's nearness, but he pulled her into the curve of his arm. He passed a concerned gaze over her face. "Did I hurt you?"

"Just a bit, and not at all anymore," she rushed to assure him.

He hesitated, and she looked at him searchingly, knowing the subtle nuances of his body enough to know there was more he wished to say. "Were you...did you...?" A dull flush marked his cheeks.

Her heart swelled with even more love as she realized his question. "How can you doubt that I did not enjoy that?" she murmured against his lips. "And do you know what, Auric?"

"What?"

"One cannot learn *that* in a manual." She winked.

Laughter rumbled up from his chest and then melded with her own breathless giggles. With a contended sigh, she nestled against him and for the first time in seven years, knowing peace. For so many years she'd loved him with a girl's heart. Now she loved him every way a woman could love a man. She'd never needed a gypsy's bauble to capture that which she'd longed for the past ten years...Auric's heart.

TWENTY

The following afternoon, Auric sat behind his immaculate, mahogany desk. He drummed the tip of his pen back and forth upon his open journal, just as he'd done for the better part of the morning and now early afternoon.

It had been inevitable. At last, the guilt threatened to consume him. He tossed his pen down and flipped through the pages of the loyal, leather volume. Auric skimmed the pages containing his lists of suitors for Daisy, all men he hated just for having been hypothetically marked as a husband to her. He continued turning the pages and then froze. His gut clenched and he stuck his finger in the middle of the page.

I killed her brother. Those four words inked in black stared damningly up at him and he fixed on them so intently, the marks upon the page blurred before him.

There were a million reasons he shouldn't have wed her, but the sheet needn't have had any further reasons beyond the one. He turned the page over and studied the other letters he'd written.

Dear Lionel,
I promise to wed her. Because she has long been neglected and uncared for. I know she requires protection. And also, how very lonely and sad her life is.

Odd, when he'd jotted down all the reasons to wed Daisy, in his ducal haughtiness, he'd thought of her in terms of a responsibility, denying the very real and very obvious truth—he loved her. Those words belonged on this useless sheet he'd hastily put together at Wessex's insistence.

With a curse, Auric quickly turned the pages over and over, frantically reading, and then at last settling on the accusatory words penned in his own hand—*I killed her brother*. Had the reasons to wed Daisy outweighed the role he'd played in Lionel's death?

Guilt bunched and twisted inside his stomach and he stared blankly down at the damning admission. He'd owed her the truth. Not after their marriage, but rather before, when it would have been her decision as to whether she could set aside the crimes of his youth, forgive him, and love him, even as he was undeserving of that love. He'd clung to the fleeting moment of madness in which he'd assumed what had come to pass in the Seven Dials could remain buried.

When the morning had come, he should have risen and shared every dark, sordid detail of that night with her. For even though she was a lady, as Lionel's sister, and more, Auric's wife and friend, he owed her the truth. Instead, he'd rushed from her bed, leaving her snoring, curled in a contented ball, and sought to put some distance between them.

He set the journal down on the corner of his desk and scrubbed a hand over his eyes. Wessex had maintained that Auric hadn't been to blame. He, however, knew the truth. Yet, when she'd been simply Daisy, Lionel's younger sister, sharing details that would ultimately shatter her heart had never been something he'd intended. All these years, he'd seen her as no more than a responsibility, a debt to be paid, an obligation owed to his closest friend. Nor was the truth fit for a young lady's ears. He shoved back his chair with such force it scraped along the wood floor. Restless, he climbed to his feet and stalked over to the empty hearth. He stared down into the cold, dark grate.

Everything had changed so swiftly he'd not allowed himself to consider the ramifications in loving her or worse, in marrying her. He'd demonstrated the same self-centeredness that had driven him, a then bored, young student in university to a seedy hell no decent or indecent person belonged. Auric reached into the front of his jacket and withdrew the quizzing glass he carried close to his heart. He held the delicate piece in his palm, the cool metal etched in daisies from that day he'd ceased to see the world in shades of gold and seen only Daisy—forever Daisy.

"There you are."

Her soft contralto froze him where he stood. There was a shyness, a hesitancy, in her tone that he'd never known of her, but then, weren't there so many pieces of each other both didn't know?

Auric schooled his features and turned around. "Daisy," he greeted, tucking the quizzing glass into its familiar place beside his heart. She hovered in the doorway, holding her embroidery frame close to her chest. He sketched a bow.

A little frown marred her full lips. Lips that drew forth all manner of wicked memories of how she'd felt in his arms, and how he longed to bury himself in her once again and…"Did you just bow?"

Her words were eerily reminiscent of that night not too long ago inside Lady Harrison's ballroom.

"Yes, a bow." He quirked an eyebrow. "A general expression practiced upon a polite greeting."

Some of the tension seemed to leave her shoulders and she wandered deeper into the room, coming to a stop several steps away. "Ah, yes. The ever important bow usually preceded by a polite *curtsy*."

Thick and prolonged silence fell between them. They'd never been without words—until now. He cleared his throat, suddenly uncomfortable. "I trust you slept w—?"

"Oh, yes, very well," she hastily interrupted and then her cheeks blazed red. "And did you—?"

"Also well." Auric folded his hands behind his back and rocked forward on the balls of his feet.

They both went quiet, once more.

Daisy lowered her arms to her side and beat her embroidery frame against her leg. "You weren't there," she blurted. "This morning, when I arose, and then I'd expected you'd break your fast with me, that is…because it is afternoon and you've surely already broken your fast and…" She clamped her lips into a line.

She wanted to know why he'd left her—again. *Tell her. Tell her all the truths and mistruths between you.* Surely, she could forgive him.

Except, how could she forgive him, when he could never forgive himself? "I had matters of business to see to," he said instead. Which wasn't altogether untrue. There were any number of estate matters and responsibilities he had to attend to. Those matters, however, came nowhere near the import of taking precedence over her.

"Oh," she said. She motioned to the sofa. "May I join you?"

"Join me?" he echoed back, following her gesticulating hand. "Of course," he said.

With a smile, Daisy sailed over to the seat, embroidery frame in her hand. She promptly sat and proceeded to pull the tip of her needle through the white fabric. He studied her a long moment, head bent over her work, and something tugged at him. In her blue skirts and companionable silence, she presented a bucolic tableau he'd not allowed himself to believe for himself. He'd envisioned a life in which he wed a proper, English miss who'd make him a sufficient duchess, but where no true emotional bond connected them.

And all along, Daisy had been there.

Peace. This was the peace he'd not allowed himself to believe possible. Not for him. Only, the moment she knew everything, all of this would fade.

She peeked up from her work and looked at him questioningly, effectively jerking him from his reverie. He returned to his desk, the journal containing all his sins glared up at him. Auric reached for a pen and dipped it into the crystal inkwell, and proceeded to see to his accounts.

Except now, with her here, the neat rows of columns held even less appeal than they had since the moment he'd entered his office earlier that morning. How was he to think with Daisy so close, the lavender scent drifting over to him, permeating his senses and consuming his thoughts? He glanced up at her. She sat with her knees drawn close to her chest, her trim ankles exposed while she worked intently on that embroidery frame.

Feeling his gaze upon her person, Daisy picked her head up. She smiled at catching his stare, but then her smile dipped. "What is it?"

Auric forced a smile. "I merely wonder what you've set your efforts to now?" He tightened his grip upon the pen in his hand, abhorring how effortlessly the lie slipped out. The pen snapped in his fingers and he released it swiftly.

Daisy swung her legs over the side of her seat in a noisy rustle of muslin. She held up the wooden frame for his inspection.

Auric tossed his pen down and leaned back in his seat. "Hmm." He made a show of studying the red and gold stiches. "A flower?" he ventured. There was not a thing he did not love about her. Even her horrid ability to stitch and the joy she seemed to find in it.

She pointed her eyes to the ceiling. "Does this appear to be a flower, Auric?" she asked, her tone filled with exasperation. She hopped to her feet and proceeded over to his desk.

Well, in fairness, the misshapen…shape, didn't appear to be much of anything. He rolled his shoulders, his attention fixed not upon that damned embroidery but upon her. The modest, muslin gown clung to every curve of her voluptuous frame, the fabric kissing her skin as she moved. He would never have enough of her.

Daisy stopped at the edge of his desk and propped her hip against the edge. She held the frame under his nose.

Auric captured her wrist and raised it to his lips. He placed a lingering kiss upon the wildly beating pulse. "Beautiful," he murmured against her satiny soft skin.

The muscles of her throat worked up and down with the force of her swallow. "W-well," she whispered breathlessly. "Have a look." All attempts of hers to command was lost on a breathless, little whisper, that roused images of how they'd spent the evening, entwined in one another's arms.

Auric swallowed a groan and released her, shifting his attention to those familiar threads. He captured the delicate wood frame in his hand, careful to avoid the dangling needle. Then, he sat back in his seat and proceeded to study her efforts.

"I'm rather horrid at it, I know," she confessed. He'd always admired her forthrightness which set her apart from any other lady he'd ever known. When most women prevaricated, particularly around him as a duke, Daisy had been unrepentantly honest. From the corner of his eye, he detected her distracted little movements as she wrung her hands together. "I do enjoy it, though."

He recalled a seven-year-old Daisy behind the blue drapes in the Marquess of Roxbury's office as she hid from a nursemaid intending to drill proper lessons into the then girl, on embroidering and singing and all manner of things young Daisy had detested. "You detested it as a child." What had changed?

She ran her palm over the surface of his desk in a back and forth movement, her gaze fixed on her own distracted motion. "When…my brother died I found myself unable to sleep."

He stilled. How many nights had he lain awake himself, riddled with nightmares made all the more horrific by their truth. Even then, when sleep had come to him, he'd been tortured by his own cries that merged with the memories of that night.

Her hand paused. "I would stitch," she admitted. "Sometimes I'd jab my finger with the needle." A wistful smile played about her lips. "Or rather, *most* times I'd inadvertently jab my finger with the needle. But, as much as I've abhorred needlework through the years, it gave me something to focus on. Even if it was something as inane and senseless as stitching." Silence met her admission. She glanced up at him. "Silly, isn't it."

"Not at all, silly," he said, his voice gruff with the agony of regret. He looked down once more, his gaze drawn back to the frame.

…Yes. A heart. I've been told it is this big. And gold with faint etchings…

At last, it made sense. It was a heart.

Daisy used her husband's preoccupation to study him. There was a sadness to him. He wore it on the harsh, angular planes of his face and in the somber set to his mouth. She hated the sadness that had lingered all these years.

"Do you know in the early days of Lionel's death," she said softly, "I would sometimes find myself smiling or laughing about something, sometimes nothing. And then I would immediately feel guilty." He gave no outward reaction that he heard. The slight tensing of his shoulders, however, indicated he focused intently on her words. "One time, however, I entered his rooms." It had been the first time and last time since his passing that she'd entered those quiet chambers. "I spoke to him and apologized for still finding happiness when he was gone. But when I lay upon his bed and stared up at the ceiling, I realized he didn't want me to be unhappy or sad. He would have wanted me to laugh, as he would have wanted you to be happy, too."

A muscle jumped at the corner of his eye. He swallowed several times as though besieged by a wave of emotion. "You're wrong."

She ached with a physical need to take him in her arms and drive back any and every sadness that remained, so that all they knew was happiness with each other, in each other. "Of course he would, Auric. He loved you." She stood and wandered around the desk.

He spoke, his words bringing her up short at the edge of the massive, mahogany piece.

"There is something I would tell you, Daisy." Auric's words, barely a whisper reached her ears.

She rested her hand on the edge of his desk. Her fingers brushed a piece of paper. "What is it?" she asked, as the first frissons of unease traveled along her spine. Those same, dangerous, volatile, knowing sentiments she'd known once in her life that spoke of inevitable doom. She forcibly shoved aside such inane panic.

"I have withheld the truth from you." He released her embroidery frame. The delicate, wood piece clattered to the desk.

It was the reason Daisy glanced down and why she happened to note the page under her hands and why she then caught the handful of words scratched upon the sheet, in her husband's handwriting. And it was why she saw those four words strung together.

I killed her brother.

A dull, humming filled her ears and she shook her head in a bid to make sense of the words on that page. With tremulous fingers, she picked the book up.

"Daisy," Auric said hoarsely and leaped to his feet. He reached for the page.

She held it out of his reach and backed away from him. Her heart pounding loudly in her ears, Daisy skimmed the page and then moved to the next. She gave her head a clearing shake. No. This was a mistake. A lie, dashed upon a page. Daisy lifted her gaze from the opened book. Her husband stood, stoic and unmoving, guilty in his silence. She returned her eyes to the page.

I am sorry I killed you. I will fulfill the role of brother and promise to treat her as my own sister.

Except, no matter how many times she read them, nor how many times she willed them gone, the dark ink remained the same. The silence threatened to drive her mad. "What is this?" she whispered, picking her head up once more.

His face was a ravaged mask of grief.

"What is this?" she cried, waving the page about, and then she glimpsed the words upon the opposite side. She flipped the damning sheet over and the air left her on a swift, exhale.

I promise to wed her. Because she has long been neglected and uncared for. I know she requires protection. And also, how very lonely and sad her life is.

Oh, my God. She recoiled. He'd wed her out of a sense of responsibility for his role in Lionel's death. The room dipped and swayed under her feet and she sought purchase then found it against the wall. She borrowed support from the hard plaster, her ragged breath coming fast.

"I can explain," he said, his tone deadened. "I owed you the truth before we wed."

The truth? His words blended and blurred together. "What truth?" She hardly recognized that high, panicky cry as her own.

He resumed walking and came to a stop several feet away from her. Daisy flipped her head back and forth, seeking escape. Oh, God, he'd killed her brother. The details of that night that no one knew of but Auric. She'd believed Wessex had remained shrouded in secrets and mystery and…

"Do not look at me like that," he pleaded, his voice a hoarse entreaty. "As though I'm a monster."

"What truth?" she demanded again, proud of the steady, unwaveringness in that question this time.

He held a hand out to her and she recoiled. She'd spent her life loving him, desiring him, wanting him, and all along he'd been a stranger.

"You were deserving of the truth before this." He sucked in a slow breath and remained silent for so long, restlessness filled every corner of her being until she wanted to run from him, and this room, and back to last evening when he'd been simply Auric and she'd been Daisy, and they'd both been in love.

Lies. Lies. Lies. All of it.

"We went to a…" Auric flushed. "A place fit for no man or gentleman and certainly no place a lady should ever know about." She cocked her head, trying to follow this disjointed exchange. "Lionel did not want to go. He wanted to remain in the fashionable end of London with…" He closed his eyes. "…the more fashionable light of loves." Oh, God. "I insisted that we visit a…a…place," he stumbled over his words. "I even paid the coins for the woman he went abovestairs with, and sometime during that," He choked on his words. "exchange, he was stabbed." A strangled sound, half-sob, half-laugh, escaped him. "All for a bag of coin and his gold timepiece."

Daisy groaned. The sound tore from her throat, painful. "No. No. No," she moaned, tossing her head back and forth. She released the journal and clamped her hands over her ears to blot out his voice.

A heavy sheen of tears filled his eyes, those useless, empty, meaningless expressions. More lies. "I didn't kill him." He dragged a hand over his face. "But he was there because of me…and, ah, God Daisy the guilt of that will always be with me."

Tears flooded her own eyes and she blinked them away. A drop streaked a path down her cheek, followed by another, and another, until the torrents opened, and she openly sobbed. She folded her arms about her waist and hugged herself tight, but it did little to drive back the pained agony threatening to rip her apart. She'd heard nothing more than faint whisperings about that dark night. For what had transpired had been too dark and too vile for even the gossips to boldly bandy about before polite Society. Now, she knew the truth. Auric and Lionel and Marcus had gone to the unfashionable ends of London… to know the pleasures of a whore and, in the end, her brother, who by Auric's account had not wanted to go, had paid with his life.

She pressed her eyes closed, her body wracked with silent sobs, as at last it all made sense. "Th-that is why y-you came around," she managed to rasp out between shuddering cries. That loyalty, that sense of obligation to her, and Mother, and Father, had been his attempt at an absolution of his guilt. And ultimately, that guilt had led him to marriage—to her, neglected and uncared for, sad, lonely Daisy Meadows.

Auric reached out for her and she swatted his hand away.

"Is that why you came 'round all these years?" she demanded in a soft, steady voice.

He allowed his fingers to drop to his side. "At first," he conceded, his eyes tortured. He was tortured? He who'd lied, and then ultimately wedded her, out of guilt, was tortured? He cared nothing more than she'd discovered the truths of his deception.

Daisy wrenched her gaze from his and alternated it to the book in her hands. "Of course, how stupid I was to not see," she whispered to herself. "You all but threw suitors into my proverbial path, coming by with Lord Astor and speaking to me of marriage…because you felt obligated to see me cared for." If she'd been married, then he'd not have to pay her visits.

"I enjoyed seeing you, Daisy," he said lamely.

A mirthless laugh bubbled past her lips, scaring her with the vitriol there. "You enjoyed seeing me?" Her laughter redoubled.

Auric took another step toward her and when she again held her hand out to stop him, this time he continued coming anyway. "Stop," she pleaded. He captured her shoulders in a grip that was both gentle and firm, staying her retreat.

"I'll not lie to you." He flushed again. "Any more than I already have. Guilt brought me to visit. When I saw you, I remembered everything I'd cost you and your family." And still he'd wed her anyway.

Goodness his guilt must be great. She slid her gaze away from his. Bitterness tasted rusty and dry in her mouth.

Auric spoke on a rush. "Then I saw you at Gipsy Hill and initially I was fearful of your well-being, but then I saw you, Daisy." He gave her a gentle squeeze. "I truly *saw* you. And I hated Astor and every other man who might be a husband to you, because I wanted that role."

She shook her head, dispelling more of his lies. How could he expect her to believe anything uttered from his traitorous lips?

"I love you," he said, lowering his brow to hers. "I always loved you, Daisy, even when you were a girl dogging my footsteps. It just took me a bit longer to open my eyes and see you'd become the woman I adored, the woman I could not live without, the woman—"

She wrenched herself from his grip and spun away from him, needing to put distance between them and the riotous emotions churning through her. "Stop," she pleaded. For when he spoke he made her want to forget everything that had come to pass and continue on as the couple they'd been last night. Had it only been a night ago?

Daisy retreated another step and another, until she'd placed the leather, winged back chairs between them. She glanced blankly down at the damning pages that contained more truths than anything else Auric, the Duke of Crawford, had uttered in the past seven years. "You didn't love me," she said softly, to herself. "Not truly. You never saw me as anything more than Lionel's sister." She closed her eyes. "Where I, I only saw you." All these years she'd simply wanted someone to see her, truly see her, Daisy Meadows. She'd not wanted to be an object of pity or sympathy. In the end, with Auric's obligatory offer of marriage, he'd consigned her to a marriage based on those very sentiments she detested. Daisy opened her eyes. Auric stood, commanding and powerful in all his masculine glory. She bit hard on the inside of her cheek, wanting him to say something, anything. Except no words were coming. No profession of love. As much as she would hate him for his deception, he would always own her heart. "What a fool I've been," she whispered.

"No." That word emerged a garbled croak.

Daisy tightened her grip on the leather volume. "You speak of love and obligation, but none of that was ever about me or love, Auric." Her lip peeled back in a sneer. "It was only about you. It was about your guilt and your regret and trying to find peace inside yourself." She tossed the book at him, where it landed ineffectually at his feet. The thick sheen of tears blurred his image and she swiped angrily at the flowing signs of weakness. "You sought to replace Lionel, failing to realize that I didn't want a brother. I had a brother. I had a brother and he died." Daisy held his gaze. "I wanted a husband, Auric." *I wanted you.*

"Please—"

"Please what?" She arched a single, cynical eyebrow. "Forgive you? For lying to me? For Lionel?" With a rusty, broken laugh she gave her head a shake. "I won't forgive you any of that, Auric, and I suspect that won't matter much to you, anyway. The only one who can give you the absolution you need is you…and you'll never find it."

With that, she swept from the room, leaving him with the remnants of her broken heart for his company.

TWENTY-ONE

D aisy sat at the edge of the Serpentine River. Crimson red and hues of orange painted the dawn sky in a blaze of colors both majestic and sad. She looked down at the embroidery frame, the image of a heart at last perfectly captured. After seven years of struggling with the too small needle and her awkward fingers she had managed what she'd deemed an impossible feat. For so long she'd found solace and comfort in this skill that really was no skill; neither for her, nor the way it was for other ladies. When she'd lived, an invisible shadow in her parents' household and missed Lionel, her embroidering had represented a challenge. Something so very difficult that it required her full attention and, in so doing, forced her attention on the inane.

She set aside the wooden frame and drew her knees close to her chest. She rested her chin atop her skirts and stared out at the vast, empty grounds of Hyde Park. A spring breeze rustled the beech tree, stirring the leaves overhead. Now, the task was completed, and when her thoughts should be of Lionel and the aching hole that would forever dwell in her heart, she thought of another.

A man, who by his admission, had killed Lionel. Her heart spasmed. Since she'd read those damning words on the pages of Auric's journal and listened to his claims of guilt, she'd alternated between a mind-numbing shock and, God help her, hatred for the man who should have been a friend to Lionel, who had instead ushered him to his death. Her life, and the subsequent years of pain and loneliness she'd known, that he'd so casually written upon the pages of that book were secondary to Lionel. She would have traded every last smile if it meant she could have her brother back in her life for even one day.

After a night of too many tears, she'd fled her new home and Auric, needing to put space between them so she might sort through her husband's damning words. She'd lain abed, staring blankly up at the mural upon the center of the ceiling. How could she look upon him and see anything but the darkness of that night? A chill stole through her at the truths he'd uttered. And yet, in the clear light of day, even as she wanted to blame him for the loss of Lionel, she could not. As long as she'd known her brother, he'd never been one to go anywhere or do anything he didn't wish to. He'd gone of his own volition and his death was a result of his own actions.

Oh, there was little solace to be found in that. For there would always be a need to make sense of an unconscionable act commit-ted against a man who'd been just twenty-two years of age. The wind tugged at her coiffure and loosened a single curl. It tumbled over her brow. She closed her eyes thinking of Auric and all the times he'd captured a strand in his hand, studying the lock as though it were the rarest of artifacts on display at the Egyptian Hall. Daisy opened her eyes. A pink pelican glided along the smooth surface of the river. It dipped its enormous head under the surface and emerged a moment later with a fish inside its enormous, orange bill. She could not hate Auric or blame him or hold him in contempt for that night of revelry and carousing. They'd been young and no different than most young gentleman out of university. They'd merely partaken in activities she'd never heard whispers of because of the scandalous nature of them.

Daisy picked up her completed fabric and ran her fingers over the flawless heart. She could not, however, forgive or accept this marriage of obligation he'd forced upon her. A union in which he saw her as a responsibility, a debt owed Lionel, that now he'd spend the remainder of his life paying for in the form of marriage to lonely, unprotected her. Lies. Lies. All of it.

I love you, Daisy. She winced. Had any of it been real?

She paused with her fingertip at the dip in the red heart. She'd convinced herself Auric wedded her of love, and because he felt the same desperate emotions she'd long carried in her own heart. Only the truth was their marriage had been carefully constructed upon lies and deception and a tragic past. Where could there ever be happiness in such a union? A viselike pressure tightened about her heart. She deserved more of a marriage. Just as Auric deserved more. The golden haired beauty who'd captured his affections flitted through her mind. Lady Stanhope. The kind, lovely, flawless, English beauty was the woman he would have had in his life. Oh, on their wedding night he'd spoken of his love for Daisy and issued protestations of any real emotional regard for the countess.

But she had been the woman he'd courted…and there had been no Lionel or guilt or obligation prompting his suit. The pressure tightened once more, squeezing off her airflow. Whereas Daisy always was and now, as his wife, always would be, an eternal responsibility.

A little yawn cut into her sad musings and she looked over at her maid seated at a distance. The poor woman leaned against the base of one of those tulip trees, her eyes closed a moment as though exhausted.

Guilt tugged at Daisy. She'd dragged the poor woman out at an ungodly hour. She looked to her maid. Agnes shoved away from the tree and rushed over. "Do you require anything, Your—" The young servant's mouth formed a small moue of surprise. She looked to the embroidery frame in Daisy's hands and then back to Daisy. "My goodness, you've done it, Your Grace. It is a heart."

Agnes had been with her for nearly six years. She'd seen those earlier attempts at a heart when they'd been more of an amorphous sphere, and when Daisy had required kerchiefs to blot digits wounded by her inept fingers.

"I did it," she repeated quietly. Where was the sense of accomplishment? Where was the joy? Daisy froze. Only was this truly joy? This empty scrap of fabric with her perfectly etched heart? The one sliver of happiness she'd clung to hadn't been this or even the memories of Lionel, but rather of Auric…as he'd been before, and who he'd been after.

Everything between them had been false. *Or had it?* She thought of the accusations she'd hurled at him, the hurt she'd seen reflected in his eyes, eyes that were usually indecipherable masks that gave no glimpse of thought or emotion. Daisy drew in a slow breath. For the pain she carried over their marriage crafted upon obligation and responsibility, she needed to see her husband if for no other reason than to take back those horrific charges she'd leveled at him, holding him guilty for crimes that were no one's but the person who'd murdered Lionel.

"It is time to return home, Agnes," she confided. She murmured her thanks as the young woman set to work folding up the blanket and packing up the handful of belonging they'd brought that morning.

And what, then? What happened after they spoke? Did they simply become friends as they'd once been? She shook her head, clearing the thought. They could never have the uncomplicated, trusting relationship they'd once known. Or were they to be one of those polite, proper dukes and duchesses who attended polite, Society functions together and hosted the requisite dinner parties and balls, while never being anything more?

"Are you ready, Your Grace?" Agnes asked.

Daisy nodded and reached for her embroidery kit, relieving Agnes of that burden. They strolled in silence through the empty park. The soft morning cry of a kestrel punctuated the peace in the empty, expertly manicured grounds. She followed Agnes to the waiting carriage and allowed the liveried servant to hand her inside. He made to close the door. Daisy held her hand out, staying the moment. "The Marchioness of Roxbury's first."

The driver nodded and a moment later, the carriage sprang into motion. She pulled back the curtain and peered out at the passing London streets. Empty and quiet, there was an almost eerie peace that allowed one to forget, if even for a moment, that they dwelled in the dark, dirty city of glittering falsity. She looked on as Auric's carriage returned her to the familiar row of townhouses, before ultimately rocking to a stop before her former home. The driver pulled the door open and Daisy stepped down. "I'll not be long," she stated and then started forward.

Daisy drew in a slow breath and stared up at the white stucco structure and then continued forward, up the handful of steps. She rapped once.

The door opened immediately. Frederick looked at her a moment, his mouth agape and then colored. "Your Grace," he swept aside, allowing her entry.

Daisy tugged off her gloves. "There is no need for such formality, Frederick," she said gently to the servant who'd looked after her with far more care than even her own parents had over the years.

He widened his eyes as though she expressed her intentions to lob off the Queen's head and make off with her crown.

She started toward the stairs and then began the slow climb. "I've returned for something," she explained and marched upward, fearing if he asked questions or said even a word, her resolve would desert her. She reached the main landing and then continued down the corridor, finally stopping beside one familiar, long-closed door.

Knock three times...

But what if you are not around...

I'll always—

Daisy pressed the handle and stepped inside. It took her eyes a moment to adjust to the darkened chambers. The emerald velvet curtains still drawn as they'd been seven years ago. She pushed the door closed and the soft click thundered through the hallow space.

She lingered at the door. She closed her eyes a moment and drew in a breath seeking a hint of Lionel here. She didn't know what she expected. A trace of the sandalwood scent he'd favored, perhaps? Or the echo of his laugh. Nothing but dark, empty silence met her. Daisy tossed her gloves onto a small side table and wandered the perimeter of the room. She trailed her fingertips along the plaster walls and stopped beside the mahogany armoire.

Unthinking, Daisy opened the doors. Immaculate, white shirts and sapphire and emerald waistcoats, those dark hues always favored by Lionel, hung perfectly within. But for the slightly out of fashion lines of the breeches, the garments may as well have belonged to a man still attending *ton* functions and visiting his clubs. She reached a reverent hand out and stroked the white linen of one shirt.

Then she gave her head a slow, sad shake and closed the door. She rested her forehead against it. "You silly, silly man. Why would you go to that place?" Silence met her pained question. She knocked her head against the wood panel. "You didn't allow anyone to drag you anywhere, ever." As the sister who'd dogged his steps, she knew he'd never alter whatever path he'd set.

Daisy stepped away and moved over to the untouched bed. She hesitated, afraid to disturb the coverlet he'd once lain upon and steal the ghost of his memory. With a quiet sigh, she sat on the edge. A hint of dust drifted from the fabric, the silver specks danced in the air. Auric hadn't forced Lionel there. He had gone of his own volition. Just as Marcus and Auric had. Blame was useless and futile and wouldn't right the past. Daisy lay down. Only, she wished they'd made altogether different decisions, for then Lionel would now live and there would still be the uncomplicated laughs and smiles they'd all once shared. She rolled onto her side and stared at the nightstand alongside Lionel's bed. When all she craved was a tangible memory of him, something she could cling to, the mahogany piece may as well have belonged to any other young man and any other chambers, just as the armoire and garments.

"You're gone," she whispered. *Not gone.* "You died." Those two words, unspoken until now, sucked the breath from her lungs. Through the years of listening at the keyhole to her parents speak of Lionel's murder no one had dared utter the words, as though in speaking them, they became true.

Only, they'd always been true. There could be no undoing. Whatever guilt carried by Auric would not bring Lionel back. A sob escaped her. She sat up and drew Lionel's pillow close to her chest and rocked back and forth, crying so hard her chest hurt. He was gone and it was not Auric's fault. And then she cried all the more, the sobs threatening to tear her in two at the guilt she'd thrown upon his already weighted shoulders. She wept until she thought she might break and then there was nothing left but a shuddery, wet hiccough. None of them had truly lived these seven years. Not her mother, not her, and not Auric, and she'd venture not Marcus. Even though she'd put forth a fine act of laughing and attempting to enjoy life, she never really had, truly, deeply. Rather hers had been a carefully constructed façade of a woman who sought to prove to her family and Society that her heart was healed and there was no need for pitying stares and whispers.

"I want to live again," she said softly into the empty chambers. "I think you would want that, too, Lionel." Reluctantly, Daisy sat up and remained perched at the edge of his bed. Loathe to leave for this felt more a parting than she'd ever truly had with Lionel. She ran her palm over the surface of his side table and absently pulled out the drawer. From within the darkened confines of the compartment, a stark, white kerchief embroidered in the bold, black letterings of Lionel's name, snagged her notice. With trembling fingers, she withdrew the cloth. Something slid to the floor and landed with a metallic clang upon the hardwood. Daisy dropped her gaze to the floor and her heart stopped. A daisy pendant attached to a gold chain lay in a sad little pile upon the floor. Emotion clogged her throat and she swiftly retrieved it, involuntarily crushing the delicate piece in her hand.

Her gift.

I've gotten you something special, Daisy-girl...
I don't need anything special...
You deserve something special because you are special...but you'll have to wait to see, my girl...

Daisy stood, cradling the piece close to her. It was time to go home. Both of them—she and Auric. She crossed to the chamber door, pulled it open, and stepped out into the hall.

"Daisy."

She started and then turned.

Her mother stood in the corridor, her head tipped in consternation. As though she sought to make sense of her daughter's presence outside the sacred door, she alternated her gaze between Daisy and Lionel's chambers.

"Hello, Mother." They studied each other a long while until Daisy spoke, breaking the silence. "He is gone."

She furrowed her brow. "Who is—?"

"Lionel." The woman aged by grief jerked as though she'd been struck. Daisy walked over to her mother. She took in the wrinkled lines of once smooth, elegant cheeks. "He is gone, Mama," she repeated words that had needed to be said by all of them some years ago.

"Wh-what are you on about?" her mother squawked, clutching her neck.

"Lionel is—"

"Of course I know he's gone," she snapped with more force of emotion than Daisy recalled, more than she imagined the broken woman capable of. "Do you think I can forget that?"

Daisy shook her head. "Not forget. You should always remember him, but he'd not have wanted you," *Nor me, or Auric,* "to become this." With her free hand she took her mother's cold fingers in her free one. "Let go of your grief, Mama. It is time."

Her mother wrenched her fingers free and spun away. "How dare you, Daisy?" she hissed. "You'd come here and berate me for loving my son. You'd have me smile again? What is there to smile for?" The halls echoed with her cry.

There is me. There is me to smile for.

And standing there, amidst the sad, quiet corridors with her mother's chest heaving with the force of her angry, shallow breaths, Auric's silence all these years at last made sense. She took in her mother's tightly drawn features and the bitterness seeping from her blue eyes. Pain pulled at her heart as she imagined the guilt and responsibility her husband must have felt through the years coming here, brave enough to bear witness to her mother's and when he'd been alive, father's, agony. Of course Auric would live with the guilt of Lionel's passing. How could he not have felt the weight of it pressing down on him?

He'd kept his secrets from her because he'd feared she would react—precisely as she had. Daisy closed her eyes and shook her head slowly, back and forth. When she opened them, she looked at her mother and truly saw her. The older woman stared at her with fire snapping in her eyes. Mama could never be free and if Daisy held onto the pain and bitterness, then she too would become no different than this woman she no longer recognized. "Goodbye, Mama," she said softly. She walked over and placed a kiss on her cheek. Her mother stiffened. "It was not my intention to upset you."

The truth would have never given her parents any form of solace. Auric had known that and it likely accounted for his silence. "I love you." Daisy started down the corridor, ready to put the sadness of these years behind her and attempt to set her world with Auric to rights. He might not have wedded her for love, but their relationship had been forged on something so much deeper than most all other wedded couples. He was her best friend. And that had to mean something.

Then from the corner of her eye, Lionel's grinning visage stared back at her and she stopped suddenly. Drawn to the portrait of her brother forever frozen as the lighthearted, loving, young man he'd been, Daisy wandered over. The painting, once hung on the walls among the marquesses of Roxbury, was to have been the last one of Lionel until he ascended to the title. Instead, it had been his last sitting ever.

"Auric petitioned the current Marquess of Roxbury for it."

Daisy spun about. "Wh—?"

"The day of your wedding," her mother murmured.

Emotion clogged her throat, making speech difficult. This was the man Auric was. As long as she'd known him, he'd been one to always consider the happiness, well-being, and feelings of others. That was the man she'd fallen in love with, and he was the only man she would ever love. Reluctantly, Daisy drew her gaze away from the image of Lionel and forced her legs into motion.

"Daisy?" her mother called out, staying her movement.

She turned around.

"I love you, too," her mother whispered.

Daisy gave her a smile. "I know, Mama." With that, she took her leave. It was time to find her husband.

TWENTY-TWO

A uric sat in the library, head buried in his hands. The half empty bottle of brandy he'd lost himself in for the better part of the day lay forgotten at his feet alongside the open journal that had both saved him these years and had now destroyed him before the woman he loved.

Daisy's accusations and words echoed around the chambers of his mind, just as they'd done since she'd taken her leave of him yesterday afternoon, with loathing teeming from her once loving brown eyes.

He dragged his hands through his hair and swiped for his glass of brandy. He downed the remaining contents in a long, slow swallow, grimacing as it burned a fiery path down his throat. Had he expected a different reaction from her? And more, was he deserving of an altogether different reaction?

And the worst part of it all was there had been a hideous truth to those charges she'd leveled at him. All these years, he'd thought there was something honorable in his dedicating himself to Lionel's family. In actuality, those things hadn't been for Daisy, or the Marquess and Marchioness of Roxbury—they had been for him.

He swept the book up and stared at those words that had forever killed the love Daisy had carried in her heart.

I killed her brother…

Auric crushed the leather book in his hand. Daisy had the right of it, however. There was no absolution. There was no forgiveness. But

237

now there was truth between them. Yet, he'd not been freed by those truths as all those great tales told. Instead, it had shackled him into a loveless marriage, with the sin all the blacker for his role in Lionel's death and in his deception.

He wished the lies remained between them. For then, at least those untruths would continue to eat away at him, but Daisy would remain untouched by the vileness of that night. Now she knew things no young lady had a right to know, and saw him for the self-centered bastard he was, and always had been. Auric fanned the pages of his journal, his finger stopping randomly upon a page.

Lionel,
Daisy requires a husband...I shall see she wed an honorable, respect-
able, resolute gentleman as she desires and deserves...

Just one more lie. For knowing Astor or another would have made her a better match, giving her freedom from the pain of her past, Auric had gone and wed her anyway. Their marriage would forever remind Daisy of what she'd lost and what he'd cost her. He slammed the pages closed. *Thwack.* The echo of that gave him little satisfaction. Auric surged to his feet with the damning pages in his hands and stalked across the room to the hearth. A soft fire cracked and snapped in the metal grate, casting off warmth from the low, orange flames. Odd, he could be so warm on the outside and yet frozen cold from within.

He fixed upon one flame that reached above the others. All these years he'd fought for some semblance of peace and normalcy in his life. From the moment of that great mistake, he'd devoted his life to being a man who might be respected for the moral and proper life he led. Every part of his life after Lionel had been a carefully orchestrated façade, meant to deceive—polite Society, Daisy, her family, himself. He'd always known as much and the guilt of even that deception ate at him. Auric turned the journal over in his hands and studied the warm, familiar pages of a book that had been more friend and confidante to him. When his life had been crafted of lies, these pages had known truths. When the nightmares had threatened to consume and destroy him, this book had kept him from falling over the precipice of madness.

Odd, the book that had brought him comfort and solace these years had inevitably destroyed him. He caught his visage in the reflection of the gold mirror. A hard, bitter smile twisted his lips. This journal hadn't destroyed him. He'd destroyed himself, because that is what he always did. Lionel's life, his own, Daisy's, her parents'.

Auric held the edge of the book to the fire. The crimson flame licked at the corner, smoldering the edge black. He fixed on that rapidly growing charred mark, expanding, until it sparked orange. With a curse he tossed it to the floor and stomped the small flame out with the heel of his boot. He stared blankly down at his journal. Burning the book would never manage to undo everything that had been done.

A knock sounded at the door and his head shot up, his heart suspended in hope. Then, his butler stepped through the door and the organ fell.

The old servant widened his eyes at catching a glimpse of his employer. "The Viscount Wessex," he murmured, studiously avoiding the gaze of his disheveled employer. He admitted the viscount and scrambled from the room, hastily pulling the door closed behind him.

His lips twisted in a wry, mirthless grin. Ah, yes, the servants, just as all of polite Society still saw the polished, refined Duke of Crawford. They didn't see this drunken, unkempt, rumpled, pathetic figure of a man.

Where the servant had looked away in horror, Wessex ran a cursory glance over him. He took several steps toward Auric and then jerked to a stop. "Good God, man." He wrinkled his nose. "You smell as though you've been bathing in spirits."

Brandy and whiskey to be precise.

"What do you—?" His words trailed off as Wessex's gaze fell to the floor and the burnt journal at Auric's feet. When he looked back to Auric, his expression was carefully blank.

The viscount wandered to the sideboard and sifted through the crystal decanters. He held them up, one at a time, as though studying their color and quality, and then settled on Auric's oldest, finest

French brandy. Wessex grabbed a glass and then the tinkle of crystal touching crystal sounded as he poured a glass to the brim. He turned back to face Auric and propped his hip on the edge of the Chippendale sideboard. "You look like hell," he said without preamble, his words an observation more than an accusation.

Well, looking like hell was appropriate for a man living in hell and as there was no question there, he bent down and retrieved the book. He carried it to his desk and tossed it atop the otherwise immaculate surface. All the while his skin burned under the other man's scrutiny. Auric sat.

"She knows," Wessex murmured without preamble.

He gave a terse nod.

"How—?"

"She discovered my journal." He'd been careless. Not that such a detail should matter. What was contained within the pages of the journal mattered less than the fact that he'd kept secret the details within those pages.

Wessex said nothing for a moment, merely sat there so casually, sipping his brandy, when Auric's entire world had tumbled down around him. "She loves you," he said at last.

The loathing teeming in her gaze and the sneer on her lush, full lips all alluded to the truth—she'd once loved him—but no longer. He shook his head again. "Quite the opposite," he managed. "She hates me." *I love you...* Hated him, when there had once been love in her eyes and heart and on her mouth with those three words that had breathed life back into him and made him believe that he could be happy. That they could be happy.

Fool. Fool. Fool.

His friend shoved off the sideboard. "Come now," he scoffed. "Surely, you know the lady has loved you for years. That night at Lady Harrison's ball, she searched the crowd for a certain gentleman."

Auric tightened his fingers painfully upon the arms of the chair. She would have been better off with any one of the gentlemen on the damned lists comprised by both he and his friend. His stomach tightened and he raised his eyes to meet the other man's curiously blank stare. "I believed her wedding another would destroy me." He trailed his palm along the black leather book. "How could I have failed to realize that wedding her would destroy the both of us?"

A sound of impatience escaped his friend and with his free hand, he jerked out the leather, winged back chair and sat on the edge. "She was upset, Auric."

Hope stirred in his chest. Perhaps Wessex was correct. He tried to imagine the shock of learning everything Daisy had in the matter of moments. Of course she'd be filled with shock, disgust, loathing, but perhaps, in time she could come to see…realize…Auric shut his eyes a moment and gave his head a shake. When he opened them, he found the viscount's somber, blue gaze trained on him. "There is no forgiving what I've done," he said his voice hollow.

"What you've done?" Wessex hissed, leaning forward in his seat so swiftly, the aged leather crackled in protest. He planted his palms on the edge of the desk. "You do not have exclusivity to the guilt of that night, Auric. You were not the only one eager to visit that hell that evening, nor did you force Lionel to go. He went. We all did."

The memories intruded, as they often did. Sporadic and inconsistent. Auric scrubbed his hands over his face, trying to bring that bloody night into focus. "I forced him—"

Wessex's chuckle cut into his admission of guilt. "Come, man. I know it is likely a product of your lofty title as duke, but you could not force me to do anything, and you certainly were never able to force Lionel."

Auric's breath froze as he tried to sort through his friend's words. Then, he quickly thrust aside the generous pardon. "I recall that night," he said flatly.

The leather groaned in protest once more as the viscount leaned closer. "Do you?" he repeated, propping his elbows on Auric's desk. "Do you truly remember that night?" With a dogged intensity, he held Auric's gaze.

How could he forget that fateful evening in the seedy streets of London? "Of course." Except, the memories only lived in fragmented parts that he'd assembled into some frame that made sense.

"Bah," Wessex said, slashing the air with one of his hands. "Do you truly recall what transpired? Or have you selectively chosen that which you wish to remember?"

Those words gave Auric pause.

"You've based the man you became on a night that you can't piece together. And do you know the truth?" He didn't wait for Auric to respond. "The truth is, Auric, you'll not let yourself remember," his voice cracked and he cleared his throat. "Just as you'll not discuss what happened, as I'd tried to do in those earlier days."

A swell of emotion lodged in his throat. In the early days after Lionel's passing, Marcus had come to him, trying to speak of that night and matters of the living. In the end, Auric had not made himself available. How many times had he silenced the other man, shifting the topic away to something, anything, that wasn't that night? Until eventually, the topic of Lionel and that night never again came up. Who had Marcus turned to after Auric betrayed their friendship? "I'm sorry," he said, his voice hoarse with remorse.

Only, Wessex continued. "I lost him, too. You didn't love him more, even though you've convinced yourself in your mind. I'm your friend, too...and I not only wanted to help you see the truths of that night...not just for you, but for me, as well." The guilt redoubled in Auric's breast and he took each lash. "You'd not speak to me." He jerked his chin to the burnt, black leather book on Auric's desk. "You would, however, confide on the pages of your journal there, content to live here alone, in your closed-off world, erecting this protective fortress about you, constructed of guilt. In your arrogance you'd take all this on, when in truth," he stopped and leaned across the desk, looking Auric squarely in the eye. "We were all guilty. You. Me. And Lionel."

No.

"Yes," Wessex said, that one word utterance, quiet, and yet so powerful as to carry through the room. He straightened and smoothed his hands over the front of his jacket. "Perhaps if we'd spoken of this before..." Daisy. "*This* moment, then there would not be the tumult there is. For any of us. Surely, you know the blame does not lie solely with you."

Auric slid his glance away, for the truth was, he did not know it. All he knew were the memories that flitted through his mind, disjointed and senseless, but when pieced together only pointed at his culpability.

"My God," Wessex said quietly. The air left him on a slow exhale, calling Auric's attention back. "You don't remember all the details of that night, do you?"

"I remember enough," he bit out.

"Lionel *wanted* to go to that club." *At my insistence.* His friend shook his head back and forth slowly. "No, Auric." He sat once more. "At his insistence."

Auric cocked his head. "We argued about—"

"You did argue," Wessex interrupted. He reached for his brandy. "But you're misremembering what you argued about."

The wheels of Auric's mind churned slowly as he tried to pluck remnants of his broken memories. They were there, within his grasp as they always were, but any time he danced close to the truth, the black curtain would descend. He struggled through the thick, black, filmy shadow and with a growl of annoyance leaped to his feet. They had argued, the teasing jocundity of two young men vying for control and position.... jockeying back and forth. For what? For what? Auric began to pace rapidly behind his desk. What had there been to argue over when he'd relented and...He drew to an abrupt stop and stared unblinking at the floor-length windows.

"It was Lionel's idea to visit that hell."

Did those words belong to Wessex? Or were they his own. He spun to face the other man. "It was Lionel's decision to go there."

Wessex stared into the contents of his glass, swirling the amber drops in a slow circle. "You wanted no part of the filthy underbelly of London."

Auric dragged trembling fingers through his hair and closed his eyes once again, as he tried to pull together the rest of the pieces of that night. He'd wanted to visit one of the upscale brothels...Then he let his hand fall back to his side. "The woman."

His friend's silence stood as confirmation of the niggling memory.

The lithe creature with midnight black curls falling about her shoulders, and a promise in her eyes. They'd both wanted a place in the lady's bed that evening. Ultimately, Lionel had ceded the opportunity, going with another, and ultimately meeting his death.

It would have been me. Oh, God. The room dipped and swayed, and he shot a hand out, grasping for the wall to keep his legs from crumpling under him. Nausea churned in his belly as at last the curtain lifted and the past was revealed. "It should have been me," his voice emerged in a hoarse croak.

Wessex cursed. The floorboards creaked, indicating the other man moved. "You would still take on the guilt of that night? Even knowing—"

"If I'd gone to her rooms instead—"

"Then you'd be dead," his friend said bluntly.

And Lionel would be alive.

He thought of Daisy, his wife, and the secrets he'd withheld from her. In truth, there was no greater crime than this. Emotion cloyed at his insides, clutched at his mind and drove back logic and reason. If he did not leave, he'd descend into madness. He stalked across the floor.

"Where are you going?" Wessex called out.

Auric ignored him, needing to be free of the memories that now surged through him with a staggering clarity, more horrific and nauseating for the realness of them. He yanked the door open and collided with Daisy.

Auric shot his hands out and steadied her shoulders. He released her suddenly, taking in her wan complexion. Her freckles stood out in stark contrast to her pale white cheeks. She opened and closed her mouth several times.

He swallowed hard and without another word, stepped around her and fled—from the truths, his wife's agonized eyes, and a guilt he'd never be free of.

Daisy stared after her husband's swiftly retreating figure as he disappeared down the corridor. Her heart thundered, pounding painfully on the walls of her chest. She leaned against the doorframe, borrowing support from the wood, as everything she'd heard played out in her mind.

All these years Auric had taken on the guilt as his own. He'd dwelt in a hell crafted in his mind, where, of some misguided guilt at surviving, he'd taken ownership of his, Lionel's, and Marcus' actions that night. It had been Lionel's decision and but for some slight and significant twist of fate, Auric had went abovestairs with a different woman, and in doing so now lived. It could have been him.

It should have been me.

She pressed her fingers to her mouth, as pain rolled through her in slow waves. That is what he believed? That a world in which he was not in it was the preferable one? Loving Lionel as she did, and always would, God forgive her, she would never have sacrificed Auric, so that her brother could live. She needed him. In every way and any way she might have him. Now. She made to leave.

"Daisy," Marcus' low, baritone froze her. She whirled around to face him. He stared back at her with concern and something indefinable in his blue eyes. "You heard." A dull flush stained his cheeks.

His was no statement and yet incapable of words or any sufficient response, she nodded. She cast another glance over her shoulder, wanting to set out after her husband. Daisy closed the door behind her and leaned against the hard, solid wood panel.

"You were angry," he said without preamble.

Those words would have been insolent had they come from anyone else. For his annoyance with her when she'd been a child however, Marcus had still been more brother than anything else to her. "I was shocked," she said, a trace of defensiveness in her tone.

He steeled his jaw. "It was not his fault." He stooped down and retrieved a now blackened journal. The same article that not even one day ago had upended her world. "For your presence and mine, and his visible role in polite Society, he has been alone these years now."

Her heart tightened at the truth of that. With the jealousy and regret she'd carried over his courtship of Lady Anne, Daisy would have traded her own happiness, her very own heart, if it could mean Auric had that which he deserved—the peace he craved, love with Lady Anne.

"Here, take this." Marcus held the book aloft.

She shook her head jerkily, thinking of the reconciliation she'd made with his, theirs, and Lionel's past. "I do not need to read his words." She'd read enough, heard enough to know that they were his words and belonged to him. They'd all managed through their grief, in their own ways, or in her parents' case, not at all. She would not rob him of his privacy to bring herself empty solace. Daisy folded her arms about her chest. She only needed him.

"He loves you, Daisy." It took a moment to register those words belonged to Marcus and were not merely the yearnings she'd carried so long in her heart.

She picked her head up, her heart racing. "Did he say as much?" The question emerged hesitantly.

A pained laugh escaped Marcus and he swiped a hand over his face. "Oh, Daisy, this is rich."

She cocked her head.

He slashed the air with his hand, motioning in her direction, noisily rustling the pages of Auric's book. "He's always loved you. Just as you've always loved him. You two have both been blind to the truth seen by everyone who has ever known you."

Daisy fisted the daisy pendant in her hand so tightly, the metal bit into her palm. "I was an obligation," she whispered to herself.

"If you believe you were an obligation, then you are as big of a fool as he was with his damned insistence on finding you a husband, other than himself," he said.

She started unaware she'd spoken aloud. "Where has he gone, Marcus?" There was a faintly pleading note to those words. "I need to see him." Needed to tell him she loved him, and there was no blame, so that perhaps he could begin to heal.

Marcus lifted his shoulders in a shrug. "I don't know." A pensive expression settled over his face.

She rushed over in a whirl of skirts and took his hands. "Find him, Marcus. Bring him home." To her. Where he'd always belonged.

He searched her face a moment and then gave a brusque nod. With a short bow, he turned over Auric's journal and took his leave.

Daisy turned her attention to the badly burned leather volume, heavy in her hands. She fanned the pages and bits of black ash flaked off. Where would he go...where would he go...? Daisy's fingers froze mid-movement. The steady tick-tock-tick-tock of the long-case clock grated in the stillness of the empty room. Guiltily, she dropped her gaze to the book in her hands. She'd vowed to not read Auric's words.

She wet her lips and guilt snaked through her. Except, this was no longer about the past. This was about the future. Daisy opened the book and turned the pages, skimming dates, and turning pages.

And paused.

22 April 1816

Her heart started. The day he'd reentered her life. She scanned the sentences, feeling like the worst sort of interloper in his private thoughts, a thief, stealing words she had no right to.

Saw the world in shades of russet... Her heart thumped a funny rhythm. *At Gipsy Hill...*

Daisy's heart kicked up a beat. *Of course.* She snapped the book shut and started for the door.

TWENTY-THREE

Auric stood on the edge of the cobbled street. The calls of gypsies hawking their wares blurred in his mind in a cacophony. He glanced down at the quizzing glass in his hand, turning it over in his palm. The morning sun's rays played off the smooth lens, glinted off the metal, and momentarily blinded him.

It is a quizzing glass. It helps you to see…

Only, how little he'd truly seen these many years. Everything he'd ever wanted, everything he'd never known he needed had always been there, right before him. *She* had been there. And yet, he'd lost her. Lost her, long, long ago.

"Can I help you find something, good sir?" The woman's voice, aged and quiet cut across his silent musings.

Auric stuffed the quizzing glass back into the front pocket of his jacket. "No," he murmured. He wasn't even sure what had called him here to this precise place. No, that was just another lie. He knew what had brought him here. This had been the place when he'd ceased to see Daisy as a small girl in need of protection and discovered Lady Daisy Laurel Meadows, the woman who'd cracked open his heart and reminded him of what it felt to…feel again.

And damn if he did not detest all that went with living again.

"Perhaps a gift for yer lady?"

He stiffened, returning his attention to the insistent woman with her straggling, gray-black hair. He opened his mouth, but she brandished a long, yellow ribbon, ending the words on his lips. "Perhaps a ribbon for the lady's hair?"

He shook his head. "I—"

She held up a small, ivory-plated, hand mirror. "A mirror then to capture her beauty?" She didn't allow him to speak but continued on. "Or a pair of hair combs."

An image she'd been on their wedding day, glowing and grinning with the butterfly combs tucked in her dark brown curls flitted through his mind and a pressure settled in his chest. He managed to shake his head and she returned her attention to her colorful collection of goods.

Auric reached into his coat and withdrew a small bag of coins. "Here," he said gruffly, staying the old woman's movements.

She looked up expectantly and then eyed the purse for a long while.

"Take it," he said quietly, and pressed the bag into her gnarled fingers.

The old gypsy hesitated and then tucked the bag into the pocket of her colorful, purple gown. He started down the cobbled street.

"My lord."

He ignored the woman and took one step, another, and then stopped. Auric closed his eyes a moment and wheeled around to face her.

She smiled at him, displaying a row of crooked, yellow teeth. "Perhaps a necklace for yer lady?" The chain twisted back and forth in her bent fingers, the sun reflecting off the gold piece.

It is a heart pendant…About this big, and gold with slight etchings upon it…

He sucked in a breath and of their own volition, his legs carried him forward.

Wordlessly, she held the necklace out and Auric automatically accepted the small bauble. The muscles of his throat moved painfully. A heart. It was a heart. The very talisman his wife had tried to capture upon her embroidery frame. "It is perfect," he said quietly. He fished around the front of his jacket for additional coins for the woman, but she held up both palms.

"No, no. There will be no further coin for that." She lowered her voice and spoke in such hushed tones he strained to hear. "There is a legend behind that necklace." A slow, mysterious smile turned her lips up. "Some even say magic, that portends the wearer of it will—"

"Auric!"

He spun around and searched the clogged streets for the woman who that husky contralto belonged to.

Daisy stood several carts away, hesitancy in her proud, narrow shoulders. She drew her reticule close to her person and took a tentative step toward him. Their gazes caught and a painful longing for a life with her besieged him. She wet her lips and continued walking toward him. "You left." There was a faintly breathless quality to her words, an accusation, heated by the intensity in her eyes.

There had been no reason to stay. His fingers curled reflexively about the gold pendant in his hand.

Daisy held her palms up in supplication. "There was every reason to stay, Auric." The reticule twisted and twirled in the faint spring breeze.

His throat closed with emotion. They'd always shared a connection in which they could complete the other's thoughts. "Was there, Daisy?" His voice emerged, hoarse and unrecognizable to his own ears. How could she forgive everything he'd cost her?

Daisy let her reticule slip to the ground where it landed with a thump at her feet. She reached on tiptoe and captured his face between her hands. "Do you believe I could live in a world in which you were not in it? Do you believe I could or ever would have sacrificed you for Lionel?"

Agony knifed through him. She tightened her grip upon his face. "I loved my brother, Auric," she said quietly. "I always will and the pain of his loss will always, always be with me."

The muscles of his stomach tensed. "I'm s—"

She gave her head a brusque shake, staying that useless apology.

Yes, at some point, he too had reconciled that one was never truly free of such a loss. The jagged, empty hole left in Lionel's absence would never be fully healed. "That pain will always be with *us*," she softly amended. Daisy looked at him squarely. "But I don't want to imagine a world without you in it." She let her hands fall to her side and he mourned the loss of her touch.

Ah, God he did not deserve her.

Daisy's chest rose up and down with the force of her emotion. She took a step closer so only a hairsbreadth of space separated them. "Perhaps you only wed me of obligation," she began.

"No." The denial burst from his lips. Auric could not live knowing she believed herself a responsibility and nothing more. How could she not know how much she meant to him? *Because you never let her in the way she deserved...* He drew in a breath. "I convinced myself that was all it was, Daisy." He dragged a quaking hand through his hair. "What was the alternative? Loving you, the woman who—"

She pressed her fingertips to his lips, stopping the flow of those words. "I know you love me, Auric." A tremulous smile hovered on her lips. "And I'll have you any way I can have you. If yours is just the love of a friend—"

He took her lips under his in a slow, silencing kiss. The noisy call of vendors hawking their wares and the rattle of carriages along the cobbled roads faded and he, who'd spent years valuing and honoring propriety and respectability because he couldn't face the truth, kissed his wife, uncaring of anyone and everyone around them. Daisy leaned into his touch and met his kiss. He drew back and ran his gaze over her precious, heart-shaped face. Her lashes fluttered wildly, and when she opened her eyes, they were glazed with passion. He caressed her lower lip. "I love you, Daisy Laurel Meadows."

She said nothing for a long while, studying him with an assessing silence, and then that slow, mischievous, patently Daisy smile turned her lips up at the corners. "And I love you, husband."

Auric dropped the inexpensive bauble given him by the gypsy woman into his pocket. She narrowed her old, knowing eyes now intently studying them, but then a young woman stepped up to the wagon and called her attention away and she rushed to assist the young woman. He rescued Daisy's reticule and handed it over to her. "Shall we go home?" He held out his hand.

Daisy looked at his fingers a moment and then placed her fingertips in his. "Haven't you realized, Auric?" she whispered.

He furrowed his brow.

"We already are," she said softly.

Her words washed over him, and a lightness he'd never thought to again feel filled his chest, freeing, and at last he knew peace.

EPILOGUE

17 January, 1817

“**I**t is time we say goodbye,” Auric murmured. His voice carried off the walls of his office. “I will forever appreciate everything you have done, the friend you've been to me.” He drew in a slow, steadying breath. “I will no longer require your assistance, however,” he said quietly. Even as the words left his mouth, he recognized how ungrateful they seemed, how formal, and very aloof. “You see, I've another who listens and I will give myself wholly to her.” He paused. “And I know you would approve.”

Auric sat back in his chair and studied the slightly charred, black leather book atop the mahogany surface of his desk. He ran his palm over the front of this piece that had been with him for eight years. Odd how an inanimate object had pulled him from the edge of despair and provided him some sliver of solace. He stood. However, he no longer required a mere sliver of solace. Daisy had filled his life with the peace and happiness he'd thought forever beyond his grasp. With purpose in his movements, he stood and carried the book across the room to the blazing hearth.

He touched his lips to the cover of the volume and tossed it into the fire. The crimson red flames licked at the edges of the book, swiftly devouring the pages, until it burned bright in an orange-red blaze. “Goodbye,” he whispered.

A sense of peace filled him. With that, he turned and started for the door. He pulled it open and made his way through the empty, quiet corridors of his London townhouse, passing portraits of his stern, frowning, ducal ancestors and their prim, unsmiling, and very un-Daisy-like duchesses. Auric climbed the stairs and made his way to a set of chamber doors.

Mindful of the late hour, he pressed the handle and quietly stepped inside. It took a moment for his eyes to make order of the darkened chamber. He located Daisy propped amongst a cluster of pillows with a precious bundle in her arms. "Hullo," she whispered softly, a smile wreathed her plump, freckled cheeks. He returned her smile. She returned her attention to the tiny babe cradled against her heart. Joy swelled in his chest, powerful and all-consuming. He swallowed back a wave of emotion. The roaring fire snapped and hissed angrily, thoroughly warming the room.

Auric made his way carefully over to the bed. "You are awake?" he asked quietly, as he sat at the edge of her bed. The mattress dipped under his weight.

Daisy looked up from the babe in her arms, just two days old. "I could not sleep," she said with another smile.

Then, they both wore a perpetual smile these days. He brushed his hand over the small tuft of hair atop the tiny babe's head. Nay, his and Daisy's babe. She opened her gray, cloudy eyes with effort and her lips moved in a slow, quiet suckle. Then she found him. Ah, God he loved her. She and Daisy were more joy than he, or any one man, had a right to. "Hullo, Lionella," he said quietly. Her lashes drifted closed once more and she slept. A light sheen of tears marred his vision and he blinked them back.

This was peace. They three, in this moment he would forever freeze in time if he could. He reached into the front of his jacket. "I've brought you something."

Daisy looked to him expectantly.

"I found it at our Gipsy Hill, and waited for the right moment to give it to you." There would never be a more right moment than this one. He held up the gold chain given him by the old gypsy woman.

A gasp escaped her lips and she alternated a disbelieving gaze between him and the necklace. "I know you sought a heart pendant." Daisy had demonstrated a singular interest in the heart. "And though it is not fancy and of the rubies and diamonds you deserve," he murmured and leaned forward to hang it about her neck. "It seemed perfect." Just as she was and always would be. He snapped the clasp closed with a soft click that echoed in the quiet.

He reached for Lionella and Daisy turned the precious bundle over. Love swelled in his chest as he rocked her in his arms. His body warmed at the sweet, gentleness of her diminutive frame against him.

Daisy touched her fingertips to the necklace. The muscles of her throat moved. He brushed his knuckles over Lionella's satiny soft cheeks. "The Heart of a Duke," Daisy whispered.

He looked at her quizzically.

"The necklace," she explained, her fingers still at her neck. "Whoever wears it shall possess the heart of a duke."

His lips turned up at the romantic dreamer she'd always been. He wanted his daughter to bear every characteristic of her brave, bold, spirited mother. Well, but for the taking it into her head to dash off through the streets of London without a chaperone.

"Do you know," Daisy said softly. "I never wanted the heart of a duke, though."

Her words froze him.

She layered her hand to his, as together they cradled their babe. "I only wanted you, Auric. Only you."

And finally...he was complete.

The End

BIOGRAPHY

C hristi Caldwell is a USA Today Bestselling author of historical romance novels set in the Regency era. Christi blames Judith McNaught's "Whitney, My Love," for luring her into the world of historical romance. While sitting in her graduate school apartment at the University of Connecticut, Christi decided to set aside her notes and try her hand at writing romance. She believes the most perfect heroes and heroines have imperfections and rather enjoys tormenting them before crafting a well-deserved happily ever after!

When Christi isn't writing the stories of flawed heroes and heroines, she can be found in her Southern Connecticut home chasing around her feisty six-year-old son, and caring for twin princesses-in-training!

Visit www.christicaldwellauthor.com to learn more about what Christi is working on, or join her on Facebook at Christi Caldwell Author (for frequent updates, excerpts, and posts about her fun as a fulltime mom and writer) and Twitter @ChristiCaldwell (which she is still quite dreadful with).

OTHER BOOKS BY
CHRISTI CALDWELL

"Winning a Lady's Heart"
A Danby Novella

Author's Note: This is a novella that was originally available in A Summons From The Castle (The Regency Christmas Summons Collection). It is being published as an individual novella.

For Lady Alexandra, being the source of a cold, calculated wager is bad enough...but when it is waged by Nathaniel Michael Winters, 5th Earl of Pembroke, the man she's in love with, it results in a broken heart, the scandal of the season, and a summons from her grandfather – the Duke of Danby.

To escape Society's gossip, she hurries to her meeting with the duke, determined to put memories of the earl far behind. Except the duke has other plans for Alexandra...plans which include the 5th Earl of Pembroke!

"A Season of Hope"
A Danby Novella

Five years ago when her love, Marcus Wheatley, failed to return from fighting Napoleon's forces, Lady Olivia Foster buried her heart. Unable to betray Marcus's memory, Olivia has gone out of her way to run off prospective suitors. At three and twenty she considers herself firmly on the shelf. Her father, however, disagrees and accepts an offer for Olivia's hand in marriage. Yet it's Christmas, when anything can happen...

Olivia receives a well-timed summons from her grandfather, the Duke of Danby, and eagerly embraces the reprieve from her betrothal.

Only, when Olivia arrives at Danby Castle she realizes the Christmas season represents hope, second chances, and even miracles.

"Forever Betrothed, Never the Bride"
Book 1 in the Scandalous Seasons Series

Hopeless romantic Lady Emmaline Fitzhugh is tired of sitting with the wallflowers, waiting for her betrothed to come to his senses and marry her. When Emmaline reads one too many reports of his scandalous liaisons in the gossip rags, she takes matters into her own hands.

War-torn veteran Lord Drake devotes himself to forgetting his days on the Peninsula through an endless round of meaningless associations. He no longer wants to feel anything, but Lady Emmaline is making it hard to maintain a state of numbness. With her zest for life, she awakens his passion and desire for love.

The one woman Drake has spent the better part of his life avoiding is now the only woman he needs, but he is no longer a man worthy of his Emmaline. It is up to her to show him the healing power of love.

"Never Courted, Suddenly Wed"
Book 2 in the Scandalous Seasons Series

Christopher Ansley, Earl of Waxham, has constructed a perfect image for the *ton*–the ladies love him and his company is desired by all. Only two people know the truth about Waxham's secret. Unfortunately, one of them is Miss Sophie Winters.

Sophie Winters has known Christopher since she was in leading strings. As children, they delighted in tormenting each other. Now at two and twenty, she still has a tendency to find herself in scrapes, and her marital prospects are slim.

When his father threatens to expose his shame to the *ton*, unless he weds Sophie for her dowry, Christopher concocts a plan to remain a bachelor. What he didn't plan on was falling in love with the lively, impetuous Sophie. As secrets are exposed, will Christopher's love be enough when she discovers his role in his father's scheme?

"Always Proper, Suddenly Scandalous"
Book 3 in the Scandalous Seasons Series

Geoffrey Winters, Viscount Redbrooke was not always the hard, unrelenting lord driven by propriety. After a tragic mistake, he resolved to honor his responsibility to the Redbrooke line and live a life, free of scandal. Knowing his duty is to wed a proper, respectable English miss, he selects Lady Beatrice Dennington, daughter of the Duke of Somerset, the perfect woman for him. Until he meets Miss Abigail Stone…

To distance herself from a personal scandal, Abigail Stone flees America to visit her uncle, the Duke of Somerset. Determined to never trust a man again, she is helplessly intrigued by the hard, too-proper Geoffrey. With his strict appreciation for decorum and order, he is nothing like the man' she's always dreamed of.

Abigail is everything Geoffrey does not need. She upends his carefully ordered world at every encounter. As they begin to care for one another, Abigail carefully guards the secret that resulted in her journey to England.

Only, if Geoffrey learns the truth about Abigail, he must decide which he holds most dear: his place in Society or Abigail's place in his heart.

"Always a Rogue, Forever Her Love"
Book 4 in the Scandalous Seasons Series

Miss Juliet Marshville is spitting mad. With one guardian missing, and the other singularly uninterested in her fate, she is at the mercy of her wastrel brother who loses her beloved childhood home to a man known as Sin. Determined to reclaim control of Rosecliff Cottage and her own fate, Juliet arranges a meeting with the notorious rogue and demands the return of her property.

Jonathan Tidemore, 5th Earl of Sinclair, known to the *ton* as Sin, is exceptionally lucky in life and at the gaming tables. He has just one problem. Well...four, really. His incorrigible sisters have driven off yet another governess. This time, however, his mother demands he find an appropriate replacement.

When Miss Juliet Marshville boldly demands the return of her precious cottage, he takes advantage of his sudden good fortune and puts an offer to her; turn his sisters into proper English ladies, and he'll return Rosecliff Cottage to Juliet's possession.

Jonathan comes to appreciate Juliet's spirit, courage, and clever wit, and decides to claim the fiery beauty as his mistress. Juliet, however, will be mistress for no man. Nor could she ever love a man who callously stole her home in a game of cards. As Jonathan begins to see Juliet as more than a spirited beauty to warm his bed, he realizes she could be a lady he could love the rest of his life, if only he can convince the proud Juliet that he's worthy of her hand and heart.

"A Marquess For Christmas"
Book 5 in the Scandalous Seasons Series

Lady Patrina Tidemore gave up on the ridiculous notion of true love after having her heart shattered and her trust destroyed by a black-hearted cad. Used as a pawn in a game of revenge against her brother, Patrina returns to London from a failed elopement with a tattered reputation and little hope for a respectable match. The only peace she finds is in her solitude on the cold winter days at Hyde Park. And even that is yanked from her by two little hellions who just happen to have a devastatingly handsome, but coldly aloof father, the Marquess of Beaufort. Something about the lord stirs the dreams she'd once carried for an honorable gentleman's love.

Weston Aldridge, the 4th Marquess of Beaufort was deceived and betrayed by his late wife. In her faithlessness, he's come to view women as self-serving, indulgent creatures. Except, after a series of chance encounters with Patrina, he comes to appreciate how uniquely different she is than all women he's ever known.

At the Christmastide season, a time of hope and new beginnings, Patrina and Weston, unexpectedly learn true love in one another. However, as Patrina's scandalous past threatens their future and the happiness of his children, they are both left to determine if love is enough.

"Once a Wallflower, At Last His Love"
Book 6 in the Scandalous Seasons Series

Responsible, practical Miss Hermione Rogers, has been crafting stories as the notorious Mr. Michael Michaelmas and selling them for a meager wage to support her siblings. The only real way to ensure her family's ruinous debts are paid, however, is to marry. Tall, thin, and plain, she has no expectation of success. In London for her first Season she seizes the chance to write the tale of a brooding duke. In her research, she finds Sebastian Fitzhugh, the 5th Duke of Mallen, who unfortunately is perfectly affable, charming, and so nicely…configured…he takes her breath away. He lacks all the character traits she needs for her story, but alas, any duke will have to do.

Sebastian Fitzhugh, the 5th Duke of Mallen has been deceived so many times during the high-stakes game of courtship, he's lost faith in Society women. Yet, after a chance encounter with Hermione, he finds himself intrigued. Not a woman he'd normally consider beautiful, the young lady's practical bent, her forthright nature and her tendency to turn up in the oddest places has his interests…roused. He'd like to trust her, he'd like to do a whole lot more with her too, but should he?

"In Need of a Duke"
A Prequel Novella to "The Heart of a Duke" Series by Christi Caldwell

In Need of a Duke: (Author's Note: This is a prequel novella to "The Heart of a Duke" series by Christi Caldwell. It was originally available in "The Heart of a Duke" Collection and is now being published as an individual novella.

It features a new prologue and epilogue.

Years earlier, a gypsy woman passed to Lady Aldora Adamson and her friends a heart pendant that promised them each the heart of a duke.

Now, a young lady, with her family facing ruin and scandal, Lady Aldora doesn't have time for mythical stories about cheap baubles.

She needs to save her sisters and brother by marrying a titled gentleman with wealth and power to his name. She sets her bespectacled sights upon the Marquess of St. James.

Turned out by his father after a tragic scandal, Lord Michael Knightly has grown into a powerful, but self-made man. With the whispers and stares that still follow him, he would rather be anywhere but London...

Until he meets Lady Aldora, a young woman who mistakes him for his brother, the Marquess of St. James. The connection between Aldora and Michael is immediate and as they come to know one another, Aldora's feelings for Michael war with her sisterly responsibilities. With her family's dire situation, a man of Michael's scandalous past will never do.

Ultimately, Aldora must choose between her responsibilities as a sister and her love for Michael.

"For Love of the Duke"
First Full-Length Book in the "Heart of a Duke" Series by Christi Caldwell

After the tragic death of his wife, Jasper, the 8th Duke of Bainbridge buried himself away in the dark cold walls of his home, Castle Blackwood. When he's coaxed out of his self-imposed exile to attend the amusements of the Frost Fair, his life is irrevocably changed by his fateful meeting with Lady Katherine Adamson.

With her tight brown ringlets and silly white-ruffled gowns, Lady Katherine Adamson has found her dance card empty for two Seasons. After her father's passing, Katherine learned the unreliability of men, and is determined to depend on no one, except herself. Until she meets Jasper...

In a desperate bid to avoid a match arranged by her family, Katherine makes the Duke of Bainbridge a shocking proposition—one that he accepts.

Only, as Katherine begins to love Jasper, she finds the arrangement agreed upon is not enough. And Jasper is left to decide if protecting his heart is more important than fighting for Katherine's love.

"More Than a Duke"
Book 2 in the "Heart of a Duke" Series by Christi Caldwell

Polite Society doesn't take Lady Anne Adamson seriously. However, Anne isn't just another pretty young miss. When she discovers her father betrayed her mother's love and her family descended into poverty, Anne comes up with a plan to marry a respectable, powerful, and honorable gentleman—a man nothing like her philandering father.

Armed with the heart of a duke pendant, fabled to land the wearer a duke's heart, she decides to enlist the aid of the notorious Harry, 6th Earl of Stanhope. A scoundrel with a scandalous past, he is the last gentleman she'd ever wed...however, his reputation marks him the perfect man to school her in the art of seduction so she might ensnare the illustrious Duke of Crawford.

Harry, the Earl of Stanhope is a jaded, cynical rogue who lives for his own pleasures. Having been thrown over by the only woman he ever loved so she could wed a duke, he's not at all surprised when Lady Anne approaches him with her scheme to capture another duke's affection. He's come to appreciate that all women are in fact greedy, title-grasping, self-indulgent creatures. And with Anne's history of grating on his every last nerve, she is the last woman he'd ever agree to school in the art of seduction. Only his friendship with the lady's sister compels him to help.

What begins as a pretend courtship, born of lessons on seduction, becomes something more leaving Anne to decide if she can give her heart to a reckless rogue, and Harry must decide if he's willing to again trust in a lady's love.

"The Love of a Rogue"
Book 3 in the "Heart of a Duke" Series by Christi Caldwell

Lady Imogen Moore hasn't had an easy time of it since she made her Come Out. With her betrothed, a powerful duke breaking it off to wed her sister, she's become the *tons* favorite piece of gossip. Never again wanting to experience the pain of a broken heart, she's resolved to make a match with a polite, respectable gentleman. The last thing she wants is another reckless rogue.

Lord Alex Edgerton has a problem. His brother, tired of Alex's carousing has charged him with chaperoning their remaining, unwed sister about *ton* events. Shopping? No, thank you. Attending the theatre? He'd rather be at Forbidden Pleasures with a scantily clad beauty upon his lap. The task of *chaperone* becomes even more of a bother when his sister drags along her dearest friend, Lady Imogen to social functions. The last thing he wants in his life is a young, innocent English miss.

Except, as Alex and Imogen are thrown together, passions flare and Alex comes to find he not only wants Imogen in his bed, but also in his heart. Yet now he must convince Imogen to risk all, on the heart of a rogue.

"Loved By a Duke"
Book 4 in the "Heart of a Duke" Series by Christi Caldwell

For ten years, Lady Daisy Meadows has been in love with Auric, the Duke of Crawford. Ever since his gallant rescue years earlier, Daisy knew she was destined to be his Duchess. Unfortunately, Auric sees her as his best friend's sister and nothing more. But perhaps, if she can manage to find the fabled heart of a duke pendant, she will win over the heart of her duke.

Auric, the Duke of Crawford enjoys Daisy's company. The last thing he is interested in however, is pursuing a romance with a woman he's known since she was in leading strings. This season, Daisy is turning up in the oddest places and he cannot help but notice that she is no longer a girl. But Auric wouldn't do something as foolhardy as to fall in love with Daisy. He couldn't. Not with the guilt he carries over his past sins…Not when he has no right to her heart…But perhaps, just perhaps, she can forgive the past and trust that he'd forever cherish her heart—but will she let him?

Non-Fiction Works by Christi Caldwell
Uninterrupted Joy: Memoir: My Journey through Infertility, Pregnancy, and Special Needs

The following journey was never intended for publication. It was written from a mother, to her unborn child. The words detailed her struggle through infertility and the joy of finally being pregnant. A stunning revelation at her son's birth opened a world of both fear and discovery. This is the story of one mother's love and hope and…her quest for uninterrupted joy.

AND COMING JUNE 2015...

BY CHRISTI CALDWELL

Book 1 in a New Series "The Lords of Honor" Series
"Seduced By a Lady's Heart"

Featuring Lieutenant Lucien Jones from "Forever Betrothed, Never the Bride" and Lady Eloise Yardley.

After he'd returned from fighting Boney's forces, Lieutenant Lucien Jones lost not only an arm but also his wife and son, who died in his absence. He languished in a hospital, until he was given purpose once more, in the form of employment on the Marquess of Drake's staff.

Yet what happens when the friend of his youth, now the Lady Eloise Yardley forces him to confront the world he'd left behind? Sparks fly and passions flare as this servant is Seduced By a Lady's Heart...

43507428R00157

Made in the USA
Middletown, DE
11 May 2017